Vladislava

The Invisibles

The Web

The Nihilists

The Mirages

The Dragons

The Chroniclers

Thorn's
father

The Narcotics

Thorn's
mother

FAROUK
Familiy spirit
of the Pole

Thorn's cousins

"I loved *A Winter's Promise*, which felt simultaneously fresh and also like a classic along the lines of Narnia."

—*Geekly Inc.*

"Dabos draws her fantasy world and cast of characters in life-like, vivid detail . . . Ophelia is able to grow as a character without betraying her values. I would absolutely recommend this book to readers who enjoy well-built fantasy worlds and family and political dramas."

—*Children's Book World's Teen Readers Council*

"The unusual settings, original characters, dark intrigue, originality, and fast-moving plot result in a book that leaves readers eagerly awaiting the next volume."

—*School Library Journal* (Starred Review)

"Dabos's darkly enchanting debut, a French bestseller, employs vibrant characters, inventive worldbuilding, and a sophisticated plot that will dazzle readers."

—*Publishers Weekly* (Starred Review)

"Your next YA obsession . . . An irresistible mix of character development, imaginative world-building, and tightly-wound suspense."

—*Entertainment Weekly*

"Dabos has managed the rarely seen triad of complex worldbuilding, nuanced character development, and enthralling plot, even making it look easy."

—*Kirkus Reviews*

"I was too engrossed to interrupt myself with thoughts on how I was going to review it. I was under the spell of a master-story teller, a spell only the turning of the final page would break."

—Lizzy Siddal, blogger

THE MIRROR VISITOR
BOOK 2

THE MISSING
OF CLAIRDELUNE

Christelle Dabos

THE MIRROR VISITOR
BOOK 2

THE MISSING
OF CLAIRDELUNE

Translated from the French
by Hildegarde Serle

Europa
editions

Europa Editions
214 West 29th Street
New York, N.Y. 10001
www.europaeditions.com
info@europaeditions.com

Translation by Hildegarde Serle
Original title: *La Passe-Miroir. Livre 2. Les Disparus du Clairdelune*
Translation copyright © 2019 by Europa Editions

Library of Congress Cataloging in Publication Data is available
ISBN 978-1-60945-507-1

Dabos, Christelle
The Missing of Clairdelune

Book design by Emanuele Ragnisco
www.mekkanografici.com

Cover and inside illustrations by Laurent Gapaillard © Gallimard Jeunesse

Prepress by Grafica Punto Print – Rome

Printed in Italy, at Puntoweb

Contents

Volume 1 Recalled: *A Winter's Promise*   9
Fragment: A Reminder   15

The Storyteller
  The Game   19
  The Kid   28
  The Contracts   39
Fragment: First Reprise   53
  The Letter   56
  The Theater   70
  The Doll   81
  The Tales   89
  The Forgotten One   101
  The Pipe   112
  The Question   125
  The Affront   138
  The Promises   145
  The Bell   157
  The Client   176
Fragment: Second Reprise   182
  The Train   185
  The Family   194

The Reader

The Date 209
The Weather Vane 216
The Mothers 229
The Caravan 243
The Disgraced 253
The Invitation 264
Vertigo 270
Fragment: Third Reprise 288
The Absentees 293
The Seal 312
The Pin 323
The Workshop 330
The Sandbeds 340
The Dead End 347
Fragment: Fourth Reprise 360
The Cry 363
The Non-Place 380
The Dark 393
The Announcement 401
The Mattresses 417
The Genteel Death 429
The Heart 436
The Deal 448
The Reading 458
Fragment: Fifth Reprise 470
The Memory 472
The Parent 487
The Sentence 497
The Mirror Visitor 508
Fragment: Postscriptum 512

Author's Postscript 513
Acknowledgments 515

VOLUME 1 RECALLED
A WINTER'S PROMISE

After the Rupture, which put an end to the old world, life was concentrated on a few distinct territories, or arks, suspended in the firmament. Inhabited by families endowed with particular powers, each ark is governed by a distant ancestor called a "family spirit."

Young Ophelia is a Mirror Visitor, a rare talent among the inhabitants of Anima. Clumsy, solitary, and reserved, she is also an excellent "reader": when she touches an object, she can read its past history, picking up the trace of all those who have touched it before her.

When a forced marriage obliges her to leave her home and family for the faraway ark of the Pole, her world is shattered. Thorn, her fiancé, is a stern and enigmatic man. With him, Ophelia discovers the floating city of Citaceleste, a place of spatial distortions and optical illusions. There, a court composed of rival clans gravitates around their common ancestor, Farouk, the all-powerful and immortal family spirit, while they conspire against each other with a grim mix of cunning, manipulation, trickery and treachery. To make matters worse, Thorn is Treasurer of the Pole, so he is hated by everyone.

Thrown into this ruthless world, where she can trust no

one, Ophelia explores behind the scenes. While waiting to be married, she is made to conceal her identity and, disguised as a servant, she begins to see the true face of the city and its denizens. In this way, she learns of the existence of Farouk's Book, a very ancient and mysterious tome with which the family spirit is completely obsessed. The awful truth becomes clear to her: Thorn wants to marry her to inherit her power as a reader, thus enabling him to decipher the Book.

As Ophelia receives a telegram announcing the imminent arrival of her family, tragic events hit Thorn and his aunt, Berenilde. Now that they are the last surviving members of the Dragon clan, they have to seek Farouk's protection. Ophelia prepares to be officially presented at court; with renewed resolve, she is determined to find her way in this labyrinth of illusions.

THE MISSING
OF CLAIRDELUNE

ON BOARD THE CITACELESTE

7. Farouk's Apartments
6. Gynaeceum
5. Jetty-Promenade
4. Family Opera House
3. Thermal Baths
2. Hanging Gardens
1. Council of Ministers' Hall
0. Embassy of Clairdelune

a. Treasury
b. Police Station
c. Workshop of Hildegarde & Co.

FRAGMENT: A REMINDER

In the beginning, we were as one.

But God felt we couldn't satisfy him like that, so God set about dividing us. God had great fun with us, then God tired of us and forgot us. God could be so cruel in his indifference, he horrified me. God knew how to show his gentle side, too, and I loved him as I've loved no one else.

I think we could have all lived happily, in a way, God, me, and the others, if it weren't for that accursed book. It disgusted me. I knew what bound me to it in the most sickening of ways, but the horror of that particular knowledge came later, much later. I didn't understand straightaway, I was too ignorant.

I loved God, yes, but I despised that book, which he'd open at the drop of a hat. As for God, he relished it. When God was happy, he wrote. When God was furious, he wrote. And one day, when God was in a really bad mood, he did something enormously stupid.

God smashed the world to pieces.

*

It's coming back to me—God was punished. On that day, I understood that God wasn't all-powerful. Since then, I've never seen him again.

THE STORYTELLER

THE GAME

Ophelia was dazzled. If she just risked a peek from under her parasol, the sunshine came at her from all directions: down it streamed from the sky; back it bounced off the varnished-wood promenade; it made the entire ocean sparkle, and lit up the jewelry of every courtier. She could see enough, however, to establish that neither Berenilde nor Aunt Rosaline were any longer by her side.

Ophelia had to face facts: she was lost.

For someone who had come to the court with the firm intention of finding her place, things weren't looking too good. She had an appointment to be officially presented to Farouk. If there was one person in the world who absolutely mustn't be kept waiting, it was certainly this family spirit.

Where was he to be found? In the shade of the large palm trees? At one of the luxurious hotels lining the coast? Inside a beach hut?

Ophelia banged her nose against the sky. She'd been leaning over the parapet to look for Farouk, but the sea was nothing but a wall. A vast moving fresco in which the sound of the waves was as artificial as the smell of sand and the distant horizon. Ophelia readjusted her glasses and looked at the scenery around her. Almost everything here was fake: the palms, the fountains, the sea, the sun, the sky, and the pervading heat.

The grand hotels themselves were probably just two-dimensional facades.

Illusions.

What else could be expected when one was on the fifth floor of a tower, when that tower overlooked a city, and when that city hovered above a polar ark whose actual temperature never rose above minus fifteen degrees? The locals could distort space and stick illusions all over the place, but there were limits to their creativity.

Ophelia was wary of fakes, but she was even more wary of individuals who used them to manipulate others. That was why she felt particularly ill at ease among the courtiers now jostling her.

They were all Mirages, the masters of illusionism.

With their imposing stature, pale hair, light eyes, and clan tattoos, Ophelia felt even more diminutive, more dark-haired, more nearsighted, and more of a stranger than ever in their midst. Occasionally, they would look snootily down at her. No doubt they were wondering who this young lady, desperately trying to hide under her parasol, was, but Ophelia certainly wasn't going to tell them. She was alone and without protection; if they discovered that she was engaged to Thorn, the most hated man in the whole city, she'd never save her skin. Or her mind. She had a cracked rib, a black eye, and a slashed cheek following her recent ordeals. Best not to make things even worse.

At least these Mirages proved useful to Ophelia. They were all moving towards a Jetty-Promenade on pilings, which, due to a pretty convincing optical effect, gave the illusion of extending over the fake sea. By squinting, Ophelia realized that the sparkling she saw at the end of it was the light reflecting on a huge glass and metal structure. This Jetty-Promenade wasn't just another trompe l'oeil; it was an actual majestic palace.

If Ophelia stood any chance of finding Farouk, Berenilde, and Aunt Rosaline, it would be over there.

She followed the procession of courtiers. She'd wanted to be as unobtrusive as possible, but hadn't taken her scarf into account. With half of it coiled around her ankle and the other half gesticulating on the ground, it gave the impression of a boa constrictor in full courting display. Ophelia hadn't managed to make it release its grip. Delighted as she was to see her scarf thriving again, after weeks of separation, she'd have preferred not to shout that she was an Animist from the rooftops. Not until she'd found Berenilde, at least.

Ophelia tipped her parasol further over her face when she went past a newspaper kiosk. The papers all carried the headline:

TIME'S UP FOR DRAGONS:

HUNTERS BEATEN AT OWN GAME

Ophelia found it in extremely poor taste. The Dragons were her future in-laws and they'd all just perished in the forest in dramatic circumstances. In the eyes of the court, however, it was only ever one less rival clan.

She proceeded along the Jetty-Promenade. What had earlier been but an indistinct shimmer turned into architectural fireworks. The palace was even more gigantic than she'd thought. Its golden dome, whose finial darted into the sky like lightning, vied with the sun, and yet it was but the culmination of a much vaster edifice, all glass and cast iron, studded here and there with oriental-looking turrets.

'And all this,' Ophelia thought as she surveyed the palace, the sea, and the throng of courtiers, 'all this is just the fifth floor of Farouk's tower.'

She was starting to feel really nervous.

Her nervousness turned into panic when she saw two dogs, as white and as massive as polar bears, coming towards her.

They were focusing intently on her, but it wasn't them that terrified Ophelia. It was their master.

"Good day, miss. Are you walking alone?"

Ophelia couldn't believe her eyes as she recognized those blond curls, those bottle-bottom glasses, and that chubby cherub's face.

The Knight. The Mirage without whom the Dragons would still be alive.

He might seem like most little boys—clumsier than most, even—but that didn't make him any less of a scourge whom no adult could control and his own family feared. While the Mirages were generally happy to scatter illusions around themselves, the Knight would implant them directly into people. This deviant power was his plaything. He'd used it to inflict hysteria on a servant; imprison Aunt Rosaline in a memory bubble; turn the wild Beasts against the Dragons hunting them; and all without ever getting caught.

Ophelia found it incredible that there was no one, in the whole court, who could prevent him from showing himself in public.

"You seem to be lost," the Knight commented, with extreme politeness. "Would you like me to be your guide?"

Ophelia didn't reply to him. She couldn't decide whether saying "yes" or saying "no" would be the signing of her death warrant.

"There you are at last! Where on earth did you get to?"

To Ophelia's great relief, it was Berenilde. With a graceful swish of her dress, she was making her way through the crowd of courtiers, as serenely as a swan crossing a lake. And yet, when she slid Ophelia's arm under her own, she gripped it as tightly as she could.

"Good day, Madam Berenilde," stammered the Knight. His cheeks had gone very pink. He wiped his hands on his smock with an almost shy awkwardness.

"Hurry along, my dear girl," Berenilde said, without even a glance at or reply to the Knight. "The game is nearly over. Your aunt is saving our seats."

It was hard to make out the expression on the Knight's face—his bottle-bottom glasses made his eyes look particularly strange—but Ophelia was almost certain that he was crestfallen. She found the child unfathomable. Surely he wasn't expecting to be thanked for causing the death of a whole clan, was he?

"You're not speaking to me anymore, madam?" he still asked, anxiously. "So you don't have a single word for me?"

Berenilde hesitated a little, and then turned her most beautiful smile on him. "If you insist, Knight, I even have nine: you will not be protected by your age forever."

On this prediction, offered almost casually, Berenilde set off in the direction of the palace. When Ophelia glanced back, what she saw sent shivers up her spine. The Knight was looking daggers at her, and not at Berenilde, his face contorted with jealousy. Was he about to set his dogs after them?

"Of all the people with whom you must never find yourself alone, the Knight is top of the list," murmured Berenilde, gripping Ophelia's arm even tighter. "Do you never listen to my advice, then? Let's hurry up," she added, walking faster. "The game is coming to an end, and we absolutely mustn't make Lord Farouk wait."

"What game?" gasped Ophelia. Her cracked rib was increasingly painful.

"You are going to make a good impression on our lord," Berenilde decreed without dropping her smile. "Today we have many more enemies than we have allies—his protection will swing the balance, decisively. If you don't please him at first sight, you're sentencing us to death." She placed a hand on her stomach, including the child she was carrying in this statement.

Hampered as she walked, Ophelia kept having to shake the scarf that had wound itself around her foot. Berenilde's words did nothing to help her feel less nervous. Her apprehension was all the greater for still having the telegram from her family in the pocket of her dress. Concerned by her silence, her parents, uncles, aunts, brother, sisters, and cousins had decided to move their arrival at the Pole forward by several months. They were, of course, unaware that their security also depended on Farouk's goodwill.

Ophelia and Berenilde entered the palace's main rotunda, which was even more spectacular seen from inside. Five galleries radiated within it, each one as impressive as the nave of a cathedral. The slightest murmur from the court or rustle of a dress became greatly amplified beneath the vast glass canopies. In here, only the great and the good were to be found: ministers, consuls, artists, and their current muses.

A butler in gold livery came towards Berenilde. "If the ladies would care to follow me to the Goose Garden. Lord Farouk will receive them as soon as his game is over."

He led them along one of the five galleries, having relieved Ophelia of her parasol. "I would rather keep it," she told him, politely, when he wanted to take her scarf, too, perplexed at finding this accessory placed somewhere as inappropriate as an ankle. "Believe me, it gives me no choice."

With a sigh, Berenilde checked that Ophelia's veil was properly concealing her face behind its lace screen. "Don't show your injuries—such poor taste. Play your cards right, and you can consider the Jetty-Promenade your second home."

Deep down, Ophelia wondered where exactly her first home might be. Since she'd arrived at the Pole, she'd already visited Berenilde's manor, the Clairdelune embassy, and her fiancé's Treasury, and she hadn't felt at home in any of them.

The butler led them under a vast glass canopy just as there

was a burst of applause, punctuated with "Bravo!" and "Good show, my lord!" Despite the white lace of her veil, Ophelia tried to work out what was going on between the palms of the indoor garden. A group of bewigged nobles was gathered on the lawn around what looked like a small maze. Ophelia was too short to glimpse anything over the shoulders of those in front of her, but Berenilde had no trouble clearing a path for them to the front row: the nobles, as soon as they recognized her, withdrew of their own accord, less for decorum's sake than to be at a safe distance. They would await Farouk's verdict before aligning their behavior to his.

Seeing Berenilde return with Ophelia, Aunt Rosaline hid her relief behind a look of annoyance. "You must explain to me someday," she muttered, "how I'm supposed to chaperone a girl who's forever giving me the slip."

Ophelia's view of the game was now unrestricted. The maze comprised a series of numbered tiles. On some of them, there were geese attached to stakes. Two servants stood at specific stages along the spiraling path and seemed to be waiting for instructions.

She turned to see what everyone was looking at right then: a small, round rostrum overlooking the maze. There, sitting at a dainty table painted the same white as the rostrum, a player was shaking his fist and taking obvious delight in annoying the spectators. Ophelia recognized him from his gaping top hat and cheeky, ear-to-ear grin—it was Archibald, Farouk's ambassador.

When he finally opened his fist, a rattling of dice rang out in the silence.

"Seven!" announced the master of ceremonies. Immediately, one of the servants moved forward seven tiles and, to Ophelia's astonishment, disappeared down a hole.

"Our ambassador's really not lucky at this game," said

someone behind her, sarcastically. "It's his third turn and he *always* lands on the pit."

In one way, Archibald's presence reassured Ophelia. He was a man not without faults, but in this place he was the closest thing she had to a friend, and he at least had the merit of belonging to the Web clan. With very few exceptions, there were only Mirages among the courtiers, and the whiff of hostility that hovered around them made the air unbreathable. If they were all as devious as the Knight, it promised some delightful days to come.

Like the rest of the spectators, Ophelia now concentrated on the table of the other player, further up the rostrum. At first, due to her veil, the only impression she got was of a constellation of diamonds. She finally realized that they were attached to the numerous favorites cradling Farouk in their entwined arms, with one combing his long, white hair, another pressed to his chest, yet another kneeling at his feet, and so on. Leaning his elbow on the table, which was far too small for his stature, Farouk seemed as indifferent to the caresses being lavished on him as to the game he was playing. That, at any rate, is what Ophelia inferred from the way he yawned noisily as he threw his dice. From where she was, she couldn't see his face that clearly.

"Five!" sang out the master of ceremonies in the midst of applause and joyful cries.

The second servant immediately started leaping from square to square. Each time he landed on a tile occupied by a goose, honking furiously and trying to snap at his calves, but he was straight off, going from five to five, until he finished bang on the final square, in the centre of the spiral, to be hailed like an Olympic champion by the nobles. Farouk had won the game. As for Ophelia, she found the spectacle unreal. She hoped someone would bother to get the other servant out of his hole soon.

Up on the rostrum, a small man in a white suit took advantage of the game ending to approach Farouk with what looked like a writing case. He smiled broadly as he had a word in the lord's ear. Baffled, Ophelia saw Farouk casually stamping a paper that the man held out to him, without reading a single word on it.

"See Count Boris as a model," Berenilde whispered to her. "He waited for the right moment to obtain a new estate. Prepare yourself, our turn's coming up."

Ophelia didn't hear her. She'd just noticed the presence of another man on the rostrum who was absorbing all her attention. He stood in the background, so dark and still that he might almost have gone unnoticed had he not suddenly snapped his watch cover shut. At the sight of him, Ophelia felt a burning flash surge up from deep within her until even her ears were red-hot.

Thorn.

His black uniform, with its mandarin collar and heavy epaulettes, wasn't suited to the stifling heat—an illusion, certainly, but a very realistic one—beneath the glass canopy. Stiff as a poker, starchy from head to toe, silent as a shadow, he seemed out of place in the flamboyant world of the court.

Ophelia would have given anything not to find him here. True to form, he would take control of the situation and dictate her role to her.

"Madam Berenilde and the ladies from Anima!" announced the master of ceremonies.

As all heads turned towards Ophelia in a deadly silence, broken only by the honking of the geese, she took a deep breath. The time had finally come for her to join the game.

She would find her place, despite Thorn.

THE KID

As Ophelia walked up to the rostrum, she felt eyes on her that were burning with such curiosity, she wondered if she might end up catching fire. She tried to ignore the cheeky wink Archibald gave her from his gaming table, and climbed the rostrum's white steps while concentrating on a single thought: 'My future depends on what takes place here and now.'

Perhaps it was due to the nervousness Thorn brought out in her, or the lace veil obscuring her vision, or the scarf coiled around her foot, or her pathological clumsiness, but the fact is, Ophelia tripped on the final step of the stairs. She would have fallen flat on the floor had Thorn not caught her in full flight by grabbing her arm and forcibly putting her back on her feet. This near miss, however, went unnoticed by no one— not by Berenilde, whose smile froze; not by Aunt Rosaline, who buried her face in her hands; not by Ophelia's cracked rib, which throbbed furiously against her side.

Laughter rippled across the Goose Garden, but was swiftly stifled once it was noticed that Farouk himself didn't seem to find the situation remotely amusing. With elbow still on table and a look of utter boredom, he hadn't moved an inch since the end of the game, while his diamond-adorned favorites clung to his body as though a natural extension of it.

As for Ophelia, she'd forgotten Thorn the moment the family spirit had focused his inscrutable eyes, with their pale blue, almost white irises, on her. In fact, everything about Farouk was white—his long, smooth hair, his eternally young skin, his imperial garb—but all Ophelia noticed were his eyes. Family spirits were, by nature, impressive. Each ark, with just one exception, had its own. Powerful and immortal, they were the roots of the world's great family tree, the ancestors common to all the great lines. On the rare occasions when Ophelia had met her own ancestor, Artemis, on Anima, she'd felt minuscule. And yet that was nothing compared with how Farouk made her feel right now. Ophelia was separated from him by the distance demanded by protocol, but even so, his psychic power crushed her as he contemplated her with the fixed stare of a statue, without blinking, without a qualm.

"Who's this?" Farouk asked.

Ophelia couldn't reproach him for not remembering her. The only time their paths had crossed, it had been at a distance: she'd been disguised as a valet, and they'd exchanged not a glance. She was taken aback when she realized that his question also referred to Thorn and Berenilde, on whom Farouk had turned his blank eyes. Ophelia knew that family spirits had very bad memories, but all the same! Thorn was the Superintendent of Citaceleste and all the Pole's provinces, and thus was responsible for its finances and a good deal of its judicial administration. As for Berenilde, she was pregnant by Farouk, and the previous day, once again, they had spent the night together.

"Where's the Aide-memoire?" asked Farouk.

"I'm here, my lord!" A young man, who must have been about Ophelia's age, sprang out from behind Farouk's chair. He had the forehead tattoo and the blond beauty of the Web clan. Probably one of Archibald's cousins. "Mr. Ambassador has requested an audience to converse with you on the subject of the situation of your treasurer Mr. Thorn, his aunt Madam Berenilde, and his fiancée Miss Ophelia."

The Aide-memoire had spoken gently and patiently, indicating each person to Farouk as he named them. First to come forward was Archibald, his top hat askew on his tousled hair. Ophelia was convinced he hadn't shaved on purpose: the more solemn the occasion, the more the ambassador defied convention.

"On what subject?"

"On the subject of the disappearance of the Dragon clan, my lord," the Aide-memoire reminded him with angelic sweetness. "The disastrous accident that cost your hunters their lives. Mr. Archibald explained it all to you this morning. Read here, my lord—you noted it down in your memorandum."

The Aide-memoire passed a notebook, dog-eared from much handling, to Farouk. Painfully slowly, Farouk dragged his elbow from the gaming table and began to leaf through it. The favorites adapted to the slightest movement of his body, releasing their embrace here only to tighten it there. Ophelia watched the scene with both fascination and repulsion. Under their diamond tiaras, diamond necklaces, and diamond rings, they no longer really looked like women.

"The Dragons are dead?" asked Farouk.

"Yes, my lord," replied the Aide-memoire. "That's the last thing you wrote."

"'The Dragons are dead,'" repeated Farouk, this time reading out what he'd written. He paused for a long while, still as a block of marble, and then turned another page of his memorandum. "'Berenilde belongs to the Dragons clan.' I wrote that, there."

Farouk had separated each syllable as he had made that statement. Coming from his mouth, the Northern accent took on a thunderous resonance. Distant thunder, barely audible, but truly menacing. When he raised his eyes from his memorandum, Ophelia detected a worrying glint that hadn't been there a moment ago.

"Where is Berenilde?"

With not a word, not a curtsey, Berenilde went forward to stroke his cheek with the tenderness of a real wife. This time, Farouk seemed to recognize her immediately. He gazed at her, uttering not a word himself, but Ophelia sensed there was much more in their silence than in all the conversations in the world.

It was Thorn, impatiently snapping his watch cover shut, who broke the spell. Farouk, with the slowness of a drifting iceberg, then moved once again, seizing the fountain pen his Aide-memoire held out to him and adding a new note in his memorandum. Ophelia wondered whether he was writing, "Berenilde is alive," never to forget it again.

"So, madam," Farouk continued, "you have just lost your whole family. I offer you my condolences." His cavernous voice betrayed not a single emotion, as if an entire branch of his own line hadn't just been wiped out in a bloodbath.

"Most fortunately, I'm not the sole survivor," Berenilde was quick to clarify. "My mother is undergoing treatment in the provinces, unaware of recent events. As for my nephew, here present, he is soon to take a wife. The continuation of the Dragons is assured."

Ophelia almost felt bad. One day she'd try to break it to Berenilde that the marriage would remain unconsummated and there'd be no children.

As murmurs of protest rose among the nobles gathered around the players' rostrum, the word "bastard" was clearly enunciated. Thorn didn't even attempt to defend his honor. With forehead dripping in sweat, his eyes were glued to the dial of his fob watch, as though enduring a considerable delay to his schedule.

"Here's why I requested this audience," Archibald broke in, with a broad smile. "Whether you like it or not, my dear Berenilde, your nephew has never been recognized by the Dragons, and your mother is no longer a spring chicken. Before very long, you will be the sole representative of your clan. This is what calls into question your position at court, as you'll accept in good faith."

His speech was greeted with scattered applause. As the worthy representative of the embassy, Archibald had expressed out loud what everyone was quietly thinking. Ophelia turned round when she heard the sound of a typewriter behind her: a clerk was sitting at a gaming table and recording all that was being said.

"For that reason," Archibald continued, more stridently, "I have offered the official friendship of my family to Madam Berenilde and Miss Ophelia."

This statement cast a terrible chill over the Goose Garden and any applause immediately stopped. Until then, the Mirages were unaware that an alliance had been forged between Berenilde and the Web clan. "It's a diplomatic friendship, not a military alliance," Archibald explained, with the joviality of someone telling a good joke. "The Web wants to ensure that nothing unfortunate happens to these ladies, but it also wants to maintain its political neutrality and to stay out of your little backstairs murders. We thus formally undertake neither to threaten the life of anyone nor to hire someone to do so on our behalf."

Ophelia was staggered by the offhand way in which Archibald tackled such a serious matter. She also noted that he'd said nothing of the linchpin of the aforementioned friendship: Berenilde making him the official godfather of her future child. The direct descendant of a family spirit—it was certainly no minor detail.

"The friendship of my family has its own limitations, my lord," Archibald said, directly to Farouk. "Would you consent to take these ladies under your personal protection, here, at the court?"

Farouk was barely listening to him. He was slumped with boredom, elbows on knees, and any concentration was only for his memorandum, which he was limply leafing through.

Ophelia wondered where the pain in her arm was coming from, and then realized that it was Thorn's hand. He'd not let go of her since her stumble, and was digging his long, bony fingers into her flesh. He tightened them even more when Farouk froze, mid-memorandum, and his white eyebrows shot up, sky-high.

"The reader. I wrote down here that Berenilde would bring a reader to me. Where is she?"

"She's here, my lord," said the Aide-memoire, indicating Ophelia. "Beside her fiancé."

'Here we go,' thought Ophelia, clutching her hands to control their shaking.

"Oh," said Farouk, closing his memorandum. "So it's her."

Silence filled the entire glass canopy as he went over to Ophelia and crouched down in front of her, like an adult drawing level with a child. She hadn't expected such a face-to-face encounter.

Without a qualm, Farouk lifted the lace veil to study Ophelia's face. While he was staring at her, lengthily and attentively, Ophelia struggled, with all her might, not to run for her life. Farouk's mental power was blurring her sight, splitting her head, overwhelming her, body and soul.

"She's damaged," he declared in a disappointed voice, as though sold shoddy goods. The clerk conscientiously tapped these words out on his typewriter. "And also," Farouk continued, "I don't like kids."

Ophelia could see now why no one mentioned Berenilde's pregnancy in front of him. She took a deep breath. If she didn't speak up, right here, right now, her entire future would be in jeopardy. She exchanged a glance with Aunt Rosaline, who indicated that she should speak frankly, and then looked straight at Farouk's face, with its inhuman beauty, forcing herself, above all, not to look away.

"I may not be what one might call a grown-up, but I'm not a kid anymore." Ophelia had a tiny voice that didn't carry far and that often obliged her to repeat herself; so she'd now dug deep in her lungs for enough breath to be heard by all those present on the rostrum. She wasn't merely addressing Farouk, but also Thorn, Berenilde, Archibald, all the people who'd got into the regrettable habit of treating her like a little girl.

Farouk tapped his bottom lip, pensively, and reopened his memorandum at its opening pages. Ophelia was close enough to make out, upside down, the clumsy handwriting and impressive number of sketches. Farouk lingered on the drawing of a little figure with stick arms, orangey-brown colored-in curls, and a giant pair of glasses.

"That's Artemis," he explained, in his drawling voice. "Since she's my sister, and since she's your family spirit, I suppose that makes you a sort of great-great-great-great-grand-niece? Yes," he finally conceded, squinting at the drawing, "I suppose you remind me a little of her. Particularly the glasses."

Ophelia wondered when Farouk had last seen his sister, because Artemis looked nothing like that scribble and didn't wear glasses. Family spirits never left their arks. They may once have shared a childhood together, before the Rupture, but they didn't seem to retain a very vivid recollection of it. They had no memory, a possible side effect of their prodigious longevity, and that gave an aura of mystery to their past—to the past of the whole of humanity, in fact. Even Ophelia, despite being a reader, knew nothing of their personal history. She sometimes wondered whether they themselves had had parents, at some very distant time.

"So, Artemis's girl," Farouk continued, "you can read the past of objects?"

"To my great regret," Ophelia sighed, "it's the only thing I can get my ten fingers to do properly." That, and escaping through mirrors, but the latter was trickier to include in a professional reference.

"Don't regret it." A spark had just lit up beneath Farouk's drooping eyelids. With interminable slowness, he plunged a hand inside his great imperial coat and pulled out a book, its binding encrusted in precious stones. In proportion to Farouk's height, it was the size of a paperback; on the Ophelia scale, it was equivalent to an encyclopedia.

"You could, for example, 'read' my Book."

Ophelia's apprehension on seeing this object was almost as intense as her curiosity. Such a Book deserved its capital "B." Ophelia had long thought that only one of its type existed, on Anima, within Artemis's private archives; a tome so singular and so ancient that the best readers, including Ophelia, had never succeeded in deciphering it. On arriving in the Pole, Ophelia had not only discovered that there were others across the various arks, but also, more importantly, that Farouk's volume was the raison d'être of her marriage.

So, when she finally saw, with her own eyes, this Book, to which her destiny was linked, Ophelia could feel her hands itching and reaching instinctively towards it. By penetrating its secret, maybe she could free herself?

"Not her."

That lugubrious voice had rung out like a funeral gong. It

was the first time Thorn was speaking since the start of the audience. He seemed to have waited for that precise moment to pull suddenly on Ophelia's arm, dragging her back and placing her behind him, well hidden in his shadow. "Me."

Still crouching and clutching his Book, Farouk blinked as he looked up at Thorn, dazed, as if roused from a nap.

"It is I who will read your Book," Thorn continued, his tone unequivocal. "When I have inherited my wife's power, in four months and nine days, and when I have learnt how to use it. It's in our contract."

Thorn put his fob watch away, plunged his fingers into an outside pocket of his uniform, and promptly produced an official document. His other hand still hadn't let go of his fiancée. Ophelia knew that this gesture was neither affectionate nor protective. It was a clear warning to Farouk and his entire court: he, Thorn, had exclusive ownership of her reader's gift.

Ophelia seized up, from head to toe. Of all the discoveries she'd made in the Pole, this was by far the most repugnant. The Ceremony of the Gift was a nuptial ritual during which husband and wife passed on their respective family powers. Thorn had carefully avoided telling Ophelia that he'd organized their marriage with the sole intention of inheriting her Animism and of proving himself as a reader. He had his mother's phenomenal memory, and seemed to think that the combining of their family powers would allow him to go back far enough in time to decipher Farouk's Book.

Thorn wasn't interested in historic discovery itself. He was thinking only of his personal ambition.

"Will you take my fiancée and my aunt into your protection from now until my marriage?" he continued. "Along with all the Animists who will be coming to the Pole, in order to maintain good diplomatic relations with them?"

His Northern accent was, of course, particularly strong,

hardening each syllable, but requesting this favor of Farouk actually seemed to burn his lips. As for Berenilde, she maintained a calm silence; one had to know her well to be aware that her silky smile concealed a certain anxiety.

Ophelia was aware that they were acting together on a theatrical stage, before an audience waiting for just one slip to boo them. Every word, every inflection, every movement mattered. But on this stage, Thorn remained her greatest adversary. Because of him, the only image retained of her would be that of a woman cowering in her husband's shadow.

Sullenly, Farouk reread the terms of the contract Thorn had given him, and then put the Book away inside his coat and straightened up, muscle after muscle, joint after joint, until standing fully upright. Thorn was big; Farouk was gigantic.

"If all she's good for is reading, and I can't ask her to read," he said, slowly, "what am I going to use her for? I only accept, within my entourage, people who can entertain me."

It was now or never. Ophelia stepped out of Thorn's shadow, obliging him to let go of her arm, and then raised her eyes up to Farouk to look squarely at him, and never mind the pain involved.

"I'm not entertaining, but I can make myself useful. I ran a museum on Anima; I could open one up here. A museum, it's like a memory," she stressed, choosing her words carefully. "It's like your memorandum."

Ophelia couldn't see Thorn's expression, as he was behind her, but she could see that of Berenilde, who was smiling no more. This was definitely not what she'd had in mind when asking her to make a good impression. Ophelia tried to ignore the shocked murmurs rising from the audience surrounding the rostrum. With this request, she'd probably broken half the rules of etiquette.

"What kind of museum did you run?" asked Farouk.

"Primitive history," Ophelia swiftly replied, relieved at having succeeded in arousing his curiosity. "Everything relating to the old world. Of course, I can adapt myself to your historical resources."

Farouk seemed truly interested and, for a brief moment, Ophelia thought she'd finally obtained her museum, her independence, and her freedom. So she was incredulous when she heard the response, faithfully recorded by the clerk's typewriter:

"History, then. Perfect, Artemis's girl, you will tell me stories. That will be the price of the protection I give you—you and your family. I appoint you Vice-storyteller."

THE CONTRACTS

Barely had Ophelia descended the rostrum steps when, hampered by her scarf and stunned by what had just happened, she was blinded by a sudden flash of light. It was the first time in her life that she was being photographed and it had to be precisely when she looked most despondent. With black box under arm and shrouded in magnesium smoke, the photographer made a beeline for her. He was a Mirage, bald as a coot and bubbling like a cauldron.

"Miss Animist! I'm Mr. Chekhov, director of the *Nibelungen*, the newspaper with the highest readership of all Citaceleste. Would you answer a few questions? Our Lord Farouk has just appointed you Vice-storyteller," he babbled, without even giving Ophelia a chance to accept. "Are your shoulders broad enough to rival the most excellent Eric, our official Storyteller? You'll need a great deal of talent to share the bill with his amazing mime shows. No one, in his forty years in the business, has ever successfully competed with him! What's your strategy to defend your place on the stage?"

Ophelia didn't know how this newspaper director had managed it, but her dress was drenched in perspiration just from listening to him. A stage? Because, to top it all, she'd have to perform on a stage?

Her embarrassment wasn't helped by the courtiers staring

coldly at her as they awaited her reply. To her relief, everyone's interest in her ceased when, up on the rostrum, Farouk placed a tiara on Berenilde's head. The Mirages applauded this coronation half-heartedly. Seeing Berenilde decked in her diamonds like this, cheeks pink and eyes shining, enhanced by the glass canopy's brilliant luminosity, and with palms and bougainvilleas as a backdrop, Ophelia felt as if she were gazing at an exotic queen. A queen? No, a courtesan.

"I pity her," declared Aunt Rosaline, who, thanks to much elbowing, had finally reached Ophelia. "It can't be easy, loving a fellow who needs diamonds to remember which women he's intimate with."

"She's accepted it for my sake," murmured Ophelia. "Mr. Farouk protects me from his court, but Berenilde, she protects me from Mr. Farouk."

"In fact, I pity you even more than her. I knew Mr. Thorn wasn't very sentimental, but still, one would have to have clockwork for a heart to see you as merely a pair of hands. You're as pale as a blister," fretted Aunt Rosaline. "Is your rib hurting?"

Ophelia had just detached the veil from her hat, fed up with seeing the world through lace.

"It's my own stupidity that hurts. Our family could arrive any day now and everyone's safety will depend on my performance on a stage. Can you really see me as a storyteller?"

Aunt Rosaline opened and then closed her mouth, clearly stumped by the question, and then grabbed Ophelia by the shoulders. "Let's get away from these courtiers while they're distracted. We'll wait for Berenilde outside. And watch where you put your feet: your scarf's not behaving itself."

Ophelia had a final look at the gaming rostrum, where the nobles were flocking to congratulate Berenilde. Thorn was still there, but he was the only person paying no attention to his aunt— he was totally engrossed in reading the minutes just handed to him by the clerk. Ophelia averted her eyes as soon as Thorn raised his, glinting like metal, to peer at her over the typed sheet.

"It's no great love affair, is it!"

The woman who had cooed these words was approaching between the garden's palms. Huge in stature, she wore a veil hung with gold pendants that must have been incredibly heavy. Ophelia didn't feel that reassured when she noticed the Mirage tattoo on her eyelids. She felt even less so when the woman cupped her face in her hands and examined her wounds with a disconcerting familiarity. "Did Mr. Thorn leave you in this state, my dove?"

Ophelia would have liked to reply that it was perhaps the only thing in the world that Thorn wasn't responsible for, but all she could do was let out a sneeze. A strong, heady scent emanated from this woman that made one feel dizzy.

"To whom do we have the honor?" asked Aunt Rosaline.

"I am Cunegond," the Mirage replied, without taking her eyes off Ophelia. "I loved what you tried to do up on that rostrum, my dove. We're alike, you and I."

Cunegond's gold pendants tinkled like little bells when she raised her arm. She pointed out a Mirage among the procession of courtiers. His girth was so impressive, his bearing so splendid that one could practically see only him. A highly effective illusion made the stripes on his frock coat change into all the colors of the rainbow. Ophelia had no difficulty in recognizing Baron Melchior. She had passed him more than once in the corridors of Clairdelune, when she'd worked there disguised as a valet.

"Your bête noire is Mr. Thorn," Cunegond whispered in Ophelia's ear. "My bête noire is my brother. The Baron with the golden fingers! The great illusionist-couturier! The Minister of

41

THE MISSING OF CLAIRDELUNE

Elegance! He was even awarded the highest honor for services rendered to the family. Melchior has always been afforded the footlights while I'm condemned to remain an artist behind the scenes. And do you know why, my dove? Because these gentlemen think that only they are capable of keeping the wheels turning up here."

"What must we do to come out of their shadow?" asked Ophelia, touched to the quick by Cunegond's words.

"Join forces, my dove. Why should ridiculous clan feuding make us rivals? We're women, first and foremost. Enterprising women, what's more!"

"At last, some sense being spoken," intervened Aunt Rosaline. "I'm entirely of your opinion, dearest madam. I would return to Anima reassured if I knew my niece was able to get by on her own. What kind of art do you do?"

Cunegond's smile widened with a sliding of red lips.

"I run Imaginoirs. Establishments for risqué illusions, if you prefer. I named mine 'The Erotic Delights,' and believe me, I don't aim them exclusively at those gentlemen."

From the way Aunt Rosaline's eyes popped out of her head, Ophelia knew that Cunegond had already ceased to be a "dearest madam."

"There are two categories of women in our Lord Farouk's entourage. Those who offer up their charms and those who offer their services. If you don't participate in his pleasure, you won't survive very long here. May I see your hands, my dove?"

After some puzzled hesitation, Ophelia unbuttoned her reader's gloves. With her red fingernails, sharpened like blades, Cunegond traced the lines on her palms with a look of fascination. "They're so small and so ordinary . . . And yet you have the most feared hands in the whole of Citaceleste."

"Because of Mr. Farouk's Book?" Ophelia asked, with surprise.

Cunegond winked at her, briefly revealing the tattoo on her eyelid. "Objects hold no secrets for you. In other words, you're likely to reveal all the court's secrets, and believe me," she whispered very quietly, "they are innumerable."

Ophelia looked more carefully at the nobles gathered around the hedges of the Goose Game and noticed hostile glances being shot at her from a distance. The ladies, in particular, were nervously checking their accessories, as if simply losing a pin could compromise them.

"I have a deal to offer you, my dove," continued Cunegond, clasping Ophelia's hands in her own. "I'll put my finest illusions at your service and I guarantee you a show that will outclass that of the official Storyteller. In exchange," she went on, further lowering her voice, "you'll let your fingers linger here and there for me."

Cunegond was so close that her scent was choking Ophelia like volcanic fumes. "I thank you for your offer," she responded, trying not to cough, "but I must decline it. I never read an object without the consent of its owner."

Cunegond's smile intensified. Her fingernails, however, dug into Ophelia's hands. "You decline?"

"I decline, madam."

"It would seem I was mistaken. I thought I saw an ambitious young woman on that rostrum. May I offer you a little advice, my dove?" Cunegond dug her fingernails deeper into Ophelia's hands and Aunt Rosaline couldn't suppress an anxious gesture. "Never say 'no' to a Mirage."

"Is that a threat?"

It was Archibald who had asked the question. With hands in his frock coat's holey pockets and his old top hat skew-whiff, he had nonchalantly strolled up. Two old women accompanied him, wearing farthingales so wide and so black that they resembled funeral bells.

Cunegond instantly released Ophelia's hands.

"A suggestion, Mr. Ambassador," she replied, addressing the old ladies more than Archibald. "A mere suggestion."

With these words, Cunegond left, pendants clattering, but not without a final glare at Ophelia.

"You don't waste time, Thorn's fiancée!" Archibald guffawed. "Only just presented at court, and already you've made yourself an enemy! And not any old enemy. Nothing's more formidable than a desperate artist."

Ophelia winced with pain as she rebuttoned her gloves. Cunegond hadn't pulled her punches with those fingernails.

"Desperate?" she queried.

Archibald took a pretty blue sandglass from a pocket in his frock coat. Ophelia knew this object by reputation, even if she'd never used one. Pulling out the pin was all it took to trigger the mechanism and find oneself transported, for the duration of one turn of the sandglass, to a kind of paradise. "Try to imagine the brightest colors, the most intoxicating perfumes, the most passionate caresses," Fox had once told her. "And you'll still be way off what this illusion can do for you."

"Lady Cunegond's businesses aren't flourishing," said Archibald. "Her Imaginoirs are going bust, one after the other, since that dear Hildegarde made these blue sandglasses available. Which aristocrat would go and publicly display himself in a shameful venue when he can just, totally discreetly, pull the pin on this? Allow me to present your escorts to you," he said, suddenly switching subjects. "I promised that dear Berenilde some protection. Here it is!"

With a theatrical flourish, Archibald indicated the two old women who were standing silently behind him. Their pale eyes, between which the family tattoo seemed like some mysterious punctuation mark, focused on Ophelia with a professional coldness.

44

"So it's these ladies who are going to defend us?" asked an outraged Aunt Rosaline. "Might not policemen have been more appropriate?"

"You'll be living in the Gynaeceum, like all of Farouk's favorites," explained Archibald. "Men are not permitted to enter there. Don't be concerned—the Valkyries are the best guarantee of your security."

Ophelia, impressed, raised her eyebrows. She'd stayed long enough at Clairdelune to have heard talk of the Valkyries. These women were specialists in diplomatic escorting: they noticed every detail, listened to every conversation with scrupulous attention. They were telepathically linked to the other members of the Web, some of whom were charged with recording, night and day, all that the Valkyries saw and heard. People entrusted to their care were under effective surveillance. Their services weren't offered to just any aristocrat.

Ophelia adjusted her glasses on her nose so she could look Archibald straight in the eye. It was like gazing at the sky through two windows.

"I've been the victim of a terrible mistake. I'm incapable of telling stories. Mr. Ambassador, you offered me your friendship—could you help me to clear up this misunderstanding?"

Archibald shook his head with a smile that was half-apologetic, half-ironic. Despite his tousled hair, ill-shaven jowls, and badly patched clothes, he was outrageously handsome.

"Pardon the expression, Thorn's fiancée, but when you've made your bed, you have to lie in it. Particularly with Farouk."

"I didn't have time properly to plead my case. If I could just demonstrate the validity of my proposal . . . "

"Your proposal?" sneered Archibald. "You mean that ridiculous museum idea? Forget that right away. You'll never interest anyone here in something so boring."

45

"You . . . " spluttered Aunt Rosaline. "You're coarser than a rough-hewn plank!"

Archibald swiveled around to her, thoroughly amused by the insult.

"No, Aunt," said Ophelia. "He's right."

The intense light through the glass canopy made all the dust gathered on her glasses stand out. She took them off to wipe them on the beautiful white dress Berenilde had given her, unconcerned about getting dirty, and started seriously thinking. She'd had weeks to explore new ideas, new possibilities, but instead she'd clung on to her old life.

"I'd like you to take a close look at these," Archibald interrupted. "I 'borrowed' them from the master of ceremonies." He had just pulled out two lovely dice, the ones he had used in the Goose Game. He held them out to Ophelia, but Aunt Rosaline grabbed them so she could pass them on to her niece herself. She had witnessed enough debauchery under Archibald's roof not to tolerate even the lightest brushing of fingers between the two of them.

Ophelia saw that all the sides of the dice were blank.

"Do you understand, Thorn's fiancée? They're loaded. The master of ceremonies is a Mirage, and he decides which numbers must appear on the dice he throws."

"So that's why you always landed on the pit?" muttered Ophelia, stunned by this revelation.

"Farouk always wins. You could have suggested opening a cheese shop, he would have decided to make it a chocolate shop."

Just then, a joyful clamor rose up in the Goose Garden. Ophelia could no longer see the players' rostrum as the palm trees and fountains were blocking her view, but she presumed the game must have started again. A new game with new loaded dice.

"Unless one is smarter," she said, thinking back of Count Boris, who awaited Farouk's victory to obtain his estate. "I should have offered to read his Book, instead of talking about the museum. I allowed Thorn to get the better of me."

Archibald's eyes and smile widened in simultaneous surprise. "Come, come, so no one's told you what happened to the readers who preceded you here?"

"I was told that they all failed and Mr. Farouk took it rather badly. I could try my luck. I have no confidence in myself for all manner of things, but I do achieve excellent evaluations."

"Give up on that one," said Archibald, without the slightest hesitation. "I watched you very closely earlier, on the rostrum; you nearly passed out because Farouk looked at you. Just imagine the effect his anger would have on you. I've seen men who've wept blood and gone raving mad after having disappointed him. Our family spirit is incapable of controlling himself."

Ophelia shook her foot, still entwined in the scarf. If Archibald had sought to terrify her, he'd succeeded.

"Give up on the Book," he insisted. "My family almost ruined itself by employing the top experts to decipher it— philologists, readers, and so on. At least I learnt one lesson: that book is an insoluble equation. Impossible to date since it doesn't change as time passes. Impossible to translate since its script has no equivalent."

"Artemis, our family spirit, possesses a similar Book in her private collection," Ophelia pointed out. "Would all family spirits have one?"

"It's hard to answer that question, each ark having its little secrets," said Archibald, with an enigmatic smile. "But just let Thorn break his bones in your place. You'll make an adorable little widow."

Despite the fake sun, Ophelia was shivering all over. She

47

looked, in turn, at the two Valkyries, who were silently listening to them with professional indifference, and then, quietly, asked: "Why is Mr. Farouk so obsessed with his Book?"

Archibald burst into such riotous laughter that his top hat toppled on to the lawn. "That question, Thorn's fiancée," he replied, once he had got his breath back, "is probably the only thing you have in common with all the inhabitants of the Pole. The Book is Farouk's only obsession. I say to you, and I repeat it in your interest, never, but never, bring up the subject with him ever again."

Archibald picked up his top hat, twirled it in the air, and replaced it on his head with a clown's flourish. And yet Ophelia considered him with great seriousness. He might be provocative and egocentric, but he, at least, wasn't false.

"I haven't met many people here who care about what's in my interest. Thank you, Mr. Ambassador."

"Oh, don't thank me. The more I give you advice, the more your debt to me increases. One day, I'll ask you to settle the bill."

"What debt, what bill?" asked Ophelia, astonished. "You offered me your friendship."

"Exactly. Bad debts make bad friends. Don't worry, you'll find it so enjoyable that you'll hasten to get into debt again."

Ophelia found it distressing that the only valid support that she enjoyed at the court came from such a lustful man. His favorite pastime consisted of pushing women to commit adultery. If Ophelia hadn't been engaged to Thorn, he'd never have shown any interest in her.

"I told you not to associate with such awful people!" exclaimed Aunt Rosaline, whose indignation had turned her sallower than usual. "Mr. Ambassador, I will personally ensure that you keep your distance from my niece!"

Archibald's smile, stretchy as elastic, just kept expanding.

"I'm sorry to contradict you, Madam Rosaline, because I already like you. You won't always be able to keep your eye on this young lady. And neither will you, Mr. Treasurer."

Ophelia turned around so impulsively that the pain caused by her cracked rib winded her. Two heads higher, there was Thorn, right behind her. He loomed like a monolith in the middle of the lawn, with a typed document in his hand. Ophelia had never seen him looking at ease anywhere, on any seat, at any table, in any gathering, but she had to admit that he looked particularly ill at ease in this exotic garden. The harsh light made the two scars on his face stand out, and sweat was pouring from his pale hair. He must have been truly baking in that official uniform. Far from that softening him, he seemed, on the contrary, tense from head to foot.

Thorn handed his piece of paper to Ophelia, paying as much attention to Archibald as he would to a rug. "I've come to give you your contract."

"Just spare me any of your comments," snapped Ophelia, snatching the paper out of his hand. She'd taken Thorn on and had lost miserably. It would take just one criticism, one sarcastic remark for her to let rip.

Thorn wasn't remotely disconcerted. "I also wish to inform you that I succeeded in making radiotelegraphic contact with your family. I managed to reassure all of them of your fate and postpone their arrival until later."

This was probably the best news of the day. Ophelia, however, took this announcement as an additional affront. "And it didn't cross your mind that I might have liked to be part of this radiotelegraphic contact? Since our departure, my parents have received none of our letters and we've received none of theirs. Do you have the slightest idea of how isolated that made us feel, my aunt and me?"

"I attended first to what was most urgent," replied Thorn, without even a glance at Archibald, who seemed to be relishing the situation. "The presence here of the members of your family, in the current climate, would be as dangerous for them as for us. I'll ensure that your next letters reach them."

"And what about your contract?" asked Ophelia. "Do I have the right to read it, or is that none of my business either?"

Thorn was continually scowling, but Ophelia's remark deepened his scowl another notch. He pulled an envelope from an inside pocket of his uniform. "I intended to give you this copy. Never be parted from it, and confront Farouk with it as often as necessary."

Ophelia unsealed the envelope. She dropped the paper it contained, picked it up off the lawn, and read it with the closest attention. It was a copy of Thorn's contract. It was all there: the organizing of his betrothal with a reader from Anima (Ophelia's name wasn't explicitly mentioned); the date of the marriage, on the 3rd of August; and even, already scheduled for November, the date of the reading of the Book. It was made very clear that the fiancée chosen by Thorn would be exempt from any involvement in this contract. Ophelia's glasses darkened when compensation for the reading of the Book was referred to: "If successful, Mr. Thorn will obtain an official noble title and his bastard status will henceforth be considered null and void."

Ophelia felt a lump rise in her throat. All of Thorn's ambition contained in two lines. He'd wrenched her from her family and put her in danger just to play at being an aristocrat. Berenilde featured nowhere; he'd spared not a single thought for his own aunt, despite the personal risks she'd taken to help him with his plan.

Thorn didn't care about anyone; Ophelia decided not to care about him anymore.

"One day, I will settle the bill," she promised Archibald. "Allow me to choose in what way—I'll ensure that it's fair."

Archibald possessed a full spectrum of smiles, but never had Ophelia seen him grimacing in such a way, as if she'd embarrassed him. It lasted but the blink of an eye, as he hastily gave a comedic slap to his top hat.

"I can't wait to see your bill, Thorn's fiancée. In the meantime, I take my leave of you. I've been away from Clairdelune too long," he said, tapping his little forehead tattoo. "When the cat's away, the mice will play."

The mice were his sisters, whom he jealously protected. As he turned on his heels with a pirouette, he almost hit Aunt Rosaline, who had moved to block his path. With the tip of her chin raised, her equine, stern face, her tiny bun pointing skyward, and her hands folded on her austere dress, she was female dignity personified.

"Mr. Ambassador, you are lewder than a salt shaker. I would be lying if I claimed to harbor any deep affection for Mr. Thorn," she said with a glance at the latter, who was paying more attention to his watch than to anything else, "but he is the legitimate fiancé. Give me a single good reason why I should permit you to continue to frequent my niece."

"You will give me that permission," Archibald asserted, calmly, "since you will be the first to seek my company."

With these words, as Aunt Rosaline was already opening her mouth in outrage, he placed a little kiss on her cheek. Ophelia held her breath. Her aunt had already relegated hand-kisses to the category of obscene practices; she was never going to accept such familiarity without responding with an almighty slap.

The slap never came. Ophelia couldn't believe her eyes when she saw Aunt Rosaline's yellow complexion turn pink and her hard face soften under the effect of intense emotion.

She was gazing at Archibald as if she'd just floated off into the sky of his eyes.

Archibald gave a final tip of his hat to Aunt Rosaline, the Valkyries, and Ophelia, and then disappeared between the palm trees, gleefully swinging the chain of his blue sandglass.

"Aunt?" asked Ophelia, concerned. "Are you alright?" In truth, she looked twenty years younger. "Sorry?" stammered Aunt Rosaline. "Of course I'm alright, what a question. It's stifling under this glass canopy," she added, nervously fanning herself. "Let's get out."

Ophelia watched her moving off, totally discomfited. It was one thing seeing all the ladies at court falling under Archibald's spell; it was quite another seeing one's own aunt falling under it, too.

"I think allying yourself with Archibald was a bad idea," Thorn commented while winding his fob watch.

Ophelia looked up at him with what composure she had left. "Fine. Is that all you had to say to me?"

"No."

Thorn's steely look had hardened, now they were alone. Ophelia had expected as much. After the way she'd sought to thwart him publicly, right under Farouk's nose, she couldn't hope to avoid what was coming.

"Just tell me what you're really thinking," Ophelia said, impatiently. "Let's get it over and done with."

"What you did, earlier, on that rostrum," said Thorn, his voice leaden. "It was brave."

He tucked his fob watch into his uniform pocket and, in turn, left without a backward glance.

Fragment: First Reprise

In the beginning, we were as one. But God felt we couldn't satisfy him like that, so God set about dividing us.

A wall. The flickering light of a torch-lamp. Children's scribbles pinned up on each panel of wallpaper.

This memory's level of precision is relatively high. He must have spent dozens of hours staring at it, this wall. On the other hand, he can no longer remember what the rest of the room looked like. For the moment, nothing else exists beyond the wall, the torch-lamp and these children's scribbles.

The angle of the light changes, then stills. He must have placed the lamp on a table, so that it continued to light up the wall. No, the angle of the light is too low for a table. Rather on a chair or a bed. He's probably in a bedroom. His bedroom?

The shadow of his body, at first hazy and huge, becomes more clearly defined as he gets closer to the wall. What's so fascinating about these scribbles that he should be so fixated on them? One drawing in particular holds all his attention: a multicolored scribble that depicts them together, him and the others. Carefully, he removes the four thumbtacks, one by one.

Behind the drawing, a hole. On this particular part of the wall, there's no more wallpaper, or lining, or brick. A hiding place? He peers deep into the hole. All is black. He can't see what lies on the other side of the wall.

"Artemis?" he hears himself whisper. He has great difficulty recognizing the shrill voice, strangely accented, that comes out of his mouth. So is that how he spoke, before? "Artemis!" he hears himself whisper again, tapping gently on the wall. The slightest sound of steps, the scraping of a brick being pulled out, and, finally, an eye blinking right at the back of the hole. Artemis's eye?

"I was looking at the stars through the skylight. It's interesting." Artemis's voice is very calm, without expression, muffled by the thickness of the wall. "You should put your brick back in place as I have done. We no longer have permission to speak to each other, remember."

In fact, he would dearly like to remember. He remembers Artemis's eye, Artemis's voice, Artemis's words through the hole in the wall, but he can't remember why they were separated. "The others," he can still hear himself whispering. "Do you know if they're well?"

"They are more obedient than you," says Artemis's eye. "I haven't spoken through Janus's wall for days. He was a bit bored but, yes, he was well. He gave me news of Persephone's wall, and she was well, too. And you? Helen's wall?"

"She never replies."

"She hears everything, Helen," says Artemis's eye. "She would hear the blink of an eye from the other end of the house. If she doesn't reply, it's because she's obeying. We're going to do likewise. Go back to bed."

This time, he doesn't hear himself replying. Is the memory already slipping away? No, it's something else. He didn't reply to Artemis's eye because something unexpected prevented him from doing so.

The shadow of God.

He can see it again clearly on the wall, superimposed on his own. God is in his bedroom, just behind him. Artemis's eye disappears from the back of the hole as she hastily puts her brick back in place.

He remembers now. It's God who separated them—him, Artemis, Helen, Janus, Persephone and all the others. Seeing God's shadow on the wall, he can almost feel again the fear and anger that ran through him at the time. He must turn around, he must stop looking at this wall, he must look God in the face.

He finally turns around, but his memory stubbornly refuses to give a face, a form, a voice to God, who is approaching him, slowly.

The memory ends here.

Nota bene: "Try your dears." Who said these words and what do they mean?

THE LETTER

Ophelia's first weeks at court were certainly not what she'd imagined. This was doubtless linked to the fact that she'd not set foot in it again.

After Farouk had appointed her Vice-storyteller, Ophelia had been installed, with Berenilde, in the Gynaeceum, on the sixth floor of the tower, just above that of the Jetty-Promenade, and she'd not left it since. Every morning, the Lord Chamberlain would pass through the lift's golden gate, unfurl a sheet of paper, and call out, one by one, the courtesans chosen to serve as escorts for Farouk. While Berenilde's name was always on his list, not once was Ophelia's mentioned. And if there was one place where it didn't feel good to be forgotten by Farouk, it was definitely the Gynaeceum.

This mellow world seemed to come straight out of an oriental print. The sun never set. Each courtesan had her own dwelling, and Berenilde's was a veritable ode to relaxation, with its banquettes, cushions, rugs, and ottomans, all bathed in light filtered through the fretwork shutters.

This mellowness was deceptive. The courtesans living in the Gynaeceum were nearly all Mirages and they had viewed the intrusion of new rivals in their nest very unfavorably. Barely would the lift gate have closed on Berenilde before hostilities commenced. One morning, Ophelia was covered head to toe in pustules. The following day, she started giving off a ghastly whiff of dung. The day after that, she couldn't move without letting off thundering flatulence noises. Thankfully, they were just temporary illusions cast on her when her back was turned, and they disappeared in a few hours, but the resourcefulness shown by these courtesans to humiliate her was boundless.

"It's intolerable!" Aunt Rosaline finally exploded when Berenilde returned one evening from the Jetty-Promenade. "What use are they to us, your Valkyries, if everyone here can mistreat this girl when the fancy takes them?"

She had pointed an accusatory finger at the old ladies, who didn't even do her the honor of batting an eyelid. The Valkyries followed Ophelia and Berenilde wherever they went, slept by their sides, ate at their table, as discreet and silent as two shadows, but they never got involved in their daily affairs.

"For now, it's nothing more than childishness," Berenilde asserted, turning to Ophelia who, on that occasion, sported a pig's snout. "However, this situation can't go on forever. I know these ladies—their attempts to intimidate are going to get increasingly bold, and that will continue so long as our lord hasn't given you another look. If he loses interest in you as a person, you won't be able to honor your contract and his protection will no longer pertain. I attempted to slip him a note about you, but how do you expect the lord chamberlain to put you down on the list when your appearance is so unappealing?"

Sitting at the salon's tea table, Ophelia didn't respond, concentrating instead on the letter she was trying to write to her parents. Thorn had promised to safeguard any correspondence, but it was a real headache recounting her life here without totally horrifying them.

For her part, Ophelia was far less preoccupied by the illusions disfiguring her than by the role of vice-storyteller, which, sooner or later, she would have to fulfill. She'd not found a single book in the Gynaeceum to help her put some ideas together, so, for want of anything better, she was putting her free time to good use by improving her diction with pronunciation exercises. She would have liked to know, at least, what kind of stories Farouk enjoyed listening to. She didn't even know herself what kind she'd like to tell.

The Pole's family spirit is requesting that I tell him Animist stories, she ended up writing to her great-uncle. *You wouldn't have some ideas for me?*

Her great-uncle was an archivist, and the family member to whom Ophelia felt closest. And yet she didn't dare tell even him what was really going on here.

With each day, she missed Fox and Gail more. They were the only true friends Ophelia had made in the Pole, but they existed in a different world from hers, and led a life already hard enough as it was. She relieved herself in gold lavatories, while they scoured those of Clairdelune.

Occasionally, Ophelia would find herself missing Mime's livery, which, for a long time, had guaranteed her total anonymity. For example, when she came across Cunegond in the Gynaeceum. The Mirage supplied the other courtesans with saucy illusions, and had easy access almost everywhere. Ophelia shuddered whenever she heard the tinkle of her pendant-hung veil, or smelled her strong scent at the turning of a gallery. Cunegond never said a word to her, but never missed a chance to let her know, with a telling look, that she hadn't forgotten her affront in the Goose Garden.

If Cunegond made Ophelia feel uncomfortable, it was nothing compared with how the Knight made her feel when she saw him. And she saw him much too often for her liking.

At the Gynaeceum, there were visiting times set aside specially for the children. These were never Farouk's actual offspring—the child Berenilde was carrying was the exception that proved the rule—but some courtesans had previously been wives and mothers. The Knight took advantage of this to bring gifts to Berenilde. He created the most beautiful illusions of flowers and perfumes for her, but she stubbornly refused each of his gifts.

"Never open the door to him in my absence," she continually advised Ophelia and Aunt Rosaline. "This is the first time anyone has stood up to that child, so he could react unpredictably."

Berenilde didn't know how right she was. The Knight was so obsessed with her, so distraught at her disdain, so pathologically jealous that, one day, he took it out on another child at whom she had made the mistake of smiling. The child started running across the patio and rolling on the ground while calling for his mother's help, as if he were burning with invisible flames. He was left with no aftereffects, at least visible ones, and the Knight insisted that it was "for a laugh," but Ophelia was horrified by the spectacle. Since then, she'd woken with a start every night thinking she could see bottle-bottom glasses glinting at the end of her bed.

"I don't know how you manage to control yourself like that," muttered Aunt Rosaline, glancing nervously through the half-open shutters. "That little Mirage makes the pins on my head stand on end. One day you must explain to me why you all call him 'Knight.' He's a real public hazard, more like!"

"He's the one who proclaimed himself as such," sighed Berenilde. "And you don't even know the funniest part. He did it in my honor. He claims to be my liege knight."

"So there's not a single adult to control him? We're surely not going to spend our time hiding from him."

"Count Harold is his uncle and guardian. He's an old man who's a little hard of hearing. He rarely shows himself in society and dedicates more time to the breeding of his dogs than to the upbringing of his nephew. I suppose I have contributed to making that child what he has become," murmured Berenilde, stroking her rounded stomach. "A willfulness that knows no limits."

"Why do you say that?" Ophelia asked her.

Berenilde didn't reply. In her beautiful eyes there was an unfamiliar touch of sadness that left Ophelia deep in thought. This situation probably had something to do with the manor Berenilde had inherited from the Knight's own parents. Ophelia still recalled her great surprise on first discovering that strange estate, with its artificial autumn and mysterious child's room that seemed to await the return of its former occupant. Berenilde had every reason in the world to hate the Knight, but, actually, she didn't reject him that vehemently.

This was true, at any rate, until the evening when the Knight moved a little too close to Ophelia. He'd taken advantage of Berenilde's brief absence to sneak into her apartment, without Aunt Rosaline or the Valkyries knowing. With total astonishment, Ophelia had seen him enter the room in which she was busy having her bath, and start to chat to her as though it were the most natural thing in the world. When Berenilde had discovered the Knight resting his elbows on Ophelia's bath, she had become livid and, incapable of containing her power any longer, had flung him to the other end of the corridor. When he'd got up, very shaken, his thick glasses were broken.

"If you start on this child," Berenilde had hissed, "I will kill you with my very own claws. Get out and don't show me your face ever again."

The Knight, tormented with both rage and sorrow, fled the Gynaeceum, and didn't return either the next day, or on any of those that followed. As for Ophelia, she never saw Berenilde in the same way again. This difficult woman, who had frequently given her a hard time, had defended her as she would her own daughter.

"What you did is admirable," Aunt Rosaline had congratulated her. "At last we're going to have a little peace!"

Ensuing events proved her not entirely right.

One morning in April, the clatter of the letter box echoed through the apartment. Ophelia's heart leapt sky-high when she saw her name on the envelope. But she soon realized that it was far from a letter from her family:

Miss Vice-storyteller,

Your marriage with Mr. Treasurer is scheduled for August 3. I regret to inform you that you will be dead before then, unless you follow my advice. Leave the Pole without delay and never come back.

GOD DOESN'T WANT YOU HERE.

"What was it?" asked Aunt Rosaline.

"An error," lied Ophelia, having hidden the letter. "Which phrase should I focus on for elocution, do you think? 'The Dragon will come when he hears the drum,' or 'Six sick sea serpents swam the seven seas'?"

Ophelia waited until she was in bed to reread the letter several times.

GOD DOESN'T WANT YOU HERE.

Ophelia had received threats in the past, but never before with such a tone. Was it a hoax? Religion and theology were but ancient folklore on Anima, as on many arks where the family spirits alone embodied the absolute. Was the "God" in this letter supposed to designate Farouk?

The message was obviously not signed and no sender was

indicated on the envelope. Ophelia pulled off the reader's gloves she wore to sleep and fingered every inch of paper. It surely wasn't using her power dishonestly to apply it to a letter addressed to her, was it? Especially a death threat.

But she was disturbed not to sense anything special: no strong impression, no particular vision. The letter had been typed, but its writer must have touched it in some way. After closer examination, Ophelia did pick up some traces on the sheet of paper, and on the envelope, as if they had been handled with the help of pincers.

Despite the fake sun filtering through the slits in the shutters, which flooded the bed's mosquito net with light and drowned Ophelia in the oppressive warmth of an eiderdown, she felt an icy shiver. It was impossible for her to read objects that had been manipulated at one remove. This anonymous messenger seemed very well informed about what she could and couldn't do with her hands.

It wasn't what the letter said that troubled her the most; it was more what it didn't say. Why this desire, at all costs, to thwart Thorn's marriage? Was it simply clan rivalry, in that endless battle for influence that surrounded Farouk?

Ophelia leapt out of bed and rummaged in her mess until she found the copy of the contract Thorn had given her. "If successful," she read again, "Mr. Thorn will obtain an official noble title and his bastard status will henceforth be considered null and void."

Now that Ophelia thought about it, this payoff was, in fact, derisory. Thorn was already a feared top-ranking official, and his ennoblement would fundamentally change nothing for his enemies. And that could mean only one thing. What concerned the opposing camp wasn't Thorn rising in rank; it was the actual reading of Farouk's Book.

But then again, why?

'Thorn, into what soup have you gone and dropped me?' Ophelia thought.

The following week, during an interminable afternoon of "Who washed the white woolen underwear when the washerwoman went west . . . ", while Ophelia and Aunt Rosaline were, at the same time, trying to dry their own washing on the terrace, the telephone in the boudoir rang.

"I have a call for Miss Ophelia," a woman's voice announced as soon as Ophelia picked up the receiver.

"Uh . . . that's me."

"You are Miss Ophelia?"

"Yes. And to whom am I speaking?"

"You're requested to enter into communication with the Treasury, please wait a moment."

Ophelia was about to protest, having no desire to be connected to anything whatsoever to do with the Treasury, but she was distracted by a sound of hail. She'd knocked the contents of her clothes-peg box onto the floor. She was just picking up all the pegs, phone wedged between shoulder and neck, when a gloomy voice boomed in her ear.

"Hello?"

Hearing Thorn reawakened such nervousness in Ophelia that she seriously considered hanging up on him.

"Hello?" repeated Thorn.

"Have you changed your secretary?" asked Ophelia, seated on the floor surrounded by pegs.

"No. Why do you speak to me of him?"

From the aggressive tone, Ophelia could visualize the accompanying frown.

"I've just had a woman on the line."

"An operator," Thorn specified, as if it were blindingly obvious. "Farouk's tower and the Treasury aren't linked to the same telephone exchange and we have no automatic systems."

Ophelia understood nothing of this jargon. On Anima, the telephones managed very nicely between themselves, and that was it. "What did you want to say to me?"

"It seems to me that it's rather you who should say something to me," retorted Thorn's monotonous voice. "I have had no news from you since you moved in."

The final peg that Ophelia was about to return to its box suddenly came alive to bite her finger, infected by her anger. For a moment, she considered telling Thorn about the typed letter, confronting him with the danger to which they were currently exposing her, him and his damned ambition, but what difference would it have made? Thorn was already aware of the risks and he hadn't cancelled their engagement for all that.

"There's nothing you need to know."

"You are still angry with me," Thorn observed, in a neutral voice. "And yet I thought we had straightened things out. We came to an agreement that we had, both of us, taken the wrong path."

Ophelia closed her eyes, in the grip of emotion. Now out of control, the peg was twitching on her finger like an enraged crab.

"No, Thorn. You came to an agreement on your own."

"You should consider . . ."

"Listen to me carefully," Ophelia interrupted him. "I felt truly sorry for you because I believed that Berenilde had arranged this marriage, that we were her two puppets. I now know that there was only ever a single puppet from the start, and that it was me. Your wanting to marry me for my hands is a concept I can accept—I've seen the kind of world you grew up in. But learning it from a mouth other than yours," she concluded, in a subdued murmur, "for that I will never forgive you."

A deathly silence had suddenly filled the phone's ear trumpet. Instead of expending all her anger, Ophelia had expended all her breath; her diction exercises had at least served a purpose. She concentrated on the boudoir's floral wallpaper, trying to ignore that peg tearing angrily at the seam of her glove.

"Did you hear what I just said to you, Thorn, or must I repeat it to you?"

"Don't repeat it." The Northern accent so hardened his voice, it was difficult to know when he was displeased, and when he wasn't.

"Right. Is there anything else before I hang up the phone?"

Ophelia hoped there wasn't. Her hand was shaking so hard, she wasn't sure she could hold the heavy mother-of-pearl receiver against her ear for much longer.

"I think you should come," Thorn replied after a moment's reflection. "Alone, preferably."

"Excuse me?" With the poor reception and crackling on the line, Ophelia couldn't dismiss the possibility that she'd misheard.

"I'm arranging a meeting with you. An official meeting, between future husband and future wife. Can you still hear me?"

"Yes, yes, I can hear you," she stammered. "But really, why see each other? I've just told you that . . ."

"We simply can't allow ourselves to be enemies," cut in Thorn. "You're making my life difficult with your resentment; it's imperative that we become reconciled. I'm not permitted to enter the Gynaeceum; meet me at the Treasury, insult me, slap me, smash a plate over my head if you feel like it, and then let's never speak of it again. Name your day. This Thursday would suit me. Let's say . . ." The sound of hastily turned pages could be heard in the ear trumpet. "Between eleven-thirty and twelve. Shall I put you down on my schedule?"

Outraged, Ophelia hung up the phone as angrily as if she'd slammed it down on Thorn's skull.

"This sun really is useless!" Aunt Rosaline declared, as Ophelia returned. "The sheets are smarter than us—they've totally grasped that it's fake. Small wonder the washerwoman went west, when nothing dries."

The black rage in which Ophelia had been immersed since her telephone conversation with Thorn lifted one evening when a servant delivered two letters and three parcels to the apartment. At first, Ophelia feared it would be more death threats, but this time the postmark said "ANIMA."

"Come on, come on, what does it say?" urged Aunt Rosaline as Ophelia ineptly tore open the envelope of the first letter.

"Mother is furious but relieved," Ophelia summarized as she read. "She accuses me of causing her violent palpitations by my silence. She wants me to send photographs next time as my descriptions made no sense to her. She's astonished to learn that we get so much sunshine in the middle of the polar winter, and asks if I didn't go to the wrong ark. Ah, she's giving me a new coat, but apparently it's just as bad-tempered as its maker . . . That must be the big parcel, there, that's twitching. She hopes I'm making a good impression on my new family."

"She should start by hoping that your in-laws are making a good impression on you," Aunt Rosaline muttered between her long teeth. "And then?"

"And then Agatha takes over. She's expecting another baby."

"Already? Well, your sister doesn't waste time."

"She says it won't prevent her from coming to the wedding. She's made a dress to match her eyes, which she intends to wear specially for the occasion. She's already altered it to fit being six months pregnant. She's also planned pretty white dresses for our little sisters."

"Is that it?"

"No. She reproaches me for not having sent them a wedding list. She wants to replace my scarf with a shawl, but is hesitating over the color."

"Coats, dresses, shawls . . ." Aunt Rosaline repeated, rolling her eyes. "And then?"

"It's Father who takes over. He wants to know if I get on well with my fiancé and his family, he's looking forward to seeing me again for the wedding, and he's—"

"He's what? I didn't quite catch the end of your sentence."

Ophelia hadn't spoken it. *I am sorry.* She felt her throat tightening, her nose prickling, and her eyes blurring even more than usual. She had to get a grip to continue reading in an almost composed voice.

"Hector ends the letter. He asks me why it's sunny and night at the same time in the Pole, why I wrote 'Citaceleste' instead of just 'Citadel,' and why I speak of everything except Thorn. He sends me a top that he animated himself and that never stops spinning. That must be the little parcel that's humming."

"Your brother's the smartest of them all," declared Aunt Rosaline. She had taken the chance, while Ophelia was opening the second envelope, to blow her nose as discreetly as she could into a handkerchief. On her side, Ophelia hoped her aunt wouldn't notice how much her own chin was wobbling.

"It's my godfather," she said, with an irrepressible smile. "One word from me and he'll be on the first airship heading for the Pole." Ophelia would never have asked so much of him, of course. She was putting Aunt Rosaline in enough danger without getting another member of the family embroiled, too. And yet she found these few words incredibly comforting. "The last parcel is from him. He says no more than that so it's a surprise for me."

Ophelia tore off the reinforced paper of the package. It contained an illustrated book, quite a thick one, which smelt a bit of the cellar and was entitled:

TALES OF OBJECTS AND OTHER ANIMIST STORIES
(FREE ADAPTATION OF FABLES OF THE OLD WORLD)

Hoping that it will come in useful, kid, said the sloping handwriting at the top of the first page. *Artemis has a copy in her private collection, maybe it will appeal to her brother?*

If her great-uncle had been standing there, in front of her, Ophelia would have thrown herself into his arms.

"Your godfather has great timing." Berenilde had waited until Ophelia had finished reading her letters to approach her with a swish of her dress. Her two beringed fingers held out an invitation card; as soon as Ophelia took hold of it, the illusion of a miniature firework display burst out before her eyes.

SURPRISE NOCTURNAL EVENT!
*LORD FAROUK INVITES THE ENTIRE COURT
TO JOIN HIM AT THE SPLENDID OPTICAL THEATER,
TONIGHT, AT THE STROKE OF MIDNIGHT.*

"The entire court?" queried Ophelia. "Do you think that includes me?"

"You should read the whole invitation," suggested Berenilde.

Ophelia's glasses paled on her nose when she discovered the night's lineup:

THE STORYTELLER'S LUMINOUS MIME SHOWS
FOLLOWED BY THE VICE-STORYTELLER'S ORIGINAL TALES

"Is that a joke?"

"It's in an hour's time," Berenilde asserted with utmost seriousness. "And to think I've only just returned from the Jetty-Promenade! That leaves me barely enough time to change my outfit."

THE THEATER

Ophelia reread the opening sentence of *Tales of Objects and Other Animist Stories* for the twentieth time without managing to understand it. The surrounding conversations and laughter didn't help. The lift descending from the sixth to the fifth floor of the tower was packed. Squashed between the farthingales of the old Valkyries, sterner and more silent than ever, who were sitting on either side of her on a banquette, Ophelia was feverishly leafing through her great-uncle's book. Should she choose that tale? Or rather this one? She was continually interrupted by favorites coming to wish her good luck with barely concealed insincerity. Berenilde had to resort to some gems of diplomacy and flattery to get them to go away.

"Badly powdered wigs alive!" cursed Aunt Rosaline. "They never once uttered a word to us since our arrival, and now that we need quiet, they can't hold their tongues. And you, stop turning those pages," she said, tapping Ophelia's fingers, "you're getting nowhere. Choose a single tale and read it right through several times."

Ophelia applied this advice to the letter. She picked a story at random, "The Doll," skimmed through it from beginning to end without taking in a single word, and then started again. She didn't tear her eyes away from her book when the lift's gate opened on to the dazzling sunshine of the court; or

70

when she was carried along by a throng of nobles through a Jetty-Promenade arcade; or when her bootlace came undone, threatening several times to trip her up; or when she ascended a red-carpeted staircase with gold rods.

She only lifted her nose out of her book when a butler came and spluttered in her ear: "Miss Vice-Storyteller, please come this way."

Blinded, Ophelia blinked. She found herself in the theater's reception hall, where the white flagstones, white columns, and white statues were reflecting the light from the windows like snow. With champagne flutes in one hand and blue sandglasses in the other, all of Citaceleste high society was here. The women were dressed in sophisticated ensembles and hung with long pearl necklaces; the men wore white suits, black bow ties, and blue-ribboned boaters. Ophelia had rarely felt so out of fashion, in her little purple dress that buttoned her up to the chin, her old, badly knitted scarf, and her shapeless hair, which she'd forgotten to style.

"This way, Miss Vice-Storyteller," the butler patiently repeated while coughing against his fist. He was indicating a secret door, behind the reception bar. "Normally, Miss Vice-Storyteller should have gone through the stage door, behind the theater."

"Is Mr. Farouk here?"

"Yes, the lord is already settled in his seat. He is eager to hear miss's stories. Very sorry, madam," the butler added when Aunt Rosaline attempted to follow Ophelia behind the bar. "This area is off-limits to the public."

"What's this nonsense?" protested Aunt Rosaline. "But come now, this is my niece!"

"Not at the Splendid, madam. Here, miss is the vice-storyteller of Lord Farouk. Access to the stage is strictly controlled for security reasons."

"Come now, I'm hardly carrying explosives under my dress!"

"Don't worry, auntie, everything will be fine," promised Ophelia, not believing a word of it. "Try to find yourself a seat close to the stage. If I see you, it will give me courage."

"Here," Aunt Rosaline whispered, slipping a comb into her hand. "When you have a moment, try to untangle your hair."

"A final word of advice, madam?" Ophelia asked, turning to Berenilde. For the first time, the smile the beautiful widow gave her didn't seem like one of those made-to-measure expressions she produced with the ease of an actress. It was a somewhat fragile smile, quivering at the corners of the mouth. The smile of a concerned mother.

"Be impressive." Berenilde laid her velvet-gloved hand on Ophelia's cheek. "I don't say that to make you anxious. I say it because you are capable of it, as I have witnessed more than once."

Ophelia didn't feel remotely impressive as she walked unsteadily towards the secret door, and even less so when Cunegond stood in her way, pointing her big, red fingernail at her. "Well, well, my dove, is that your only material?" she asked, indicating her book. "Know that my offer still stands: your hands for my illusions. Accept," she cooed, "and I'll furnish you, starting this evening, with special effects so grandiose that they will suffice to make you the new official storyteller."

"I'm not interested," Ophelia replied.

Cunegond shook her head, looking sorry, and the golden pendants on her veil tinkled like little bells. "You're as stubborn as a mule." She leant so close up, she brushed Ophelia's ear with her lips. "Haven't you heard the rumor, then?" she whispered very quietly to her. "Your dear Archibald has apparently lost one of his guests in entirely obscure circumstances. Perhaps you should review your friendships, my dove."

Considering the conversation closed, Ophelia slipped through the secret door and plunged into the backstage area of the theater. She hadn't the slightest idea what Cunegond was referring to, and for the moment it was the least of her worries.

With heart pounding and scared stiff, she sat down on the first chair she found. Only then did she notice that she was sitting beside an old man who was meticulously cleaning a small, painted glass slide with a cloth. He bore the mark of the Mirages on his eyelids.

"Good evening," she whispered to him. "I'm Ophelia. You're Mr. Eric, the official storyteller?"

Moving slowly, the old man turned in his chair so that he was facing Ophelia. He was muscular for his age. His hair and beard, dyed blue, merged into a single plait hanging down his body and almost touching the floor. For a brief moment, he raised his eyes in surprise to the top of Ophelia's head, disconcerted, perhaps, by her mass of messy curls, then frowned with eyebrows also dyed blue.

"I hope you're very inspired, Miss Vice-storyteller," he said, rolling his "r"s as though chomping on rock. "Because for my part, I'm going to ensure that our two names are never again linked on an invitation card."

With these words, he grabbed his box of slides with one hand, a magic lantern with the other, and went off to a different backstage corner.

Now that she was alone, with only her restless scarf for company, Ophelia could feel her knees knocking, one against the other. She wasn't ready. She'd already forgotten half of her doll story, but if she reread it just one more time, she would definitely make herself sick. She remembered how much she'd suffered when Farouk had merely looked at her, on the rostrum at the Goose Game; what on earth happened when one disappointed such a creature? If she failed, would Ophelia be allowed a second chance, or would her whole future be in jeopardy?

She pulled Aunt Rosaline's comb through her thick hair, trying to keep her hands occupied, but broke one of its teeth at the first knot.

"Drink this."

Ophelia squinted at the glass that had just suddenly appeared in front of her nose. On the other side of it there was Archibald and his immutable smile.

"No thanks," muttered Ophelia, instantly averting her eyes. Her throat was dry, but Berenilde had taken her through such a long list of the poisons swilling around the court that she'd retained the gist of it: never accept a gift from a stranger. And despite all that time spent at the embassy, Ophelia barely knew Archibald.

"I promise you that it's just water," he said, cajolingly. "Look, I'm drinking a mouthful of it myself."

He matched action to words, in an exaggerated way, and then again held the glass out to Ophelia. This time she accepted it, but still refused to look Archibald in the eye.

"What are you doing here?" she asked, defensively. "Backstage is off-limits to the public."

Archibald swiveled the chair old Eric had just been sitting on and sat on it the wrong way around, casually resting his elbows on its back. "I'm not ambassador for nothing. I have access almost everywhere. And I do feel that you have the right to be in the know."

"In the know about what?"

Archibald grabbed a mirror propped against a wall, dusted it off with a sweep of his sleeve, and, theatrically, held it up. Ophelia hadn't passed through a single mirror since she'd been consigned to the Gynaeceum, but she was very tempted to dive into the one Archibald was holding for her, and never come out of it.

Her head had sprouted two ass's ears.

Ophelia would have liked to tear them off, but her hand passed through them as if they were made of smoke. An illusion, of course. "You're as stubborn as a mule," Cunegond had said. Only a Mirage would apply an expression so literally.

Archibald observed Ophelia, now fiercely gripping her glass. "You arouse a certain curiosity in me, Thorn's fiancée. It's quite a novelty for me, I'm not used to it."

He tipped his chair forward and craned his neck to look Ophelia in the eye. She had barely glimpsed, by candlelight, his puzzled smile, big sky-hued eyes, and messy blond hair, before she turned her head away and slapped her hand over her glasses, so she was blinkered.

"Is it my imagination, or are you avoiding meeting my eyes?" asked Archibald, laughing.

"I have no idea how you go about charming women, but I have no desire to fall for it myself. Particularly tonight."

Since what had occurred in the Goose Garden, Aunt Rosaline would blush furiously as soon as Archibald's name was mentioned in a conversation. Ophelia had really tried to talk about it with her, to understand what he'd done to her, but she sidestepped it every time by changing the subject.

"It's not very practical for talking," Archibald commented, calmly.

"I don't want to talk. You're actually distracting me."

With the reflexes of an acrobat, Archibald caught in midair the glass that Ophelia had just let slip.

"Quite right. I'm distracting you from your fear. Fine," he sighed, "if that's all it takes to put you at ease." Archibald placed the glass on a nearby pedestal table, gripped the rim of his top hat, and, in one go, pulled it down to his nose.

"There you are, you have nothing more to fear from my eyes."

So ridiculous was he like this, with his nasal voice and tufts of hair sprouting through the flapping crown of his hat, that Ophelia caught herself smiling.

"Stay serious for a second, Mr. Ambassador. Why are you here? You didn't just want to offer me a glass of water, now did you?"

Archibald tucked his chin between his arms, which he had crossed on the back of his chair. Due to the pulled-down top hat, all Ophelia could see of his profile was that huge slash of a smile.

"I've told you, Thorn's fiancée. Out of curiosity. Do I need to remind you that you officially made me your friend? I've been watching you for some time now. At first, it was just a glance from time to time, to check that your life wasn't in danger, but I got to enjoy it. Your pronunciation exercises, your minor mishaps, your Animist manners, your resolve in the face of every ordeal, and your aunt, too: I like this, the fabric of your daily life. The reading of your correspondence, earlier on, almost tugged my heartstrings."

Ophelia was astounded, not at what Archibald was saying to her, but at her own forgetfulness. The Valkyries! How could she have lost sight of the fact that these grandmothers were linked to each member of the Web, Archibald included? For all this time, Ophelia had spoken, eaten, slept in front of a crowd of people. She thought of the many times she'd taken something to read with her to the lavatory, and right under the noses of the old ladies, too. Due to this, she almost forgot the hubbub rising on the other side of the theater's curtains, as the courtiers gradually took their seats in the auditorium.

"It's very embarrassing."

"Why?" asked Archibald, with surprise, from under his hat.

"It doesn't bother you, having no privacy? Sharing all you see, all you do with the whole of your family?"

Swinging, blindly, on his chair, Archibald casually shrugged his shoulders. "It means we save money on telephone bills. But don't get the wrong idea, Thorn's fiancée. You seem to believe that, at this very moment, the entire Web is lapping up all we say. It doesn't work quite like that . . . How can I explain?" Beneath the top hat, Archibald's mouth puckered into a thoughtful pout, before breaking into a new smile. "I know! Imagine yourselves, you and your family, gathered together in a single room. Each one of you gets on with their own thing; the atmosphere is forever changing, confused and noisy, you get the picture? So if you wanted to know what your sister or your mother were doing at this precise instant, you'd have to turn towards them and listen carefully. It would clearly be impossible for you to know what all the others were doing at that same time. Well, that's virtually what it's like for us!"

"But Mr. Farouk," murmured Ophelia, suddenly struck by a thought, "isn't he supposed to possess a concentration of all his descendants' powers? I mean . . . What if he were listening to your every conversation? If he were listening to us, here, now?"

"He has the powers of concentration of a cherry stone," retorted Archibald. "He's already incapable of following a normal conversation. No, really, I've already traveled several times to other arks and I've never seen a family spirit so unworthy of his own power."

It was a small consolation for Ophelia to know that, if this evening had to end in disaster, she would at least have learnt one or two things.

"I received an anonymous letter," she declared, point-blank.

"What kind of letter?"

"The deterrent kind. I think it has something to do with Mr. Farouk's Book."

"Threats are all the rage around here. Stay close to the Valkyries."

Ophelia couldn't see Archibald's eyes, due to his pulled-down hat, but she could have sworn that, despite his smile, he had tensed up in his chair. She suddenly remembered what Cunegond had whispered to her. "Is it true, what they say? You've . . . um . . . *lost* a guest?"

"I'm incapable of lying," said Archibald. "Permit me not to answer that question."

The sergeant's opening knocks echoed all around, behind the big, black curtains, bringing the audience's buzzing to a stop. "My lord, ladies, young ladies and gentlemen, it is midnight!" proclaimed a cheery voice. "Let the nocturnal event commence!"

From the darkness that fell like sudden night, Ophelia realized that all the lamps in the theater had been extinguished. Only the candle on the pedestal table now enabled one to make out the outline of the ladders and furniture backstage. Ophelia held her breath as she heard old Eric's voice rise against a backing of accordion music.

"My lord, tonight you will hear how a one-eyed vagrant changed the destiny of three heroes!"

His "r"s still sounded like gravel, but his tone was completely different to the one he'd used to threaten Ophelia. Old Eric was now deploying a voice that was deep, sonorous, and spellbinding, capturing the attention from his very first words. The voice of a true storyteller. Listening to him, Ophelia would have liked to drink a second glass of water, to clear her own voice. She rose from her chair, walked on tiptoe, and glimpsed, in the gap between the big, black curtains, a small section of the stage.

What Ophelia witnessed made her understand how right old Eric was. Combining their appearances in the same show, it was an insult to the profession.

A large white canvas screen had been stretched across the proscenium, preventing her from seeing a good part of the audience. Old Eric was concealed at the back of the stage, his fingers dancing with virtuosity on the accordion's two keyboards; close by, the magic lantern's mechanism projected onto the white canvas, in a beam of light, the animated illusion from the glass slide. A tall, caped character was entering a cave in which a dwarf was busy forging a sword. Viewed from the wings, the illusion unfolded in reverse to what the audience saw, and after a few seconds, kept repeating, but that took nothing away from the beauty of the sequence. Each time, Ophelia discovered incredibly realistic new details: the sparks flying from the blacksmith dwarf's hammer; the iridescent reflections on the cave's icy walls; the swishing of the one-eyed vagrant's cape. It was hard to believe that it was all merely a two-dimensional show, without contours or depth.

Ophelia tried to catch a glimpse of the audience, on the other side of the canvas screen. What she could make out in the half-light left her deeply pensive. Not a single noble was watching the show. The spectators in the back rows only applauded, exclaimed, and laughed if the spectators in the front rows applauded, exclaimed, and laughed. It was like the ripples produced by a pebble thrown into water, and the epicenter of this strange quake was, of course, Farouk, seated in the front row. Ophelia knew it even though the canvas prevented her from seeing him. It was exactly like the evening of the Spring Opera. Everyone yawned if Farouk yawned, everyone praised if Farouk praised.

Ophelia remained watching old Eric for a long time, as he changed his illusory slides without ever interrupting the music from his accordion or the flow of his heroic epic, full of monsters and giants, and in which the dead rubbed shoulders with the living in a macabre phantasmagoria. The different episodes of the tale were each more horrifying than the last; it was nothing but honor to be regained, incestuous love affairs, and bloody murders.

Ophelia felt a little stupid with her doll story and her ass's ears.

"He's good," she muttered, once she'd returned to her chair. "He's very good."

"He's the court's official storyteller," said Archibald, bursting out laughing. "What were you expecting?"

Still sitting the wrong way round on his chair, he'd kept his top hat pulled down to his nose, but Ophelia no longer found it at all amusing. She looked at the cover of *Tales of Objects and Other Animist Stories*, as if a miracle might yet emerge from it.

"I've never felt so nervous in my life," she admitted. "I won't be able to equal Mr. Eric."

"Indeed," replied Archibald, with his usual frankness.

"Leave me alone, Mr. Ambassador," Ophelia begged. "Please."

Archibald stood up without unscrewing his top hat, and bowed his half-head towards Ophelia, his mouth revealing a row of teeth like a scarecrow's smile.

"You won't be able to equal him," he stressed in a whisper. "It's up to you to differentiate yourself."

Ophelia watched Archibald depart, arms outstretched, feeling his way, like some strange hat that had been endowed with a body.

THE DOLL

"Differentiate myself," Ophelia repeated, stroking the handwriting of her great-uncle, on the first page of the book. *Hoping that it will come in useful, kid.* Since Archibald's departure, Ophelia had drawn up a list of what differentiated her from old Eric, but none of it worked in her favor. Her story was less dramatic, her voice less charismatic, and she knew neither how to play a musical instrument nor how to work a projector of illusions.

And thanks to Cunegond, she was now sporting ass's ears.

Ophelia felt her stomach lurch when the enthusiastic applause marked the end of another tale. How many more slides did old Eric still have to show? As if in answer to her question, the butler made a furtive appearance backstage. "It will be miss's turn in ten minutes. Miss must be at the ready."

Ophelia cast a panicked look around her, searching for something that might change her thinking. On the nearby pedestal table there was only the candle, the empty glass, and some pages of a newspaper that old Eric had probably used to wrap his slides. Feverishly, Ophelia smoothed one of them out. It was from an old issue of the *Nibelungen*, dating back a few weeks.

BEWARE OF COCKROACHES!
They're everywhere. They're infiltrating our homes, our lives,

and at the very heart of power. They are decadence personified. Our Treasurer? Of bastard nobility. His aunt? Of a sinister race facing extinction. And now, here they are, presenting at court, at the holy of holies, an uneducated Animist! Don't fall for her dumb looks—this schemer will wait until your eyes are turned to get her little prying hands on your belongings. Foreigners are, dear readers, like cockroaches. Allow one of them to get into your house, and it will soon be crawling with them. And as if this invasion of vermin weren't enough, today, the disgraced are asking to return among us! Have these degenerate clans already forgotten the errors committed by their own relations? For goodness' sake, let's get a grip and keep all these cockroaches far away from our prestigious Citaceleste!

The article was illustrated with an engraving depicting Thorn. The illustrator had turned the thinness of his legs, the length of his nose, and the twisting of his mouth into a caricature.

Let's remember that the mother of Mr. Treasurer, who today is disgraced, was only yesterday the most despicable of plotters, commented the caption. *Like mother, like son?*

Ophelia tore up the newspaper page. She was so outraged that she'd completely forgotten her fear. Decadents, bastards, foreigners, vermin, degenerates: by what right did this newspaper director speak of human beings with such disdain? Ophelia knew nothing of the disgraced—she'd not met any yet—but she hadn't forgotten Berenilde's words when she'd explained to her how this world functioned: "There are the families who are favored by our spirit Farouk, those who no longer are, and those who never were." Ophelia had seen for herself just how easy it was to lose it and to gain it, that favor.

Farouk wanted to hear an Animist story? Well, he was going to hear one.

"Miss Vice-Storyteller? H'm, h'm. Miss Vice-Storyteller?" repeated the butler.

Ophelia suddenly noticed that the floorboards and her chair were vibrating due to the audience's applause. Old Eric's show was over. "My turn? I'm coming."

With her great-uncle's book under her arm, Ophelia slipped between the gap in the black curtains and bumped into old Eric, laden with his accordion and magic lantern. His long blue plait, a marriage of hair and beard, was streaming with sweat. "Your turn, now," he said, defiantly, making both "r"s vibrate.

As Ophelia advanced onto the boards of the stage, her nerves had gone. In fact, she had the curious impression of no longer feeling anything at all, as though she'd left her emotions behind in the wings. The projector had been removed; now that the white screen had gone, Ophelia had a panoramic view of the rows of spectators, stretching from stalls to balcony. Was the writer of that threatening letter among them?

Ophelia's entrance was greeted by shocked murmurs. Her ass's ears were certainly no novelty here. There was clapping from just one person to welcome her: Ophelia couldn't see her, but she knew it was Aunt Rosaline slapping her hands together like that, despite the embarrassed coughs of those around her. No one else would have risked showing the slightest sign of support as long as Farouk hadn't done so. "They all want to make him think that he pulls the strings," she thought. "He's just their puppet."

Ophelia continued right up to the front of the stage, eyes squinting behind her glasses. As she had supposed, Farouk was seated in the first row. Although *seated* wasn't the right word: he was sprawled across six chairs. His head was resting on Berenilde's dress, and she was stroking his long white hair in a motherly way. His eyes were closed, as though he'd fallen asleep, and his great white hand limply held a glass of milk, which threatened to spill over at any moment. Transformed into a blanket of diamonds, the other favorites had curled up wherever they could along his gigantic body. Apart from Berenilde, who gave Ophelia encouragement with a silent movement of her lips, all eyes glistened with contempt.

"Differentiate myself."

Ophelia knelt on the floor, blew out several candles, and, to shocked murmurs, awkwardly sat down on the edge of the stage, with her legs dangling as though on a swing. For her, Farouk was her only spectator, so she wanted to be as close to him as possible.

"Good evening," she said, as loudly as her small voice allowed. Ophelia waited for the traditional knocks with a stick, announcing the start of the show, as she'd heard done for old Eric, but as none came, she decided to improvise. She banged with her heel against the wood of the stage until Farouk half-opened one eye.

"Good evening," she repeated, clutching her book with both hands. "I have here a collection of Animist tales that I've just received in the post. I've had time to read only one of them, so my performance will be short, and perhaps not very faithful to the original. Please forgive me in advance."

Ophelia focused exclusively on the front row, on Berenilde's knees, on the sleepy face, on the half-opened eyelid, on that small spark that alone betrayed the presence of an eye. Farouk was too far, or too somnolent, for Ophelia to be able to sense his mental presence; she'd have to strain her vocal cords.

"There once was a doll belonging to a little girl," she began. "It was an ordinary doll, the sort one finds commonly on

Anima—she fluttered her eyelashes, raised her arms, or moved her head, depending on the mood of her owner."

From among the back rows, where it was darkest, a woman spectator shouted: "Louder!"

"Like many Animist toys, the doll, in the end, developed her own personality. She closed her eyes if she wanted peace. She waved her arms when her dress was dirty. She shook her head to show disagreement. She even started walking with her articulated legs."

"Louder!" shouted someone else in the auditorium.

"The time came when the doll had had enough of being a doll. She no longer felt she belonged on a shelf. She no longer wished to be a little girl's toy. She had a dream. Her own dream. She wanted to be an actress."

"Louder!" shouted several voices in unison, emboldened by Farouk's silence.

"One night, the doll left her shelf, her bedroom, and her house. She set off alone into the world on her articulated legs. She thought only of fulfilling her dream. The doll ended up crossing the path of a troupe of puppeteers."

By now, there were so many "Louder!"s in the auditorium that even Ophelia was finding it hard to hear herself. And as if the atmosphere weren't chaotic enough, Aunt Rosaline had stood up in the middle of the stalls to applaud with gusto.

Ophelia was determined not to lose her concentration. She hadn't yet delivered her message to the spark beneath the eyelid.

"The puppeteers were already envisaging the great show they could put on with a doll like that and the profit they could make. They flattered the doll. They told her that she was made to be an actress and they could help her to fulfill her dream. And the doll believed them, unaware that she'd never been more dollish in her life."

Ophelia stopped speaking. She'd rarely uttered such a long

succession of words and, as if that weren't exhausting enough, the "Louder!"s were buzzing across the auditorium, until they drowned out her voice. Nestling against Farouk's body, the favorites shouted in chorus with the others. Berenilde could no longer conceal her dismay behind her smile. When Ophelia saw the family spirit's eyelid close like a curtain over the spark of his eye, she knew she'd lost the battle.

"Louder! Louder! Louder!"

Then, two unexpected things occurred. First, the favorites in the front row started tumbling, one after the other, like a shower of diamonds. Next, the glass of milk flew across the auditorium and splashed the flabbergasted faces in the back rows with white. It had all unfolded so fast, it took Ophelia a while to grasp what had just happened.

Farouk was standing upright, towering over the spectators with all his great height. From the stage, all Ophelia could see of him was a huge imperial coat, where the whiteness of his hair blended into that of the fur. Never would she have believed Farouk capable of moving with such alacrity. When she heard the rumble of thunder that served as his voice, she was very grateful not to be in the spectators' place.

"Interrupt her just once more . . ." Farouk didn't need to say more. The stupefied silence that descended on the auditorium almost hurt the ears. Those who had been sprayed with milk didn't even dare wipe themselves down.

Extremely slowly, Farouk's head turned away from the spectators. It pivoted on his neck, with the rest of his body not moving an inch, until it was set at a seriously alarming angle. Only a family spirit could contort himself to that degree without risking breaking his bones. Once Farouk's head was facing the stage, it proved as expressionless as usual. And yet, that one look gave Ophelia the impression that lightning had just flashed between her ears.

"What happened to the doll?"

Ophelia had been so taken aback by Farouk's reaction that she'd forgotten her story. All the emotions she had left in the wings had returned with a vengeance, in an indescribable mix of astonishment, terror, and anxiety. Her scarf, equally intimidated, was almost strangling her as it tightened around her neck. "I'll tell you the end some other time, sir."

Farouk's eyebrows twitched almost imperceptibly. Ophelia couldn't tell if that was a sign of vexation or reflection, but she had plenty of time to hear her heart pounding during the long silence that ensued. If she obtained it, this *some other time*, she would have achieved her very first victory.

"Your story," Farouk finally articulated, stressing each syllable, "I'm not sure I really like it."

"But you want to know how it ends. You want to know whether the doll remains the plaything of the puppeteers, don't you?"

Ophelia hoped the quavering of her voice wasn't too noticeable. She could almost feel the spectators' hostility prickling her skin, but this time no one dared to shout: "Louder!"

Farouk's body nonchalantly turned, until, finally, it was normally aligned with his head. He advanced towards the stage at such a slow pace that time seemed to stop in his tracks. The closer he got, the more Ophelia's migraine increased dramatically; he stopped just in time, as the pain coursed through Ophelia's body like unbearable neuralgia.

"No, I don't want to know what happens next. I don't like that story. But you," he added, pensively, "you ring true."

From the astonished whispers that immediately spread across the auditorium, Ophelia presumed that that must be some kind of compliment.

"I appoint you Vice-storyteller," declared Farouk.

"I'm already Vice-storyteller."

"Oh? Perfect, so we'll avoid any unnecessary paperwork."

Ophelia clenched both hands on her book of tales. Farouk was causing her so much pain that she would have liked to entreat him to speak a little faster and to move further away. He unfolded his arm, a casual gesture whose meaning became clear to Ophelia when she saw the young Aide-memoire leap forward to hand him his notebook. Farouk dipped a quill into the inkpot the Aide-memoire, on tiptoe, held out to him, and started laboriously writing.

"You will tell me another story tomorrow evening, Miss Vice-storyteller."

Ophelia and her scarf jumped simultaneously when thunderous applause rose up across the auditorium. The people who were shouting "Louder!" just moments ago had got up from their seats to hurl bravos and fingertip kisses.

As the gas lamps slowly came back on, Ophelia no longer saw Farouk, limply closing his notebook; or Berenilde, coming towards her in a graceful rippling of dress; or Aunt Rosaline, gesticulating wildly at her with her parasol.

She saw only Thorn in his big, black uniform, at the very back of the auditorium, well hidden from view. He was not applauding.

The Tales

Change entered Ophelia's life through the slot of the letter box. From one day to the next, there were sandglasses of every hue addressed to "Miss Vice-Storyteller." A ball with illusory costumes, tea in the hanging gardens, a balcony seat at the Opera House, a literary salon at the thermal baths: the flap of the letter box never stopped banging.

Ophelia deeply admired Mother Hildegarde, but she didn't like these sandglass-invitations she had invented. And yet it was a means of transport not lacking in ingenuity: just by pulling out the pin, which set off the turning mechanism, one was instantly transported to the designated destination, and would remain there until the sand stopped flowing. The quantity of sand and width of opening were in proportion to the importance of the guest, so the invitation could range from a few minutes to several days.

Ophelia might well have got used to them if it wasn't for the blue sandglasses. Because they were forever being offered to her, she often almost pulled the pin out by mistake. If there was one kind of sandglass she'd promised herself never to use, it was definitely that one. They were to be found absolutely everywhere at court—on servants' trays, among champagne flutes, in vending machines. How many nobles had Ophelia not seen disappear for a few minutes, only to reappear in a state of total euphoria? When she asked where these sand-glasses transported them, the reply was: "To paradise, of course!", which didn't reassure her one bit.

"I won't reply to invitations anymore," she decided one morning, when she'd settled in bed to work. "All these gatherings exhaust me and I have to prepare my tales."

Barely had she opened her great-uncle's book before Berenilde snapped it shut on her fingers and made her get out of bed. "I advise you, on the contrary, to honor all of them."

"Why? I don't feel as if I fit in over there. As I see it, I am under obligation only to Mr. Farouk."

"I agree with the girl," added Aunt Rosaline. "There can be only one passenger per sandglass, and she's the only one of us to receive them. How, then, are we supposed to chaperone her?"

"I know," Berenilde sighed. "The fact is that Ophelia came to the Pole in the context of a diplomatic marriage. By declining the invitations of these ladies and gentlemen, she will cause great offense, and every offense has to be paid for, sooner or later. But don't worry," she assured Ophelia in her finest velvety voice, "it's just a fad, it won't last. And as long as our Lord likes your stories, no one will dare touch you."

Ophelia had to recognize that she'd found in Farouk an audience indulgent beyond all her hopes. Every evening, she thought it would be her last, that he would suddenly notice that she had no talent. And every evening, against all expectations, he requested new stories from her for the following day.

His face of marble never expressed the slightest emotion: not a smile when the story was supposed to be funny, not a frown when supposed to be sad. And when Ophelia closed her book to signal the end of her session, Farouk made no comment, asked no question. He simply unraveled the limbs of his gigantic body, and, before departing, slowly declared: "You will tell me another story tomorrow evening, Miss Vice-Storyteller." Only then did the applause erupt in the auditorium, like a well-oiled machine.

"I do wonder whether Mr. Farouk truly enjoys listening to me," Ophelia confided in Aunt Rosaline. "In fact, I wonder whether he listens to me at all."

"I don't know whether he listens to you, but one can certainly say that he looks at you."

That was exactly what embarrassed Ophelia. She was very conscious of Farouk scrutinizing her from the foot of the stage. It was nothing like the hungry look he jealously gave Berenilde, or the deeply bored look he gave everyone else. No, the look he gave Ophelia was at once vague and piercing, as if he sought to look right through her, to discover someone else within. She would have really liked to make him aware of all that was awry in his family. What was the point of making all this effort if he didn't listen? One evening, Ophelia had told the same story twice in a row, hoping to get a reaction out of him, but he hadn't noticed a thing.

The only story that had made an impression on him was that of the doll, and he wanted to hear nothing more of it.

'What does Farouk expect of me exactly?' Ophelia asked herself, night after night, while stroking the scarf curled in a ball beside her pillow.

Maybe she was imagining it, but it seemed that he was now seeking through her what he had previously sought through his Book. The fact is that he had never again mentioned it in her presence, as though it had, for now, completely gone out of his head.

Ophelia couldn't say the same for herself. One month after receiving her strange threatening letter, she still wondered why some people were so fearful of Thorn reading this Book. Artemis also owned one, and, to Ophelia's knowledge, no one on Anima had ever been killed while trying to decipher it. What made Farouk's Book so particular and so troubling? Did it contain, somewhere in the midst of its strange alphabet, a compromising secret? Did Farouk know this himself without being able to remember it?

'I would only have to offer him my services once,' thought Ophelia, drumming her fingers on her bed. 'Just once . . .' As a reader, she was burning with professional curiosity, and as a fiancée, she was dying to take her revenge on Thorn.

"I'm Vice-Storyteller," she finally declared to her scarf. "I'm going to concentrate on my work and try to remain alive. That would already be a good start."

Unfortunately for her, Mr. Chekhov never missed a chance to give her prime position among the headlines of the *Nibelungen*. And that May morning was no exception:

A VERY DEVIOUS VICE-STORYTELLER

"You're playing a dangerous game, my girl," commented Berenilde, once she had read the whole article. "Your little act isn't fooling anyone. You're using your tales to criticize the court, and the courtiers detest that."

"It's not the court I'm addressing," said Ophelia, who was jotting down new ideas in a notebook. "It's Mr. Farouk." It was her only means of expression, the only way she could give meaning to what she was doing.

"Do you intend to educate our family spirit?"

Wrapped in a pink silk dressing gown, Berenilde seemed more amused than angry. As she did every morning, she'd settled in her armchair to leaf through the newspaper while Aunt Rosaline styled her splendid blond hair. At six months pregnant, Berenilde's belly made such a bulge in her dresses that she could no longer hide it from the eyes of the world, and

Aunt Rosaline had started chaperoning her almost as much as her own niece: she threw all her cigarettes down the garbage chute, confiscated her glasses of liqueur, and forbade her from attempting the latest fashionable dances, which were far too boisterous for her liking. Above all, she disapproved of the way Farouk would invite her to come up to his room, on the top floor of the tower, night after night.

"If you were really brave," continued Berenilde, "it would be my nephew you would be addressing. You always find excuses to avoid having to talk to him on the telephone: yesterday you had a sore throat, the day before, earache . . . You don't think this poor boy has enough worries without, in addition, having to run after you?"

Ophelia tensed up over her notebook. Her last conversation with Thorn hadn't made her feel like repeating the experience. "Precisely. He has other fish to fry at the moment, so best I leave him in peace."

In that, she wasn't lying. The Citaceleste was experiencing a serious food shortage since the Dragons had been slaughtered. Without its usual hunters, the court found itself deprived of game, and larders were emptying with alarming speed. The Mirages had certainly given the art of hunting a try, but the experience had been disastrous: accustomed to their cozy little illusions, far removed from the harsh realities outside, they'd all nearly ended up with their throats slit. Ophelia had never seen wild Beasts, apart from in sketches, and those had been enough for her to grasp that the hypnotic talent of the Mirages was no match for the monstrous fauna of the Pole. The Mirages only succeeded in enraging the Beasts even more. The result: while attempting to find a solution, the Treasury requested that everyone tighten their belts.

"I warn you," said Berenilde, calmly looking at her over the top of her newspaper, "if you break what serves as a heart to my nephew, I'll cut you to ribbons."

Ophelia poured the coffee outside her cup. She knew only too well that this wasn't mere rhetoric: Berenilde had already sunk her claws into her for less than that.

"Oh, don't pull that face," exhorted Berenilde. "Living with Animists isn't that relaxing either for a pregnant woman. The doors slam over the slightest thing; the clocks show totally whimsical times; the taps run as soon as one approaches the sink; and that coat, my godfathers, that coat!" she sighed, looking disapprovingly at the garment writhing furiously on its hook. "I sometimes feel as if I'm living in a haunted house."

Ophelia had to admit that her mother had sent her an appallingly bad-tempered coat. As soon as she had taken it out of its wrapping, it had struggled like one possessed, and Aunt Rosaline had to grab it from behind to hang it on the hook. Since then, all of the apartment's occupants, including the Valkyries, had made a habit of carefully skirting that corner of the room to avoid the heavy buttoned sleeves that angrily swung out.

Ophelia got back the *Nibelungen* and skipped the countless caricatures ridiculing both her and Thorn. It was hard to find any news worthy of interest in this paper. Chekhov was content to churn out hateful articles on the disgraced nobility, foreign arrivistes, and, generally, all those who weren't Mirages. His preferred target remained Mother Hildegarde: on every page, he urged his readers to stop buying blue sandglasses, citrus fruit, spices, and new houses from her.

Ophelia finally fell on an article that was neither caricature nor counter-advertising:

POACHING: THE DISGRACED, AS PER USUAL!
"With famine at the door of our beautiful Citaceleste, the

disgraced merrily throw themselves into poaching," Ophelia read out quietly. *"They steal the meat destined for our plates and redistribute it among the population of the powerless. This crass manipulation is patently aimed at regaining prestige. The disgraced claim that they are filling the gap left by our former hunters, but we won't fall for that one!"*

"What a liar," she said, closing the *Nibelungen* with annoyance. "They've merely succeeded where the court's hunters failed. I'd like another opinion on the disgraced, apart from what this paper puts out."

"In what way are these poor people your concern?" asked Berenilde, disapprovingly. "They are the past and we are the future."

"They are partly my future, though," retorted Ophelia. "Some of them will soon be members of my family. You told me once that Thorn's mother was a Chronicler, and I still know nothing about that clan."

Berenilde gave a nervous look toward the Valkyries, seated on one of the salon's banquettes, ever attentive and silent, as if she found it highly embarrassing having such a conversation in front of witnesses.

"The disgraced are nobles who have committed particularly serious offenses, my dear girl. So serious that they are condemned, along with all their descendants, to permanent banishment from the court. They have lost their privileges, their properties, and they are forbidden from entering any towns."

"In other words," said Ophelia, frowning, "they have to live out in the wild, among the Beasts, with no right to hunt? That's condemning them to death."

"Don't you worry about them," Berenilde said, sarcastically, raising a cup of tea to her lips. "They manage to survive perfectly well."

"Including my future mother-in-law?"

Berenilde's smile twisted and she placed her cup back on its saucer, as if the tea had suddenly become too bitter. "Your future mother-in-law is a topic of conversation to be avoided. Just mentioning her in public could seriously harm Thorn's reputation."

"But why?" insisted Ophelia. "What did she do that was so terrible?"

"Thorn will soon be your husband," Berenilde stated, in a tone brooking no response. "It's to him that you should ask your questions."

Ophelia let it go. She'd promised herself she'd have nothing more to do with Thorn as long as was diplomatically possible.

Her clumsiness decided otherwise.

The fact is that Ophelia had finally given up on the sand-glasses that came through the letter box. She had frequented the social venues enough to be very familiar with their mirrors. She soon returned to her habit of using her power as a means of transport, making both dandies and coquettes jump as they saw her emerging from the reflections that they were just admiring.

Ophelia found regaining her freedom of movement intensely satisfying, but she probably wasn't careful enough. Going from one mirror to another required being both well focused and at one with oneself. The sleep deprivation, the endless parties, the fear of not fitting in—all of that should have prompted her to use her mirror-visiting power sparingly, instead of springing from one place to another.

The fact remains that, one afternoon in early June, Ophelia found herself stuck.

Her head and shoulders had become jammed, bang in the middle of the mirror in a smoking room, and the rest of her body refused to follow. She tried to retreat from her mirror of departure, where her foot was still standing on tiptoe, but her other leg and both arms seemed to be floundering in the void. It took a moment for Ophelia to understand that they had each got stuck in a different mirror. Try as she might to wriggle her shoulders in order to bring her weight forward, she freed herself not an inch. She was in too many places at once, so was unable to coordinate her movements.

"Please?" Ophelia called out from the mirror in which her head was trapped. That part of her had emerged in one of the many smoking rooms of the Jetty-Promenade and, as though by design, the place was deserted. Balanced uncomfortably on each leg, Ophelia called for help for what seemed like an eternity when, finally, someone somewhere decided to pull on one of her hands. She abandoned her whole body to this sudden impetus, getting the painful impression of being wrenched from multiple worlds, and then fell backwards onto a wooden floor.

Completely dazed, Ophelia could see only blurred silhouettes around her, emitting shocked noises and angry barks. She felt around the floor for her glasses, but then some good soul handed them to her and helped her onto her feet. The "I'm you sorry" and "Thank so kindly" that Ophelia confusedly stammered died on her lips as soon as she recognized Thorn as her savior.

"What are you doing here?"

That was the first question that came to Ophelia's mind. Two heads above her, Thorn knitted his endless eyebrows, which did nothing for his naturally tense features. Under his arm he was carrying a batch of forms that made it pretty clear that he was in the middle of doing his job.

"It's rather for me to ask you what your hand was doing in that mirror," he grumbled. "These ladies may well be accustomed to eccentric behavior, but they were verging on apoplectic."

Ophelia became aware that she'd just burst right into the middle of a dog show. A crowd of elderly lorgnette-bearing aristocrats and large beribboned dogs were all staring at her with looks of indignation. When she raised her eyes, she realized that she was in the hanging gardens . . . or rather, *under* the hanging gardens. The second floor of the tower would have been just a classic exhibition room, with its fine polished floors and large wall mirrors, had the ceiling not been entirely covered in tropical jungle. One just had to lift one's nose to be immersed in a natural world that was all cedars, mahoganies, carnivorous flowers, and multicolored parrots. Once, Ophelia had even thought she'd glimpsed the striped coat of a wildcat among the waving ferns.

"Please forgive me, ladies, I was completely stuck," she said, pushing back the streaming hair that had escaped from her bun. "That hasn't happened to me for a long time."

At twelve years old, when attempting her first passage through a mirror, she'd got stuck in two places at a time. She'd come out of it all topsy-turvy, unable to coordinate her right side with her left. She couldn't recall what had possessed her, throwing herself into such a ridiculous endeavor in the middle of the night; but she did clearly recall the lengthy physiotherapy sessions that had followed. She already owed her incurable clumsiness to a mirror accident; she hoped this blunder wouldn't make her even clumsier.

Thorn turned, rigid as an automaton, to the elderly aristocrats. "If you would kindly excuse me," he said, in a tone that excused itself of nothing whatsoever. "Please fill in your forms, and I will come and collect them in five minutes."

Without asking Ophelia her opinion, Thorn grabbed her by the shoulder and directed her into an empty antechamber, in which fake exotic birds fluttered between the fine parquet floor and the ceiling's creepers.

"Right," said Thorn, taking his neutral accountant's tone. "When Miss Vice-Storyteller has honored her engagements with every inhabitant of the Pole, might she deign to spare me, finally, a little of her time?"

It seemed to Ophelia that his hair, always neatly combed back, was turning increasingly silver. Even the steel in his eyes had lost some of its edge. Was it the food shortage that was leaving him in such a state?

"You helped me to free myself. I daresay I can give you a moment."

"Not here and not now," said Thorn, with a wary glance towards the door of the antechamber. "Come to the Treasury tomorrow. The time doesn't matter, I'll cancel all my appointments."

"I'll speak to Berenilde about it," sighed Ophelia. "We'll try . . ."

"I want neither my aunt, nor yours," he cut in, gesturing adamantly. "You will come alone. This situation can't go on any longer, I insist that you reconcile with me."

Ophelia didn't appreciate this authoritarian tone at all. If Thorn hadn't had such a terrifying head on his shoulders, she would have refused point-blank.

"What were you in the middle of doing, exactly?" she asked, taking the forms from his hands.

"I'm doing an inventory of all the domestic Beasts."

Ophelia almost burst out laughing, imagining Thorn busy counting poodles, but when she guessed why he was doing it, she stared wide-eyed with horror.

"You're surely not thinking of . . ."

"I'm considering all options to save us from famine," he replied, consulting his fob watch. "If it were just up to me, I would first select the fattest minister, but cannibalism is an illegal practice, even in the Pole."

Ophelia glanced through the antechamber's half-opened door and saw the elderly aristocrats continually stopping, mid-form, to comb and compliment their enormous dogs. "Do they know what you're expecting of them?"

"They will know it as soon as I have finished with you," Thorn grumbled, without a qualm, the hardness of what he was saying underlined by his accent. "My five minutes are over, may I have your response? Will you come to see me, yes or no?"

Ophelia stared at him with a combination of revulsion and pity, as if she had before her a grim funeral director. "I really wouldn't like to be in your shoes."

Thorn was such an inexpressive man that, at first, Ophelia interpreted his rigid immobility as him waiting for something; when she noticed that he was staring intently at her, no longer blinking or breathing, she understood that, in reality, she had taken his breath away.

"I'll concede to you that they're not very comfortable," he finally got out, after a very long silence. "A bit worse than that, even." He checked his mandarin collar, already perfectly buttoned; smoothed his hair, already perfectly combed; wound up his watch, already perfectly accurate; and then cleared his throat. "I take it then that your response is no. May I?"

Thorn had held out his hand to retrieve his forms, a professional gesture that was so automatic that Ophelia felt absurdly guilty. She did, however, have to admit that Berenilde had got it right: it was indeed out of cowardice, more even than anger, that she'd spent recent weeks avoiding him.

As she was returning his papers to him, Ophelia looked him straight in the eye. "You're right, we can't spend the rest of our lives avoiding each other. Together we must find a compromise. I will come to the Treasury tomorrow, before my storytelling. And I will come alone."

One had to be observant to spot the infinitesimal relaxing of Thorn's frown.

"See you tomorrow, then," he said.

THE FORGOTTEN ONE

Like the highest wind, Ophelia flew over the old world. The land was intact, as it must once have been, before it inexplicably shattered to pieces. From the sky, Ophelia gazed at its towns, forests, oceans, and fields, which remained out of her reach. For as long as she could remember, she'd always had this dream, but this time it took an unusual turn. The clouds turned into a carpet, and barely had Ophelia set foot on it when, suddenly, there was no more old world—no more oceans, no more towns, no more fields. She now found herself in a bedroom. Not any bedroom: it was her childhood bedroom, on Anima. Ophelia was standing before the wall mirror and her reflection was much younger, wrapped in a dressing gown, with hair that was still red, curling around her face. What was she doing here, in the middle of the night? Something had woken her, but what? It wasn't her sister Agatha, who slept in the top bunk; or the furniture, which sometimes moved on the quiet. No, it was something else. It was the mirror.

Ophelia opened her eyes wide, her heart racing. In a daze, she watched the tabby kitten that was playing with her scarf. It leapt off the dining table when Ophelia sat up in her chair. She had fallen asleep halfway through both breakfast and her book of tales.

"I had a strange dream," she told Aunt Rosaline, as she arrived with the coffee pot.

"If you saw a cat, it wasn't a dream. It got in through the window. Berenilde has shut herself in the bathroom, waiting for it to be chased away. She really doesn't like animals."

"No. Well, yes, I saw the cat, but that wasn't my dream. I thought . . . I don't know . . . I heard something," mumbled Ophelia, rubbing her eyes behind her glasses. Now that she was waking up, the dream was losing its clarity and intensity. She couldn't really remember what she'd found so perturbing. "It must be due to the mirror accident yesterday. It brought back memories."

"Yes, it's mentioned in the 'Strange but True' column," sighed Rosaline. She had placed that day's *Nibelungen* on the table, with its mocking headline:

THE FOREIGNER LEAVES BITS OF HERSELF EVERYWHERE!

"Last week, it reported a logjam of mattresses in a lift," responded Ophelia, casually leafing through the paper. "I think I'm going to stop reading this load of nonsense—it's not what I call news."

Ophelia tried to concentrate on the pile of letters and sand-glasses heaped on the tray used for the day's mail. It wasn't going to be easy to find a free moment, between two invitations, to visit Thorn without Berenilde and Aunt Rosaline knowing.

"Have you seen how you've dressed yourself?" her aunt asked her, pointing at the seams along her sleeves, which were inside out. "I think you should stay away from mirrors as long as you're not rested," she continued, pouring her some coffee. "You do realize that they could leave you with aftereffects? Since I don't like those sandglasses, either, I suggest we take lifts together, alright? And too bad if you arrive late to your appointments."

Ophelia's coffee went down the wrong way, she shut her book on her scarf, and got up so abruptly that she knocked her chair over.

"I'm sorry, aunt, I have to go. Let Berenilde enjoy her bath—you can tell her afterwards."

"Sorry? But where? How?" stammered Aunt Rosaline, astonished.

Not even bothering to reply, Ophelia went over to the two Valkyries, seated on their usual banquette, arms crossed on their large, black dresses. They were as stiff, silent, and vigilant as on their first day.

"Archibald?" Ophelia called out, leaning towards the old women. "Archibald, if you're listening to me, I'm letting you know that I'll be outside your office in one minute. If you want to spare me being arrested by your policemen, meet me there as soon as possible. Come with your steward; I'll explain everything there. Thanks in advance."

The Valkyries looked at each other, frowning sternly, shocked to be taken for a telephone exchange.

"What's got into you?" Aunt Rosaline asked, impatiently, as, still clutching her coffee pot, she followed Ophelia to her room. In reply, Ophelia merely handed her the note she'd just opened, with its few hastily scribbled words:

F. is in a fix. You owe him one, so get him out of there.

Signed G.

"Who is F.? Who is G.?"

"My friends from Clairdelune," said Ophelia, pulling off her dress to put it back on the right way.

Until that moment, she had chosen never to speak openly of either Fox or Gail. She'd always thought she'd cause more harm than good by revealing her interest in the servants of another family. Such friendships were forbidden up here, and her reputation would have suffered less than theirs. And yet, from the moment she'd read Gail's message, Ophelia had felt her whole body catch fire. She could no longer think coldly about the consequences of her deeds and words. Fox had helped her like no one else at Clairdelune. The invitations, the sandglasses, the protocol, the decorum no longer counted; all that mattered was the urgent need to do the same for him.

Standing in the middle of the corridor, Aunt Rosaline looked in turn at the note, at her niece, and at the door of the bathroom in which Berenilde was singing the latest fashionable opera to herself.

"We'll go together. It's out of the question that you wander around alone in the lair of that libertine."

Ophelia couldn't help noticing how her aunt's waxen cheeks had reddened. Her turmoil was more eloquent than any warning: frequenting Archibald was playing with fire.

"No, aunt. You can't pass through mirrors and the lifts are too slow. What with the connections and the checks, it would take me almost an hour to get to Clairdelune. My friend needs my help, it may be urgent," she cut in, firmly, as her aunt was about to respond. "I'm not stopping you from meeting up with me over there, but please, don't slow me down."

Aunt Rosaline clenched and unclenched her long teeth, before banging her coffee pot down on a console table. "I'll join you as quickly as possible. In the meantime, just don't let yourself be bamboozled by that ambassador."

Without wasting another second, Ophelia plunged head first into her large swing mirror. She resurfaced through the mirror of a corridor that led to Archibald's private office. The last time she'd been reflected in it was just before going up to be officially presented at court. It felt, to her, like an eternity ago.

Barely had Ophelia stepped on to the thick, blue carpet, in the midst of a golden world of wood paneling, bronzes, and gas lamps, when she saw an on-guard policeman frowning under his cocked hat and then marching towards her. Not for nothing was the embassy the Citaceleste's best-guarded place.

"Return . . . to your post. Miss . . . is the guest of . . . Mr. Ambassador."

A breathless man had just appeared at the other end of the corridor. Ophelia recognized Philibert, the steward at Clair-delune. Due to his wrinkled face, all the servants called him Papier-Mâché. He was a man so dull of complexion, dress, and character that, normally, he could disappear into any decor, but on this occasion, he was all one could see, with his lopsided wig, scarlet cheeks, sweat-soaked jabot, and wheezy breathing.

"Miss," he greeted her, stumbling, with register under arm. "I rushed here . . . as soon as Sir telephoned me. He asked me . . . to let you into his study. He will join you there . . . soon."

Ophelia sat up very straight on the seat she was offered, raised her chin, crossed her hands on her outside-out dress, and displayed a calmness she didn't feel. For the first time, she was applying to the letter the posture lessons Berenilde had tried, for months, to drum into her. If she had to play the perfect society lady in order to come to Fox's aid, she would do so.

"Mr. Steward?" she called, searching around for him.

"Does Miss require something?" Philibert was standing right beside the door, register still under arm. Now that he had got his breath and his sallow complexion back, he had already resumed his usual transparency.

"The valet Foster belongs to the permanent staff at Clairdelune, doesn't he?"

"I don't quite understand, Miss," he said, in a monotone.

"Did poor service give Miss cause for complaint on her last visit here?"

Berenilde had decided it was best not to reveal the little masquerade they had put on for weeks at Clairdelune, disguising Ophelia as a valet. This sometimes made conversations rather complicated.

"I have no complaints whatsoever, quite the opposite. I appreciated the manners of that servant and I'm simply asking you how he is. Is he still serving Madam Clothilde?"

"Now this is embarrassing, Miss," said Philibert, seeming far from embarrassed. "The late-lamented Madam Clothilde sadly departed from us several weeks ago. Did Miss not attend the funeral?"

Ophelia was speechless. She knew that Archibald's grandmother's health was delicate, but she had lived long enough under this roof for the news to come as a shock. "But Foster? What's become of him?"

It was Philibert's turn to be shocked. For a guest at Clairdelune to attach more importance to the fate of a valet than to the death of an aristocrat—to him, that probably defied every convention. "Since Miss insists on knowing." He put on his gold-rimmed spectacles and opened the register that never left him. "The man named Foster is currently residing in our dungeons."

Ophelia's glasses paled on her nose. "How did that happen?"

"In the column 'grounds', I have written 'absence of key.' Keys serve as identity papers for our staff. The police carry out checks every day for security purposes. And for the reputation of the embassy, Miss."

"Come, now, that's ridiculous," said Ophelia, with annoyance. "That valet has worked here for years. You can't throw him in prison because he once forgot to present his key."

"He didn't forget to present it, Miss," said Philibert, considering her with increasing puzzlement. "From what is recorded here, he didn't possess one." As though realizing himself the peculiarity of this state of affairs, the steward reread his register more carefully. "Ah, I understand now. Upon the death of the late-lamented Madam Clothilde, Foster deposited his old key, as is correct procedure. He must have been checked before a new position and new key had been allocated to him. That's really unlucky," he concluded, all in the same tone.

"You mean to say that he's been rotting in your dungeons for weeks because you delayed sorting out his situation?"

"Only the master can lift the sentence. And the master is terribly busy, so I've not yet had a chance to mention it to him. In any case, we no longer require Foster's services as we are fully staffed. And a servant who has frequented the dungeons would look awfully bad for our establishment."

Ophelia was so outraged that it was all she could do not to snatch Philibert's register from his hands and tear up every page. Archibald, a busy man? For twenty-three years, Fox had been working for that family, and he was treated with less consideration than a laundry basket!

"You have a sense of the unexpected, Thorn's fiancée." Archibald, smiling sleepily, had just entered his study. Apart from his irremovable top hat, he was wearing old, ragged, red-and-black-striped pajamas. His hair was as messy and his chin as stubbly as ever. Even in an inside-out dress, Ophelia would have looked more presentable than him.

"I woke you up," she observed, politely. In her haste, she'd forgotten how early it was. She didn't apologize in the slightest. It was the first time she felt such anger at someone other than Thorn.

"And in a highly unorthodox way," sniggered Archibald, collapsing onto his usual chair. "I didn't place you under the watch of the Valkyries for you to make personal use of them." He stretched with a long yawn, rested his elbow on an arm of the chair, and looked at Ophelia with a twinkle in his eye. "Coming to see me, so many floors down the Citaceleste, with no one chaperoning you? You're putting your respectability in jeopardy."

"I had an urgent favor to ask you. I'll do you one in return to make up for it."

Archibald's eyebrows and smile expanded in parallel. "Unpredictable, nonconformist, and enterprising. Watch out, one of these days I could end up falling in love with you. And so, what favor can I do for Thorn's fiancée?"

It wouldn't have been very smart to come out with all the Animist insults that Ophelia had in mind at that second. She forced herself to take a deep breath to get rid of the nasty red tint that had flooded her glasses.

"We're short of staff at the Gynaeceum, so I've come to borrow a trustworthy man from you. Please," she added, after a slight hesitation, arming herself with all the politeness she could muster.

Propped up in his chair, Archibald considered Ophelia with a look of fascination. "You got me out of bed at six in the morning over some staffing problem?"

"I've discussed it with your steward. You have an unoccupied valet who has been the victim of a technicality. With your permission, I would like to employ him."

"Foster is the man in question, Sir," Philibert clarified, with his cold professionalism. "He served your late—lamented grandmother."

Archibald shrugged his shoulders while using his toe to play with his slipper.

"No recollection of him, I'll take your word for it. I can see no objection to letting Thorn's fiancée have him. On one condition," he added, with a mocking smile for Ophelia. "You promised me a favor in return: I want it now."

Ophelia slid her hand into her twitching scarf to calm both her and its irritation. She made sure she kept up the bearing and smile of a well brought up young lady. She'd maintain this illusion as long as Fox hadn't been freed from his dungeon.

"You're catching me short. If you'd allow me a little time . . ."

"Now," Archibald interrupted her, with redoubtable sweetness. He leapt on to his slippers, bowed down theatrically, and gallantly held out a hand to invite her to stand. Ophelia was too ill at ease already to accept a man's arm; this one being clad in ragged pajamas didn't really help matters. "I'm afraid I haven't brought anything with me that could interest you."

"You're quite mistaken," declared Archibald, tapping her amiably on the head. "You brought yourself, I wish for nothing else! Follow me, Thorn's fiancée; my steward will do what's required for your valet in the meantime."

In the meantime of what, Ophelia wondered. Archibald was already leading her out of his study, his arm around her shoulders, with a familiarity at once tender and commanding.

"What do you want of me, Mr. Ambassador?"

"Don't be concerned. I'm certain you're going to adore it."

Dubious, Ophelia averted her eyes as far from Archibald's as possible. She'd witnessed Aunt Rosaline once succumb to the appeal of that azure, and she had no desire to lose her head in turn. Gently, he directed her into the billiard room. There, everything was green, from baize to velvet banquettes, and from damask drapes and wallpaper to lampshades. When Ophelia realized that they were alone, she immediately covered her glasses with her hands.

"Come on, now," said Archibald, with a burst of laughter, "you're not back at that again!"

"Would you promise me not to use your charm on me?

Please, Mr. Ambassador, it would really put me at ease to proceed with our meeting."

There was a long silence, during which Ophelia had ample time to contemplate her gloves, pressed against the surface of her glasses.

"I didn't realize that you feared me that much."

Ophelia hadn't heard this sentence with her ears; it had reached her from within. She'd forgotten that Archibald could impose his thoughts on her, and, for a moment, she feared that his bewitchment could seep into her using the same shortcut. "Please, Mr. Ambassador."

"Contrary to what you imagine, Thorn's fiancée, I have neither the power nor the desire to steal women's hearts. If they succumb to me, it's not because they love me, but because they feel lonely."

Ophelia screwed up her eyes, behind her glasses. This time, it was Archibald's true voice talking, but it sounded different, almost serious.

"You don't believe me? My family received the invaluable gift of transparency from Farouk. You deem this lack of privacy embarrassing, but I will never feel alone as long as one member of my clan is alive. What I offer all those poor wives is simply this: a moment of pure transparency, in which I erase the barrier between us, separating the 'me' from the 'other.' I don't feel like making you a promise that both of us could one day regret. A communion of souls . . . it's quite romantic, don't you find?"

Ophelia mainly found it extraordinarily shameless, much more so than anything she had imagined. She detested the idea that Archibald had imposed himself on her aunt in this way. He claimed to take women away from their loneliness, but he was listening only to his own egotism. Although Ophelia was dying to say that, she obviously refrained from doing so. She wasn't in a position to offend her host, she was here for Fox, and only for Fox. So she played along when Archibald pulled away her hands to look her straight in the eye. With top hat askew, he put on a relaxed smile that jarred with the seriousness of his voice.

"You're here to return a favor to me, must I remind you?" Suddenly, he twitched his eyebrows, looked around the deserted billiard room, and then returned to Ophelia with an apologetic expression. "Oh, I'm beginning to understand. You think I brought you here to cuckold Thorn? No, no, that's not the plan today. If that's all that's needed to reassure you, I have other preoccupations on my mind at the moment. In fact, we're waiting for someone."

Ophelia was so taken aback, she forgot her anger. "Who?"

"Me."

A nightmarish apparition had just entered the billiard room.

THE PIPE

Ophelia couldn't make head or tail of anything anymore
once she recognized Mother Hildegarde. She was such an outlandish mix of fat and bone, curlers and cigars—she smoked
two at a time—that it was impossible to determine, at first
sight, whether one was dealing with a man or a woman. Her
skin, whatever its original color, was now covered in liver spots.
How could one imagine for a moment that, behind this mum-
mified exterior, there hid an architect of genius, the famous
inventor of the sandglasses, a woman capable of reshaping
space as if it were made of rubber? Only her little black eyes
betrayed, by their intense glint, a singular intelligence.

"I'm not a morning person," grumbled Mother Hildegarde,
in a guttural voice with a strong foreign accent. "I've come
because it was you, in person, who called me, Augustine."

"Archibald, madam. Archibald. I asked you to come alone."

Ophelia had also just noticed, with a quickening heart, the
small woman accompanying Mother Hildegarde. She wore a
mechanic's uniform, and a flat cap that tried, in vain, to contain her dark curls and conceal her eyes. In truth, such eyes
were impossible to hide: between the electric-blue one and the
black-monocled one, it was hard to decide which side of her
face was the more fascinating.

Gail.

Had she left the basements of Clairdelune to see Ophelia? What madness! Gail wasn't any more working-class by birth than Ophelia was noble: she was a Nihilist, the last survivor of a clan whose family power allowed them to cancel out the powers of the Pole's other clans. Only her monocle could filter her "evil eye," as she called it herself. Merely showing herself in public meant she risked being recognized and suffering the same fate as her family. Ophelia would have liked to beg her to stop hanging her head and pulling the peak of her cap over her eyes: it was a real invitation to stare at her.

"She's my granddaughter," declared Mother Hildegarde. "All that concerns me also concerns her."

It wasn't the first time that Ophelia had caught this old lady lying to protect someone. Judging by Archibald's skeptical smile, she presumed he was used to it.

"She could be your concubine, but it wouldn't alter the fact that I didn't request her presence here. But since you're here, Miss Mechanic," he said to Gail, "could you check the toilets on the first floor? I've been told the flush is playing up."

"Yes, *señor*," Gail muttered, with the same accent as Mother Hildegarde, as if they really were related. She set off, hugging the walls, hands in pockets, but not without a furtive last glance at Ophelia. The latter got the message as clearly as if Gail had whispered it in her ear: it was her move to get Fox out of his dungeon.

"This is the girl you spoke to me about on the telephone?" asked Mother Hildegarde, fixing her black eyes on her. "The one who gets stuck in mirrors?"

Archibald laid a possessive hand on Ophelia's brunette head, as if it were to him she was engaged, not Thorn. He took no notice of the furious slaps the scarf was giving him.

"Madam, allow me to present to you Anima's best reader. As soon as I heard she was coming to visit us, I thought it would finally be a chance to clarify our . . . situation." He chose his words very carefully, which made Ophelia increasingly confused.

"I hope, for your sake, that it won't take long," said Mother Hildegarde, stubbing out her two cigars, one after the other, in a standing ashtray. "I was working until the middle of night on Count Boris's plans."

"Just don't move," Archibald whispered to Ophelia, strengthening his hold on her head.

Mother Hildegarde locked the door very carefully, having first glanced suspiciously out into the corridor, and then clicked her fingers. There was no movement of air, no change of light, and yet Ophelia's heart lurched as violently as if she'd just fallen to the bottom of a well.

"Breathe slowly," Archibald told her, amiably ruffling her hair. "It will pass."

Ophelia looked at her surroundings with renewed attention. The billiard room still featured the same green fabrics and the same murky light, but certain details were different. The colored balls, gathered in the billiard table's pockets a moment ago, were now in play formation, as if a game had just been interrupted. The smell of the place had also changed. It was redolent of stale smoke, and for good reason: the ashtray, brimming with cigarette butts, hadn't been emptied. And yet, when Mother Hildegarde had stubbed out her cigars in it a few seconds ago, Ophelia could have sworn that it was perfectly clean.

A double room. They were now in a space that was the billiard room's twin, but, as disturbing as the resemblance was, it wasn't the same place. Ophelia knew that Mother Hildegarde could superimpose one room on another—indeed, she'd once almost remained trapped in the double of a library—but she didn't know that the architect could bring about a flip from one space to another with just a snap of the fingers.

Archibald pushed Ophelia towards a divan, on which someone had left behind a very pretty porcelain pipe.

"Thorn's fiancée, I present you with your part of the deal!
Read this pipe for me. And before you ask me the usual question: yes, although I did lend it to a guest during their stay
with me, I remain its happy owner."

It was such an unexpected request, Ophelia didn't know
what to say. She looked questioningly at Mother Hildegarde;
from the center of the curler-covered head, the little black
eyes stared back at her. The old woman seemed expectant, as
though waiting to see the young girl prove herself. Ophelia
realized that she herself wanted to gain the esteem of this
brilliant woman, this untamed character, this foreigner who
had fulfilled herself through her profession.

She took a seat on the divan, beside the porcelain pipe.
"You've deliberately avoided touching it since it turned up
here, yes? Is there anything I should know before I start my
reading?"

"No," said Archibald, sending a warning sign to Mother
Hildegarde. "We'll give you explanations afterwards. I prefer
not to influence you."

Ophelia examined the pipe by the light of the closest lamp:
it was indeed marked with the Clairdelune coat of arms. Once
her hands were free of her reader's gloves, she gripped it again,
and was instantly rocked by an emotional shock so powerful,
she had to rest the object on her dress while she recovered.
"They're not my feelings," she repeated to herself several
times. "It's not me."

Because she was out of practice, she was making beginner's
errors. She waited for her fingers to stop shaking, and then
continued her reading where she'd left off. The anxiety was
still there, but this time Ophelia observed it at a distance,
like someone viewing a dark and disturbing painting. The

tobacco no longer had any effect on her. She could inhale day after day—or rather, day before day, since readings progressed in the opposite direction of time—but it no longer calmed her at all. All this because of two confounded letters! But she'd been at the embassy for a month now, and nothing had happened to her yet. Ophelia mustn't stop smoking. As soon as the effect of the tobacco wore off, she saw again those bluish bodies floating on the surface of the lake. Obviously, she regretted nothing. She'd only done her job: poachers remained poachers. One really isn't going to embroil oneself in endless trials with people of that sort. The newspaper's right: the disgraced, they're like cockroaches. Apparently, they're quietly infiltrating everywhere today—the city walls, the towns, the Citaceleste, maybe even the court! Ten to one, those ridiculous letters come from them! They see themselves as divine justice, those guys? The justice is her, Ophelia! But all's well, she's been at the embassy since yesterday, she can sleep safely in her bed now. And a little pipe won't do any harm.

Ophelia placed the pipe back on the divan. Her heart was pounding. "I presume that, if you asked me for this evaluation," she said, her voice shaking slightly, "it was to gain information about the last user. Should I stop at him?"

Perched on the edge of the billiard table, elbows planted on thighs, Archibald was observing her with amused curiosity. "You no longer look like a little girl at all, when you take on that professional air. Yes, you can stop there."

Ophelia tried not to betray her personal feelings as she rebuttoned her gloves at each wrist. This reading had shaken her up.

"You can speak at ease in front of Madam Hildegarde," Archibald reassured her, as she hesitated. "After all, her reputation is as much at stake as mine in this affair."

It was hard to tell whether the roar that Mother Hildegarde let out was a laugh or a sigh.

"It's rather delicate," said Ophelia. "You may be the owner of this pipe, but what guarantee do I have that you're not going to use what I've read to harm the person who smoked it?"

"It's not to harm him," he promised, with that unshakeable composure of his. "You know that I never lie. I'm listening, what can you tell me?"

"Evidently, this man was extremely anxious. His conscience wasn't clear and that's why he asked you for refuge here, at Clairdelune. He feared . . . well . . . reprisals."

"Impressive," murmured Archibald, his eyes half-closed like a cat's. "Did you learn of whom he was afraid and why?"

"It would perhaps be preferable for you to ask him that directly."

"Ophelia, I wouldn't be asking you if it weren't important."

Hearing her first name in this conversation sounded wrong to Ophelia's ears. Until now, she had always been "Thorn's fiancée" for Archibald. Was he finally starting to take her seriously, or was he trying to play the sentimental card? In any case, it didn't take Ophelia long to decide between getting Fox out of his dungeon and protecting the private life of a criminal.

"Poachers. The disgraced."

Mother Hildegarde let out an appreciative whistle. "It's true that she's talented, the little reader."

"You already knew that?" asked Ophelia, astonished.

"I take meticulous care in researching my guests," Archibald, still perched on the billiard table, said smoothly. "I knew this one had behaved like a swine towards some of the disgraced, and I knew his deed was sufficiently serious for him to fear for his life."

"Why ask me to do this reading, then?"

"To answer a very simple question. What exactly was my guest doing before leaving his pipe on this divan?"

Ophelia frowned. To answer that question, she would have to recall her first impression on beginning her reading. "I sensed great agitation throughout his stay with you. This gentleman smoked a good deal to calm his nerves, but he found tobacco less and less effective. That was his last thought: tobacco was no longer enough for him."

"And that's it?"

"And that's it."

"Well, that's annoying."

"Why?"

Archibald exchanged a knowing look with Mother Hildegarde, before returning to Ophelia. "Because you may have just read the last moments of the Provost of the Marshals."

Ophelia stared, wide-eyed. "Your guest who disappeared!" she suddenly realized. "Then it was him?"

"The old *señor* won't be missed by anyone," sniggered Mother Hildegarde. "It's because of people like him that this ark is rotten to its icy core." Her particular accent made her pronounce the "r" of "rotten" as though clearing her throat.

"Madam Hildegarde," Archibald said, with an angelic smile, "I have already asked you to keep your personal comments to yourself."

Ophelia saw the pretty porcelain pipe, left on the green velvet of the divan, from a entirely new angle. "This guest . . . Mr. Provost . . . he was killed?"

"We don't know," replied Archibald, with a shrug. "He was seen for the last time by his valet, two weeks ago, sitting on this divan, smoking the pipe. The next moment, he was gone. Disappeared without trace! Maybe he left of his own accord, on a whim, but his valet seems to know nothing about it. You'll understand that if criminals managed to enter my home and abduct one of my guests, under the very noses of my policemen, it's a serious blow to my family's honor. As it is to that of the architect who was supposed to make the embassy impregnable," he added, with a knowing wink for Mother Hildegarde. "We came up with the idea of putting a twin room above this one, for the duration of the inquiry. It's a bit more discreet than barring the door, and will minimize gossip. Luckily for us, Mr. Provost has no close relations to spread news of the affair."

"There were some letters," Ophelia murmured, pensively. "Letters that Mr. Provost received and that obsessed him. Threatening letters."

Ophelia felt chilled just speaking of them. Why had this man thought of a "divine justice"? Was it possible that the writer of these letters was the same one who had asked her to leave the Pole? *GOD DOESN'T WANT YOU HERE.* No, she was surely getting worked up over nothing. There was absolutely no connection between punishing a man for having killed poachers and preventing a woman from getting married.

"He spoke to me once of those letters," Archibald confirmed, "but he was determined not to show them to me. I daresay he found them embarrassing. It would strengthen the hypothesis of an abduction."

Mother Hildegarde snapped her fingers and Ophelia was hit with dizziness again as the surroundings changed subtly in appearance. The colored balls had gone from the billiard table, back into the side pockets; the cue was neatly stored in the rack with the others; and there was no more porcelain pipe on the divan. They were back in the first room.

"You should think twice before harboring a shady official, Augustine," grumbled Mother Hildegarde. "If you had any

119

pride, it would be to the disgraced that you would give your protection. Fellows who know true cold and true hunger."

"You're no philanthropist yourself," retorted Archibald. "You don't distribute them free of charge, your citrus fruits and spices."

Ophelia knew that there was, indeed, a very special Compass Rose, somewhere at Clairdelune. This shortcut covered thousands of miles, and enabled the Pole to be linked to Mother Hildegarde's native ark, the LandmArk. Everything exotic to be found in the court's larder came from there.

"As if I had the choice," laughed Mother Hildegarde. "It's *your* steward who possesses the key to *my* Compass Rose."

"*My* steward, as you put it, madam, integrated the embassy on *your* recommendations."

Mother Hildegarde broke into an enigmatic smile. "One of these days, Augustine, my family may well close off the route and I may take Arkadian leave. The Pole's air agrees with me less and less. It stinks too much of arrogance around here."

With those words, she unlocked the door and departed, limping. Ophelia saw her rejoin Gail, already waiting for her in the corridor, with the peak of her cap still over her eyes and overalls splashed with dirty water.

"Why does Mother Hildegarde call you Augustine?" asked Ophelia, once the two women had gone.

With his hands deep in the pockets of his pajamas, Archibald pensively contemplated the remains of the cigars in the elegant standing ashtray.

"It's my great-grandfather's name. Apparently, I'm the spitting image of him, and I think they once had a little passing love affair. Madam Hildegarde is a very old lady, you know. She has complete mastery of space, but time's a different matter." Archibald gave such a deep sigh that the blond locks flopping on his face fluttered in all directions. "All the same, she should really hold her tongue—she's certainly skilled at making enemies for herself. Me, I can afford to be provocative, but her . . . who will defend her the day she has serious problems?"

Archibald went quiet and, across the blue of his eyes, a shadow passed, like a cloud. Ophelia wondered how this man managed to be at once so exasperating and so disarming.

"And Thorn? What did you do to him for him to detest you so much?"

When Archibald turned towards her, straightening his top hat with a flick, his eyes had regained their summery sparkle. "He is the embodiment of order, and I am that of chaos. Does that answer your question?"

"He did accuse you, all the same, of having harmed his aunt," said Ophelia, recalling the memorable conversation between them, just after the slaughter of the Dragons.

"Ah, that?" In a few deft movements, Archibald took a billiard cue and placed three balls on the fine baize. "You're getting to know me a little, Ophelia. I'm very contrary; one need only forbid me from doing something for me to want to defy it."

"What's the connection with Berenilde?" she asked, surprised.

"Come on, it's obvious. Farouk's favorite, a magnificent woman, dangerous, faithful in love . . . she's the forbidden fruit *par excellence*! I was very young at the time, I couldn't resist. I did overuse my power of transparency somewhat," he admitted, calmly tapping his forehead tattoo. "Berenilde was so absorbed in me that she neglected the tower for a week. Farouk didn't appreciate that and, just for good measure, excused her from going up there for a year. Berenilde almost didn't get over this humiliation. Her dear nephew holds me responsible, and rightly so, indeed."

Archibald slid the billiard cue between two fingers, and the white ball sent a red one into a hole. The noise on impact resounded with such clarity, Ophelia got the impression she'd been jolted out of a trance.

"Don't go thinking I have no regrets," continued Archibald, as he sent another ball into another hole. "This business went pretty far. Thorn proved even more reckless than I myself have been. He attacked me in front of witnesses, with punches and claws; I've got two fine scars to show for it."

Ophelia found it really hard to picture the scene. Thorn rarely lost his cool and had never lifted a finger for his aunt. The most affectionate gesture Ophelia had ever noticed between him and Berenilde was when he'd handed her the saltshaker, at the dining table.

"A bastard, who, what's more, is the son of a disgraced woman, must not attack a person of high birth," concluded Archibald's voice above another clattering of balls. "Even if it's to avenge the honor of a member of his family. I didn't press charges for fear he'd be sent to prison, but he received an official warning from the tribunal: the next time he raised his hand to a noble, it would be Mutilation."

Archibald said this last word while miming the cutting of scissors with his fingers. Mutilation. It was the ultimate punishment, when a family spirit takes back his or her power from the child who has misused it. This sentence had never been applied on Anima, but Ophelia knew it was carried out on other arks. She'd always been told that a person was only mutilated if they had put their whole family in danger. So why did everything have to be so extreme here, in the Pole? By living at the other end of the world, far from other families, did one finally lose all sense of proportion?

'I don't know what worries me most,' thought Ophelia. 'That I might never grow accustomed to it, or that, on the contrary, I end up getting used to it.'

"Sir?"

She jumped on hearing the impersonal voice of Philibert, right beside her. The dull little man was standing in the billiard room, register under arm, as if he'd always been there.

Being familiar with his steward's sudden appearances, Archibald calmly opened a snuffbox and sniffed the powder through each nostril. When he pulled a handkerchief from his sleeve, Ophelia noticed that it was as riddled with holes as his top hat and pajamas.

"So, Philibert! That valet?"

The steward's only response was to signal in the direction of the door. Two policemen brought a stooped man into the light of the lamps. They were each supporting him with an arm, so shaky were his legs under his weight. Ophelia felt her heart sink to the pit of her stomach. The Fox she knew was a blazing fire; this man was but a heap of ashes. She had to look long and hard for any sign of eyes amid the tufts of shaggy beard, but when she found them, she hesitated no longer. It was definitely Fox.

"You should have washed him first," winced Archibald, pressing his holey hankie to his nose, "he smells really bad. I can't decently offer *that* to a lady, go and fetch another one."

"Our agreement entailed my evaluation and this man," Ophelia said, firmly. "Let's not go back on those conditions, if you don't mind."

Puzzled, Archibald just plunged his hands into his pajama pockets, noting with amusement the finger poking out of a hole. "I sometimes find it hard to follow you, but if that is your desire, so be it. You will understand, however, that I can't deliver the goods in this state—the reputation of the embassy is at stake. Philibert, ensure that this man is washed, shaved, deloused, combed, and dressed appropriately."

"Yes, sir."

"In the meantime, my dear, you're my guest!" Archibald

announced, giving Ophelia his flashiest smile. "Have you ever played indoor croquet?"

Ophelia understood that this final condition was nonnegotiable, and she'd have to grin and bear it for a few more hours. She solemnly promised herself that, once Fox was out of this place, she'd dispatch her mother's coat to Archibald's own bedroom.

"One moment, please," she asked, as the policemen were about to take Fox away. Ophelia slowly approached him, but he continued to gaze around the billiard room in a daze. At first, she thought Fox didn't recognize her—after all, he'd only seen her once as she really looked, and at the time he didn't know who she was—but she finally understood that, quite simply, he couldn't see her. Having been deprived of light, he was dazzled by the lamps. Fox saw nothing, understood nothing, and no one had bothered to explain the situation to him. Ophelia resisted the urge to shout out to him that she was Mime, that he had nothing more to fear, and that she'd restore the dignity stolen from him.

"Hello, Foster," she said, instead, aware that all eyes were on her. "I'm Mr. Thorn's fiancée and from now on you will work for me. I will give you more detailed explanations later."

In the middle of the bushy beard, hair, and eyebrows, Fox's eyelids blinked several times, as if he were trying to glimpse, through the fog, the person speaking to him. There was such a look of stupefaction on what remained visible of his face, here and there, between the grimy tufts, that Ophelia knew he'd finally recognized her. She waited for a spark in his eyes, a complicit smile or a relieved sigh, but instead, Fox turned his head away, looking totally despondent. "Yes, miss," he said in a hoarse whisper.

With her heart in her mouth, Ophelia was starting to wonder whether she'd made the right decision.

THE QUESTION

The silence in the lift was the most awkward that Ophelia had ever experienced. Metals grated, furniture creaked, champagne flutes clinked, the gramophone trilled, and the liftboy cleared his throat.

From behind her double-wound scarf, Ophelia observed Fox with distress. Holding his arms along his body in an almost military way, he stood between the buffet sideboard and the pedestal table with the record player, as if he himself were an item of lift furniture. His hair, washed and combed, had regained something of its flaming redness, and his beard had vanished in favor of a strong jaw. His green eyes, finally accustomed to the light, looked both straight ahead and nowhere at all. His spine had straightened into an iron rod, and although his thinner body was lost in the work uniform, he still had his hulking frame. The transformation that had taken place that day was pretty spectacular. Ophelia couldn't understand why this man, who at last looked like Fox, remained a stranger to her.

"Stop!" Aunt Rosaline suddenly ordered. Deferring to Animist authority, the lift's handbrake lowered itself, to the liftboy's amazement. The lift ground to a halt in a cacophony of wood, glass, and metal. "Don't touch that," Aunt Rosaline told the liftboy, as he grabbed the brake to release it. "This lift's not leaving until I decide it is."

Grinding her equine teeth, she considered Fox and Ophelia in turn, like two guilty children.

"Mustard pots alive, it's just impossible, you're both as bad as each other! I can't make sense of your little stories, but I do know one thing. When this door opens," she said, pointing at the lift's golden gate, "we must all hold our heads high. Young lady, you've just acquired an appalling reputation for yourself. You can't pass through the mirrors of a libertine, at the expense of all your other invitations, what's more, without suffering the consequences. Berenilde is furious with you, and, for once, I don't disagree with her. I'll support you whatever happens," she added, less harshly, having noticed Ophelia's glasses turning blue, "but at least, for pity's sake, finish what you've started!"

Fox, who had momentarily dropped his professional bearing, swiftly stood to attention once more. "If I'm a nuisance to these ladies, they mustn't burden themselves with me. I don't want to . . . "

"That's enough," Ophelia interrupted him. It was when she heard the strangled sound of her voice that she realized how much Fox's attitude was tormenting her. "I have no need of a valet. However," she continued, as Fox unclenched his great jaw, "I propose to employ you as an assistant. You will get board and lodging, and be paid, in exchange for your opinions and your advice." Ophelia heard herself speak with a sense of unreality. She'd said everything apart from what was most important. Why did the only words that mattered refuse to come out? What good was being able to address an audience of pernicious nobles every evening, if she couldn't even speak sincerely to a friend?

"I'm very sorry, miss," replied Fox. "I'm just a valet. I'm not supposed to have opinions or give advice."

Ophelia felt as if each word he uttered sank in her stomach

like red-hot coal. There were times when she wished she could express her emotions with the ease of her sisters.

"At least take some time to think about my proposal. I have to be at the optical theater," she said, glancing at the lift clock. "Come with me on a trial basis, and we'll discuss it again after my stories."

"Yes, miss."

There was such rigidity to those two polite words that Ophelia knew Fox had already decided: he didn't want the hand she was holding out to him. She would have liked to prevent the brake from being released, the lift from rising, and the gate from opening. If Ophelia had had the power, she would have stopped time, and then turned it inside out like a glove. Go back to being a little person with no responsibilities. Sheltering behind the counter of her museum. Having only objects for company. In fact, maybe that was all she was good for.

"We're not early," declared Aunt Rosaline, on seeing the deserted staircase of the theater. "Berenilde must already be in her seat. I'm going to try to find myself a vacant one. As for you," she said, dusting down Ophelia's scarf, "focus on what you've got to do. There'll be plenty of time to worry later."

"Follow me," Ophelia said to Fox. "I have access at the back."

As they walked around the theater, Ophelia had not a single thought for the stage awaiting her on the other side of the white-marble walls. She was using every step to find the words that might return Fox to her.

She lost her thread as soon as she saw the Knight on a bench, in the shade of a palm tree, just beside the stage door. He was busy playing with a cup-and-ball, and despite his best efforts, he couldn't get the ball in. His giant dogs were lying at his feet, tongues lolling out of their mouths, ailing due to the climatic illusion, which didn't suit their breed.

"I was waiting for you," he declared, on seeing Ophelia.

From the mouth of such a child, these five words were as ominous as any death threats. "I can't speak to you," she said, continuing resolutely towards the stage door. "You'll make me late."

The two dogs blocked her path. They had moved silently, not showing any sign of aggression, but they were each still the size of a bull. Fox himself, who didn't know the Knight like Ophelia knew him, showed anxious hesitation.

The Knight pushed up the thick, round glasses on his nose. They resembled in every way the pair that Berenilde had broken when she had thrown him across the corridor. "I just had a tiny little question to ask you, Miss Ophelia. Answer me and I'll let you go quietly to your work." He jerked the ball of his toy and, once again, missed. "Could you tell me the essential difference that exists between you and me?"

Ophelia already knew this conversation didn't bode well. Her scarf, which, until then, had been dozing on her shoulders, began to twitch.

"No?" said the Knight, looking crestfallen. "And yet it was an easy riddle. The difference between us," he then said with utmost seriousness, "is that Madam Berenilde likes you. It's not a compliment I'm paying you. You only hold a tiny place in Madam Berenilde's heart, you understand? She likes you, and that's it. Madam Berenilde and me, that's something totally different. We're united by a bond that's stronger than love and hatred."

There was such a sense of the absolute in these words that it was hard to believe that they came from a little boy.

"It is for her that I became a knight, for her alone. I loved her more than my own mother. I showered her with gifts. I even rid her of her family."

Ophelia froze in horror. It was the first time the Knight

was referring explicitly to his responsibility for the slaughter of the Dragons.

"So, it really was you," she murmured. Part of her had always refused to believe this child capable of such crimes.

"They were horrible," retorted the Knight, shrugging his shoulders. "They all hated her because she had better manners than them. They didn't want her to come out of that hunt alive. I *had* to protect her," he said, missing another attempt at getting the ball in, "it's my role as a knight. I took every precaution so her feelings wouldn't be offended," he thought it worth specifying. "I did what was required so she wouldn't witness the killing."

Ophelia remembered it only too well. He'd managed to get all the policemen of Clairdelune on her tail, and he'd plunged Aunt Rosaline into an almost fatal hypnotic trance. Even if Berenilde had wanted to, she wouldn't have been able to join the hunt under such circumstances.

"There were children," murmured Ophelia. "Children of your age."

She had once come across a photograph, in the *Nibelungen*, in which one saw the appallingly mutilated bodies of the hunters, partly showing in the snow. She had recognized one of Freya's triplets. She still sometimes had nightmares about it.

"They were all hunters," said the Knight, shaking his little blond curls. "Hunters risk their lives every time they confront Beasts. If they had been nicer to Madam Berenilde, I wouldn't have got involved. I had to prote . . ."

"You have no idea of the harm you did to her," Ophelia interrupted him, impulsively. "Or of the harm you continue to do to her."

Deeply shocked, the Knight knitted his fine eyebrows and his huskies instantly snarled, revealing impressive rows of fangs.

Realizing her imprudence, Ophelia was about to suggest to Fox that they flee when she suddenly noticed that he'd already gone. She couldn't believe that he'd left like that, without a word.

"How dare you say to me, to *me*, that I'm doing harm to Madam Berenilde?" murmured the Knight. "Or maybe you don't know what doing harm means. Would you like me to teach you, miss?" He had said this last sentence extremely slowly, while his eyes, magnified by the lenses of his glasses, penetrated Ophelia to the depths of her soul. With a nauseous feeling of déjà vu, she knew she must stop looking at this child straight on. She had no memory of it, but she was suddenly convinced that once, in the past, he'd already trapped her in this way.

The sun went dark, the exotic setting disappeared, and Ophelia felt herself falling into the darkest and most glacial of nights.

"Miss Vice-Storyteller, everyone's waiting for you!" exclaimed a cheery voice. The Knight jumped, the dogs pricked up their ears, and the illusion into which Ophelia was plunging shattered. She felt as stunned as if someone had stopped her, at the last moment, from falling down a well.

To her great surprise, it was Baron Melchior, coming towards them with his distinguished swagger. His frock coat, adapted to the vast proportions of his body, was woven entirely out of an illusion of the Milky Way. Shooting stars even crossed his opera hat, leaving luminous trails. He wasn't the Minister of Elegance for nothing. His blond moustache seemed to punctuate his round face with two exclamation marks.

"Good day, Uncle Melchior," said the Knight, with the politeness of a model child.

"My dear nephew, you don't have permission to walk your dogs here," replied the baron. "And also, have you seen the time? You should get home quickly, to your Uncle Harold's, and go to bed." Lifted by a smile, each side of his moustache stood up, like the wand of a magician.

"Please forgive me, Uncle Melchior, you're right. Goodbye, Miss Ophelia," said the Knight. "We'll meet again very soon." This promise, murmured with a wave of the hand and a half-smile, made Ophelia's stomach turn to lead.

As soon as the Knight and his dogs had disappeared into the striped shadows of the palm trees, Baron Melchior gave a sigh of relief. "That child is increasingly uncontrollable. Thank goodness your valet came to find me."

Seeing Fox standing behind the baron, upright and impassive as any servant, Ophelia felt totally ashamed. For a moment, she had thought he'd abandoned her.

"My nephew causes all of us great concern," Baron Melchior lamented, while smoothing his moustache.

"And what are you doing to change that?" Ophelia would never, normally, have risked talking to a Mirage in that tone. She should have felt grateful to him, but her nerves were still sending defensive impulses across her body. She hadn't forgotten, either, that Baron Melchior was the brother of Cunegond, and Cunegond was far from a friend.

Not remotely offended, Baron Melchior cast wary glances around the theater, as if he feared seeing the Knight return with a vengeance. "Excellent question. Stanislav unleashed one of his dogs onto my little niece because she had made an unfortunate remark about our dear Berenilde. Fourteen years old, Miss Vice-Storyteller, and the child will never walk normally again. All that blood, all that violence . . ." he said, with a grimace of disgust. "Because of a single remark."

"Stanislav," Ophelia repeated, thoughtfully. "I didn't know the Knight's real name. Did you know that it was he who killed the Dragons?"

She had so expected Baron Melchior to feign indignation or ignorance that she was amazed when he admitted to knowing. He glanced again over his shoulder, checking that no one was eavesdropping, and whispered: "I had my suspicions. We all did. You see, there are very few Mirages who know how to use their power on animals. Stanislav lost his parents in circumstances that were rather . . . particular. He is under the guardianship of my cousin Harold, his uncle, but I suspect the latter of having passed on some repugnant and dangerous knowledge to him. Harold is no criminal," Baron Melchior immediately clarified. "He would never have asked Stanislav to act in such a reckless way. But it's possible, even probable, that he unintentionally created that event. It is most regrettable that the Mirage name should be associated with that appalling business."

"You are that scared of him?" Ophelia asked, provocatively.

Baron Melchior kept turning on the spot, like a giant spinning top, forever checking that no one was approaching. His stoutness was such that Ophelia suspected him of not abiding by the rationing measures imposed by the Treasury since the meat shortage. Like every minister worthy of the name, the baron spent a good deal of time in the hall of the family High Council, on the first floor of the tower; there, it was said, a perpetual banquet took place, at which all excuses were good for eating and drinking.

"It's a trifle more complicated than that. A Mirage will never publicly denounce another Mirage. On the other hand," Baron Melchior added with a sidelong smile, "a Mirage can give a little nudge in the right direction to fate."

"Fate?"

"Otherwise known as 'Mr. Thorn.' I understood that our Treasurer was going ahead with the inventory of domestic Beasts. If I were him, I would go and ferret a little around

Harold's place. Of course, I never said a word to you on the subject, did I?"

"I . . . Right," said Ophelia, unsure she'd really grasped all of it. "I really must go now,"

"Just one tiny moment!" Baron Melchior moved closer to her and wiggled his fat, ringed fingers in front of her nose, as if trying to cast a spell on her. Rather puzzled, Ophelia wondered what had got into him, and then realized that he was bringing the seeds of illusions to life in the very fabric of her dress. The ethereal forms gained in precision, color, and movement, and soon two-dimensional butterflies fluttered the length of Ophelia's body, like a pattern that had come to life. It was the first time she'd witnessed the creation of an illusion. The baron certainly hadn't stolen his reputation as a great designer.

"Officially, I came *exclusively* to give you this present. A modest present from the Minister of Elegance to Miss Vice-Storyteller. We touched on no other subject of conversation, did we?"

With these words, addressed as much to Ophelia as to Fox, Baron Melchior left, with a polite tip of the hat.

"Miss Vice-Storyteller has finally arrived," sighed the butler when Ophelia had rung the bell at the stage door. "We were starting to worry over her absence. Mr. Storyteller has started his performance."

"What stage is he at?"

"The one-eyed vagrant has already changed the fate of the first two heroes, Miss Vice-Storyteller. He's about to meet the third."

That left Ophelia with still a little time. Old Eric always told the same saga, evening after evening; she'd heard it so often, she knew when she needed to be ready.

"I'm very sorry," said the butler, with a vague look at Fox, "but this entrance is prohibited to the public."

"He's my assistant," Ophelia responded, firmly. "I absolutely need him. He'll remain in the wings. Don't make me late, please," she added, as the butler seemed to be thinking it over.

"Please forgive me, Miss Vice-Storyteller," he said, stepping aside to let them through.

Indicating to Fox to follow her, Ophelia plunged into the familiar backstage darkness. Even though she'd got to know the setting well, it didn't stop her from banging into the ladders, chairs, and bits of set that turned the path into an obstacle course. Old Eric's grating voice and the mournful accordion music, muffled by the thick black curtains, made the darkness even darker.

This evening, however, it was Fox's silence that seemed to reverberate against every surface. Ophelia leant against some furniture and waited for the nervous shaking of her body to abate. Her legs, which had turned to jelly, wouldn't carry her anymore.

"Miss?" asked the voice of Fox, who had almost bumped into her.

"Give me a moment," murmured Ophelia. "It's that child. He terrifies me. Thank you for going to get help." She took a deep breath. "You would have preferred to remain at Clairdelune, wouldn't you?"

She turned slowly towards Fox's massive form, which was causing the floorboards to creak. They were now no more than shadows among shadows, faceless presences, voices without mouths. Ophelia understood that here, where all conventions disappeared, it would perhaps be possible, finally, to talk. She tugged on the scarf to bare her face and free her words.

"I know you felt at home there," she murmured to the condensed blackness opposite her. "You get on well with everyone, you know every corner like the back of your hand, you know how and when to play the game. And then there's Gail,"

Ophelia stammered, in an even lower voice. "You have always liked her. She's the one who informed me, you know? And me, Foster, I gave myself the right to tear you away from that place."

Somewhere in front of her, Fox was now nothing but tense breathing.

"You're free," whispered Ophelia. "Free to go, free to stay. I won't make you leave one cage for another one, although, as you've seen, I really don't live in great security. I decided your fate without taking time to think, or to speak to you. I was selfish . . . and I still am," she had to admit, after a few seconds' reflection. "I still am because, deep down, I would like you to choose to remain by my side. I know that apologizing can no longer change anything, but anyway: forgive me."

"No, miss." Fox had murmured a barely audible reply, but Ophelia couldn't have been more shaken if he'd shouted at the top of his voice. "No, miss," he repeated, harshly. "Even for all the sandglasses in the world, I wouldn't have wanted to remain at Clairdelune."

There was a moving of shadows as Fox leant against what must have been a ladder. The top of his head caught a little ray of light escaping between two theater curtains. Some red hair lit up as though on fire.

"Miss seems to think I'm angry. Can't she understand, then, that I'm just very embarrassed?"

"Embarrassed?" Ophelia had been ready for anything but that. She looked at Fox's profile, haloed by the faint light. He was nervously rubbing his lion's mane, thinking he was invisible in the darkness of the wings.

"After what has happened, I could never feel at ease, neither in miss's presence nor in that of her fiancé. Miss says she's making me her assistant? She wants to benefit from my opinions and my advice? If I had any decency, I shouldn't even look at her."

"What are you talking about?" Ophelia asked, taken aback. Two green lights lit up in the dark: Fox was staring, wide-eyed.

"Well," he stammered, "regarding the fact that . . . you know . . ." Now the professional mask was cracking, he'd slipped back into a Northern accent one could cut with a knife. "I . . . I got totally undressed in front of miss."

Ophelia was at once so incredulous and so relieved that she felt as though her swelling chest had just burst like a fairground balloon. "And that's all?" she asked, huskily. "Come now, Foster, I was only a valet myself. How could you have guessed?"

"That doesn't change the fact that I lacked respect towards miss. I spoke casually to her, I treated her with familiarity, I took her sandglasses, and, to top it all, I washed myself under her very nose. Of course, I didn't know who miss was. I only discovered it when ironing the newspaper; I recognized her in a photograph. The fiancée of Mr. Treasurer," sighed Fox, separating each syllable. "Valets have been hanged for less than that."

Applause made the floorboards under their feet vibrate. Old Eric had finished his story, soon he would have put away his illusion projector.

"Listen, Foster," Ophelia said, trying to make herself heard over the clamor. "You taught me the nuts and bolts of this world, and protected me from the policemen when I was nobody. That's all I remember today. I wouldn't ask anyone else but you to be my adviser. So have a good think about it, and you can give me your response after my stories. Mr. Farouk is waiting for me to take the stage."

When the safety lights came back on in the wings, Ophelia saw that Fox was astonished. "The Immortal Lord? *He* is here?"

"It's to him that I tell my Animist tales. Stay in the wings," whispered Ophelia, before slipping between the theater curtains. "I'll explain everything to you afterwards."

136

It was as she was advancing on the stage, dazzled by the footlights, amid the forced applause of the audience, that something disturbing dawned on Ophelia.

She hadn't the remotest idea what story she would tell Farouk.

THE AFFRONT

As she sat down in her usual spot, at the very edge of the stage, Ophelia could gauge the significance of her aunt's words in the lift. There were many more spectators than usual filling the rows of seats, but not a dandy stifling a yawn, not a noble consulting his watch, not a lady playing with her pearls. No, this evening, in the velvety half-light of the auditorium, every spectator was focusing his or her opera glasses on Ophelia. The previous day, she was still just a somewhat simple little foreigner to them; a day spent at Archibald's had just made her lose all her innocence. She'd had her baptism of vice, taken her first step towards depravity; in short, she was starting to become their equal, and from now on, they intended to keep a closer watch on her.

None of these nobles concerned her as much as Berenilde did, seated in the front row, her diamonds sparkling in the play of darkness and light. Until now, she had always given her an encouraging look before her performance. Not this time.

If there was an evening when Ophelia shouldn't have forgotten her book of tales back at the Gynaeceum, it was definitely this one. Only Farouk seemed to be unaware of the noxious atmosphere filling the auditorium like stagnant water. He left his seat and approached the stage, as was now his wont.

Impassive as a statue, and with his long hair enfolding him like a white cloak, he sat in the middle of the cushions that the theater's director had placed there for him, to facilitate this curious ritual.

Farouk was waiting for the story; Ophelia was waiting for inspiration.

The silence that fell between them was so prolonged that the spectators began to exchange whispers, taking care not to raise their voices too much, however—one glass of milk had been quite enough for them. Ophelia knew that she must say something soon, but her head was ringing desperately hollow. Even the stories she knew by heart, by dint of telling them, fluttered through her memory without settling, like the butterflies Baron Melchior had conjured up on her dress.

"Would you agree to our postponing the tales of objects until tomorrow?" she asked, timidly.

The courtiers, seated too far away to have heard her, continued whispering behind their opera glasses. As for Farouk, he hadn't blinked. He continued to focus his blurry eyes on Ophelia, as if he hadn't heard her, either. It was after a sustained face-off that he finally said, in an extremely deep and extremely slow voice: "Tell your story."

"I'm sorry, sir. This evening I can't manage it."

Farouk's heavy eyelids half-closed and his eyes became more attentive. This simple increase in concentration sent his mind wave out into the atmosphere. Ophelia tensed up from head to toe as the wave reached her. Farouk's power attacked the nervous system directly, and there was nothing she could do to protect herself from it.

"You can't manage it," he repeated.

"No. I offer you my utmost apologies."

Slowly, very slowly, Farouk turned his head. Reading the signal, the young Aide-memoire came over at the double and handed him his notebook. "There," he said. "I wrote: 'The Vice-Storyteller will tell me stories every evening.'"

Ophelia felt her mouth go dry. How could one person deny the will of another to this extent? Gazing at the rows of spectators, she wondered if it wasn't his egocentricity, more even than his strange family power, that this father had passed on to his offspring.

Suddenly, Ophelia was listening to herself speak, as if her mouth knew better than her what must be done: "There was once, on Anima, a doll belonging to a little girl. She was an articulated doll, able to move her head on her own, lift her arms on her own, walk with her legs on her own. The doll really liked the little girl, but the day arrived when she no longer wanted to be her toy. She wanted to have her own dream. She wanted to be an actress."

"I don't like this story," Farouk interrupted her. "Tell another one."

Ophelia took a deep breath, and continued: "One night, the doll left the little girl's bedroom. She traveled all over the world, from ark to ark. She thought only of how she could fulfill her dream. The doll ended up coming across some puppeteers."

Generally, Ophelia introduced pauses and combined several tales. Tonight, however, she was speaking rapidly and in a trance. Fury, fatigue, and fear had taken control of her tongue, and she no longer really knew at whom, whether at herself or at Farouk, this story was really directed.

"The puppeteers promised the doll that they would make an actress of her. And that is how, every evening, she performed on the stage of their little theatre. Everyone rushed to see her. And yet, every evening, after the show, the doll wasn't happy. She thought more and more often of her little girl. She didn't understand why she felt so empty. Hadn't she fulfilled her own dream? Hadn't she finally become an actress?"

"That's enough." Farouk had interrupted Ophelia for the second time. There was a nervous stir across the auditorium.

Ophelia knew that she should have stopped there. And yet, the rest of the story escaped from her, as if it had a life of its own: "And one day, the doll finally discovered the whole truth. Being an actress wasn't her own dream. From the start it had been the dream of the little girl. The doll had never stopped being her toy."

Barely had she uttered the last word of the story when Ophelia was racked with a pain so intense, she had to cling to the edge of the stage not to fall forward. She felt the blood running from her nose and spreading on her chin. Farouk's power had propagated itself like a shock wave. As he was relinquishing his extraordinary position, extricating his limbs one by one to stand upright, his face lost its marble blankness. His white eyebrows lifted, his pale eyes widened, and his facial muscles slackened, all dilating as one.

Ophelia was grabbed by the arm and pulled backwards. It was old Eric, who had leapt from the wings to remove her by force.

"If my Lord would return to his place, a new variation of the one-eyed vagrant will be recounted to him!" he announced in such a strong voice that his "r"s sounded like thunder. "The show continues!"

On the stage, scene shifters were already busy putting the illusion-projector stand back in position. Trampling on her own terrified scarf as she was bustled to the back of the stage, Ophelia saw Farouk's contorted expression one last time before the white canvas of the screen fell between them like a curtain.

"You're completely reckless," old Eric muttered into his beard, once he was sure he couldn't be heard. "You want to make the lightning strike your head?"

Ophelia had assumed he'd been grabbing the chance to get

top billing again; when she saw that he was as scared as her, she began to understand that he had perhaps just saved her life. "I was short of ideas," she stammered, sputtering blood. "I didn't think that story would put him into that state."

"If I distract him now, perhaps he will have forgotten your affront," muttered old Eric, sliding on the straps of his accordion. "He must not be allowed time to record the incident in his notebook. Or the entire theatre could suffer the consequences."

With these words, he shoved Ophelia into the wings. Barely had she been swallowed by the dark when the hypnotic voice of the storyteller rose to drown out the audience's booing. Disorientated, Ophelia moved shakily away, gradually weighing up what she'd just done. When she felt Fox's solid hands holding hers in the dark, she gripped them as if they were a life preserver.

"I think, this time, I've really done something stupid."

"You still want my opinions and my advice, miss? Here's my opinion: you're in urgent need of advice. And here's my advice: always listen to my opinion."

It was much later that night that Ophelia finally thought about Thorn.

Curled up in her bed and overcome by the tropical heat, she was suffering such anxiety that her Animism, then exceptionally febrile, contaminated all the furnishings in the room. The canopied mosquito net was billowing like the sail of a boat; the hangers on the screen were all clattering against each other; her glasses were scuttling along the bed like a demented crab; her left shoe was stamping its heel on the carpet; and the shutters were shivering on their hinges, making the illusory sunlight flicker between the slats.

Ophelia had been trying to get to sleep for a long time to

stop this commotion, but as soon as she closed her eyes, she saw Farouk's contorted face again, as if imprinted beneath her eyelids. She'd needed four handkerchiefs to stem her nosebleed, and her body was still racked with painful neuralgia. Ophelia couldn't fathom how a simple tale could have so upset this family spirit. When Farouk had told her he didn't like that story, she'd thought it was because he recognized his own courtiers in the puppeteers, and that truth disturbed him. Now she realized she'd been gravely mistaken: there was something else about this tale. Farouk's power had become so uncontrollable that the entire theater had had to be evacuated. Since then, he had shut himself away in the top floor of the tower and, according to his Aide-memoire, he was currently unapproachable.

As Ophelia had become, too. Until further notice, she was persona non grata. Fox had spent half the night answering the telephone to note down all the canceled engagements. As for Berenilde, she had lectured her as never before, calling her, in turn, insolent, stupid, and ungrateful. "If we lose our Lord's protection," she'd repeated, both hands tensing up on her stomach, "we're doomed!"

For all these reasons, Ophelia just couldn't soothe the agitation of the furnishings in her room. And it was seeing the large cheval mirror swinging furiously in its frame that she had suddenly remembered her missed meeting with Thorn.

Ophelia dragged herself out of bed and plunged one hand into her reflection. She was surprised not to feel the fabric of the coats in the Treasury wardrobe. This meant that Thorn had left the door of his wardrobe open and was still expecting her visit, despite it being so late at night. After a moment's hesitation, she caught her glasses, walking crabwise on the bed, and slipped on her dressing gown and boots.

When Ophelia traveled from the mirror in her room to the

one in the wardrobe, the temperature difference was such that it quite took her breath away. It was like leaving summer to enter the worst of winter. The Treasury was the very model of discipline, with its perfectly aligned files, locked cabinets, and labeled classifications on every shelf. So Ophelia thought she'd got the wrong mirror when she discovered, in the flickering light of a lamp, hundreds of papers dancing across the room, like birds in an aviary.

An icy wind was sweeping through it with the force of a torrent; if it had the merit of being real, unlike the court breezes she encountered all day long, it certainly whipped up all the papers into unstoppable white whirls. Ophelia positioned her feet on the ground so as to avoid creasing all this administration, and wondered where Thorn was, and why he'd opened the window.

It was as she neared the bull's eye window and heard glass crunching under her shoes that Ophelia realized that the window wasn't open; someone had broken it. That surprise was nothing compared with her astonishment when she finally found Thorn, in the middle of the paper storm.

He was pointing his pistol at her.

THE PROMISES

Ophelia was so shocked, she didn't have the presence of mind to be afraid. Thorn was barely recognizable. Blood was flowing from his forehead, nostrils, and mouth like the many tributaries of a single river, smearing his hair, clogging his eyelids, running down the steep slope of his nose, and daubing long, scarlet streaks on his white shirt.

"Ah, it's you," he said, lowering the barrel of his pistol. "You should say who you are on arrival, I wasn't expecting you anymore."

Thorn had spoken in a solemn, steady voice, hardly bothered by his split lip, as if his Treasury hadn't just been trashed in an apocalypse. With a flick of the hand, he swiveled the pistol round and presented its grip to Ophelia. "Take it. Only pull the trigger if absolutely necessary. They probably won't be back, but we must remain vigilant."

Ophelia didn't even look at the weapon; all she could see was the blood. She was trying hard not to look horrified. "Who did that to you?"

"That question no longer really concerns me," Thorn said, phlegmatically. "I gave them as good as I got. On the other hand, I would have appreciated it if they had searched my office with more care. It's going to take me hours to put everything back in order."

Realizing that Ophelia wouldn't touch the pistol, Thorn slid it under his belt, and then caught a sheet of paper as it swirled in front of him.

"Application for subsidy for exterior improvements to housing," he muttered. "That's for the telephone pile."

Incredulous, Ophelia watched Thorn stride across the administrative cataclysm and push the form under what must have once been the telephone. She noticed similar piles all over the room, under the mail tray, under the ashtray, under chair legs, like strange nests seeking to escape the wind. On every paper, there was Thorn's blood. Ophelia found it extraordinary that such a methodical man hadn't prioritized looking after his injuries, alerting security, and repairing the window *before* attempting to tidy up. Now he was sitting on the floor, busy sorting out whatever he came across.

Ophelia tied her scarf to control her hair, which the wind was blowing in all directions, and then risked a quick look through the bull's eye window. First she saw the dizzying drop of the wall, which, far down, disappeared in the mist. Those who had smashed the window from outside were serious acrobats. For a second, she'd wondered whether the Knight hadn't done it again, but it didn't look like his way of doing things.

When she turned to the wardrobe she'd arrived through, Ophelia better understood why she'd found it open: it, too, had been wildly emptied of its contents. Ophelia picked up a coat that had been flung on the floor, and managed to wedge it around the frame of the bull's eye window. The wind stopped flooding into the room and the papers fell limply to the floor like autumn leaves.

With her teeth chattering, Ophelia turned up the cast-iron radiator to its maximum and turned on the gas lamps, increasing the light and warmth produced by their flames as much as possible. How could it be this cold at the beginning of June?

Thorn let her get on with it without a word or a glance. With his limbs bent like great spider's legs, he was still on the floor, busy collecting, assessing, and classifying anything that resembled paper. His metallic eyes, partly obscured by dark crusts, glinted with concentration in the middle of the shattered surface of his face. When he pushed his hair back, it stayed stiff, forming red spikes.

"Thorn," murmured Ophelia, cautiously. "I don't want to panic you, but you . . . well . . . you're not looking very well."

"Cut forehead, fractured nose, two broken molars, and a few strained muscles," he intoned, without looking up from his sorting. "Don't be traumatized by the blood—it's only mine."

"Do you have a first-aid kit?"

"I did have one. Bottom drawer of the desk."

Ophelia crouched under the table, found a lacquer box, and accidentally spilt its contents over the floor. To her great surprise, it was just dice: dozens, hundreds of small dice. It was the strangest, most pointless collection she'd ever seen. She finally found the drawer with the first-aid kit behind the desk chair, guided by the strong smell it gave off. The phials it had contained were broken. In the hope of finding a survivor, Ophelia carefully picked through the debris, but no bottle was intact and there were no dressings, bandages, compresses, or plasters. "You must see a doctor," she concluded.

"No," replied Thorn, "I must reorganize these documents. The Treasury will reopen its doors at eight sharp, and not a minute later."

While her scarf shivered on her shoulders, Ophelia kneeled on the floor, opposite Thorn's spiderlike form. She handed him the pile of papers she'd gathered along the way. "As you please. Now, tell me: what happened exactly?"

Thorn studied a facsimile by the light of a lamp while he replied:

"Two masked individuals broke into the Treasury, having scaled the outside wall. They asked me a few questions, which I obviously didn't answer, and then they searched here for what they hadn't got out of me. My bastardized claws may not be as effective as my paternal family's, but, combined with a pistol, they can be a deterrent: those gentlemen departed, empty-handed, through the window." To illustrate what he was saying, delivered in the manner of a legal statement, Thorn dug into his shirt pocket and pulled out a black-velvet pouch. "A nose and a little finger," he announced, shaking the pouch. "My assailants now have distinguishing features that will facilitate a future inquiry."

"What did these people want from you?" asked Ophelia, trying not to look at the pouch. "What were they looking for?"

"Confidential information. I happen to be in charge of a sensitive dossier in which important people are implicated."

Ophelia held her breath as the memory of her threatening letter came back to her. "Because of Mr. Farouk's Book?"

"What?" muttered Thorn. "No connection. I'm currently focusing on the rehabilitation of the disgraced."

In the blink of an eye, Ophelia recalled all those newspaper articles warning the people of Citaceleste about the disgraced and Thorn's ambiguous position towards them. "Their rehabil-itation? Berenilde told me that the crimes of those clans were too serious ever to be forgiven."

"Not true."

If Thorn's lanky body, contorted into the position of a tailor, was almost immobile, his arms and his slender hands were endlessly coming and going between chaos and order. He smoothed out, folded, and then lined up the countless accounting documents; his meticulousness was such that not a single page stuck out from the new piles he was making. Looking more closely, Ophelia noticed that each pile even followed the lines of the strips of parquet, and all in perfect symmetry. She thought of the extraordinary collections of dice and phials she'd found under the desk and seriously wondered whether Thorn wasn't a little crazy.

"The disgraced are excellent hunters, the only ones up to confronting the fauna of this ark and protecting its inhabitants. If you visited the towns of the Pole, you would see that they are heroes in the eyes of those without powers. It's because of that, and only that, that they are feared up here."

"How could the court be convinced to give them another chance, in that case?"

"With the help of the law," replied Thorn, tackling another pile of documents. "The Constitution allows for the possibility of commuting permanent banishment to temporary banishment, if it's in the general interest. I will demonstrate this at the next Family States, on the 1st of August. The dossier, kept securely in a safe, contains some weighty arguments. Between now and then, the Treasury will represent the disgraced and place them under its official protection, whether the intimidators like it or not," he concluded, with highly professional loquacity.

Ophelia suddenly remembered that porcelain pipe she'd read for Archibald. The Provost of the Marshals had killed some of the disgraced for poaching, and, today, he was reported missing. If Ophelia hadn't scrupulously kept professional secrets, she would have been tempted to share this information with Thorn. "What are these Family States?" she asked, instead. "I've never heard of them."

"They take place only once every fifteen years. On those occasions, Farouk presides over the Council of Ministers and hears the grievances of the three states: the nobles, the disgraced, and the powerless."

"And why should it be up to you to represent the disgraced? You did kill one of their own, after all."

Frowning, Ophelia remembered as if it were yesterday the way Thorn had announced the fact at dinner, between two spoonfuls of soup, as if it were the most trivial thing in the world.

"Legitimate defense," Thorn retorted, without a second thought. "If a disgraced person places himself at the disposal of a noble, to get his hands dirty on the noble's behalf, he has to accept the consequences. And in any case, the disgraced don't have the right to enter the court, including during the Family States: they're obliged to designate a representative. They were very sensible to choose me."

Ophelia hugged her legs tighter and buried her chin in her scarf. The cold suddenly gripping her was more pernicious than that pervading the Treasury. She found Thorn's way of speaking to her like this—nose in his papers, never looking her in the eye—chilling. With his stained shirt, neutral tone, and mechanical gestures, he was like a rusty automaton condemned to perpetual movement.

After a period of silence, however, he consulted his fob watch, also streaked with blood. "Have you finished with all your questions? Good. So now it's my turn."

Thorn linked his hands around his knees and finally relaxed his big arms, now hanging from each shoulder like dead weights. His entire body, half-hunched, half-twisted, was stock-still, like a stopped machine; as for his sinister face, criss-crossed with blood and bruised from the blows, it displayed a vaguely sullen blankness.

This calmness was but a facade. Ophelia tensed from toe to head when he finally raised his long, damaged nose in her direction. His eyes cut into hers like razor blades. "What were you doing at Archibald's today?"

Thorn's neutral tone had given way to a leaden one. Ophelia was unnerved by the personal turn the conversation had taken. She couldn't even understand how Thorn could know about that, having been holed up here all day. "Oh, that? It would be a bit long to explain."

"We had an appointment," Thorn stressed, unnervingly slowly. "Why Archibald rather than me? What makes him more suitable company?"

"That's not the issue," she stammered. "Something unforeseen cropped up, that's all."

"So what must I do for you to put a stop to this punishment you are inflicting on me."

Now, Thorn's eyes were like white-hot metal. Hunched up, Ophelia tucked her chin deeper under her scarf, forcing herself, at all costs, not to turn her head away. She didn't want to show it, but Thorn was suddenly scaring her somewhat. "It really wasn't planned. In fact, I'd forgotten about you."

Hearing this reply, Thorn began to stare at Ophelia with such intensity, she felt as if she were shrinking inside her dressing gown, while he, on the contrary, seemed to keep getting bigger. He frowned so hard he made his mask of dried blood crack. "You really don't like me."

Ophelia felt an electric charge run across her skin. She knew this effect well: it was the one produced by a Dragon about to pull out his claws. Her slight, instinctive gesture to protect her face instantly made Thorn's face fall. The hardness of his features had given way to consternation.

"So that's where we are? You distrust me to that extent?"

"My nerves have been sorely tested today," Ophelia explained. "And you should take a look at yourself in a mirror when you make that face. You, too, would find yourself terrifyi . . . "

"I would never do you any harm." Thorn had interrupted her with such abrupt spontaneity, Ophelia was knocked sideways. For the first time in a long while, she believed in his sincerity.

"There are several ways of harming someone. I now only put my trust in very few people, and, for now, neither you nor Archibald is among them."

Thorn contemplated his big, bloodied hands, and with a futile, rather awkward gesture, rubbed them on his shirt as though finally aware of what he looked like. "I have many enemies," he said, scowling. "I no longer want to count you among them, so tell me what I must do. That is why you came here, isn't it? You have a deal to offer me, I'm listening to you."

Ophelia would have preferred to have this discussion some-where other than on this uncomfortable parquet floor, and with a man free of wounds and bumps, but she had no inten-tion of backing off. "I want a job."

"A job," repeated Thorn, his accent hardening both conso-nants. "You already have one."

"I am definitely not cut out to be vice-storyteller. My per-formance this evening was a disaster; in fact, it all ended very badly. I don't think Mr. Farouk will want to listen to me again."

If Thorn was annoyed by this news, he didn't show it. "He won't withdraw his protection from you. You are too import-ant. He'll end up forgetting. He always ends up forgetting."

Ophelia hoped with all her heart that he was right. Just thinking again about what had happened triggered a terrible neuralgia. "I've thought about it, and I would like to run a reading consultancy. I could carry out evaluations to authen-ticate family objects or . . ."

"Granted," said Thorn, without hearing any more.

Ophelia raised her eyebrows, astonished to have won her case so swiftly.

"Just avoid doing your work in front of Farouk," he con-tinued. "It could give him the idea of trying you on his Book, and the Book, that's my business. Anything else?"

"I've hired an assistant, but currently have no means to

remunerate him. I'm not very familiar with these money matters. Between now and when I'll be able to pay him, would you be able to provide a wage for his services?"

"Granted. Anything else?"

"Er . . . yes," stammered Ophelia, who hadn't expected that, too, to be dispatched so swiftly. "I fear that, in time, I'll no longer be able to tell illusions from reality. I want to see the outside world."

"Granted," Thorn said, in his cleaver-like voice. "The Polar night is over and temperatures are rising, so you will soon be able to get some fresh air. Anything else?"

Ophelia knew that Thorn was ready to make a few concessions, but not for a moment had she imagined that he'd give in to her like this, on all fronts, with no objections. He really was serious about their reconciliation. Ophelia decided to be so, too. She unknotted her scarf, lightened her glasses, and pushed back her forest of brown curls, to stop hiding herself.

"I have a final favor to ask of you, the most important of them all. Promise me to be honest from now on. My being just a pair of hands to you, that's no longer a problem," she said, clenching and unclenching her gloves. "I'll take on that role as long as it's clearly established between us and it suits both of us. I'm even prepared to teach you to read objects when you've inherited my Animism, after the ceremony of the Gift; and you, you will teach me to handle my claws. That will be our only conjugal duty," she stated, stressing each word. "But then, for me to trust you again, don't conceal anything from me anymore that concerns me directly."

This time, Thorn maintained a lengthy, sullen silence, broken only by the wind seeking, with its gusts and eddies, any give in the seams of the coat.

"Granted," he finally muttered.

They remained staring at each other for a long while, as

a new awkwardness hovered around them. Ophelia would have gladly initiated some symbolic gesture—a hand offered, a friendly smile—but Thorn was as unyielding as a block of marble.

Since they were speaking frankly, might as well make the most of it: "You're counting on your personal memory to enhance the reading of the Book. So it's that exceptional?"

Thorn winced on hearing Ophelia mention the Book. "A bit more than that, even."

"But this memory," insisted Ophelia, "am I going to inherit it, along with your claws, at the Gift ceremony?"

"It will all depend on your receptivity. It's not an exact science."

"And what do you do with your own receptivity? After all, your memory may not make you a good reader. And," she added, recalling the contract, "you only gave yourself three months to learn to use my family power. Personally, it took me years."

"Failure is a possibility," conceded Thorn.

Ophelia looked at him intensely. He was moving heaven and earth to meet Farouk's needs, but he didn't seem really bothered about the outcome of such an enterprise . . .

"And what will happen if you disappoint Mr. Farouk after promising him so much? You think he will ennoble you in spite of everything?"

"Of course not," Thorn said, with the same steady voice. "You will then be rid of a burdensome husband."

If that was sarcasm, Ophelia didn't find it at all amusing. "You shouldn't take this reading lightly. Others will take it very seriously for you, starting with Mr. Farouk. I received a strange letter . . . Never mind . . . The fact is that this Book and the secrets it holds seem to disturb some people. More even, perhaps, than your disgraced do," concluded Ophelia, indicating the broken glass on the floor.

Thorn let out a sigh that, coming through his broken ribs, sounded like the whistle of a kettle. "Stop going on about the Book. And if it's not too much to ask of you," he said, grabbing a bundle of papers, "stop attracting attention to yourself. Now, with your permission, I would like to get back to my sorting."

"I saw the Knight today. He admitted everything to me." Ophelia had never really had the opportunity to talk with Thorn about how losing his family had affected him. Of the little she knew on the subject, his half-brother and half-sister had made his childhood difficult and they had virtually not spoken to each other since they reached adulthood. So now, Ophelia was disconcerted by the way Thorn's entire body had suddenly tensed up.

"In front of witnesses?"

"No. I wonder, however, whether he isn't a bit mad." Just as she was saying that, Ophelia was struck with a thought. Who other than a madman would send a threatening letter and conclude it: *"GOD DOESN'T WANT YOU HERE"*?

"But I also had a very interesting conversation with Baron Melchior," she continued. "He told me that the Mirages dread the Knight as much as we do. He left me a message for you."

"What message?"

"The baron recommends making a search of the home of his cousin Arnold . . . no . . . Harold. He told me it could help you in your inventory of domestic Beasts, and maybe even beyond that. Do you understand what he meant to say?"

"I take note," was all Thorn muttered while leafing through what remained of a catalogue.

Ophelia frowned. Really? That was it? For someone who had committed to no longer concealing anything, he wasn't making much of an effort. She stood up, numb with cold, while dusting down her dressing gown. She was exhausted. "I'm going to bed. Don't forget your promises."

"I won't forget. I never forget anything."

Thorn had reverted to both his professional voice and his systematic sorting, as if this parenthesis of his private life was already closed. Ophelia reflected that, in two months, she would be tied to this freak for the rest of her days.

If we survive until then, she thought, gazing at the apocalyptic spectacle of the Treasury.

"You should wipe away the blood and repair the window before receiving your visitors," she couldn't resist lecturing Thorn. "Don't give people more reasons to find you suspect."

Without lifting his nose from his catalogue, Thorn pulled out his fob watch and, instead of looking at the time, clutched it forcefully in his fist.

"You wanted me to be honest with you. You will thus learn that you are not just a pair of hands to me. And I don't give a damn whether people find me suspect, as long as I am not so in your eyes. You will return this to me when I have kept all my promises," he grumbled, holding his watch out to Ophelia without noticing her stunned expression. "And if you still doubt me in the future, just read it. I will phone you soon about your consultancy," he added casually, by way of farewell.

Ophelia passed through the mirror, and returned to her bed, in the baking heat of the Gynaeceum. She looked at Thorn's watch, which was beating like a mechanical heart, and knew that tonight, again, she would find it hard to get to sleep.

THE BELL

"Ophelia, it's Mommy . . . *krshhh* . . . I did get your last letter . . . *krshhh* . . . Well done, lots of polite little words to say nothing at all . . . *krshhh* . . . You were never any good at lying . . . *krshhh* . . . I know when one of my children is hiding things from me . . . *krshhh* . . . So, just like that, you want to keep your own family out of your life? *krshhh* . . . That's not knowing us very well, my girl . . . *krshhh* . . . We'll be arriving on the *Boreal* on the 4th of July, at two in the afternoon . . . *krshhh* . . . Don't bother cancelling this time, we'll be staying until the wedding . . . *krshhh* . . . As I don't trust your fiancé, I prefer to use this Animaphone . . . *krshhh* . . . Organize accommodation for twenty-one people, your brother and sisters are coming with us . . . *krshhh* Ophelia, it's Mommy . . . *krshhh* . . . I did get your last. . ."

Ophelia stopped the constantly turning cylinder of the miniature phonograph with her finger, and put the Animaphone into her pocket. The mechanism had no starting device—no crank, or key, or pull—so only an Animist could make it work. Being rather slow with her power, Ophelia had had to persevere finally to hear her mother's message, after the little parcel had been handed to her by the mailman.

"There you are," she said to Aunt Rosaline and Berenilde.

"What do you think?" Ophelia wasn't sure herself which emotion, joy or panic, was making her heart beat fastest.

"What I think is, the 4th of July, that's next week," said Aunt Rosaline, looking annoyed. "They're all already aboard the *Boreal*. This time, we can no longer delay their coming. And your mother, kid, is not going to be a piece of cake."

"My feeling," said Berenilde, smiling insincerely, "is that it couldn't fall at a worse time." She threw a telling glance at the store window, on which a sign writer was busy painting the words "EVALUATION AND AUTHENTICATION," which would have made a better impression had ectoplasms not stuck their ugly grimaces on the other side of the glass. These illusions had been cast during the night, and none had yet disappeared.

"Excuse us, ladies."

Aunt Rosaline and the Valkyrie had to move aside to let two workmen moving a desk pass by. No, not a desk, thought Ophelia. *My* desk. She had obtained this little office to launch her reading consultancy; it was still a construction site, and already someone was trying to sabotage it. Berenilde was right, it really wasn't the ideal time to be receiving her family.

It was now three weeks since Farouk had shut himself away on the top floor of the tower, and given no sign of life. According to the newspapers, such a thing hadn't happened for decades. The Jetty-Promenade guest list, which the lord chamberlain usually drew up, depending on the family spirit's schedule, had been put on hold indefinitely. The palace's countless reception rooms and gardens had immediately been invaded by all of Citaceleste's aristocracy, including nobles who had yet to be invited there. There was a tense atmosphere around the place, with everyone feeling that they were king, and arguments on protocol had become daily occurrences. The Mirages and the Web had always been clans possessed of a keen sense of family; now, their members were endlessly quarrelling over issues of precedence.

Thorn had taken advantage of this chaotic climate to set up Ophelia's consultancy in a former cloakroom on the Jetty-Promenade. Sufficiently well positioned to attract a minimum of clients, sufficiently discreet to escape Farouk's notice.

Disturbed by the smell of fresh paint, Berenilde pressed an embroidered handkerchief to her face. "Provoking our Lord with that ridiculous doll story . . . What on earth were you thinking of? Because of you, we have lost virtually all our protection."

Since the scandal that Ophelia had created at the optical theatre, the Web had withdrawn her personal surveillance. Much as Archibald tried to plead her case, his family had proved inflexible: they would now have just one Valkyrie allocated to them, whose sole mission would be to watch over Berenilde and the unborn baby.

Ophelia resisted pointing out that it made no great difference, as far as she was concerned. The Valkyries hadn't prevented either the humiliations, or the threats, and those old women were chilling, following them like shadows without ever saying a word. If one had to wait to be killed in front of their very eyes to be proved right, Ophelia preferred to manage on her own. "Don't worry, madam," she said instead. "Mr. Farouk is enormously attached to you, he'll never stop protecting you."

"What on earth do you imagine? It's been a while now that he no longer touches me, and, recently, he barely looks at me. The moment I become a mother, I will cease forever to exist in his eyes. My days of grace were always numbered," Berenilde murmured, bitterly. "I knew that from the start. I just didn't think it would end in this way."

Ophelia glanced guiltily at that rounded stomach, which Berenilde endlessly cradled, as if the child it sheltered could escape from her at any time.

"What's done is done," continued Berenilde, lifting her chin. "As for your family, Thorn will find a solution. Ah, and here he is!"

The entrance bell had indeed just sounded, and the Treasurer was bending his endless body through the frame of the door. With his black epauletted uniform and hair combed back, he was already more presentable than the last time Ophelia had seen him, even if his wounds had left dark traces, here and there, on his skin. Briefly, he took in the nightmarish illusions splattering the store window.

"Don't expect to be inundated with clients," he said, by way of a greeting. Aunt Rosaline opened her mouth, about to speak, but Berenilde slipped her arm under the aunt's and led her away. "Come, let's leave my nephew and your niece to talk at ease."

Ophelia watched them zigzagging around the workmen on the site. It was a charming thought, but she no longer felt at all at ease.

From the front, Thorn was impassivity itself, with his severe profile and big nose elevated far above mere mortals. From the back, however, his index finger was continually hammering the wrist of his other hand. Somewhat embarrassed, Ophelia wondered whether he felt as nervous in her company as she felt in his. Now that they had made a deal, everything should have been clear between them; but their conversation at the Treasury had left her with an indefinable aftertaste. And the closer the date of the marriage became, the more absurdly anxious she felt.

"I received a message from my mother," she said, diving straight in. "She'll be here next week. She and twenty other members of my family."

Thorn remained so silent, Ophelia thought for a moment he hadn't heard. "Twenty-one," he finally grumbled. "Twenty-one

Animists that will have to be housed, fed, and protected for more than a month. Do these people not have any obligations back at home?"

"Our family works in the conservation of our heritage. The department closes in the summer. Do you never take holidays?" Seeing Thorn knit both brows and scars, Ophelia felt as if she had uttered a profanity.

"Your family will attempt to repatriate you to Anima," he declared. "They don't like me and your mother is impulsive. However strong the temptation, don't give them any reason to make you leave the Pole before we've got married. If you could avoid broaching certain subjects in front of your family, that would be ideal."

Ophelia frowned. "And in front of the Doyennes of Anima?" she asked, stiffly. "It's through their mediation that you and your aunt organized the marriage. They must already know the true reasons."

"No," replied Thorn, to her surprise. "They didn't ask us any questions. In fact, they seemed relieved to know what to do with you at last."

Ophelia gripped the little Animaphone in the pocket of her dress. "We have granted you a final chance," the Doyenne had said just before her departure. From whatever angle she considered her present situation, it didn't really seem like a lucky chance.

"I'm a bad actress. I, myself, can't really find a good reason for staying. So convincing my parents of the opposite . . ."

"You're contractually bound to Farouk. The diplomatic repercussions, in a case of withdrawal, would be very serious, for your family as for mine."

"I already know all that," said Ophelia, annoyed. She was talking "homesickness," and Thorn was responding "affair of state." He must have noticed her irritation, because he finally deigned to lower his big nose towards her. "Would you prefer to hear me say that I would like to be your reason for staying? I doubt it."

" . . . letter . . . *krshhh* . . . Well done, lots of polite little words to say nothing at all . . . *krshhh* . . . You were never any good at lying . . ." Ophelia snatched her hand from her pocket to shut the Animaphone up. Her tension had restarted the mechanism. "No," she said, stiffly, "you will have to help me to reassure my parents when they're here. I'm not asking you to play the perfect son-in-law, but might you at least manage to smile?"

Ophelia didn't know whether Thorn had heard her question; the entrance bell had just found its voice again. She couldn't believe her glasses when she saw that the visitor coming through her door was Lazarus himself, the arks-trotter with an interfamilial reputation.

"Knock, knock, is it open?" he asked, cheerily, while raising his huge top hat. "Good day, *chères dames!*" On top of his very particular accent, which dodged each "r" and distorted each vowel, Lazarus was endowed with long silvery hair, a beardless face that extended into baldness, a large white frock coat, and two eyes that sparkled mischievously behind their pink spectacles. Behind this appearance of an old conjuror hid a tireless traveler and brilliant entrepreneur. He came from the City of Babel, which he pronounced "Baball," a cosmopolitan and avant-gardist ark that Ophelia had heard about since childhood. It was the first time Lazarus was visiting the Pole, but he was one of those rare passing tourists that the court welcomed with open arms.

"I'm here on business!" he exclaimed, looking with great curiosity at the grimacing illusions on the shop window. Ophelia took her most professional look. She couldn't have imagined a better start to her new career. Lazarus was only in the

162

Pole for a few weeks at the most, and every aristocrat vied to receive him in their salon. And yet it was the consultancy door belonging to her, the tainted one, that he'd chosen to walk through.

On top of that, Lazarus hadn't come alone. Walter, his mechanical butler, fresh from a Babel factory, followed him with stiff, jerky movements.

"Was it you saying I shouldn't expect any clients?" Ophelia muttered to Thorn. He didn't reply. From the moment the bell had sounded, he had returned to his statutory distance and police-officer posture, as if speaking to his fiancée in public were improper.

"Good day, Mr. Lazarus," Ophelia said in greeting, moving towards him. She tried not to stare at Walter for fear of seeming impolite. It was her first encounter with this mechanical butler, which everyone in Citaceleste was already talking about. He looked like those articulated manikins used for learning to draw: his metallic head was faceless and he had visible cogs at each joint of his limbs. So people said—and, particularly, so Fox said these people said—Walter was capable of carrying suitcases, serving tea, and playing chess, which in itself was an amazing feat, even if he never won a single game.

"You are Mademoiselle Ophelia, the reader from Anima?" asked Lazarus, studying her over his pink spectacles.

"Yes, sir."

"That's marvelous!" he chirped, handing his top hat and cane to Walter. "I visited Anima twice, it's so picturesque. Your little brick houses are full of character . . . I mean literally, actual character, and not always of the best sort. A door pinched my fingers, once, because I'd forgotten to wipe my shoes on the doormat. So, you came from the end of the world to settle here? I greatly admire people who are open to the cultures of other families!"

As old Lazarus was frenetically shaking her hand in his, Ophelia refrained from telling him that it wasn't due to open-mindedness that she had landed in the Pole. He was going to make her even more homesick if he continued speaking of Anima to her in this way.

"You're like that incredible architect I heard so much about when I arrived here," he continued enthusiastically, pronouncing it "incredibeul." "This Citaceleste, it's a real masterpiece, I marvel at every floor! Mademoiselle Hildegarde, is that it? An authentic Arkadian, can you imagine? I hope to meet her, too, but she is elusive! I've travelled a great, great deal, but I've never visited LandmArk. It's an indiscernible ark, said to be wedged in a hidden recess of space. And yet the Arkadians have created shortcuts all over the world! You know about the interfamilial Compass Roses?" he asked, fervidly, as if speaking of the greatest wonders ever invented by man. "There's one installed on every ark. Yes, yes, on every ark, miss, even on yours, on Anima! If the Arkadians agreed to open their Compass Roses to the public, they would revolutionize the transport system. No more airships! But alas, it's a highly secretive family that doesn't want to be disturbed. The Arkadians readily import and export, but beware, at the slightest unrest, they pack up their things and close the Compass Roses. Have you ever tasted the tangerines from LandmArk? They're the finest!"

"What can I do to help you?" Ophelia interrupted him, as politely as she could. Lazarus had delivered his speech in one breath without ceasing to shake her hand, and her fingers were starting to hurt.

"You?" he asked, surprised. "Nothing in particular, I won't trouble you much longer. In fact, I was looking for Mr. Treasurer, I was told I'd find him here."

Dreadfully disappointed, Ophelia watched Lazarus liberating her hand to set off in pursuit of Thorn's.

"Dear sir, we meet at last! You are as elusive as Mademoiselle Hildegarde. I have been hoping to see you since the day I arrived, I . . ."

"The Treasury will not purchase your automatons." Thorn had interrupted Lazarus in a gloomy voice, without touching the arm thrust towards him. Far from being offended, the old explorer seemed, on the contrary, more amused by this refusal.

"You live up to the portrait people paint of you, Mr. Treasurer. Allow me at least one minute of your precious time. Don't stop at commercial considerations, but try to envisage what Walter truly represents," declared Lazarus, with a theatrical gesture towards the liveried mannequin. "He's not a grown-up's toy. He is the end of the servitude of man by man, no more, no less! Walter will undertake lowly tasks, and will do so with the most civilized manners in the world. Walter!" called out Lazarus, with two exaggerated mouth articulations. "Greeting!"

In one rigid movement, the mechanical butler bent over at a right angle . . . and dropped Lazarus's hat and cane, as if incapable of carrying out more than one instruction at a time.

"*La barbe!*" cursed Lazarus, pulling an enormous key from his frock coat. "I forgot to wind him up."

"The Treasury will not purchase your automatons," Thorn merely repeated.

Ophelia jumped on hearing the entrance bell ring once again. It was Fox, triumphantly brandishing a leather notebook at the half-opened door.

"And that makes four, miss!" Although he was no longer really a valet, he'd adopted the honey-yellow livery of the court servants, the better to melt into the background. With his gold braiding and red mane, he was as dazzling as Thorn was dark. Ophelia sensed herself coloring just looking at him.

Thanks to him, the three long weeks she'd just gone through, banished from society, had been just about bearable.

"I've dug up four potential new clients, miss. Their employees are mates of mine, so it's a solid lead," he whispered, thumbing the pages of the notebook. "They're art dealers, pawnbrokers, and bankers. With these illusions all over the place, they can't tell the authentic from the counterfeit anymore. Your little hands will tell them all they need to know, you'll be the queen of demystification!"

"In other words, public enemy number one," Thorn commented, lugubriously.

Fox might be built like a wardrobe, but he still had to bend backwards to look up at Thorn. It was as if a winter wind had just blown on his fine confidence and sent him back to his former status. "Would . . . would sir please forgive me," he stammered, immediately lowering his eyes. "I didn't, of course, intend to put Miss, his fiancée, in any difficulty. I was trying . . ."

"Don't listen to him, Foster," Ophelia was quick to jump in. "I think it's an excellent idea. And also," she added, with a meaningful gesture towards the window daubed with illusions, "it's not as if I were in anyone's good books."

"Excuse me, Mr. Servant," interjected old Lazarus, with a friendly smile. "What is your personal opinion on the servitude of man by man?"

Looking warily at the mechanical butler Lazarus was presenting to him, Fox was saved by the entrance bell ringing several times. Baron Melchior was struggling, as elegantly as possible, to get his considerable bulk through the door frame. Clad entirely in rainbow-hued clothes, he looked like a hot-air balloon on legs. His large, waxed moustache lifted into a smile as soon as he spotted Thorn.

"Mr. Treasurer, I was wondering where you were!"

"Here," Thorn replied, as though stating the obvious.

"Ladies," Baron Melchior said in greeting, tipping his hat at Berenilde, Aunt Rosaline, and then Ophelia as he made his way across the building site of an office, taking care not sully his smart white shoes. "Ah, Mr. Lazarus, you're here, too? Delighted to see you again. Oh dear, oh dear, Mr. Treasurer, we don't have the *Nibelungen!*"

"Help yourself," suggested Thorn, indicating with his chin the layers of newspaper protecting the parquet from the works.

"I'm talking about today's edition. It didn't appear. My cousin Chekhov has directed the *Nibelungen* for more than thirty years and this has never occurred before."

"What do you want me to do about it?"

"Nothing," Baron Melchior admitted, frankly. "The snag is that my other cousin, right here, had booked a small ad for today's paper, specially addressed to you. As the *Nibelungen* didn't appear, he's come to read it out loud to you."

So corpulent was Baron Melchior, Ophelia hadn't noticed that he was closely followed by another Mirage. And yet the latter was hardly easy to miss, with his jewelry that made him sparkle from head to toe. He bore the tattoo of his clan on his eyelids, rings on all his fingers, and pearls threaded on each strand of his blond beard. Even his lovely silver cane was inlaid with precious stones—or, more likely, illusions of precious stones. His face, framed by two gold pendant earrings, was a picture of offended solemnity. Like nearly all of the nobles, he had a fine blue sandglass in his fob pocket.

Ophelia recognized him as the first ever Mirage she had come across, the night she'd escaped from Berenilde's manor to explore the Citaceleste. At the time, she'd taken him for a king.

"I demand rrreparrration!"

"Calm down, cousin Harold," Baron Melchior stayed him. "We're among civilized people, we'll sort all this out in a friendly fashion."

Ophelia pushed her glasses up on her nose. So he was Count Harold, guardian of the Knight? He didn't seem inclined to listen to his cousin's advice, since he continued in an even louder voice, hammering the ground with his cane, and rolling his "r"s like earth tremors:

"I rrrefuse that a bastarrrd lodges a complaint against a man of my rrrank and my imporrrtance!"

"It's the Treasury, not me, that's lodging the complaint," corrected Thorn, with supreme composure. "For 'undeclared breeding of numerous domestic beasts and unauthorized animal experimentation,'" he recited from memory. "Your dogs have been subjected to repeated hypnotic manipulation. Such practices are strictly forbidden by law."

"Rrreturn my dogs to me! And rrreturn my nephew to me!"

"I wasn't personally involved in his arrest," Thorn responded, calmly. "You can visit him at the police station."

Ophelia stared wide-eyed. The Knight had been arrested? Aunt Rosaline let out a "Holy safety pin!", and Berenilde herself had to sit down on a chair covered in plaster, stifling an exclamation of surprise.

"You didn't teach your ward very well how to use his power," continued Thorn, before Count Harold once again made the walls of the reading consultancy shake. "He admitted responsibility for serious, potentially fatal injuries. The Treasury decided to present a Mutilation case," he concluded, with professional neutrality. "You will get your nephew back as soon as this request has been dealt with."

"Rrreturn my dogs to me and rrreturn my nephew to me, bastarrrd!" demanded Count Harold, who had clearly not listened to anything. "If you don't rrreturn them to me," he said, pointing at Ophelia with his cane, "it's I who will take this little wench of a forrreigner from you!"

"Count Harold!" protested Baron Melchior, smiling all the

while. "As Minister of Elegance, I won't tolerate that language to a senior official and a diplomatic guest. And as a cousin, I beg you not to put our family into an awkward position. Your nephew is seeing to that quite enough already."

The count briefly clenched his ringed fingers around his blue sandglass, as though resisting the temptation to pull its pin right there and then. In fact, a vein was bulging at his temple, and Ophelia wondered whether it wouldn't end up bursting. She wouldn't have minded seeing him unpin his sandglass, disappear for a few moments, and then reappear in a state of gentle euphoria.

"What are you trrrying to do, then, bastarrrd?" he persisted. "Prrrovoke a Mirrrage?"

"I have gathered some most interesting confidences," Thorn replied, without losing his composure. "Two mercenaries confirmed to me that they had been employed by you to dissuade me from defending the cause of the disgraced at the forthcoming Family States. Count yourself lucky that I wasn't able to get signed confessions from them."

"You arrre nothing," said Count Harold, stroking the pearls on his beard with his ringed fingers in a very disdainful way. "Yourrr fatherrr was a barrrbarian and your mother a conspirrrator. Wherrre are they today? The Mirrrages *are* the State!"

Lazarus, who had stopped winding up Walter a while ago, was observing the scene and taking notes with an almost scientific interest. Ophelia felt as if she were watching a zoologist studying the behavior of a rare species of animal.

Baron Melchior, who was becoming increasingly embarrassed, decided to take control. He searched the count's pockets himself, pulled out a splendid silver ear trumpet, and stuck it in his ear. "We heard you," he said into the horn, "now let me take care of the details with Mr. Treasurer."

Count Harold pursed his lips with a look of outrage, but

finally kept quiet, giving a rest to everyone's eardrums. A workman took advantage of the lull to slip behind him with a
bucket of glue and some rolls of wallpaper; continuing with
the work showed admirable professionalism.

"Please excuse what my cousin has been saying, Mr. Treasurer," continued Baron Melchior, hands gripping the lapels of
his vast rainbow jacket. "He was very shocked by the arrest of
his nephew and the seizing of his huskies. The Mirages won't
obstruct you," he assured, lowering his voice so that Count
Harold couldn't hear him, despite his ear trumpet. "Beasts are
more unpredictable than ordinary animals and their intelligence doesn't lend itself to our illusions. We officially condemn these clandestine experiments."

Stuck between Thorn's lofty figure and Melchior's enormous belly, Ophelia was careful not to intervene. She could
clearly see the efforts the baron was making not to get too
involved. Despite his smiles and his habit of smoothing his
endless moustache between thumb and index finger, he
seemed even more nervous than at their last encounter. His
eyes never stopped rolling in their sockets, as if he feared being
stabbed by his shadow. Ophelia found this anxiety somewhat
over the top, but she didn't forget—she would never forget—
that it was Baron Melchior who had made the Knight's arrest
possible. She hadn't felt so relieved for a very long time.

She was surprised not to find the same emotion in Berenilde's eyes. She was still sitting in her chair, staring at the
pattern of the freshly hung wallpaper and pensively stroking
her stomach.

"Rrright, what about yourrr complaint?" growled Count
Harold, back on the attack and holding his ear trumpet the
wrong way round. "What have you decided, bastarrrd?"

"And what about my automatons?" Lazarus started again,
shaking Walter's key.

"And what about our family?" asked an exasperated Aunt Rosaline.

Ophelia was flummoxed. She felt as if the whole world had arranged to meet in her reading office to talk about everything but reading. And as if the atmosphere weren't confusing enough, the telephone started ringing like a bell. It was the first time Ophelia had heard it. She hunted for it for a while under the sheets of newspaper protecting the furniture from paint, and finally found it, a brand-new phone, on the bottom step of a ladder.

"Yes?" she asked into the funnel of the phone. Due to the general hubbub, Ophelia couldn't hear the name the operator was announcing to her. She put a finger in her ear and Archibald's voice finally rang out in a brassy tone.

"You look so distraught, little miss, that I can't resist the urge to stick my oar in! And like that, I'm the first to use your new telephone line."

Ophelia glanced reproachfully at the Valkyrie escorting Berenilde, as if Archibald was hiding behind her voluminous black dress. Knowing that he was always lying in wait, on the other side of those eyes, made her feel uncomfortable. In addition to Archibald's attention, Ophelia noticed that she had also just attracted Thorn's, despite the noisy and repeated entreaties he was being subjected to. Seeing him tighten every feature of his grim face, she turned her back on him and became intensely interested in the gas lamp a workman was screwing into the wall. "You've chosen a very bad time. Please call back later."

"You'll have to speak much louder for me to hear you," Archibald sniggered in the receiver. "Or rather, no, stay silent and listen to me. Do you recall the little favor you did me the other day?"

"Er, yes, why? Have you had news of Mr. Provost?"

"No," replied Archibald's beaming voice. "It's started again."

"What's started again?" mumbled Ophelia, pressing her mouth to the copper receiver. "What have you done?"

"The problem isn't what I've done, but what I've not managed to prevent. I was going to ask you to pass Thorn on to me, but there's no point," Archibald added, casually. "He's coming straight at you."

Ophelia didn't have time to turn round before the phone was snatched from her hands.

"Who is this?" Thorn asked, his tone authoritarian. He was so high up on those legs of his that Ophelia had to climb the steps of the ladder to raise herself to his level. By the tensing of his jaw muscles, she understood that all his concentration was now focused on the phone caller. He no longer even seemed to hear Lazarus, Count Harold, and Aunt Rosaline, who were continuing to speak to him of automatons, dogs, and family, like a scratched operetta record.

Ophelia unhooked the phone's second receiver to hear what Archibald was saying to Thorn.

". . . exactly the difference between you and me. You're as predictable as an astronomical clock! You want to control everything—I'd wagered that you wouldn't be able to resist the temptation of snatching that phone."

"That's enough," hissed Thorn. "I'm giving you ten seconds to convince me not to slam the phone down on you."

"About Mr. Chekhov, ghastly director of the *Nibelungen*: his cousins can stop looking for him; he really has been abducted. Have I convinced you not to hang up?" Archibald asked, sarcastically.

Perched on the stepladder, Ophelia had a clear view of Thorn's eyes, usually so narrowed, as, slowly, they widened.

"When, where, by whom, and why?" he said, methodically.

"Last night, at Clairdelune, I don't know, and I don't know" Archibald replied, as jokily as if playing a guessing game.

Ophelia was slowly weighing up this news. After the Provost of the Marshals, this was the second Mirage to disappear from within the best guarded bastion of all Citaceleste. If the embassy could no longer provide diplomatic sanctuary to its guests, court intrigues would no longer know any bounds.

Why, Ophelia asked herself, closing her eyes. Why is this happening now that the Dragons are dead and the Knight's been arrested? Why do new enmities always have to take the place of old ones?

"What was Mr. Chekhov doing at Clairdelune?" Thorn asked, more pragmatically. "And what makes you so sure that it's an abduction?"

From the moment he uttered these words, an abrupt silence fell on the reading office, and the workmen suspended their activities. Only Count Harold, despite Baron Melchior's signaling him to shut up, continued to shout, demanding that Thorn apologize to him.

"Mr. Chekhov was receiving malicious letters," Archibald's carefree voice declared down the phone. "When you read his rag, you can understand why. He told me he feared for his life and asked me for sanctuary. I suspect him of seizing this excuse to come and nose around my place. He moved his newspaper works here, complete with rotary press, spools of paper, and the rest."

"Get to the point," Thorn ordered.

"The fact is that, last night, I organized a fancy-dress ball . . . Indeed, now that I think of it, I'd invited you and you didn't come."

"Get to the point," Thorn repeated, between his teeth.

"Right in the middle of the ball, Mr. Chekhov went to the lavatories and never returned. My policemen searched the estate from top to bottom, but he remains nowhere to be found. If you need a description, the last time he was seen, he was wearing a white wig and a woman's dress with blue flounces."

From the way Thorn's huge forehead creased, Ophelia knew that he was cogitating on all cylinders and that the prospects he could already envisage pleased him not at all. Somewhat despite herself, she felt a certain admiration for his capacity to manage every crisis without ever losing his cool.

"Was there any notable incident before his disappearance? A quarrel? A threat?"

"We're talking about Mr. Chekhov here," chuckled Archibald. "Quarrels and threats are his bread and butter! Indeed, I was about to expel him, as he kept insulting Madam Hildegarde, and I permit no one to insult my personal architect under my own roof."

"You mentioned letters to me," Thorn prompted.

"Ah, yes, we found them among his personal effects. Patience!"

"I am being patient," said Thorn, becoming more impatient by the minute.

"No, I'm not talking to you, I'm talking to my sister. Patience, pass me one of those letters. It doesn't matter which one. Thank you." In Ophelia's receiver, there was a rustling of paper. "'Mr. Chekhov,'" read Archibald, "'you have taken no notice of my previous warnings. If you insist on producing your appalling newspaper, I will personally take the steps required.' Typed, no signature, but a strange sentence in capital letters, just below: 'GOD DEMANDS YOUR SILENCE.'"

Thorn was so taken aback that, for once, he didn't immediately know how to respond. He wasn't aware that Ophelia, for her part, had almost fallen off the stepladder. The letter. Chekhov had received the same letter as her. And he'd disappeared.

"The Treasury is going to have to launch an inquiry and hear all the witness statements," decreed Thorn. "I'll be right there in an hour. In the meantime, leaving the embassy is strictly prohibited."

Barely had Thorn hung up the telephone before the entrance bell was ringing out. Ophelia vowed to herself to get it removed so she'd never have to hear it again.

"Visiting time is over," Thorn announced, categorically. "My presence is required elsewhere."

"I'm not here for you, Mr. Treasurer, but for Miss, the reader," responded a small, polite voice. "A client wishes to see her."

This time, Ophelia tumbled down the ladder. It was Farouk's young Aide-memoire, standing at the door of her office.

"Our Lord awaits you outside," he said with an angelic smile, holding the door open for her. "He wishes to speak to you."

THE CLIENT

If her window hadn't been covered in several layers of illusions, maybe Ophelia would have noticed how much the atmosphere had changed outside. The cloakroom that was now her office was right at the end of a gallery in the Jetty-Promenade palace. One had to negotiate almost a kilometer of carpet, glass doors, tea tables, and colonnades before reaching it. So Ophelia was shocked to see the whole court gathered outside her door. The crowd was so dense and the gallery so narrow that the nobles had invaded the mezzanines, armed with opera glasses so they would miss nothing of the show. However, it wasn't so much their number that struck Ophelia, but their silence.

"What an impressive family reunion," commented Lazarus, donning his white top hat, as though he were observing some local custom. "Walter, add this scene to my picture library, please." The mechanical butler produced a camera and, in a flash of light and puff of smoke, took a photograph of his shoes.

As for Ophelia, she wondered whether she hadn't banged her head when tumbling down the stepladder: her glasses were endlessly darkening and lightening. When she took them off her nose, she finally understood that it wasn't her glasses going crazy, but the entire palace. The fifth-floor sun, which she'd never seen either setting or hazing over, was flickering behind the windows, like a badly screwed bulb. These light changes allowed one to

176

glimpse, intermittently, the true nature of the place. Ophelia discovered, in just one flicker, a gray ceiling instead of the glass dome, and a brick wall where the sea usually sparkled on the other side of the picture windows. Without its makeup, the Jetty-Promenade looked more like a hangar.

From the moment she saw Farouk, between two blinks of the sun, Ophelia knew that it was he who was disrupting the illusion. This giant, whom she had always seen slumped over and forever yawning, was standing in the middle of the gallery with all the solemnity of a commemorative statue. At that moment, his demeanor was so imperial, his beauty so inhuman, his whiteness so dazzling, and his expression so icy that he alone embodied the Pole.

Ophelia shivered all over as soon as he thundered: "I find you at last."

With a total lack of manners, Thorn presented himself to Farouk in such a way as to eclipse Ophelia behind him. "I have just been informed of disturbing events at Clairdelune," he declared in his most administrative tone. "I present you with my report."

Ophelia contemplated the black back of the uniform in astonishment. Where did Thorn get the nerve to divert Farouk's attention on to himself? The latter's psychic emanations were so oppressive that, for her part, she was struggling to breathe.

"Who are you?" Farouk asked, slowly.

"Your Treasurer."

"I am not here for that."

"Mr. Chekhov disappeared last night," Thorn continued, with as much feeling as a typewriter. "It may just be a false alarm, but we are going to have to launch an inquiry."

"I am not here for that."

"If the disappearance is confirmed, I recommend reinforcing the security on all floors of the Cita . . ."

Thorn's big body staggered to one side, as if he had been thrown off balance by a punch in the face. Farouk's mind wave had propagated so violently that even Ophelia's ears were ringing like bells. She barely heard the applause of the nobles on the balconies and Berenilde's horrified cry. However, she saw very clearly the blood spurting from Thorn's nose.

"I did not come for that," repeated Farouk. "I want to speak to *her*."

If every muscle in her body hadn't seized up, Ophelia would have seriously considered escaping through the first mirror she came across. Incredulous, she saw Thorn pick up the gold epaulette that had fallen off his uniform, take out a handkerchief, and dab his nostrils as calmly as if dealing with a mere cold.

"I got wind of my fiancée's poor performances on stage. I'm busy finding her a different occupation. I ask that you allow me a little more time."

It was clumsily put, but Ophelia would have felt reassured if Farouk had gone along with it. Instead, he walked slowly around Thorn and made straight for her. The silence surrounding them was now so oppressive that Ophelia heard her own vertebrae cracking as she looked up at the magnificent face of marble. Farouk blew a polar blizzard into the furthest depths of her being.

"How dare you?" he said between his teeth. "By what right do you put your hands at the service of people other than me?"

Ophelia would have liked to have pleaded her case, but Farouk's mind paralyzed her will. She was no longer able to speak, or move, or think. Her body and her soul now formed but one and the same block of ice.

"Do you consider yourself superior to me? Do you take me for your toy?"

Ophelia had already had a few frights in her life. She'd

choked on a peach stone; electrocuted herself plugging in a lamp; crushed her fingers in a sash window; and things had only got worse since she'd left Anima for the Pole. However, nothing she had experienced until now was comparable to the fear that gripped her, right here, right now. She could detect no anger, no disdain, nothing even remotely resembling an emotion, in Farouk's eyes.

No, what lay deep in those eyes was a desert.

Ophelia felt sucked into this infinite space. In a heartbeat, she gauged the chasm between their two temporalities: an immortal destined for eternity, a human condemned to disappear. "You are but a small, ephemeral thing," a voice whispered to her. "And Farouk has the power to make you even more ephemeral." All he had to do was frown, and Ophelia's mind would splinter like hoar frost.

Farouk plunged a hand inside his big coat and pulled out the Book. "You are presumptuous enough to run your own consultancy? Excellent, I will be your first client."

"That's not in our contract."

Ophelia barely heard Thorn's tense voice. She was entirely in the grip of Farouk's ice; all that wasn't his eyes seemed faraway and unreal to her.

"Take this Book."

"She is not ready," Thorn stressed, solemnly. "*I* am not ready. Look again at your notebook."

"I'm not sure it would be reasonable, my Lord," Berenilde intervened, controlling as best she could her quavering voice. "This dear girl is not capable of being your reader. My nephew, he soon will be."

"And my niece's consultancy hasn't opened yet," added Aunt Rosaline, with her usual pragmatism.

Farouk ignored them all. Ophelia would have liked to turn to them and reassure them with a smile, to tell them that it would all be fine, that it was only an evaluation, and that if she failed, so what, she would apologize like a professional.

She was incapable of doing so.

Farouk was terrorizing her. She'd had the audacity to stand up to him in public, and it was in public that he was going to make her pay the price.

"Do you accept, yes or no, to work on my Book?" he asked, his eyes boring into hers.

"No."

Ophelia had croaked the word in a voice that mortified her. The icy aura instantly fell away, like a receding tide, and Farouk put the Book back under his coat. Ophelia almost ran for her life when he stretched his giant hand towards her. He tightened his fingers around her skull, like the talons of an eagle.

"I scared you. Please forgive me."

Murmurs of astonishment spread like wildfire across the entire walkway, but no one could have been more stunned than Ophelia at that moment. Her body was reeling so much, she concentrated on her feet so as not to collapse under the weight of the hand.

"It would seem you reminded me of someone else," Farouk explained, distractedly. "Evidently, you are not who I thought you were."

Ophelia couldn't have said whether it was disappointment or relief that she detected in his voice.

"I withdraw your appointment of Vice-Storyteller. You make me much too nervous."

If she hadn't been on the verge of tears, Ophelia would have burst out laughing. "Me, I make you nervous?" she heard herself reply in a strangled voice. "Do you have any idea how I feel now, in your presence?"

"Look at me."

The big hand left Ophelia's head to slide under her chin and firmly lift up her face. If Farouk's face was still but a mask of expressionless beauty, his eyes had regained a small glimmer of humanity. Now that his mental hold had relaxed, Ophelia became conscious again of the world around her. The sun had stopped flickering like a lightbulb, and the ceiling looked once more like a glass canopy full of sky. The light twinkled on the nobles' opera glasses; cast the palms' striped shadows onto the ladies' lavatories; and accentuated Berenilde's pallor as much as Aunt Rosaline's redness. Wherever Ophelia looked, she saw only tension and anxiety. She expected Thorn to be the most tense, so she couldn't believe her glasses when she saw him straining to reattach his epaulette, as if the symmetry of his uniform was his number-one priority.

"Even now," murmured Farouk, tightening his grip on her chin. "Even now, you remind me a little."

"Of whom?" asked Ophelia, startled.

"I don't know," he admitted, somewhat perturbed. "Artemis, I suppose. The fact is, I prefer to put a stop to your tales."

"They were in return for your protection," Ophelia reminded him, in a tiny voice. "The contract . . ."

"Do stop annoying me with your contracts. I have absolutely no intention of getting rid of you. I will find a better way of employing you, that's all. I'll think about it when the time comes."

With these throwaway remarks, Farouk let go of her chin and, very slowly, moved off. Amazed, Ophelia stared after him for a long, long, long time, as he left the gallery, taking all the courtiers with him. Even Lazarus started to run after them, calling out to Walter; the mechanical butler was following on the heels of a man wearing the same hat as his master.

Still shocked by what she'd just been through, Ophelia jumped when Thorn announced:

"You are leaving Citaceleste, this very day."

Fragment: Second Reprise

God had great fun with us, then God tired of us and forgot us.

Stones. They fall on him like rain. He watches them flying through the sky, and then bouncing off his body. Judging from this memory, there's no shortage of stones where he finds himself: the ground is a medley of bricks, tiles, and broken glass. Here and there, a few remnants of facades are barely standing, with gaping holes instead of windows. He recalls the silhouette of a building-site crane in the distance. The aftermath of a war. Men rebuild what other men have destroyed.

Where is the wall with the drawings? Where is the bedroom? Where is God?

He forces his memory to retrace the stones' trajectory in reverse, from their impact on his body, rising up in an arc in the sky, and back down to their source. Kids. There are four of them in the middle of the rubble. Correction: there are five of them. A little girl is on the floor, crying. They all have messy hair and are poorly dressed.

Does he look like them?

No. Now that he thinks of it, he remembers his impeccable clothes, his neatly plaited long hair, and his dazzling white hands. He is as clean as they are dirty. The kids shout words at him that he doesn't understand. The more he focuses on this memory, the more he remembers just how strange they seemed to him, those kids, when he saw them the first time. They are so small, so brittle, so fragile . . . extremely fragile.

The little girl crying on the floor, now it comes back to him: it's his fault. He didn't want to hurt her, he didn't even touch her; he just approached her to look at her, out of simple curiosity, and she burst into tears. The stones, they were probably due to that. The kids want to keep him away from the little girl.

He's just thinking that that memory is of no great interest when, suddenly, Artemis appears on the scene. This time, she's nothing like an eye at the back of a hole. Her red hair is so abundant, it leaves nothing more of her to be seen but patent shoes, lace on a dress, and a pair of gold-framed glasses. She walks calmly over the debris towards the kids. They have stopped throwing stones, riveted by this apparition, but they are on their guard.

Artemis crouches beside the little girl. They are both children, but the first is as tall, as radiant, as refined, as the second is small, grubby, and bedraggled. Artemis wipes her tears firmly, without tenderness. Once sure she has all her attention, she unwinds a ribbon from her hair and brings it to life. The kids are instantly wide-eyed with fascination and cry out in wonderment. Artemis gives it to them, and they scarper, chattering in their strange language.

As for him, he was happy to watch the scene from afar. He feels at fault and his guilt increases when Artemis comes towards him. The bricks form into a path under her feet as she advances.

"You must make a bit of an effort. We're not like them, Odin."

Odin? So that's what he was once called? This memory won't have been completely pointless, in the end. "No," he hears himself reply. "It's they who are not like us. I want to go home."

"You can't."

"What are we being punished for? First we're separated, now we're abandoned."

Artemis removes her glasses, and he glimpses what her face will be like one day: a masculine beauty.

"You always have to dramatize," she adds, with her unshake-able composure. "We have to mix with men, understand how they function. It's less fascinating than the stars, but it's still instructive. See it as a new challenge. In fact, it's the last time I'll help you, Odin. You must learn on your own to get along with men."

"I can't understand a thing they're saying."

"Teach them our language."

"They snivel as soon as I go near them."

"Control your power."

"Why should it be me making all the effort?"

With her red eyebrows, Artemis frowns slightly, and again pulls her glasses away from her eyes. "They don't work any-more. Have you noticed how quickly our bodies change? I can't wait to finish growing. Little lace dresses, definitely not for me."

"Why?" he hears himself insisting. "Why must one always obey orders?"

Artemis suddenly looks at him seriously, plunges her hand into the waves of her hair, and pulls out a book made of flesh.

"Because it's written."

The memory ends here.

Nota bene: "Try your dears." Who said these words and what do they mean?

THE TRAIN

Ophelia was viewing the old world from the clouds. She would have liked to lose some altitude, to dive into the maze of towns, mingle with ancient peoples, and penetrate the mysteries of the past, but that all remained inaccessible. While she was concentrating with all her might on the world down below, a carpet spread beneath her feet and Ophelia found herself once more in her childhood bedroom, on Anima. She stood before the wall mirror, staring at her reflection. She was very young, in her dressing gown, with curly hair that still hadn't darkened and good eyes that didn't yet need glasses. What was she doing up, at this hour?

Oh, yes. It had got her out of bed. It was to be found there, in the mirror, just behind her reflection. It wanted to ask her something.

"Could you tell me the time, please?"

Ophelia awoke with a start and turned her head towards Aunt Rosaline, who was restless on her train banquette.

"Oh, sorry, you were sleeping?"

"Just dozing," she mumbled. Which hadn't stopped her from having that dream again. Since her last mirror accident, it was always the same final vision: the bedroom, the mirror, the reflection. She really wondered what it meant.

Ophelia pulled on the chain of the watch she'd put in her coat pocket, and, with difficulty, lifted its cover. There were four miniature dials incorporated within the main time dial: a chronograph, a calendar, and two whose function Ophelia still couldn't work out. Thorn's watch. "If you still doubt me in the future, just read it." That man had his own peculiar way of trying to gain someone's trust.

"Nearly midnight," she said, pushing her glasses back up her nose.

"Oh, these trains!" moaned Aunt Rosaline. "One gets as bored as a table mat on them. Pass me another magazine. Find one that's in a really bad condition, so it keeps me awake."

Ophelia searched, among the old issues of the *Ladies & Fashion Journal*, for the most creased and torn. Some passengers passed the time leafing through magazines; Aunt Rosaline, whose Animism made her excel at restoring paper, passed hers patching them up.

The *Northern Express* was forever leaving one tunnel to enter another; when there were no more tunnels, unscalable ramparts took over on either side of the tracks. Ophelia had seen only walls since their hasty departure from Citaceleste the previous week. An airship had dropped them off in a small mining town surrounded by factories, and, early that morning, they had caught the train bound for Opal Sands, a seaside resort situated in the southernmost part of the ark. The Pole's railways were veritable strongholds, designed to protect travelers from wild Beasts.

Ophelia looked again at the watch, and her heart began to beat faster than the second hand. According to the telegram Thorn had sent to their last hotel, the twenty-one members of her family had landed earlier that day, and had been asked to take the connecting train for Opal Sands. If their train hadn't been delayed, they would all already be there.

"Still determined to say nothing to your mother?" asked Aunt Rosaline, as if reading Ophelia's mind.

"I don't intend to lie to her, but neither can I see the point of going into the smallest detail."

Aunt Rosaline slid her long, slender fingers across a creased page. Not even an iron would have been more efficient than her patient, meticulous Animism.

"We didn't write to them about any of that *detail* because the postal system couldn't be trusted," she pointed out. "I'll be quieter than a clapperless bell, if that's what you want, but you, my dear, you should speak frankly while you have the chance. Thorn keeping you away from the court until your wedding is all very nice, but it doesn't resolve the main problem." Aunt Rosaline glanced briefly at Ophelia, who was nervously nibbling at the seams of her glove. "Farouk is besotted with you."

A shiver ran across the entire surface of Ophelia's skin. "I remind him of someone, which is different. It's a little as if he were searching for himself, as much through me as through his Book."

Every time she thought back on her confrontation with the family spirit, she experienced contradictory emotions. Part of her, probably her survival instinct, wanted to stay as far away as possible from his Book. Whatever this truth was that Farouk was confusedly seeking between its pages, Ophelia felt that going anywhere near it was putting one's life in danger. But another, inordinately professional part of her felt frustrated at having let the most fascinating reading of her whole career pass her by.

"If only it were just that Book business," muttered Aunt Rosaline. "Now, nobles are even being abducted under the very noses of the police! Clairdelune may be the least reputable place in the Pole, but it's also the most protected. Truly, what's going on in this ark doesn't sit well with me."

Ophelia took a sudden interest in the flashes of grit outside the window. Even if no formal link had been established between the disappearance of the director of the *Nibelungen* and the mysterious letters found among his belongings, Ophelia hadn't dared tell anyone that she'd received a very similar warning. Three months had gone by since then, and she hadn't disappeared, but all the same, she often thought about it.

"Mommy, Daddy, and the others will all have left in a month's time," she said. "I don't wish to terrify them during their stay here. If all goes well, they'll see neither the court nor Mr. Farouk. The fewer people there are mixed up in all these goings-on, the better."

"And me? Will you keep similar secrets from me when I'm no longer part of your life?"

Ophelia looked with amazement at the yellow, dry face concentrating on a tear in the *Ladies & Fashion Journal*. "Aunt . . . I didn't want to . . ."

"No, it's me," stammered Aunt Rosaline, "accept my apologies. In one month, you'll be a married woman and my mission as chaperone will come to an end. After all I've lived through with you here . . . well, my restoration studio is going to seem pretty dull."

In Ophelia's eyes, Aunt Rosaline had always been a woman who was as solid as a roof beam. Seeing her crack like this, on this train banquette, brought a lump to her throat. She would have liked to find the right words, there and then, to mend that break quickly and give Aunt Rosaline back all her solidity, but Ophelia didn't know what to say to her. It was always the same with her: the heavier her heart, the emptier her head.

Her aunt's brief smile uncovered her equine teeth. "It's ironic, isn't it? All you hope for is to return to live on Anima, and me, I'd almost be sorry not to be able to remain here."

In the heat of the moment, Ophelia almost admitted that

she didn't want to see her go either, but she checked herself in time. If there was one thing she wished on no one, and especially not her aunt, it was to live within the same walls as her.

When Aunt Rosaline finally looked up from her magazine, it was to turn anxious eyes towards the end of the boudoir-carriage. "And who will watch over her?"

Ophelia leant forward to look, in turn, at Berenilde, languishing on a mass of cushions and with the Valkyrie seated beside her like some sinister governess. She was stroking her rounded stomach with a deeply pensive look. When Thorn had decided to send Ophelia to the other side of the Pole, Berenilde had immediately taken control of things. She had chosen their destination herself, organized the preparations for the trip, and booked an entire hotel to accommodate Ophelia's family until the wedding. And yet, since they had left the court, Berenilde had sunk into a strange melancholy, and the further south they traveled, the more preoccupied she seemed. Was it distancing herself from Farouk that was making her unhappy?

"A stressed nephew, a dead husband, and an impossible lover," commented Aunt Rosaline. "Do you promise me that you will confiscate her cigarettes and glasses of wine when I'm not there anymore?"

Ophelia consented. It wasn't the first time she'd got the feeling that Aunt Rosaline and Berenilde had become closer, but now she was certain: despite all their differences, a very real friendship had blossomed between the two widows. "I need to stretch my legs," Ophelia said, getting up.

"Don't go too far, we should be arriving shortly."

The private carriages were very well guarded. Ophelia had to show her ticket to four fastidious inspectors before accessing the rear end of the train. In contrast to first class, in which the smallest spent bulb was immediately replaced, here there was no light at all. However, one's other senses were assailed with chatter, sweat, and smoke. The second- and third-class carriages were solely occupied by workmen and women fruit pickers, traveling home after work.

Those without powers belonged to a section of the population that weren't descendants of a family spirit, and who had thus not inherited any family power. So different were they from the courtiers, Ophelia found it hard to believe that they were inhabitants of the same ark. At the Citaceleste, due to the high level of consanguinity, everyone resembled everyone else: the nobles were pale from top to toe. On these train benches, the entire palette of colors was represented, from platinum-blond to coffee-brown, from pink skin to bronzed skin, from big light eyes to small dark eyes. On their faces there were traces of coal, plaster, or grease, indicating that they'd come from a mine, a building site, or a factory. And all these colors were animated, they debated, they sang. The accent of the powerless was so strong, their dialect so distinctive, Ophelia could barely understand them. She elbowed her way through the carriage to reach the train's back gangway, where Fox's huge form was leaning. The wind caused mayhem with her dress and messed with the pins in her hair.

"Miss will catch cold!" he shouted over the wind, seeing Ophelia gripping the guardrail.

"I need your advice."

"Oh? About what?"

Ophelia didn't reply straightaway. She looked out at the succession of tracks, between the ramparts' two massive walls, which seemed endlessly to unwind under the wheels of the train. Despite the late hour, it was still light, but it was a light that bore no resemblance to the tropical illusion of the Jetty-Promenade and the Gynaeceum; it was a never-ending dusk, never entirely night, never entirely day.

"I feel as nervous as a coffeepot."

"I beg your pardon, miss?" shouted Fox.

"I'm feeling extremely nervous," Ophelia repeated, straining her voice. "I can't manage to like my new life. So seeing my mother, my father, my brother and my sisters . . . I fear I won't be able to put up a good show."

"Twit!"

Ophelia raised her eyebrows before realizing that it wasn't her whom Fox was addressing. He had pinched between thumb and index finger a little tabby ball that was trying to escape from his traveling cap. Twit was a kitten that was forever getting into scrapes; he'd got into such a habit of coming into their apartment, at the Gynaeceum, that Fox hadn't had the heart to get rid of him, despite Berenilde's entreaties.

Fox placed Twit in the middle of his mass of red hair and put his cap back on top of it. "He's so clumsy, he'd be capable of falling off the train. You know, kid, I'm bubbling away inside as well," Fox declared, leaning towards Ophelia. "I've never been outside longer than the turn of a sandglass, and it's my first time going so far away from Citaceleste. It's as if I weren't breathing as I normally do." He inhaled deeply the smell in the air, a curious mix of hot rails and melted snow, and then knitted his red brows. "I . . . I called you 'kid' again?"

"I like it," Ophelia assured him.

"I'm embarrassed, miss, it's because of Mime, I got into such a habit . . ."

The locomotive's horn drowned out Fox's voice, and a tunnel's noisy draught engulfed them.

"If I still had a family, I wouldn't let all that whole caboodle bother me!" Fox shouted, to be heard over the racket of the train. "Nice playacting and little secrets, save them for the court! If something's weighing on your ticker, speak to anyone who'll listen!"

191

Ophelia was just thinking about this advice when she lost her balance. The weight of her body suddenly lurched against the guardrail of the gangway and if Fox hadn't caught her in the dark, she would have surely fallen overboard.

"What's going on?" she asked, anxiously. The train's leaning?"

"It's going up," said Fox. "A jolly steep incline, hold on tight. Twit, you're scratching my scalp!"

Ophelia gripped the guardrail with both hands. This ascent into the darkness seemed interminable to her, when, finally, the track returned to being horizontal and the tunnel opened into a flood of light.

"Blimey!" muttered Fox.

As for Ophelia, she was lost for words. There were no more ramparts around them. It was their train that was now running along the top of a vast fortification. Walls, abolished! The world was now but sea and mountains to the west, forest and sky to the east: a meeting of all that is vast. Ophelia pushed away the eddy of brown curls caught up in her glasses. Staring wide-eyed, she would have liked to capture every detail of this unexpected landscape: the glaciers reflecting their dazzling whiteness in the mirror of the water; the flight of a snowy owl beneath the foaming wave of the clouds; the pealing from a church tower surrounded by multicolored little houses; the heavily resinous scent of the firs and deliciously salty scent of the sea. Ophelia even glimpsed, at the foot of the wall, a giant elk—the size of the luggage van—with its huge legs sunk in a peat bog, shaking its antlers.

"I was born on the most beautiful ark in the world," said Fox, with a proud smile, "and I didn't even know it."

Ophelia kept her eyes wide open to drink in the landscape. The knowledge that these infinite spaces were all made up of a mosaic of minuscule elements—drop, thorn, sap, spark, twig—made her dizzy. So this, then, was the Pole, seen from beyond its walls and illusions? The coexistence of the infinitely small and the infinitely large?

"Foster, I still need your opinion on one matter."

"Yes, miss?"

"Do you believe in God?"

Fox raised his bushy eyebrows. "Whoa," he said, gripping his peak to stop the wind carrying off both cap and cat. "God, as you put it, feels a bit like old folklore. I'm like most people, myself. Above all, I believe in the family spirits."

It was obvious. When one had an immortal ruling an ark, he or she would be considered a deity. The mythologies of the old world had become obsolete. Who, then, was this "GOD" referred to in the anonymous letters, if it wasn't Farouk? Another family spirit?

Ophelia was so absorbed in her thoughts, she didn't notice that the train was slowing down to enter the station. So she was flabbergasted when her mother appeared before her on the platform in a cloud of steam, hands on hips, looking like a candy jar in her Sunday-best dress.

"I knew it! You're not even wearing the coat I gave you!"

THE FAMILY

Ophelia's mother was a naturally plump woman, with full cheeks, a frog's throat, and an enormous light-auburn bun, sprouting from her head like a mushroom. She always wore extraordinary hats, and red dresses as wide as parasols, as if seeking to occupy as much space as possible. Ophelia felt as if she were being swallowed whole in a mix of flesh and fabric as her mother hugged her.

"You're looking dreadful! What's this scar on your cheek? You've got thinner, aren't they feeding you, then? And how ungrateful you are! I come from the other side of the world for you, and you don't even meet me at the air terminal? And then two hours I've been waiting on this freezing platform for my daughter to deign, finally, to show up! How do you expect me to scold you properly when I'm exhausted?"

"Hello, Mommy," Ophelia panted, with her remaining breath.

She'd barely left her mother's embrace before she was being passed from one pair of arms to another. Her father timidly murmured that, yes, it was true, she had got a little thinner. Her brother Hector, ever practical, asked her why there was no snow in the Pole, and why the sun hadn't set since their arrival. Whereas her grandmother Antoinette examined her grubby gloves with a disapproving frown, her grandmother

Sidonia, all smiles, gave her a new pair. Her little sisters clung to her scarf, all talking over each other. Her uncles and aunts each repeated in turn that the court hadn't changed her one bit, a little disappointed, deep down, not to find their niece transformed into a fairy-tale princess. As for her cousins, all muffled up in their coats, they greeted her from a distance with little embarrassed smirks; they would probably have preferred to spend their holidays on a tropical ark.

"Hello, my dear!" a middle-aged lady exclaimed, jovially. "I'm delighted to meet you and keen to hear all about your adventures! Those dear mothers of us all, the Doyennes, were sadly not able to make this long journey themselves, but I am here in their name. I am the Familistery's Rapporteur, have you heard of me?"

Oh, yes, Ophelia knew all about her. The Rapporteur was a pretty unpopular character on Anima. She let her eyes and ears linger around every street, every shop, every crack in a door, and then reported all she had witnessed to the Doyennes.

For her part, Ophelia responded wrongly to every greeting, shaking the hands of the women, kissing the men, answering to some the questions asked by others, and mixing up everyone's names. Seeing her family again after all she'd just lived through gave her the strange feeling of being in a time warp.

"My darling sister, I missed you so much!" cried Agatha, hugging Ophelia so tight that her hair tickled her nose. "Not a day goes by when I don't regret not being in the Pole with you!"

"Really?"

"Sumptuous dresses, endless balls, society life—I was born for such an existence! If it weren't so cold . . ."

Ophelia wondered what Agatha would have said if she'd come to the Pole in the middle of winter.

"Come, come, sweetheart," Charles gently protested, while

trying to pacify the baby wriggling in his arms. "You're not unhappy with wee Tom and me, are you?"

"You couldn't understand, you're so easily pleased. Employee in a lace factory, what a fine ambitious one you are!"

"Assistant manager, sweetheart. Wouldn't you like to carry wee Tom? He's asking for you."

"I'm *already* carrying a child," grumbled Agathe, indicating her stomach.

"Where's my godfather?" Ophelia asked, with concern. "He didn't come with you?"

"Oh, my goodness, I've got so many questions to ask you!" exclaimed Agatha, not listening to her. "Do you think this dress will be suitable for dancing? I brought others, naturally, but I've put on a lot of weight these last few weeks. Will we be able to see some nobles soon? Are we at the court, here?"

"No, my dear child. You're at a seaside resort, here." It was Berenilde who had spoken, rolling her "r"s splendidly, as she stepped off the train. As pregnant as she was, she seemed as light as her luggage trolley was heavy. "I am honored to meet you," she purred, directing her most radiant smile at Ophelia's parents. "I am Thorn's aunt."

"I still haven't seen either your nephew or your properties," Ophelia's mother said, begrudgingly. Faced with Berenilde's ethereal pallor, she seemed to make it a point of honor to be even ruddier and more materialistic than usual.

"Our family spirit requires Thorn's services in the capital, Madam Sophie. Your son-in-law will soon be here to pay his respects to you, as is right and proper. In the meantime, if you don't mind, allow me to be his representative among you."

"How beautiful and elegant you are!" exclaimed Agatha. She had completely forgotten her sister's existence the moment she laid eyes on Berenilde.

"And I, myself, find you charming, my child," the latter

replied, stroking her cheek with a finger. "Your skin is cool, are you cold, then?"

"As if in an ice-cream maker, madam."

"It's already late," Berenilde said, consulting the station clock. "Do you have all your luggage? Perfect, I'll ensure that it is delivered with mine. Come, dear friends, let's head to our hotel! We'll be more comfortable talking there."

"Our little Ophelia couldn't have hoped to find a better relative than you in the Pole," the Rapporteur complimented, unctuously. "Is she herself a credit to our two families?"

"Of course," replied Aunt Rosaline, instead of Berenilde.

As for Ophelia, she wouldn't have proclaimed it from the rooftops. She'd committed numerous blunders since being introduced at court. That mysterious melancholy, always lurking deep in Berenilde's eyes, wasn't she partly responsible for it?

As her family members hastened to leave the platform in a jolly general hubbub, Ophelia watched them moving off with the same nagging feeling of being in a time warp. Where did she fit in?

"They can rabbit on, all of them, but personally, I do find you changed."

Her heart quickening, Ophelia looked around for the person who had uttered these words. She found him behind her, standing back a little on the platform, his cap hugging his skull, his moustache fluttering in the wind like two white flags. Without thinking, Ophelia dived headfirst into her great-uncle's big belly.

"Crash, bang, wallop! You almost sent me flying, m'dear."

"I thought for a moment you hadn't come. I'm pleased to see you."

That was an understatement. Just from breathing in the smell of ancient paper with which the archivist's pullover was impregnated, and hearing that voice vibrating with gruff affection and old dialect, Ophelia could feel her eyes smarting. She had to breathe in several times against the big belly to stop herself from bursting into tears like a little girl. He was right: she had completely changed. She felt the thick, gloved hand stroking her tousled hair.

"So, the Pole," her great-uncle murmured. "Is it as ghastly as I think it is?"

Ophelia hesitated, and then remembered Fox's advice. "Yes," she gurgled, with a weak smile. "Ghastly."

She pulled away reluctantly, straightened her glasses, which she'd bent, and frowned when she noticed that her great-uncle's eyes conveyed a certain awkwardness.

"What is it?"

"I myself have some bad news to tell you, m'dear."

With the Opal Sands station being situated at the top of the great railway wall, one had to take a cable car down to the town. There were several cabins for each convoy, but they couldn't carry many passengers each, which wasn't such a bad thing—Ophelia and her great-uncle had succeeded in being just the two of them in that small space, suspended there, above the world.

It was when the cabin began its descent from the terrace that the view was most spectacular. From this altitude, it became clear to the passenger that the Opal-Sands station was at the junction between two high walls: one protecting the town from the forest, the other protecting the town from the abyss. It was impossible to go any further south on the ark without falling into the void. The resort was both at the edge of the sea and at the edge of the sky.

Leaning on her elbows at the window of the cabin, her hair whipping her cheeks, Ophelia would have liked to soak up all these very real sensations of which she'd been deprived for so long. The thrill of vast spaces. The screeching of the wind in the cables. The sweet-salty air of firs, spindrift, and mountain. The stormy colors of the sea, seen from the sky. And of all that, nothing was artificial. Not a single illusion. Not a single trompe l'oeil.

Yes, Ophelia would have attempted to savor them even more, those true things, if she hadn't been beset with entirely different concerns.

"I can't believe my museum has been closed." She turned from the sea to look once more at her great-uncle, who was considering her solemnly from the opposite bench.

"But, for goodness' sake, why?" cried Ophelia.

"For an inventory, I tell you. That's what's written on the sign on the door since you left Anima."

"No, I want to know the *true* reason. The museum's collections haven't changed for decades. It's become so hard to find artifacts from the old world . . . And who's in charge of this inventory, anyway?" Ophelia added, with a frown. "I haven't even been replaced."

Her great-uncle merely crossed his arms over his big belly, his golden eyes studying Ophelia with a knowing look.

"Oh," she said. "The Doyennes, of course." Just imagining the airplanes in her museum rusting away, from lack of maintenance, made Ophelia's stomach lurch. "So it wasn't enough for them to send me to live on the other side of the world?" she murmured, holding her forehead in her hands. "That museum belongs to the whole family, the Doyennes have no right to take it for themselves. Why do they have it in for me like this?"

"Because you're a sympathizer."

Ophelia stared at her great-uncle, not understanding, but this time, it was he who looked far out of the window. The wind took mischievous delight in making his hair, eyebrows, and moustache stand on end.

"What I'm going to say to you, m'dear, is merely a personal intuition. I'd like you to listen to me, but then, come to your own opinion. In fact, it would almost reassure me if you didn't agree with me."

"Agree about what?" Ophelia had never heard her great-uncle speaking with such solemnity, and yet he was hardly the kind of man to split his sides laughing.

"We're living in a *bizarrre* setup, y'know. One day, the world's running smoothly, and the next, bang, it shatters like a plate! So, yes, the rest of us, we've had time to get used to the idea. Arks dangling in the void, indestructible family spirits, powers galore, it all seems normal to us today. But basically, we're all living in a *bizarrre* setup."

The midnight sun filled the cabin from every opening. Its twilight glow forced the great-uncle to squint, dazzled, but he didn't turn his head from the window for all that. Ophelia realized that it wasn't the landscape he was contemplating in that way, but his inner self.

"I was a very young archivist when it happened to me. You weren't born yet, m'dear, no more than your mother was. I'd just completed my apprenticeship, but I already knew the archive collection like the back of my hand. In those days, it wasn't arranged as it is today: the family files were kept on the ground floor, and Artemis's private collection was in the first basement."

"The second basement didn't yet exist?"

A spark lit up in her great-uncle's eyes. "Yes, it did. It was even my favorite place. All the archives of the old world were stored there. Oh, it was mainly war administration, y'know!" he added with a sad smile, not noticing Ophelia's stunned expression. "Staff correspondence, military-campaign journals, registers of regimental numbers, and officers' personal files. As it was written in the old language, and it's now taught less and less, that lingo, no one ever came to consult that collection of archives. It seemed such a shame . . ."

"You've never spoken to me of these archives," murmured Ophelia. "What became of them?"

"Me, I was young and stupid," continued her great-uncle, still looking deep within himself. "It made me dream, all that! I didn't see the war, I saw the human adventure. I embarked on translating every document, partly using my basic knowledge of the old language, partly reading with my hands. Years, I spent on it! I was so proud of my translations and so keen to get a little recognition, to be honest, that I submitted my work to the Council of Doyennes. I still wonder what I was hoping for. A medal, perhaps?"

Ophelia sensed, from the way his voice was growing hoarse, that he was touching on a wound that had never really healed.

"Sympathizer," he said, clearly, looking daggers at the sky. "That's what the Doyennes dubbed me, and, believe me, there was nothing nice about it. 'Morbid obsession with the war'; 'reprehensible commemoration of the past'; 'deplorable example to the young'; 'enterprise of an antifamilial nature'; and that's not the half of it! I was advised to devote myself to the family's everyday papers. I never saw any of my translations again."

"I'm so sorry," whispered Ophelia.

Her great-uncle turned to look at her in surprise, blinking, as though aware once more of her presence. "Oh, that's nothing. Most infuriating is what happened next. A few months after the incident, lo and behold, a new family decree gets put out. I don't know what had got into the Doyennes at that time, but they were forever reforming this, reforming that. Oh, they often had good ideas, don't get me wrong, huh, but when it concerned me, I sensed it had got into them worse. 'Any document without direct relevance to Artemis's lineage will no longer come under the auspices of the Family Archives and must be stored in a special department designed for that purpose,'" her great-uncle recited in a single breath. "Everything that predated the Rupture, out!"

"So the archives in the second basement were transferred somewhere else?" said Ophelia. "Where?"

"To a town on the Great Lakes. Except they never reached their destination. The boat transporting them by river suffered a technical failure. No one drowned, but all the papers floated away. Forever lost to posterity. I later learnt that my translation work was also in those crates."

Ophelia closed her eyes. If her museum's collections were destroyed in a fire, only then would she be able to grasp fully what her great-uncle must have felt at that time. She was beginning to wonder whether it wasn't due to this business that he'd become so grumpy.

"A technical failure," she repeated, pensively. "You didn't believe it."

"Well, yes, I did, actually," her great-uncle muttered, leaning forward, elbows on knees and fingers linked. "The Doyennes may be straitlaced, but they are still sacred. To me, it was just a matter of bad luck. The years flew by, I tried to forget that terrible waste. Until I spied the sign on your museum: 'Closed for an inventory.' When I read that, it was as if they'd written: 'Closed for *sympathizing*.' The Doyennes got rid of you because of your predilection for the old world, dear girl. You were a little too good at reading that past they don't approve of. Well, that's my personal intuition," he was keen to stress. "Of course, I've said nothing of all this to your mother, who already worries over nothing, but I'd stake my reader's hands on it. What d'you think about it?"

"I don't know . . . I no longer know."

Ophelia gazed at the Opal Sands. The coast was a jumble of rocks and scrub, a wild terrain to be avoided without good shoes on one's feet. All along this rugged area, little houses huddled together, putting up a united front against the onslaught of the wind, the cold, and the damp. They were in the image of the passengers on the train, those houses: robust, close-knit, and colorful. And then there was the sea, to which the cable car now drew very close. A real sea, odorous and cantankerous as a living being.

"You've not lost your bad habits," the great-uncle sighed, seeing Ophelia gnawing the seams of her gloves. "Don't spoil them, they're work tools."

Ophelia felt disorientated. She'd felt so bitterly towards the Doyennes since they'd arranged this forced engagement to Thorn that her judgment was distorted. As she was furiously thinking, her glasses went through all the colors of her feelings.

"Of course, all that is disturbing," she finally admitted, "but . . . it makes no sense. One doesn't punish someone because he supposedly has 'sympathies' for the old world. The Rupture occurred centuries ago, what would old ladies have to fear of such a distant past?"

"Have you ever been to the library, dear girl?"

"Er . . . once or twice."

Ophelia wasn't proud of it. Her parents, uncles, and aunts all worked at Anima's big Family Library, in the restoration and cataloguing department, but she herself had always been more interested in the stories contained within objects. She wasn't much of a reader, for a "reader" . . .

"Well, as for me," muttered her great-uncle, "I've been ferreting around there a lot, recently. Educational series, moral novels, only right-thinking literature! Never a crime scene, never a swear word, never a saucy illustration. And I'm not just talking about the books of Father Albert, who publishes Anima's most tedious scribblers. No, I'm also talking about the translations from the old world: poems, essays, memoirs, plays. Reading those books, you'd think our ancestors from before the Rupture cared only for pastoral lyricism and affairs of the heart."

The scarf gave an impatient nudge to Ophelia's hand, which had left off stroking it for a while. "You think that my parents . . . that the librarians . . ." Ophelia couldn't bring herself to say it. Over these last months, she had clung with all her might to the values instilled in her by her education: sincerity, honesty, and a love of work well done. If there were censors in the family, she would consider it a betrayal.

"Oh, y'know, your dear parents, they're like the rest of them," sighed her great-uncle. "They're quite happy to patch up what they're asked to patch up, to classify what they're asked to classify, full stop. No, my dear, look higher up. All the books submitted to the library, they first have to go past an approval committee. And who chairs the committee? The Doyennes. Are you starting to understand why I'm so preoccupied?"

"All the books," Ophelia repeated, slowly. "Have the Doyennes, by any chance, ever given you any warnings or recommendations about the Book? The one with a capital 'B.'"

"The Book in Artemis's private collection?" her great-uncle asked with surprise. "Not in particular, no. In any case, it's indecipherable and 'unreadable,' that one."

"And Artemis?" she insisted. "Has she ever asked you, or anyone else, to investigate this Book?"

"Never, far as I know. She's always given more importance to the vast universe of the stars than to my little world of paper."

Ophelia opened and then closed her mouth. She couldn't have explained why, because it was so crazy, but, for a fraction of a second, she'd had the intuition that between the closure of her museum, Farouk's Book, the archives accident, the library manipulations, and the recent disappearances of nobles, there was but one common denominator.

That's completely absurd, she immediately told herself, rubbing her eyes behind her glasses. The Doyennes aren't responsible for the Pole's backstairs murders, and Farouk cares as much about my museum on Anima as about his first fur coat.

"Because in the Pole, too, there are some strange goings-on," she finally replied to her uncle, "and it's muddling all my thoughts."

Ophelia watched their hotel get bigger as the cable car neared its destination. Standing on overhanging rocks, it was linked by a long covered walkway to a thermal establishment. The whole place looked more like a factory than a place of relaxation, with its great brick walls and tall chimneys belching out smoke. Ophelia had feared that the Opal Sands seaside resort would be a pale imitation of the court's fifth floor. Now she knew that there was no possible comparison. Here, among these people, there'd be no need endlessly to "watch out for" or "pretend to," and that was a great relief.

"I think I'm going to make the most of this holiday beside the sea to clear my head," she decided, out loud.

THE READER

THE DATE

"Thorn in a bathing costume!" cried three voices in unison.

Ophelia swallowed some boiling-hot water, snorted it back out of her nose, and then, through the drops distorting her vision, contemplated the steam suspended in the air and the mosaics of the thermal baths. Of course, there was no Thorn in a bathing costume here; no Thorn at all, for that matter.

Ophelia wiped her glasses and turned to her three little sisters, all wearing mobcaps, who burst into laughter, leaping around in the water. "You definitely had me there," Ophelia willingly admitted. "The steam was sending me to sleep, so I almost believed it."

Leonora waded over to her and hugged her at the waist. "But really, when do we get to see him, our new brother-in-law? He hasn't yet visited us once!"

Touched, and a trifle embarrassed, Ophelia tucked the little red ringlet, which had escaped from her cap, behind her sister's ear. It seemed like only yesterday that she was teaching her—very badly—how to animate her toys. There were several years between them, and yet Leonora would soon be taller than her, as her other sisters already were. Sometimes, Ophelia wondered why she was the only child in the family to have been given such a brief growth spurt, the vision of a mole, and impossible hair, as though Mother Nature had taken a sudden dislike to her.

"Ah, well," she said. "Thorn is a frightfully busy man."

"And frightfully impolite," Domitilla added, sternly. "Mommy is becoming increasingly livid because of him. Is it true he doesn't want to see us?"

Beatrice was furiously blowing bubbles underwater to underline this statement.

Ophelia's little sisters resembled each other like triplets, but each had a very particular personality. Leonora, the youngest, was very sensual, and liked touching everything and pressing her ear to the workings of mechanical objects. Beatrice expressed all her emotions in the raw: she laughed, she cried, she screamed, she swore, but one couldn't get a complete sentence out of her. As for Domitilla, the eldest of the three, she was endowed with a strong protective instinct.

"That's not really the issue," said Ophelia. "He just has . . . um . . . a great deal of work to do."

For two weeks, Thorn had no longer answered Berenilde's telegrams, and the Animists were starting to see this silence as a serious lack of respect. Hadn't he listened to Ophelia when she'd asked him to make a better impression on her family? The wedding was in just five days' time . . .

"You don't seem to be aware," Domitilla said, frowning. "It's now nearly a month we've been here. It's fun swimming together, walking on the rocks together, picking berries together, and all that, but you never tell us anything!"

"There's not much to tell," stammered Ophelia. She already regretted having spoken to her great-uncle about the blackmail, the threats, the claws, the lies, the intrigues, the illusions, the disappearances, and the murders that had punctuated her life at Citaceleste. She'd had to make him promise to hold his tongue in front of the family. He was raging in silence, for now, but his anger was contaminating any objects he went near. At the hotel, a cousin had fallen over due to a banister willfully tripping him up.

"Does Thorn at least treat you gallantly?" Domitilla persisted. "Does he take good care of you?"

"Do you already give each other cuddles?" Leonora was quick to ask, in turn. "Are you going to give us lots and lots of nephews?"

As for Beatrice, she cleared her throat noisily, like a teacher, waiting for some answers worthy of the questions. Ophelia sought some support from Aunt Rosaline, who was doing a few strokes in the pool, but she nodded in agreement. "Your sisters aren't completely wrong. From wanting to be too good a chaperone, I made a bad godmother. Mr. Thorn is the very opposite of Agatha's husband. I think . . . well . . . that you'll need to be prepared for what comes next."

Ophelia would have liked to disappear into the hot-spring water. The closer it got to the date of the wedding, the more she was bombarded with conjugal advice. She hadn't been able to admit to her family, for fear of creating a scandal, that Thorn and she would never be more than just a couple in appearance.

Fortunately, she was saved this time by the pool attendant, leaning over beside the pool. "A message has arrived for you at reception, miss."

It was Thorn finally making contact.

Ophelia slipped on the steps, pulled off her bathing cap, pulled on her reader's gloves, and then crossed the long tiled gallery, scalding her toes in the puddles on the floor caused by a leaking pipe. This spring water gave off a strong smell, but it was excellent for the health, and so hot that it never froze, even in the depths of winter.

"Thank you," Ophelia said to the receptionist who handed

her the message. She was just opening the envelope when she sensed a presence behind her. One of the establishment's clients was watching her with an intensity and at a proximity that were most uncomfortable. Wrapped in a red coat, with fur hat on head and long black boots on feet, she wasn't even appropriately dressed for the baths. Her eyes, hard as rough diamonds, were focused on Ophelia's letter as though entitled to read it. Maybe Ophelia was imagining it, but it seemed that this nosy parker had kept appearing and disappearing behind her since she'd arrived at Opal Sands.

Ophelia went outside the baths for a little privacy, and sat on a step of the stairs; she took her letter out of the envelope again, and put it back in before even laying eyes on it. She'd just spotted Archibald's seven sisters, lined up on a walkway bench like a collection of dolls on a shelf. From youngest to eldest, they all looked so alike that they seemed to represent the different stages of a single girl's life. Dulcie, Clarimond, Melody, Gaiety, Relish, Grace, and Patience were all staring wide-eyed at Ophelia. If Archibald's pupils evoked a glorious summer sky, theirs recalled the iciest of winters.

"Hello," Ophelia said cautiously to them. The sisters didn't reply. They never replied. It was rare to see them outdoors. They generally spent the day shut away in their hotel room. Accustomed to the velvet cocoon of Clairdelune, they loathed this windswept coast to which their brother had sent them to keep them away from danger. If they gladly sought the company of Berenilde, who, for them, was the sole representative of civilization here, they hadn't spoken once to Ophelia, as if she were personally responsible for the misfortunes that had struck their home. Occasionally, at the bend in a corridor, they all turned to look at her in fits of laughter, as if they had all had the same hilarious thought about her.

She had no desire to read a letter, particularly a letter from Thorn, in front of such an audience.

Ophelia moved away from the stairs and went along the arcaded walkway that connected the baths to the hotel, looking for a corner hidden from view. To her left, the sea roared against the resort's rocky beaches; to her right, at the edge of the conifers, the water of the salt marshes reflected the clouds without a ripple. Rock-salt dunes glittered in front of a refinery; the town owed its name to these formations resembling iridescent sandbanks. And above this world of water, salt, vegetation, and brick, the febrile sky kept veering from sunshine to rain. Ophelia breathed in deeply; it was no more than fifteen degrees and her damp skin was already reddening, but this sweet-salty mix, half-fir, half-sea, made her with quiver with delight . . . After all of Citaceleste's illusions, Ophelia did feel very real here.

Her eyes lingered briefly on the men of her family playing boules beside the walkway. As worthy Animists, they were roaring with laughter, gesticulating a lot, and swearing loudly, particularly when the jack changed position of its own accord. With hands deep in pockets, her father and great-uncle were the only spectators, the former out of shyness, the latter glumness.

"Hey, Ophelia! Don't stand there all alone! Join us!" Her uncles and cousins had just noticed her, stopped in her tracks on the walkway. She declined with a polite gesture, her envelope concealed behind her back, and then responded to her father's anxious frown with a smile.

In a way, Ophelia was relieved to see that she'd remained a fully fledged member of the family, despite being so far away. And yet she felt as if she couldn't quite make up for the slight distance that had grown between them. No one seemed to realize that she was no longer quite herself. Or that maybe, deep down, she'd never been it so much.

Ophelia sat on the walkway's balustrade, leaning against a column, and took out the letter for the third time. Now that she was finally at leisure to read it, she no longer dared to open it. She felt terribly nervous. Was Thorn going to announce his imminent arrival to her? He was perfectly capable of waiting until the morning of the wedding to suddenly appear in front of the altar, a pile of files under each arm.

On the 3rd of August, in five days' time, barely five days, they would be married.

Ophelia thought of nothing now but that fateful date. What would married life be like with someone like Thorn? Ophelia was incapable of imagining it, just as she was of imagining herself with hunter's claws where her nerves ended, and maybe a better memory, too.

She glanced, with some embarrassment, at the windows of the hotel, where the silhouettes of her aunts and grandmothers, amid much gesticulating, were busy with the preparations. Their Animism was so aroused that, from there, Ophelia could see the ribbons fluttering on the ceiling and the white tablecloths shuddering like ghosts. Workmen were hanging crystal chandeliers, carrying musical instruments, lining up hundreds of golden candelabras. Berenilde had spent lavishly, wanting to offer her nephew a wedding worthy of those held at the court.

Breathing in, Ophelia decided finally to unfold her message. It didn't take her long to realize that, contrary to what she'd believed, it hadn't come from Thorn.

Miss Ex-Vice-Storyteller,
I cannot help but notice that you didn't take my first warning seriously enough. You are obliging me to send you this ultimatum. Break off your engagement and never set foot in the court ever again. I give you until the 1st of August to make your arrangements, failing

which Mr. Treasurer will find himself a widower before even being married.

GOD DISAPPROVES OF THIS UNION.

Ophelia breathed out to still her pounding chest. This time, she really was starting to feel afraid.

The Weather Vane

Ophelia raced up the stairs of the baths. Who had delivered this message for her? Just a courier, the receptionist assured her. And he'd given no indication of its source? None, miss. Wasting no time on the changing room, Ophelia slid the letter under her glove and ran to the hotel. She had to speak to Berenilde, and only to Berenilde. She alone would understand the situation.

In her haste, Ophelia banged her nose, knees, and back inside the hotel's revolving door. She passed the displays and counters of the large lobby. As well as being the reception for those taking the waters, the ground floor served as municipal administration office, power station, post office, telephone exchange, newsagent's, and even, occasionally, ironmonger's. It was always bustling, and several workmen raised their eyebrows as Ophelia went by. So disturbed was she by this message, she'd forgotten that she was still going around in her bathing costume.

"Well, well, well!" cooed a husky voice. "You're not as prudish as you seem, my dove."

With a sinking heart, Ophelia inhaled Cunegond's potent perfume before even seeing her. The Mirage was standing at the reception counter, busy filling in the hotel's register. Under her usual veil hung with golden pendants, she didn't look that well, despite the makeup.

"What are you doing at Opal Sands?" Ophelia asked, on the defensive. She couldn't bring herself to be polite. "Occupational illness," sighed Cunegond. "I'm forever manipulating illusions, and they're not very good for the nerves. I know some people who claim to come here for rheumatism. The truth is," she said, returning the register to the receptionist, "they're here to detoxify the mind, away from prying eyes."

Ophelia had to admit that, aside from Berenilde and Archibald's sisters, the few nobles she came across here had the clammy faces of opium addicts.

"You're all anyone's talking about at court, since that memorable show our Lord put on for you," Cunegond continued, in a confidential tone. "He's become infatuated with you, my dove. When you go back there, expect to face hell."

Hearing these words, Ophelia could almost feel the letter burning her hand. She was about to ask Cunegond whether she wasn't its author, when a racket stopped her short. The overzealous porter had seized Cunegond's large tapestry bag without noticing that she hadn't closed it. An impressive quantity of blue sandglasses spilt from it on to the carpet.

"Clumsy oaf!" Cunegond hissed between her teeth, glancing furtively around, while her pendants clattered together like chimes. "Tidy those all away immediately! And do take care not to pull the pin of a single one."

The porter hurriedly put all the sandglasses back in the bag, apologizing repeatedly. Ophelia wasn't sure what surprised her the most: Cunegond losing her cool or having all those sandglasses. For someone supposedly detoxifying herself from illusions, it was surprising.

"I know, my dove, this collection may seem somewhat incongruous to you, but it is strictly for professional use. Dear Hildegarde's blue sandglasses are such competition for my Erotic Delights! I'd be unwise not to . . . well, to 'research' them, so to speak. Haven't you finished tidying those sand-glasses away yet?" Cunegond asked the porter, impatiently. "Oh, my Imaginoirs are doing really badly, my dove," she purred, returning to Ophelia. "An art critic accused me of doing down-market illusions, can you imagine! Have you ever heard mention of 'Confusion Bubbles'?"

"Er . . . no."

Ophelia didn't know why Cunegond was confiding in her like this. Since she'd refused her offer in the Goose Garden, she'd always treated her like an enemy.

"They're illusions that produce exactly the same effect as inebriation. That's what that detestable critic compared my very latest creation to—my paradise of the senses, my palace of pleasures, classed in the same category as a bad table wine!"

"I've finished, madam," said the porter, closing the bag securely this time. "If madam would care to follow me, I will show her to her room."

"I ask you as a favor, keep all this to yourself," Cunegond whispered to Ophelia, with a great fluttering of eyelashes. "I wouldn't want people to imagine that I'm so desperate as to resort to using the illusions of my greatest competition."

Ophelia nodded. In truth, she was too preoccupied with her letter to be interested in all this. And yet she couldn't help feeling a certain pity as she watched Cunegond laboriously making her way to the hotel's staircase, to the tinkling of the golden pendants of her veil.

"Excuse me," said Ophelia, standing on tiptoe at the reception counter. "I'm looking for Madam Berenilde."

"Well that's lucky," replied the receptionist. "Madam Berenilde is looking for you, too."

"Oh, really? And do you know where I can find her?"

"She's taking a walk with your sister, but she'll soon be back. She asked me to request that you wait for her here."

Ophelia sat down on one of the uncomfortable benches in the hotel's lobby, intrigued to know what Berenilde herself suddenly had to say to her. She leafed through the newspaper someone had forgotten there. It was just a local paper, not as prestigious as the *Nibelungen*, but it would help Ophelia keep her impatience at bay.

She stared wide-eyed when, between two snippets of court tittle-tattle, she fell on a photograph of Thorn.

"LORD FAROUK'S BOOK WILL SOON HOLD NO SECRETS FOR THIS MAN," announced the article in capital letters. *"Our Treasurer, currently on an inspection tour in our provinces, has never readily confided in anyone. He did, however, prove to be uncommonly talkative when we questioned him yesterday on court news. If Mr. Treasurer did avoid certain thorny subjects, such as the issues coming up at the Family States, due on August 1, or the worrying abductions seemingly affecting the Mirage clan, he didn't hold back on the cardinal role he will soon be performing for Lord Farouk. It is public knowledge that our Lord attaches prime importance to his Book, a unique piece in his collection that, to this day, has not been deciphered. Our oldest readers may recall previous attempts to decipher this enigmatic document, attempts that always ended in defeat. 'I will succeed where all the others have failed,' Mr. Thorn declared to us, however, with utmost confidence. His marriage to an Animist, on August 3, will be the keystone of this ambitious enterprise, but Mr. Treasurer didn't wish to expand on this 'minor detail,' as he himself calls it. So, watch this space!"*

Ophelia couldn't believe her glasses. Why had Thorn ordered her not to speak of the Book to anyone around her when he himself was boasting about it to the press? Thank goodness no member of her family had read this article; it would have meant a whole load of awkward questions for her . . .

She was just thinking this when she caught sight of the vast scarlet dress of her mother, who was deep in conversation with the Rapporteur from Anima. Ophelia immediately hid behind her newspaper, taking care to conceal the photograph of Thorn.

"You could at least stress the absence of this man, who thinks he's going to become my son-in-law!" cried her mother. "He's supposed to be marrying my daughter in five days' time, and he leaves all the wedding preparations to us! Now that really isn't right!"

"Come now, my dear Sophie, Madam Berenilde explained to us that it wasn't up to him. The fellow has an important job, I have no reason to convey any reservations about him."

The Rapporteur couldn't be described as an old lady, but she addressed every single person as though surrounded by inexperienced children. She made it a point of honor to don the same black garments and the same golden spectacles as the Doyennes of Anima, despite not having the title herself. Her hat, on the other hand, was one of a kind. Stuck on her curly hair like a lampshade, it was topped with a weather vane in the form of a stork, which was forever turning. This weather vane didn't respond to the direction of the wind, but to the Animism of its mistress: it was as nosy as she was, and didn't hesitate to indicate with its beak anything that seemed worthy of interest.

"Let's talk about that Berenilde!" exclaimed Ophelia's mother. "She's been trying to impress us since our arrival, but I don't trust her at all."

"We're all being treated perfectly well," replied the Rapporteur, holding up a slip of paper. "And that's all I intend to say to the Familistery."

"So, I'm the only one who can see that something's not right here?" said Ophelia's mother, exasperated, her complexion turning redder than her vast dress. "I'm certain that my daughter is being badly treated. She is so fragile and so secretive!"

Concealed behind her newspaper, Ophelia suddenly felt ashamed. Since their reunion on the station platform, she'd put up with her mother's possessiveness like an ordeal. A few months away from the parental home had left her unaccustomed to this authoritarian endlessly cutting her short, choosing her dresses for her, and forever wanting to know where she was and in whose company. On several occasions, Ophelia had surprised herself by standing up to her, when, not that long ago, she would have just shrugged her shoulders. Deep down, they had both never stopped wanting to protect each other, without being able to talk to each other.

"I don't like the look of this marriage at all!" her mother insisted, as the Rapporteur went up to the telegraphist. "Since the day I met that boorish Mr. Thorn, I've regretted not putting my foot down. Maybe the Doyennes could look into it again, hold an inquiry, or . . ."

"My dear Sophie," the Rapporteur interrupted her in a honeyed voice, "are you now telling our dearest mothers what to do?"

Over the top of her newspaper, Ophelia saw her mother's large face turn white as quickly as it had turned crimson. The metallic beak of the stork on the Rapporteur's hat had suddenly stopped to point in her direction, like an accusatory finger.

"But of course not," she stammered, like a little girl caught in the wrong. "I didn't want to seem insolent. It's just that . . ."

"No one, not even our venerable mothers, can call this marriage into question. Do I need to remind you, my dear, that the conjugal contract was ratified by Madam Artemis and Mr. Farouk in person? They alone have the authority to prevent this union, and the diplomatic consequences would be most unfortunate if our lovebirds were to provide them with a single reason to invalidate this contract. Good day, Mr. Telegraphist!" shouted the Rapporteur, placing her paper on the counter. "Would you kindly send the following message, please? The addressee is the Familistery on Anima," she articulated very loudly to make the telegraphist understand, since he struggled with her accent. "Fa-mi-li-ste-ry on A-ni-ma."

Ophelia's mother left the hotel lobby in a frightful huff. While Ophelia had succeeded in evading her vigilance, that was no longer true of the weather vane: it had turned abruptly towards her newspaper, and the stork, reacting to a fiendishly clever mechanism, started pecking at the Rapporteur's hat to attract her attention.

"Aha, you were there, dear girl? Could you put your reading aside for a moment? I would like to converse with you."

Realizing that she had no choice, Ophelia put down her paper and went over to the telegraph counter.

"Well, that's an unseemly outfit at your age," sighed the Rapporteur, looking disapprovingly at her bathing costume. "Did you listen to us, me and your mother?"

"Despite myself."

Behind the counter, the telegraphist was tapping away on the lever of his machine with totally professional impassivity.

"Oh yes, I also see and hear many things despite myself," the Rapporteur tittered, with an air of complicity. "Rest assured, I didn't want to throw oil on the fire with your mother, but the fact is, I myself am a little concerned about the absence of your fiancé. Do you know why he's taking so long to make an appearance?"

Beneath her mass of very curly hair, trimmed like a hedge,

the Rapporteur's face had assumed a concerned expression. Her large, bulging eyes gleamed with a strange zeal, as though wanting to absorb the most intimate secrets of her interlocutor. And if there was anyone Ophelia wanted to confide nothing to, it was this gossip.

"No, Madam Rapporteur. I don't know why." Ophelia felt uncomfortable. The metallic stork, nesting on the Rapporteur's ridiculous hat, hadn't returned to its usual spinning, continuing instead to point at her with its beak.

"My dear, dear girl," the Rapporteur sighed, sympathetically. "How can I do detailed reports for the Doyennes if you don't make an effort? You benefited from a probationary period to get to know your fiancé gradually, because *we*, at Anima's Familistery, we didn't want to rush you. And yet, we could have done so."

Rubbing her bare arms, Ophelia consulted the counter's clock. She was longing for Berenilde to return from her walk. She started seriously contemplating taking her anonymous letter out from under her glove and waving it under the stork's beak. The Doyennes didn't want to rush her? Others would take care of that in their place!

"I studied your file closely, you know, before embarking on this great journey," the Rapporteur continued, with a half-smile. "I learnt that you had already rejected two requests, from cousins with whom you could have led a nice, quiet life, if you had shown willing."

"The past is the past," said Ophelia.

The Rapporteur's smile widened. "Is it really? Maybe, if Mr. Thorn isn't to be found among us today, it's not his fault. Are you absolutely sure you're doing everything required to appeal to him?" she asked, examining Ophelia over the hooped rim of her glasses. "Because I'm going to tell you something, my dear girl, and this is a warning that the Doyennes are giving you through my mouth: if you make this marriage come to nothing as you did the previous ones, whatever the excuse, you'll have to settle the score with Mr. Farouk on your own. Don't expect any help from us, and don't even think about returning to Anima after having shamed us all. Do you understand?"

The Rapporteur had stated all that in a very gentle, almost sad voice, as if she found it truly regrettable to have to say such things.

Between outrage and distress, Ophelia didn't know which emotion was wrenching her stomach the most. *I give you until the 1st of August to make your arrangements,* the author of the letter had written. That left her barely three days to find a response to the ultimatum, and she didn't know to whom she should turn.

"Your telegram has been sent, madam," announced the man at the counter. "That will be five crowns."

"What does this man want from me?" the Rapporteur, frowning, asked Ophelia. "These foreigners all have an appalling accent, one can't understand a word they're saying!"

"You owe him some crowns for the telegram," Ophelia repeated.

"Five," the telegraphist stressed, showing all the fingers of his hand. "Usually, it's four, but there was an echo. They cost paper, the echoes." The man pointed to the strip of punched paper his telegraph had spat out of its own accord. "They're around all the time at the moment," he grumbled. "It causes interference with the instruments."

Echoes were a phenomenon that caused split images on photographs, or the untimely duplication of radio waves; no one really understood how they worked, but everyone agreed that they were very annoying.

"Put it on the Treasury's bill," Ophelia suggested to the telegraphist, hoping that those five crowns wouldn't ruin Thorn.

She might be about to marry the Pole's chief accountant, but coins and banknotes remained, in her eyes, an esoteric mystery.

Ophelia sat back down on her bench. She thought she was done with the Rapporteur, and so was exasperated when she settled down beside her. Once this lesson-giver had aimed her weather vane at someone, she never laid off.

"My dear girl, I know the locals here are very disconcerting," she said, with a significant glance at the telegraphist, "but you mustn't push your fiancé away with the excuse that he's not part of our family. The Doyennes themselves, in their infinite wisdom, don't hesitate to open their door to foreign influences, and it's the whole of Anima that benefits!"

"Which foreign influences?" asked Ophelia.

"I obviously can't go into the details," the Rapporteur murmured, with the enigmatic expression of the great initiated. "What takes place at the Council of Doyennes is strictly confidential, and even I, despite being a Rapporteur, have no access to it. Not yet, at any rate," she hastened to qualify. "I'm retaking the family-service exam in four years' time, and I feel sure that this time I'll make it! What I can tell you, returning to the matter at hand, is that our dearest mothers do occasionally receive a visit from a stranger who really is . . ." The Rapporteur seemed to be searching for the most suitable adjective, while her weather vane swiveled hesitantly on her hat. ". . . from a stranger who really is strange, in fact. Never have I witnessed a family power such as his . . . I couldn't even tell you his age. Oh, I've never indulged in listening at doors," she protested, so vehemently that Ophelia strongly doubted it, "I merely served them tea. But I know that our dear mothers afford this stranger's advice their most serious consideration. He doesn't visit them often, but each time he does, they pass a new family law, or repeal another. So, follow the example of such splendid open-mindedness!"

Ophelia frowned. Promulgating laws because a visitor advises you to, between two cups of tea? That was surely a little more than open-mindedness. Ophelia had enough to think about, what with her death threats and her forthcoming marriage, but she could no longer refrain from a little sarcasm: "I see. And it's also perhaps on the advice of a stranger that the Doyennes decided to move the archives, censor the library, and close my museum?"

The Rapporteur's bulging eyes opened so wide that, for a brief moment, she resembled a frog in a curly wig. "I find you very insolent and very ungrateful, my dear. That museum is benefiting, like the archives and the library before it, from a well-deserved cleanup."

"What cleanup?" Ophelia asked, anxiously. "I always looked after the collections with the utmost care."

"But without any discernment!" the Rapporteur sighed, tapping her spectacles in a teacherly way. "That I also read in your file. The men from before the Rupture created veritable masterpieces, but they also committed atrocities. Atrocities that they perpetuated by means of weapons and of books. Putting those things, even if they are several centuries old, under the noses of the young could sow the seeds of war in impressionable minds. Our dearest mothers are right to decide only to validate the heritage that all must follow as an example! In any case, it no longer concerns you," concluded the Rapporteur, as her weather vane turned resolutely away from Ophelia.

Ophelia clasped her hands so tightly, her gloves squealed. If she had honed her skills in the art of reading objects, it was because she had never felt as close to her own truth as when exploring that of objects. The past wasn't always beautiful to look at, but the errors of the people who had preceded her on Earth had also become her own. If Ophelia had learned one thing in life, it **was that** errors were indispensible for personal development.

She suddenly **remembered** the intuition that had struck her in the cable **car, that** common denominator she had sensed between the **scheming** of the Doyennes on Anima and the threats lurking **here,** in the Pole, around Farouk's Book. This impression stuck **to her** like tar, without her managing to establish any **causal link** between the two sides.

Ophelia didn't **get a** chance to go deeper into the subject. A shrill voice crossed **the hotel** lobby like a siren: "Fi-na-lly, here you are! We looked **eve-ry-where** for you! "

Agatha trotted **over** between the luggage trolleys, with an impressive **clattering of pearls.** She was wearing the same necklaces, the same **floaty dress,** the same cloche hat, and the same gauze scarf as **Berenilde,** now coming through the revolving door herself.

"Little sister, **we've** been yearn-ing for you! Good day, Madam Rapporteur, **may we** borrow Ophelia from you?"

The Rapporteur **clearly** couldn't have been more delighted. She took **advantage of the** diversion to take Arcadian leave, her weather vane **seeking** out a new destination for her.

"Sweetie, **what on earth** are you doing in a bathing costume, here, in **full view of everyone?"** Agatha exclaimed, fists on hips. "It's **in-de-cent."**

To the great **annoyance** of her husband, who wearily followed her **everywhere** with wee Tom in his arms, Agatha had picked up some **strange** mannerisms. From one day to the next, she had **started splitting** syllables like some actress on a stage, and **wearing new** dresses. Lost in admiration for Berenilde, Agatha was **trying** to mold herself into her—to dress like her, to speak **like her, and** to move like her.

"Now that **we've finally** found her," Agatha continued, excitedly, **"where did** you want to take us, madam? Are we finally going to the court? I can-not wait to see something other than those rocks!"

Bowed by the weight of her stomach, Berenilde smiled indulgently at her. "Forgive me, my dear child, but today's not yet the day. In fact, I would like to have a tête-à-tête with your sister."

"What," said a peeved Agatha, "I'm not coming with you?"

"Not this time. Enjoy some time with your husband and your little Tom," Berenilde suggested, gently. Her eyes lost all their unctuousness as she turned them to Ophelia. "Put a coat on."

THE MOTHERS

Berenilde asked Ophelia to join her in a troika, pulled by snow-white horses. The Valkyrie was already sitting in it, looking as delighted as if she were about to follow a funeral procession. Ophelia hesitated slightly when she spotted a large trunk at the back of the carriage. They weren't setting off on holiday, surely?

Once the troika had left the hotel and was travelling along the town's bustling avenues, men doffed their fur hats and women hoisted their cascading dresses to curtsey as it went by. Like a real patron saint, Berenilde had a benevolent smile for every one of them. The more Ophelia surveyed the byways of Opal Sands, the more she became aware that there was a whole side to Berenilde that she hadn't known existed. There wasn't a wall or shop window that didn't feature old notices bearing her name: "Berenilde's soup kitchen," "Berenilde's hospice," "Berenilde's educational establishment." This aristocrat, whom Ophelia had always seen sleeping in silk and just lounging around, was metamorphosing here into a benefactress who invested all her energy into keeping the heart of the resort beating.

And yet that mysterious melancholy was still there, in the shadow of her eyes.

"We must talk," Ophelia said to her. "I received a . . ."

229

"Not here," Berenilde interrupted. "Let's wait until we've arrived."

Ophelia just had to put up with it. The troika was being driven very slowly, out of consideration for Berenilde's pregnancy. It took a road leading out of the town, went along the salt marshes, and then back up around the top of a fjord. The snow never melted up on high, and the fir trees soon took on a half-emerald, half-silver hue. Ophelia curled up her feet; she'd remembered to take her scarf, but forgotten her shoes.

On one side of the road, the high railway wall was an extension of the natural rock of the shore; on the other, the ribbon of sea reflected the cliffs opposite like a mirror. It was a sea so salty that, apart from plankton and seaweed, nothing living was to be found in it; and yet it reigned supreme here. When the sun pierced through the clouds and cast its blades of gold on the water, the colors of the landscape instantly turned from pastel to gouache. For all that Ophelia had witnessed this spectacle day after day, it still had the same effect on her.

The spell was broken as soon as the troika went up a driveway of firs and stopped outside the porch of a residence with round windows.

SANITARIUM

VISITORS' ENTRANCE

Those three words carved into the facade's pediment made Ophelia want to run a mile.

"We're . . . visiting your mother?" Ophelia had ended up totally forgetting her existence. If there was one person she really didn't want to talk to, it was that old imposter. She'd never felt able to reveal to Berenilde that her own mother hated them, Thorn and her, to the extent of having put their lives in danger. And one death threat was quite enough for her, for now.

Escorted by her Valkyrie, Berenilde entered the sanitarium with all the majesty of a queen. Ophelia couldn't fathom how a woman with such a considerable stomach could move so gracefully; she herself felt very awkward, with her bare little legs sticking out from her makeshift coat. Once inside, she squinted, blinded by the immaculate whiteness of the place. The sanitarium, all picture windows and clean tiles, allowed the daylight to flood in. There was a smell of disinfectant wafting in the air, making Ophelia miss the resinous aroma outside.

She followed Berenilde and the Valkyrie along an endless succession of loungers, on which elderly people were sunning themselves with the rigidity of sepulchral statues. What was she supposed to say to Thorn's grandmother when she saw her again? "How are you doing, dear madam? Are you planning to kill me today?"

Berenilde went into another wing of the establishment, which was totally deserted. Or almost: a nurse in a large, white cornette came towards them, her clogs ringing out on the tiles.

"Good day, Madam Berenilde. Your mother will be pleased to see you."

"I have brought a few personal belongings. You are certain there is no risk to the baby?"

"No, madam, we treat breathing conditions, but none that are contagious. You'll be perfectly comfortable here, rest assured."

"We're not going back to the hotel?" asked Ophelia, astonished, as the nurse led them along a corridor.

"You are," replied Berenilde. "I will explain it all soon, but first I would like to speak with my mother."

The nurse gave two discreet little knocks on a door, and

231

then opened it without waiting for an answer. Berenilde entered the room, holding her stomach with both hands, and before Ophelia and the Valkyrie could follow her in, gently pushed the door behind her. "Wait for me," she whispered through the crack. "I won't be long."

Ophelia agreed, silently. She'd had time to glimpse, behind Berenilde, a scene that she wouldn't easily forget: the withered body, whiter than the sheets on the bed, of an old lady, staring at the ceiling with her bulbous eyes, her breathing reduced to a mere wheeze. Had Ophelia not known that this woman was Thorn's grandmother, she wouldn't have recognized her.

Shaken, she walked a few steps along the corridor and sat on the ledge of a huge, round window. To think that she'd felt threatened by this woman just a few minutes earlier . . .

"I didn't know her health was that bad," she admitted to the Valkyrie, who had followed her with a rustling of dress. "I knew she suffered with her lungs, but . . . but that . . ." Ophelia was racked by a series of sneezes before she could finish her sentence.

"Here."

Ophelia stared wide-eyed at the handkerchief the Valkyrie had just offered her. They had lived together for months and this was the first time she was hearing the sound of her voice. She blew her nose gingerly, uncomfortable with dirtying such fine handiwork: the handkerchief seemed to be fashioned from the same black, lightly embroidered fabric as the farthingale.

"Thank you, madam."

Her surprise increased when the Valkyrie gave her a mischievous smile that spread wrinkles across both cheeks. "Come, come, no 'madam' between us. It's me, Archibald."

"What?" Ophelia had been told, repeatedly, that a well brought-up young girl never says, "what?", but she felt there were certain circumstances that excused any impoliteness. The

Valkyrie sat down beside her. It was a surreal spectacle to see this old lady, normally so dignified and starchy, struggling so inelegantly in her voluminous dress.

"I'm borrowing this body for a moment. It's not very comfortable, but I wanted to speak to you in private."

When she saw the Valkyrie cheekily eyeing her bare calves, Ophelia no longer had the slightest doubt. It really was Archibald. "You're able to do such a thing?" she stammered, pulling her coat down as much as possible. "Possess a body other than your own?"

"Yes," Archibald replied in the Valkyrie's croaky voice. "When its owner is a member of the Web and I have their consent. I can't do it for long, so listen to me carefully. I'm doing my own little investigation into the matter of the disappearances from Clairdelune. What I suspect doesn't smell at all good."

"What's going on back there?" Ophelia asked, anxiously. "Whom do you suspect?"

"Let's say that I have an avenue of thought, but I prefer to explore it alone for now. I won't speak about it to anyone, not even my family, as long as I can't be certain."

Ophelia reflected that it couldn't be easy, keeping little secrets from people who can permanently watch your every move and deed. Suddenly, the Valkyrie's old face was taken over by spasms, while, all the while, continuing to smile. It was the strangest expression Ophelia had ever come across on a human being.

"I would ask you to be extremely careful. Stay far away from the court for as long as possible."

Ophelia tensed up. After the letter she'd received, she wanted nothing more than that. For now, Farouk still hadn't sent her any message about that new role he'd promised her, but that in no way solved her problem. Could Ophelia trust

Archibald? Should she tell him about the blackmail she was enduring?

"And Berenilde must take great care of the baby that's due," he added, before she'd decided. "I want to be the godfather of a healthy child! As for my sisters, ensure that they're never too far from you."

"They're only here because you forced them to come. I have no authority over them—we barely speak."

"They're jealous," said Archibald, laughing.

If it was surprising to see a Valkyrie speak, it was even more disturbing to see her laugh.

"Jealous?"

"My sisters don't understand why I'm so interested in you. They deem you uninteresting and unsightly."

"Ah," Ophelia replied, simply. "And do you have any news of Thorn from your side?"

The Valkyrie cracked a grimacing smile, her eyelids flickering with nervous twitches. Archibald's possession was putting her body under great strain.

"I'm not the one he's engaged to, if I recall. Mr. Treasurer is doing goodness knows what, goodness knows where. I don't wish to seem rude, but he seems to care as little about my missing people as about his marriage to you."

Ophelia dug her hand into her coat pocket, in which Thorn's watch was discreetly ticking. She'd almost broken it, stopped it, or jammed it countless times, but, so far, the delicate mechanism had survived her clumsiness. Ophelia had put Thorn's silence down to his inquiry at Clairdelune, but if Archibald himself didn't know where he was . . . Somewhat despite herself, she recalled the papers flying in all directions and Thorn, covered in blood, pointing his pistol at her. What if he had also received letters, himself?

"We're not connected to the Citaceleste by telephone

here. Could you contact the Treasury, Mr. Ambassador? Just to make sure . . . how can I put it . . . that nothing serious has happened."

The Valkyrie raised her eyebrows so high that her forehead concertinaed. "No, seriously? You're worried about Thorn?"

"And about you, too," Ophelia sighed, reluctantly. "I'm not sure that you deserve it, either of you, but you must be careful where you poke your noses."

She jumped when the Valkyrie leant over, deposited a kiss on her forehead, and winked at her. "Avoid showing yours at the court, little Ophelia. And most of all, keep it well away from illusions."

"From illusions? Why illusions?"

The Valkyrie's face closed like a window, her eyes stopped sparkling, and her wrinkled hands rearranged her farthingale correctly. "Your correspondent is no longer here."

"But I don't understand," insisted Ophelia. "What did Archibald mean?"

"I don't share his thoughts, thank goodness," the Valkyrie declared, taking back her handkerchief. "I was engaged to keep an eye on Madam Berenilde, not to make conversation with you." With these words, the old lady left the window and sank back into a dignified silence. Ophelia fiddled with her gloves. Perhaps she should have spoken about her letter to Archibald. Would he contact the Treasury, as she had asked him to? The Citaceleste floated too far from Opal Sands for Ophelia to be able go there via a mirror. She turned and contemplated the forest of conifers through the window. Whenever the sun left a cloud, it dazzled Ophelia with its light and threw her reflection onto the glass: a slip of a woman with messy hair, an anxious expression, and, around her neck, a scarf that was starting to wriggle with impatience.

Ophelia jumped up like a spring on hearing a door open

and then close in the corridor. It was Berenilde, clinging to her stomach as though to a lifebelt, and so pale that she appeared bloodless.

"Madam?" Ophelia inquired, anxiously.

"I would like . . . just a breath of fresh air," Berenilde said, wearily, as she leant on the arm Ophelia offered to her. "Do come with me. As for you, madam," she added, addressing the Valkyrie, "could you follow us at a respectable distance, please? We need a little privacy."

Concerned, Ophelia accompanied her out of the sanitarium. They walked in silence through the gardens. The damp grass was sticking to Ophelia's feet, but Berenilde was so heavy on her arm, it didn't enter her mind to complain about it. "You wouldn't like to sit down, madam?"

"Let's walk a few more steps, if you don't mind." Berenilde was looking around; her eyes were less big and less blue than usual. She scanned the silhouettes stretched out on the loungers, sunbathing along the terraces of the sanitarium. She seemed to be looking for someone.

Ophelia sensed her stiffening as soon as laughter erupted close to where they were standing. Kneeling in the grass, her white dress soaked from the humidity, a woman was picking Arctic blackberries under the watchful eye of a nurse. The woman examined each berry in the sunlight with a child's look of wonderment, and then bit into it and burst into delighted laughter, as if she'd never tasted anything more amazing. Her long blond hair was streaked with silver; she couldn't be far off from fifty. She had the most disturbing tattoo Ophelia had ever seen: a big, black cross, spanning her face from forehead to chin.

It was clear that this woman-child was who Berenilde was looking for in the gardens, and yet she was happy watching her from a distance, not wishing to get any closer.

"I have never been a good mother."

Ophelia had expected all manner of declaration but that one. She looked up at Berenilde, in the hope of finally meeting her eyes, but she continued to show only her profile, pure and proud. Ophelia felt as if she were holding the arm of a statue.

"I have observed yours with great interest," Berenilde continued, steadily. "I wager that, when you were little, she was already determined to keep her eye on you at all times. The customs at the Pole's court are rather different. We send our children to the provinces, we entrust them to nannies and tutors, and then we wait until they are old enough to bring them back to us and present them to society. That is how my mother brought me up, and that is how I myself brought my children up." Her smile widened, but without lighting the slightest spark of joy in the eyes that remained focused on the woman with the berries. "Thomas was taken from me first. I wasn't there when it happened; he died, poisoned, in the arms of his nanny. And do you think I changed my ways at all?" she asked, with Olympian calm. "Of course not. I withdrew into my grief and left my little Peter and my little Marian far away from me. I kept telling myself that they would be safer in the provinces than at the court. I had promised to see them soon, once I had pulled myself together."

Ophelia already knew how the story ended, but she wouldn't have interrupted her for the world. After weeks of things remaining unsaid, Berenilde was finally opening up to her.

"Not a single morning do I wake up without asking myself the same question. Would they still be alive today if I hadn't taken so long to keep my promise?"

The sun slipped behind the clouds. A low wind swept across the lawn, chilling Ophelia's calves. Berenilde's cloche hat flew off, like a giant lily-of-the-valley blossom; the woman-child followed it with her eyes, mesmerized, and abandoned her berry-picking to chase after it, despite the nurse's protestations. As for Berenilde, she hadn't moved an inch, her beautiful golden hair rippling freely around her shoulders.

"I got my revenge. As soon as I discovered the identity of the culprits, I took pleasure in challenging them to a duel and slashing them to pieces. Both of them, one after the other."

Both of them? Baron Melchior's words came back to Ophelia like a slap in the face: "Stanislav lost his parents in circumstances that were rather . . . particular."

"The Knight's father and mother," murmured Ophelia. "So it was they who attacked your children? Is that the reason you inherited their estate?"

"I am responsible for what that little Mirage has become," Berenilde admitted, losing none of her poise. "He has always expected me to fill the void that I carved into his life. I have now learnt, by telegram, that his Mutilation sentencing is soon to take place; he will probably be sent far away from the court. With him, a page of my life is turning." She inhaled the earthy smell of the wind, and, very gracefully, smoothed her ruffled hair. "The loveliest memories I have of my children are to be found here, in this town, deep in these woods, on these beaches. That is all that I wish to preserve today."

That was all Ophelia needed to understand the source of the melancholy that had shrouded Berenilde since they had come down south, and why she dedicated herself, body and soul, to this place. It was a pilgrimage.

Ophelia shuddered as she saw Berenilde clenching her hand on her stomach. "Are you in pain?"

"Nothing that isn't in the natural order of things. The birth is imminent. Just look at me," Berenilde murmured, producing a slight dimple. "I am at last going to be a mother again, and I have learned nothing from my past mistakes.

I lead a life of excess and debauchery, I have changed none of my ways. If your aunt weren't keeping such a close watch on me . . ." She sighed, without dropping her serene smile. "My mother is going to die. Her lungs are in a very bad state. It's now just a matter of days, maybe hours. I must stay close to her."

"I'm sorry."

Ophelia had said this with impulsive spontaneity, even though she didn't know what she was really sorry about. This drama couldn't have come at a worse time. Berenilde had too much to think about, and Ophelia no longer dared to share her anxieties with her.

"You don't need to be," Berenilde declared, in a noticeably less gentle voice. "Mother has just confided in me. Do you remember those oranges that almost poisoned Madam Hildegarde, and almost condemned you to death? It is she who was responsible for that. She is not apologizing to you," Berenilde decided to make clear. "She even regrets having failed to discredit you, but she wanted to tell me about it while she still could."

"Oh?" Ophelia stammered, caught off guard. "Um . . . I . . ."

Berenilde, usually in perfect control of her claws, was now filling Ophelia's head with a migraine. Nothing, on the surface, indicated that she was annoyed—she was still watching, with a detached curiosity, the woman-child, who had finally caught her hat and now seemed to be wondering what she was supposed to do with it.

"Back in her youth, my mother was a woman greatly feared," Berenilde continued. "In her eyes, all that mattered was the clan of the Dragons, the future of the Dragons, the honor of the Dragons. I thought she had calmed down with age, but I am appalled by her hypocrisy. Never will I forgive her for having caused you harm . . . I am already struggling to forgive myself for it."

Berenilde's eyes finally looked down at Ophelia, and she, heart beating like a drum, suddenly understood that that shadow dimming their brilliance had never been directed at her.

"I ask your forgiveness, Ophelia. For all the times that I forced you into things, treated you roughly, and rebuked you. That evening, on that theatre stage, when you stood up to Farouk, I realized that you had never ceased to be the stronger of the two of us. It was a rather painful lesson in humility that you gave me then, but I finally accepted it. I claimed to be protecting you, when it is I who will need you to help me."

"Me to help you?" Berenilde was her superior when it came to charm, power, and influence; it was hard for Ophelia to imagine how she could be of use. She played along when Berenilde tenderly took her hand and placed it on her stomach.

"Find me a name."

"Me? But isn't it up to the godfather . . ."

"No. I don't want it to be Archibald's choice, but yours, Ophelia. I am asking you to be the godmother of my child."

Ophelia's glasses turned crimson from the emotional impact. She did her best not to show how panicked this request made her feel. It was the first time someone had considered entrusting her with such a responsibility. Even Agatha had chosen to turn instead to an aunt, deeming her sister far too clumsy to hold a baby in her arms.

"A girl's name," Berenilde specified, while stroking her stomach. "I have always been able to sense those things before the birth. Do you know what that means?"

Ophelia didn't reply. She had so many thoughts in her head, she could no longer focus on just one of them.

"In the Pole, it is the male children who inherit the whole

240

estate," explained Berenilde. "Since I am to give birth to a daughter, it means Thorn is already the unofficial owner of the Dragons' entire heritage. He will become so officially with the nullification of his bastard status, once he has fulfilled his part of the contract with our Lord Farouk."

"And you, madam? And your daughter?"

"Oh, I have no concerns there. Thorn will provide for our needs. And I remain the owner of my manor at Citaceleste. So, Ophelia, do you agree to be the godmother of my child?"

"Well, the thing is, madam . . . It's a big responsibility."

"You are the most responsible person I know. Please, my dear Ophelia, help me to be a better mother, and help our Lord Farouk to be a better father. But above all, help Thorn," Berenilde implored her, her voice suddenly cracking. "The boy gives me plenty to worry about—sometimes I feel as though I don't really know him. I have no idea what's going on in his head, but for the rest, trust me, I understand him better than he does himself. It's your heart that he really needs, not your hands."

Ophelia stammered out a reply that made no sense at all. Having feared that she hadn't earned Berenilde's esteem, she now felt crushed under the weight of her expectations.

"For the moment, unfortunately, I won't be of any help to you," Berenilde sighed, sliding a finger along Ophelia's cheek. "I have a mother to bury in the earth, and a child to bring into the world. Stay quietly at the hotel and wait for me. I would have liked the Valkyrie to accompany you back there, to guard your safety in my absence, but it's to my baby that the Web has offered its protection. I promise you, however, that I will be at your side on the day of your nuptials. Soon, in addition to your Animism, you will have the benefit of Thorn's claws. We will teach you how to use them so that you can protect yourself from your enemies."

Ophelia forced herself to smile, but she couldn't have been that convincing: Berenilde placed both hands on her shoulders, like an adult trying to comfort a little girl. "If the law allowed it, I would make a gift to you of my own family power. You see me, perhaps, as a force of nature, but my claws as a young girl weren't worth much before being combined with those of my husband. The Ceremony of the Gift has always had the advantage of making a mutual power twice as potent. But don't underestimate the advantages that may ensue from the combining of your Animism with Thorn's abilities—you may be astonished at the result."

Ophelia jumped when a face marked with a cross suddenly loomed in front of hers. It was the woman-child, who, following the patient instructions of her nurse, held Berenilde's hat out to her. "Thank you, madam," she said, shyly taking it.

This woman's tattoo was even more impressive close up. It featured a vertical line so thick that it covered her nose entirely, and a horizontal one that looked like a mask across her eyes. This face would have still been magnificent, even if not marked in this way. Against a background of silver-blond hair, pale skin, and white dress, all one could see was that black cross. The woman-child didn't seem bothered by it. Barely had her eyes left Ophelia than she seemed instantly to forget her existence, and, seized by some new whimsy, ran off, across the lawn.

"Oh, yes, by the way," Berenilde said, her voice perkier. "Ophelia, meet your future mother-in-law."

THE CARAVAN

It's not easy to fall asleep in an ark where the nights are as bright as mornings for half the year. But right now, Ophelia had other reasons for remaining awake in her little hotel bed. She could hear the sea, she could hear the wind, she could sometimes even hear the sighing of a snowy owl or the squeaking of lemmings, somewhere inside the walls, as if all of nature had decided to meet up in her room. What didn't help, either, was Ophelia not being able to breathe easily because of her blocked nose. After all that walking around barefoot outdoors, she'd fallen properly ill.

She saw once again, in the darkness behind her eyelids, that face marked with a cross. "Neither you nor I will ever know her," Thorn had once said to her, when she'd questioned him about his mother. She understood now the significance of those words. Thorn's mother had undergone the Mutilation, and her tattoo was a mark of infamy impossible to hide behind any makeup, behind any illusion.

"Like all Chroniclers, the power of her clan is linked to the memory," Berenilde had explained to her in the gardens of the sanitarium. "In losing the first, she lost the second. Don't feel too sorry for her, my dear, she has more than one death on her conscience."

It was hard to imagine that this harmless creature, stuck in an eternal present moment, without a past or a future, could have been that fearsome. Berenilde had told Ophelia how Thorn's mother had dragged all the Chroniclers down with her in her fall, about fifteen years earlier. This clan's prime vocation was to preserve and pass on the collective memory, as Ophelia's branch of the family did. After a long trial, it was proved that the Chroniclers had used their position to distort the past and attribute great deeds accomplished by others to themselves.

They would have got off with a warning from the tribunal had Thorn's mother not committed the ultimate offense. She took advantage of her position as favorite to falsify the note-book of their family spirit. Because of her, misfortunes started raining down on all the courtiers, as Farouk no longer trusted his own descendants. Things could have gone much further had Thorn's mother not ended up being found out, judged, and disgraced.

"What I myself will never forgive that woman for," Bere-nilde had concluded with barely concealed hatred, "is what she did to Thorn. By seducing my brother and having a child by him, she wanted to reinforce her own lineage, endow the Chroniclers with the power of our hunters. When she realized that her child was sickly, she treated him like something just fit for the trash."

Ophelia wondered whether there was a single member of her future family whom she could one day present to her parents without the fear of totally horrifying them. Thinking about it, she also wondered how different the activities of Anima's Doyennes really were from the memory-doctoring of the Chroniclers.

The tick-tock of the fob watch rang out in the silence, and soon, instead of the face marked with a cross, Ophelia was assailed with the image of a sandglass trickling, grain after grain, hour after hour.

The sandglass of her life. With August the 1st as the end point.

She had resolved to throw her threatening letter into the coal-burning stove, having failed to extract its secrets: its author knew only too well her limits as a reader, having left no trace of any contact on the paper. Ophelia could see no solution to the ultimatum. If she broke off her engagement, she would have to face the consequences alone, and this time she wouldn't be able to count on Farouk's clemency. If she didn't break it off, she would probably meet the same fate as the Provost of the Marshals and the director of the *Nibelungen*. It wasn't what she called a choice. She only had forty-eight hours left to make her decision. Forty-eight grains in her sandglass of life.

Ophelia rubbed her eyelids, determined to banish this image, but it was immediately replaced by a vision of the woman in the red coat and black fur hat. Ophelia had again caught her walking right under the window of her room just as she was closing the shutters, but when she had leant out to see where she was going, the woman had vanished into thin air. She was under surveillance, she was sure of it now.

GOD DISAPPROVES OF THIS UNION.

Ophelia stared at the fob watch, its cover gleaming on the bedside table. Thorn had assured her that she wasn't merely a pair of hands to him, but where was he right now, as she wrestled alone with her anxieties? Ophelia couldn't rid herself of the disturbing impression that she'd soon be marrying—if she hadn't disappeared by then—a perfect stranger.

"If you still doubt me in the future, just read it."

Hesitantly, Ophelia pulled off her night glove and stretched out her arm towards the watch. Since she had the permission of its owner, touching it wouldn't be dishonest, would it? She would read it for no more than a few seconds, just long enough to reassure herself that Thorn hadn't lied to her this time, too.

Ophelia closed her hand around nothing. No. Not like that. That was the worst way of learning how to trust again.

She turned her back on the watch, not to be tempted any more, and buried her face in her pillow. Why was Thorn no longer giving any signs of life? Why was their marriage feared to this extent? Why were nobles disappearing without a trace? Why was Archibald wary of illusions all of a sudden?

"Why don't you ever do anything with me?"

Ophelia sat up in bed, put on her glasses, and stared at Hector, who was looking keenly at her in the half-light of the room. He was wearing his favorite pajamas, a blue one-piece with a white collar that had grown at the same time as him. Unlike Ophelia, Hector never looked scruffy: his shoes tied their own laces, tears in his clothes repaired themselves, and his pockets, despite hiding many a silly mistake, allowed nothing at all to spill out. He knew how to command obedience from any item of clothing . . . and from any locked hotel door.

"You went with the girls to the baths, and you went off with Madam Berenilde. Why shouldn't it be my turn?"

"I'm listening to you," said Ophelia, consulting Thorn's watch. "What proposal has Mr. Say-Why got for me, at twelve minutes past five in the morning?"

"I found this, yesterday evening, on the hotel notice board." Hector handed her a large poster, crumpled and torn.

BACK IN THE POLE AT LAST:
THE CARNIVAL CARAVAN!
COME AND WITNESS THE FINEST INTERFAMILIAL ACTS!

Ophelia was suddenly overcome with nostalgia. The Carnival Caravan was a travelling circus, featuring men and women from the four corners of the world, which went from ark to ark. The last time it had come to Anima, Ophelia was just a little schoolgirl, but she still had dazzling memories of it.

"I wasn't born when you saw them," Hector reminded her, as if he'd long been the victim of a regrettable injustice. "Why not come along to it with me?"

Ophelia hesitated, and then realized that not only did she feel like going to the circus with her brother, she also needed to. "We will go," she promised. "Just you and I."

The Carnival Caravan had been set up near the town of Asgard, at the mouth of the neighboring fjord, so it was just a half-hour boat ride from Opal Sands. At first, Ophelia had found the idea of this outing with her little brother pretty appealing. Now that she was running from stand to stand in search of Hector, she regretted not being escorted by an army of adults. This boy was worse than a bar of soap! He slipped into the gondola of the Seer of the Serenissima, disappeared outside the photographic studio of the Alchemists of Lead-gold, hid under the Pharoan jazz duo's piano, and rose into the air in the chair of a Cyclopean Psychokinesist. The Caravan offered a really varied palette of family powers, and Hector was insatiably curious, asking his "why"s to anyone prepared to listen.

"So?" exclaimed Fox, seeing Ophelia pass the necromancy stand. "Making the most of the festivities?" He himself was chatting with a tamer, in front of the chimera cages.

"Not really," Ophelia replied. "I'm looking for my brother."

"Still? Say, you need to keep him on a tight rein—I'd rather not get a tongue-lashing from your aunt and your mother. It's just that, today, I'm the one who's responsible for you two! Three if you count this silly billy," Fox grumbled, shaking Twit by the scruff of the neck. "I found him in the nick of time, just before he went into the chimera cage. If Madam Totemist hadn't been there . . ."

The tamer smiled from ear to ear. She was a magnificent woman, with skin as black as the night and hair as golden as the sun.

"I can't even manage to look after my own brother," sighed Ophelia. "Will I really be as good a godmother as Berenilde believes?"

"Come on, don't fret," Fox said immediately, with a big smile. "I can see him over there, your bro. At the Colossus of Titan." He pointed to a rostrum on which a puny little man was lifting an enormous mirrored wardrobe with one hand, as if it weighed nothing at all. Hector was indeed there, joining in with the polite applause of the spectators.

Apart from them and a few bystanders, not that many people were circulating between the stands and the caravans. For the most part, the crowd was made up of the performers themselves, dressed in dazzling costumes and sequined masks. Ophelia looked over to the huge railway wall, higher than the lofty fir trees, bordering the fjord in the distance. Fortunately, the Caravan was protected from the Beasts on this side.

"You're a hit," she said to Fox. She'd just caught the telling wink that the beautiful tamer had given him.

"Of course, kid, what d'you think?" Fox chuckled, putting Twit back on his head. "There's only one darned woman who still doesn't realize it. Years I've been after her, that one! She'll give in one day."

Ophelia gazed pensively at the pale disc of the sun, emerging like a watermark behind the clouds. Since leaving Clairdelune, Fox had sent a flood of letters to Gail, without ever receiving a reply. "I miss her, too," she told him. Ophelia refrained from adding that she was even very anxious about her, since knowing that Archibald was doing his own inquiry.

The disappearances at Clairdelune would probably lead him to take a very close look at his staff. What would happen if he discovered that Mother Hildegarde's mechanic not only had very good reasons to hate the nobles, but also a power capable of cancelling theirs out? She'd make a perfect culprit. Ophelia would have loved to talk openly about it with Fox, but she'd promised Gail not to reveal her secret to anyone.

"You're being followed by one of the disgraced." Fox had said it without dropping his grin, and while, kitten in hair, he pretended to remove sand from his shoe. Ophelia had to force herself not to show her surprise, and took a sudden interest in the tanks of phosphorescent fish they were walking beside.

"A woman in a red coat," he continued, in a studiedly casual way. "Near the Zephyrs' screens. I keep seeing her, right on your butt. All due respect."

"So I wasn't imagining it," Ophelia said, not daring to look away from the fish tanks. "What makes you think she's one of the disgraced?"

"She's making no attempt to be discreet, but then disappears as soon as one eyes her a bit too closely. If that's not an Invisible, kid, I don't know what is."

"A power that makes one invisible?"

Fox caught Twit, brazenly scrambling down the sleeve of his frock coat, fascinated by the phosphorescent fish, and put him back on his red hair.

"That gives the illusion of invisibility. They're always in the mind, those things."

Ophelia agreed. She'd long realized that Farouk's family power only worked from mind to mind, like a radio wave between transmitter and receiver. Unlike Animism, it had no tangible effect on matter.

"I hope that this Invisible will continue to keep her distance."

"Just let her come near," grunted Fox. "I may be without power, but I ain't without muscles."

Ophelia's nose started pouring again. She took advantage of blowing her nose to risk a quick look over at the screens. She saw no one there but a little girl in a spangled costume throwing a sugar cube at a small whirlwind. If the Invisible really was over there, her power was darned effective.

"The disgraced don't normally have the right to enter towns," continued Ophelia. "And yet I met Thorn's mother in a sanatorium, and our red-coated woman sneaks around wherever she likes."

With a practiced hand, Fox grabbed Twit by the scruff of the neck as he was calmly climbing down the leg of his trousers, and returned him to the cozy nest of his hair.

"I'm no specialist on the subject, but I've noticed a few strange things since we arrived in the provinces. Take the cobbler at Opal Sands, for example. I only went there to get a sole mended, and before I even knew what I was doing, I'd bought two pairs of new shoes off him. And then there was . . . well . . . a loose woman, you know? She accosted me in the street, devilishly beautiful she was! Me, I politely declined, because, well, you know, I'm saving myself for another. Believe it or not, as soon as she lost interest in me, she suddenly lost all her good looks. And then there was that chap who sent me straight to sleep while we were playing cards, just when I was winning and asking him for what he owed me. He squinted at me, the chap, you know, with a big sorry smile, and, bang! I was out for the count. In short, I could tell you a whole load more of strange little goings-on like that."

"Could they all be the disgraced?" Ophelia asked, amazed.

"Not necessarily of pure noble origin, but there are whiffs of power, so to speak, here and there. The Persuasives and the Narcotics, to name but two, were greatly feared clans in the days when they were playing at being courtiers, but there you go, that was way back. The Invisibles, they go way back, too. There's not even anyone left who remembers why they were actually disgraced."

Ophelia would have liked to continue this conversation, but she'd just realized that her little brother had vanished once again.

"Would you help me to find Hector?"

While Fox was questioning the pyrokinesists, as they juggled balls of lightning, Ophelia searched in the smoke-plant glasshouse. It was no easy task, looking for a little boy in the midst of a mass of giant flowers spreading thick incense smoke everywhere. Ophelia emerged from the glasshouse with tears in her eyes and petals in her hair.

When she glanced inside the neighboring tent, she found not one but two Hectors. They were busy observing each other with amused curiosity. They turned in a symmetrical movement when they saw Ophelia; the Hector on the right instantly acquired a spectacular head of hair, grew taller by a few centimeters, and soon resembled Ophelia like a twin. She knew straight away that she was dealing with Milliface, a prodigious Metamorphoser.

"This is by far the most impressive act," Hector said, with his usual placidity. "Milliface can imitate anyone. Why are you looking at me like that?"

"Because I'm forever running about after you," Ophelia said, reproachfully. "We're taking the boat back soon, so don't go off anymore."

It wasn't the first time she was witnessing Milliface's act, but she found being scrutinized by her own double no less disturbing. "You're mafiliar," Milliface suddenly declared.

"I beg your pardon?" asked Ophelia, perplexed. Not only did he look like her, in every way, but he also spoke in the same muted voice as her. His sentence, however, made absolutely no sense.

"Familiar," Milliface corrected himself. "You're familiar. We've already met somewhere."

It was said as a statement rather than a question.

"When you toured Anima," she replied, with obvious admiration. "I was a very small girl at the time and already I found your act very impressive, madam . . . um . . . sir."

A flash of light dazzled her. It had come from a large camera that Hector was carrying around his neck. "Where did you get that, you?" Ophelia asked, dragging her brother out of Milliface's tent, and still half-blinded by the flashlight.

"An Alchemist of Leadgold, who swapped it for one of my perpetually spinning tops. It's a camera that develops pictures instantly, watch." Her brother shook the paper that his camera had just noisily spat out, and then made a face. "Drat, why do my photographs always turn out wrong?"

In fact, instead of the two Ophelia's expected, there were four on the film, half the right way up, half the wrong. "It must be an echo," she explained. "The telegraphist at our hotel told me they're around all the time at the moment, and they interfere with cameras. Probably a magnetic storm, or something like that."

Ophelia tilted her head to see whether the sky was looking that menacing. She thought she was seeing things when, instead of clouds, she saw Thorn's grim face.

THE DISGRACED

"What on earth are you doing here?"

Thorn had come straight out with his question, no preliminaries. His austere uniform, bony figure, black-shadowed eyes, and scowling expression gave him an even more lugubrious aura than that of the Necromancers at the neighboring stand. He was doing his best to control an impressive quantity of papers, which the wind was flapping between his fingers.

Ophelia was so taken aback to see him here, in the midst of the attractions and the children, that she replied automatically: "I'm taking my brother to the circus."

"Is my aunt with you?"

"No, she stayed at Opal Sands," stammered Ophelia. "Well, at the sanitarium. Your grandmother is not at all well." She hesitated momentarily about mentioning Thorn's mother, but he didn't allow her the time to do so.

"Go back to the hotel," he ordered, not even glancing at Hector. "These traveling folk are not in order. I'm still missing eighty-eight identity papers and a work permit in triplicate. And I'm not even including the animals."

As he was saying this, he tried to put the forms into a leather briefcase—no simple maneuver as the wind was making his papers flutter all over the place.

Ophelia finally understood that this encounter wasn't due

to some miraculous coincidence; Thorn had come out of the caravan opposite, on which a standard, shining in the light drizzle, read: "DIRECTOR'S OFFICE." In an overwhelming mix of relief, disappointment and indignation, she became fully aware that not only was Thorn actually standing there before her, in perfect health, but on top of that, he was there as a killjoy.

"Do you have to bother these people with all your administration?" she asked, reproachfully.

Thorn frowned in the direction of the colorful dirigibles hovering over the beach. "Identity checks are imperative, today more than ev . . ."

A blinding flash stopped Thorn before he could even finish his sentence. As he furiously blinked, searching for the source of that light, his eyes fell on Hector.

"Why do you have those scars?"

"Come now," whispered Ophelia, laying a hand on her little brother's shoulder. "No 'why's on physical appearance, remember?" Hector put the dud photograph in his pocket, and then raised his placid eyes back up at Thorn, not remotely daunted by his height. "Okay. Why are you detestable?"

Ophelia was shocked. It was the first time she'd heard her brother speaking like that. As for Thorn, he didn't seem in the least upset; briefcase in hand, he looked away with a bored expression. "Could you ask your brother if he's finished?"

"Ask him yourself," said Ophelia. "He can understand you perfectly well."

She was finding it increasingly hard to remember why on earth she'd been concerned about Thorn's silence.

"I don't speak to children," he snapped back, avoiding meeting Hector's implacable gaze. "However, I would like to speak to you, just for a moment. Ask your brother to go off and play in a corner. You, come here!" Thorn suddenly ordered in a loud voice. He had just noticed Fox, who was emerging from the Funhouse with a blissful expression on his face. He must have been under the effect of some euphoriant spell, as he gave Thorn a radiant smile, not particularly surprised to see him there.

"Take this child off for a walk."

"We'll stay close by," Fox said, with a meaningful wink for Thorn. "Sir mustn't worry, I won't be keeping my eyes peeled. After all, love is sweet folly, and it's not easy holding back the impulses of the heart!" he declaimed, kissing the tips of his fingers passionately.

Ophelia concealed her embarrassment by blowing her nose. Thorn waited until they were finally alone to look coldly down at her. His hair, ruffled by the wind and shiny from the humidity, made him appear even more prickly than usual.

"I'm making an effort to keep you safe, and I would be grateful if you would make that task easier for me by not leaving the hotel anymore."

"Make that task easier for you?" Ophelia repeated, incredulous. "You were the one who was supposed to make mine easier by creating a good impression on my parents. You still haven't even come to see them. We're getting married in four days, may I remind you."

"I can't be everywhere at once," Thorn said, indicating his briefcase. "I'm proceeding with my annual provincial inspections. Let's not stay here," he added, under his breath.

Ophelia had difficulty keeping up with Thorn as his long strides were double hers. He waited until the precise moment that they were going past a giant pianola to ask: "What did the message say?"

"What message?"

"The letter you received yesterday."

"How do you know about it?"

"I have my sources. So, that message?"

"I must neither marry you nor return to court."

"Who sent you that letter?" insisted Thorn.

Ophelia had to make a considerable effort to hear him and make herself heard by him over the boisterous music and the clickety-clack of the piano's mechanism.

"I don't know. The letter was entirely typed and handled with pincers. It's 'unreadable' for my hands. It's the second one of the kind I've received. It said, '*GOD DISAPPROVES OF THIS UNION*,' in capital letters," she specified, her throat tightening.

After a brief silence, Thorn started walking again. "You didn't see anything else suspicious?"

It was typical of Thorn to do his questioning in the manner of a police officer. He forged straight ahead, briefcase in hand, as if crossing an administrative building, rather than a circus.

"A woman . . . in a red coat," Ophelia gasped, out of breath. "Foster thinks . . . she's one of the disgraced. He saw her here. I don't want to go too far . . . from my brother. You walk too fast."

Thorn deigned to slow down, not without glancing all around him. He seemed particularly tense, as if he felt watched.

"I do read the newspapers, you know?" she added. "Why did you go and boast about Mr. Farouk's Book? You ask me to be discreet, and then you, you . . ."

"I spare you from more death threats," Thorn finished for her. "Any attention I draw to myself doesn't turn against you."

Ophelia didn't know how to respond to that. In any case, Thorn didn't give her the chance.

"Count Harold has disappeared," he suddenly announced.

"The Knight's guardian?" asked Ophelia, surprised. "The man who kicked up such a fuss with you about his dogs?"

"He vanished yesterday evening from his bath. The servants thought he'd had a turn, they had to force the door open."

"He would have been abducted from a room locked from the inside?"

"And that's not the most disturbing aspect. The bathwater had apparently been used, but the tiling was dry. In other words, the count got into his bath and nothing seems to indicate that he got out of it. Even his clothes were still there. The inquest at Clairdelune had to be reopened, as if I didn't have enough to do."

Ophelia jumped at these words. "At Clairdelune?"

"Count Harold had sought sanctuary there," explained Thorn. "He felt in danger and vulnerable without his dogs. He must have been the last noble in all Citaceleste not to grasp that the embassy is no longer a safe place."

Ophelia was troubled. Only the previous day, Archibald had been warning her! Did he suspect at the time that a new crime would be committed at his home?

"He received some, too, didn't he?" she asked. "Count Harold also received threatening letters."

"Some were indeed found among his belongings." Thorn replied reluctantly. He was cautiously examining Ophelia's glasses, which had turned blue from the emotional shock.

"Letters like mine?" she insisted. "Letters with 'GOD' in them?"

"The same thing will not happen to you." Thorn's tone was totally categorical. Ophelia wished she shared his certainty; she suddenly felt as if all her insides were in knots.

"And you?" she asked, "Have you received letters?"

"Not of that sort, no."

"Why? If it's really our marriage that's the problem, why I am I being blackmailed, and not you?"

"I don't know."

Ophelia suddenly looked up at Thorn very attentively. "You're going to represent the disgraced at the Family States."

"Tomorrow evening," he replied, with a frown.

"The Provost of the Marshals, the director of the *Nibelungen*, and the Count, they all opposed that undertaking, each in their own way. I mean," Ophelia stammered as Thorn gave her a piercing look, "the Provost killed some of the disgraced, Mr. Chekhov published more and more articles against them, and Count Harold . . . well . . . he did send two mercenaries after you."

Thorn accepted this, but made no comment.

"Aren't you afraid . . ." Ophelia sneezed mid-sentence, and then blew her nose, making a mortifyingly snuffly noise. "Aren't you afraid that it's going to make you the prime suspect?"

Thorn's thin, almost invisible lips convulsed briefly. Ophelia couldn't decide whether it was a failed smile or a successful grimace.

"You think I organized these abductions to get rid of these troublesome people? You think I'm the writer of the letters and that I want to sabotage my own marriage?"

"Of course not," she said, annoyed, "but others might think it instead of me."

"No. Concerning the disgraced, I'm representing them with total neutrality."

Tired of lifting her head up to Thorn, Ophelia looked down towards the silver stretch of sea that could be glimpsed between the circus stands, beyond the vast marshy beach. She recalled the mark of infamy on Thorn's mother's face and anger surged up inside her. She couldn't comprehend how a single man managed to fill her with so many contradictory emotions at once.

"You're doing it again."

"Doing what again?" grumbled Thorn.

"Being dishonest. You're half-Chronicler, aren't you? In

attempting to rehabilitate the disgraced, you're also defending the interests of your family. At least have the guts to admit it."

Thorn frowned so hard, a crevasse appeared down the middle of his forehead. "You certainly have a very poor opinion of me. The Chroniclers don't feature in my dossier."

"Which is most regrettable, dear cousin!"

Ophelia turned with a start. The honeyed voice belonged to a tall, thin woman whose eyes twinkled mischievously under a thick blond fringe. She wore a pink dress with frills and flounces, and a matching parasol that protected her as much from the fine drizzle as from the sun. She was escorted by four men who resembled her too closely not to be members of her family. They all had the same lanky figure, the same eccentric clothes, and the same blond fringe.

"Do you recognize me, beloved cousin?" the woman sang out.

Thorn didn't reply.

"I recognize you," she clucked, "even if I must admit that you've got considerably taller. The last time I saw you, you were just a puny little four-year-old. Aren't you going to introduce us to this little young lady?" the woman asked, with a charming wink for Ophelia. "Is she your unfortunate fiancée?"

"You have no business being here." Thorn had made the statement in a measured tone, but his fingers had tightened around the handle of his briefcase. As for Ophelia, she just raised her eyebrows. Were these people Chroniclers?

"And why not, cousin?" the woman simpered, pointing at Asgard's ramparts, at the opposite end of the shore, with her parasol. "We remain more than a kilometer from the town, as stipulated by article 11 of the law relating to the living conditions of the disgraced. We've been as good as gold for fourteen years, five months, and sixteen days!"

"What do you want from me?" Thorn asked, impassively.

The Chronicler reacted with a pained pout, which made her lips, as pink as her dress and parasol, protrude. She must have been a few years older than Thorn, but she had the mannerisms of a young adolescent.

"Come again? You never read our letters?"

"Those you all started sending me once I became Treasurer? Never."

"We did have our doubts, to be honest," the Chronicler sighed, exchanging a sad glance with the four men accompanying her. "We thought, seeing all those dirigibles landing on the beach, that you'd be along soon to inspect. You're so predictable, dear cousin! We must talk, you and I."

Ophelia was starting to feel decidedly uncomfortable, not knowing whether it would be best for her to say something or keep quiet. The Chronicler slowly approached Thorn, her flouncy dress leaving a trail in the damp sand. A gust of wind lifted her blond fringe, revealing, fleetingly, a tattoo in the form of a spiral in the middle of her forehead. "Why do you refuse to represent your own family at the Family States?"

"Because that's the law," retorted Thorn, adopting the neutral tone of the perfect official. "Only the clans whose disgrace dates back more than sixty years can be represented: article 24, paragraph 3. Submit another request for rehabilitation in forty-six years, six months, and thirteen days."

"You live up to your reputation!" sniggered the Chronicler. "Quick to hide behind figures to avoid confrontation. You are a coward, beloved cousin, a coward and a liar. You deliberately keep us far away from the court, just as your mother always kept us far away from her little secrets. Mightn't she have confided one or two to you?" the woman whispered, fluttering her eyelashes. "Maybe even more? To whom if not to her only son would a Chronicler pass on her memory—and what a memory!—before losing it forever? I'm curious, so very curious, to know what such a big forehead is hiding . . ."

Ophelia held her breath. The woman had raised herself onto the tips of her pink shoes and had delicately inserted her nail, also pink, into Thorn's facial scar, to trace its path up to the eyebrow. The men escorting her had surreptitiously drawn closer to prevent any attempt to escape. A very long silence hung in the air, during which Ophelia had plenty of time to feel very small; should she call for help? Thorn and the Chronicler were defying each other with their eyes, as if a battle were taking place within their very irises. No one seemed to notice this scene unfolding against the backdrop of a funfair; the great costumed parade, passing alongside them, was attracting all the attention.

"It's not a game, cousin!" the Chronicler finally sighed, pouting sulkily. "You're like a reinforced door! But all doors, however solid, have a weak spot," she sang out, with a mischievous smile. "And I think I know yours."

Ophelia didn't have time to react before the Chronicler had spun around to her in a whirlwind of pink dress.

"Just look at that innocent little face," she chirped, affectionately tweaking Ophelia's cheek. "Reveal everything to me, my sweet . . . What dark and terrifying secrets does this man share with you?"

Ophelia would have really struggled to reply: she was no longer able to move her lips, or her fingers, or her eyelashes. Even her scarf, which had been nervously flapping around for a while, had suddenly frozen, like the pendulum of a stopped clock. All Ophelia could see were the big eyes, made-up in pink, that the Chronicler was pressing to her glasses. On the verge of falling asleep, she heard her shrill voice from afar, as memories surfaced like bubbles. Thorn snatching the telephone from her hands. Thorn pointing his pistol at her in the

261

midst of a blizzard of papers. Thorn giving her his watch as a token of trust. Thorn grabbing hold of the Chronicler's arm.

Ophelia blinked. No that wasn't a memory. Thorn really had just seized his cousin by the arm. He hadn't done it roughly, just very calmly, making her move away from Ophelia centimeter by centimeter.

"Memory-searching," he said, in a level voice, "is specifically forbidden by the law relating to restrictions on the use of family powers, article 53a. Don't make your situation worse, madam."

The Chronicler pulled her arm back so angrily that she caused her parasol to fall.

"Don't speak to me in that condescending tone, bastard! I was thirteen when they threw me out like a leper. I was young, pretty, and rich . . . I lost everything because of your mother! Are you aware how many of us died that first winter? Do you have any idea what we had to go through, my little brothers and I, just to live decently?" she asked, making every frill on her dress shake. "Our parents were the elite of the court, and they died like rats, without even having time to pass on their memory. And you," the Chronicler mocked, disdainfully, "you strut about in front of Farouk, while your mother resides in a luxurious establishment . . . What did she reveal?" she suddenly implored, clutching at Thorn's big, black coat. "You owe it to us, that memory! It's our only inheritance!"

Still drowsy from the memory-searching she'd just suffered, Ophelia had witnessed this tirade with a feeling of unreality.

"I owe you nothing whatsoever," Thorn replied, evenly.

The Chronicler let go of his coat, as if he'd suddenly become repulsively dirty. "Too bad for you. I'll extract your memories by force, if need be." She rearranged her beautiful pink dress, picked up her parasol from the sand, smoothed down her fringe flirtatiously, and winked knowingly at the other

Chroniclers. "Go on, brothers, go to town on our dear cousin. And make sure you don't spare the little face of his fiancée."

The four men made their studded gauntlets grate as they advanced. Ophelia's heart had started pounding so hard that she could feel the blood swirling inside her. *Escape.* The thought sprang into her mind like a spark. Thorn was even quicker. With a swing of his arm, he had pushed Ophelia backwards, onto the floor, and announced, in a strangely matter-of-fact tone of voice: "They're all yours."

The Invitation

Ophelia felt the soft thud of the sand on her back and, winded by her fall, gazed vacantly at the blurred image of two strings of bunting across the clouds. When the drizzle made her eyes smart, she realized she'd lost her glasses. She came back to her senses on hearing the cries of pain above the brass band of the costumed parade.

She rolled on to her side, but saw nothing around her but unidentifiable silhouettes. It seemed to her that one of them was appearing and disappearing at will, in a blaze of red, while dealing some devastating blows.

Ophelia felt around in the sand for her glasses; it was the scarf, affected by her panic, that found them for her and placed them back on her nose. As soon as she recovered her sight, she looked first for Thorn. He was standing tall, impassive as a bronze statue, still clutching his briefcase. It was unlikely to be him who had cried out. He appeared to be neither wounded nor even out of breath.

"Stay down," he advised her in a firm voice. Ophelia then realized that three of the brothers were also lying on the sand and groaning, while the fourth, with a knee on the ground, was pressing his sleeve under his nose to stem a stream of blood. Their fine blond fringes were all messed up.

The Chronicler looked as shocked as Ophelia. And for a

good reason: she was being restrained by a woman holding a dagger to her throat. Ophelia felt totally confused when she recognized the disgraced woman in the red coat, her eyes glinting with stony coldness beneath her black fur hat. So, it was this Invisible who had left the brothers in such a state? Which side was she on, in the end?

Thorn seemed to know the answer. "I would suggest that we leave it at that," he said simply, as though bringing an administrative meeting to a close. The Chronicler pursed her lips, white with rage, but stiffened as she felt the Invisible's dagger stroking the quivering skin of her neck. The spectacle of these two women entwined, the one pink and feminine, the other red and warrior-like, could have been a carefully choreographed circus act.

"V-very well," the Chronicler finally muttered, mustering a resigned smile. "Let's leave it at that, cousin."

The fourth brother, who was silently wiping his nose, immediately jumped up like a spring and aimed his studded fist at Thorn. Stuck on the sand, Ophelia opened her mouth but not a sound had a chance to come out: the Chronicler brother's head was thrown violently backwards, and the rest of his body followed, as if he had just received a brutal blow right in the face. Thorn, however, hadn't lifted a finger, or let go of his briefcase. He had merely shot a piercing look at his aggressor. It was the first time Ophelia was seeing him use his claws; she was struck by his obvious reluctance to resort to them.

"Ready to sacrifice your sister to appropriate my memory," Thorn said, looking disdainfully at the body writhing in pain at his feet. "And you wonder why your clan is doomed to disappear? It's pathetic."

At a sign from him, the red-coated woman released the Chronicler, and made her brothers stand up, one by one. Her manner matched her eyes: hard and cold as an uncut diamond.

After a final venomous look for Thorn, the Chronicler left with a brisk swish of her dress, her parasol on her shoulder and her brothers limping pitifully behind her. They were all soon swallowed up by the multicolored tide of the costumed parade.

"Return to your post," ordered Thorn. "We shouldn't see them again any time soon."

"Yes, sir." As the woman in the red coat replied, she clicked the heels of her boots together, and then discreetly withdrew. On her first step, she was there, by her second, she'd disappeared. It had all happened so quickly that Ophelia, dazed, hadn't even had time to stand up.

"You should have told me that she was working in your service. I took her for an enemy. I assume it was her, your 'source'?"

"I employed that Invisible to keep an eye on you. Her clan is among those whose case I will soon be pleading. I obtained an exceptional dispensation so she could come and go in town entirely legally."

Ophelia reflected that if those disgraced clans did get their noble entitlements back, it would mean fun times ahead at the court. In the meantime, they would make very good hunters.

"She's been protecting me for weeks," she said, vainly searching for the Invisible, "and we haven't even been introduced. What's her name?"

"Vladislava," Thorn replied, seeming to find the question most peculiar.

"She's efficient, but she doesn't pass unnoticed. For an Invisible, I mean."

"She doesn't need to. Her presence by your side is intended to be a deterrent."

"I don't quite understand what just happened," Ophelia murmured, her voice strained. "Your cousins . . . they were after your memory?"

Thorn's mouth puckered in annoyance. "The Chroniclers can appropriate and absorb memories. Some of them are even capable of falsifying them."

"You included?"

"I don't practice it, but I do know how to protect myself from such intrusions. Playing with others' memories is not only reprehensible, it's also a threat to mental stability."

Ophelia noticed that Thorn had allowed himself a moment's thought to choose his words. He was making a concerted effort to watch the costumed parade, with its brass-band music filling the air, as if this popular spectacle was a mass of problems all of its own.

"Right, let me put it another way," said Ophelia, fiddling with her glasses. "My real question was: have you effectively inherited your mother's memories, and are those memories really worth killing one another over?"

Thorn swatted a mosquito on his neck with an impatient slap. "I promised you the whole truth, and nothing but the truth," he grumbled, "on the one condition that it directly concerns you. You already know much more than you should."

Ophelia had got used to seeing Thorn as an ambitious and calculating man, but she had to bow before the evidence: he was undoubtedly the least corrupt official of the entire magistrature. Maybe he had his reasons—deep and tortuous reasons—for defending the cause of the disgraced, but, from what Ophelia could deduce, their dossier was more of a poisoned chalice. Thorn was risking his life to represent people who weren't part of his family, had no influence in high places, and would increase the number of his already considerable enemies. Did he think that, if he was successful, and once their position at court was secure, the rehabilitated disgraced would remember his help and do the same for him? If Ophelia wasn't naïve enough to believe that, he was certainly even less so.

No, quite clearly, however much she considered the question from every angle, this strength that constantly electrified Thorn's large body looked for all the world like a sense of duty.

Ophelia rubbed her arms against each other, chilled by the wind, the drizzle, and a cold feeling from within. Her anger, in leaving her, had given way to a strange melancholy. "That cousin can't know you very well to see me as your weakness. The truth is that you never rely on anyone."

Thorn immediately lost interest in the costumed parade and lowered his bird-of-prey look at Ophelia.

"You want to solve every problem on your own," she continued in a choked voice, "even if it means using people like chess pieces, even if it means making yourself hated by the whole world."

"And you, do you still hate me?"

"I don't think so. Not anymore."

"Good," Thorn grunted between his teeth. "Because I've never made such an effort not to be hated by someone."

Ophelia had barely listened to him, but it wasn't intentional. On the other side of the costumed parade, beyond the sprays of confetti and streamers, Hector had embarked on climbing a large metal structure. Fox was gesticulating most disapprovingly at him.

"It's time we went back," Ophelia said, anxiously. "We've already missed the midday boat; my mother will have the worst reception in store for us."

She breathed a sigh of relief when Hector landed on the sand after a final somersault. Then she noticed that Thorn was also watching him with great concentration, as though finally seeing this young brother-in-law in the flesh, and no longer as an abstract genealogical concept. His grey eyes were glittering strangely under the changing light of the sky, in a curious mix of rancor and curiosity.

"These little family tiffs," he said in a distant voice, "I really know nothing about them."

At that moment, Ophelia knew why he had put off coming to Opal Sands for so long. Thorn's daily life was made up of hypocrisy, fraud, blackmail, and treachery; around a family such as Ophelia's, he lost his bearings. Spurred by an uncontrollable impulse, Ophelia tugged on Thorn's big, black sleeve. "Come back with us."

If she was the first to be surprised by her own familiarity, it didn't compare to the reaction of Thorn, who lost all his composure. He suddenly seemed very awkward, with his briefcase dangling from his arm, and his other hand, prompted by an entrenched habit, groping in the lining of his coat for the fob watch that wasn't there, and for a good reason: it was in Ophelia's pocket.

"Now? But I have . . . I must go . . . My appointments."

Ophelia bit the inside of her mouth. It really was only at the Carnival Caravan that she would ever witness Thorn stammering like this, with confetti, blown by the wind, in his tousled hair.

"Stay at least for lunch," she suggested. "See it as a diplomatic duty, if your professional conscience really has to be eased."

Thorn's lips once again convulsed in that way that Ophelia couldn't quite interpret. When he finally pulled his hand out of his coat, it was obviously not his watch he was clutching, but a bunch of keys. "As it's a diplomatic duty," he said, stiffly, "I presume that I can use the Treasury's master key. There's a Compass Rose at the customs post at the entrance to Asgard. Go and get your brother."

Satisfied, Ophelia agreed to do so.

"I promise you it won't be as awful as you think it will be."

VERTIGO

As she carefully sipped the water in her glass, Ophelia reflected that she should avoid making rash promises.

Family meals were normally very animated. Literally: the salt shakers hopped from one plate to the next; the carafe stoppers quivered with impatience; and there was nearly always a duel between spoons before dessert was done. If the staff had initially been rather shocked at the way the Animists inflicted their tricks on the objects in the hotel, now it no longer surprised them. They had even taken a shine to these guests who could instantly repair the establishment's jammed locks and broken clocks.

Today, however, the diners and utensils were so quiet that Ophelia felt as if all she could hear, above the distant rumble of the sea, were the mosquitoes bouncing off the dining-room windows with an electrical crackling sound.

Ophelia cautiously considered her mother's red form, on the other side of the crystal carafe; her silence didn't bode well . . . no better, at any rate, than would a saucepan forgotten on the stove. Her little sisters nudged each other as soon as one of them stared, goggle-eyed, at Thorn for too long. Her great-uncle, in contrast, made no bones about looking hard and incessantly at him, while crumbling his flatbread, piece after piece, as though it were a body he were metaphorically dismembering. Cousins, uncles, and aunts exchanged meaningful looks among themselves, as they downed their lemming stew as discreetly as possible. Even the Rapporteur kept mum under her lampshade hat, but her weather vane kept pointing its stork's beak in the direction of the Treasurer.

Ophelia also turned her eyes in the direction of Thorn, sitting at the end of the table. Sitting? *Contorted* would have been the right word. The chair was far too small for him, and he was struggling to handle his cutlery without his elbows poking his closest neighbors' eyes out. He chewed every morsel with barely concealed disgust, as if the very act of eating was an ordeal. At regular intervals, he took a handkerchief out from his uniform, dabbed the corner of his mouth, wiped the handles of his fork and knife, repositioned his cutlery, aiming for perfect symmetry, refolded his handkerchief neatly, and put it back in its place. At no point did it enter his mind to use a hotel napkin.

Ophelia stifled a sigh. Thorn had a very personal conception of what it was to produce a good impression. Having made his presence long desired, he would have done well to offer his apologies to his future in-laws, and to address at least a few friendly words to them. One had to know him to understand that the simple act of sitting here, at this table, was the best demonstration of respect he was capable of.

"The circus was fun," Ophelia stammered, turning to Hector. "Have you shown your photographs?"

Her little brother raised his eyebrows under his bowl-cut hair, his mouth full. "Why'd I chow them? They're all chpoilt becauch of the echos."

The conversation collapsed like a soufflé. Ophelia glanced regretfully at the two empty chairs beside her. Berenilde was still at her mother's bedside, and Aunt Rosaline had gone to the sanitarium to bring her some clean linen. They alone could have helped Thorn to present himself under his least unfavorable light, or, at least, made the air breathable.

"Nine and four." On both sides of the table, all heads slowly turned, in a synchronized movement, forks suspended in mid-air. Thorn's sepulchral voice had risen out of the silence, to general amazement.

"Could you repeat that, Mr. Thorn?"

"Nine," he said, without lifting his nose from his plate. "That is the number of our family properties. They are castles, in the main, almost all of excellent construction. Three of them are to be found in Citaceleste, and I have designated one for your daughter, as a wedding present." Thorn finally raised his half-closed eyes, like two silver slits, but he turned them only to Ophelia's mother. "I suggest you visit our properties. And if you find souvenirs within that you would like to take back to Anima," he added, in a voice devoid of warmth, "help yourselves as you please."

Ophelia was staring so wide-eyed that her glasses almost fell off her nose. Why, of all the possible and conceivable subjects of conversation, was that the one Thorn had chosen?

The effect this produced on Ophelia's family wasn't long in coming. Sickened, some pushed away their plates; others removed their napkins; the great-uncle crushed what remained of his flatbread; and the youngest, realizing that hostilities had been declared, made horrible faces at Thorn. Only Agatha, her baby in her arms, had begun to tremble with excitement the moment the word "castle" had been uttered. No one dared to speak, however. All faces were now turned to Ophelia's parents, who alone had that right. Her father had turned pale and shrunk into his chair, whereas her mother had done quite the opposite: she had visibly swelled up and reddened.

"Mr. Thorn," she said, articulating the name as if it hurt

her teeth, "are you now attempting to *buy* our indulgence, as I believe to be the case?"

"Yes."

Thorn swiveled his metallic gaze at every guest, drawing nervous grimaces from some, frowns from others. The one person he was careful to avoid was Ophelia, and yet she was sparing no effort to attract his attention and silently implore him to leave it there.

"I will never make the ideal son-in-law," he continued, in the neutral tone of a report, "and I am not counting on my charm to persuade you of the contrary. These properties are the only assets I can boast to you about."

"And that's it?" rebuked the great-uncle, flushed with anger under his moustache. "That's really all you've got to say to us? Not looking for a tiff, are we?"

"Listen to me," Ophelia intervened. "I would like to . . ."

"No," Thorn interrupted her, holding, without blinking, her great-uncle's glare down the length of the table between them. "That is not all I have to say. Nine was my first argument to meet your approval. Four is the second."

"Four what, Mr. Thorn?"

Ophelia stared at her father as if he had just finally become interesting. He had expressed himself in an uncertain voice, as he did every time he spoke, but he had done so rising from his chair, pressing both hands to the table, and boring his eyes into Thorn's. The extreme solemnity he was demonstrating right now almost made one forget his balding head and bland features.

"Four days," replied Thorn, attacking a new slice of tart with his knife. "That's the time span separating us from the wedding. During this period of time, no matter how much my attitude towards your daughter shocks you or displeases you, I would ask you not to get involved."

"Thorn, perhaps you shouldn't . . ." Once again, Ophelia didn't have time to finish her sentence. Like a saucepan that's come to the boil, her mother exploded in a spectacular flurry of dress and jewelry. "I get involved in the lives of my children however I see fit! I can't oppose this marriage," she conceded, glancing at the Rapporteur, whose weather vane had started turning again. "But you're more chilling than a block of ice, and I'm not afraid to tell you that to your face."

"Four days," insisted Thorn, without raising his voice. "After the wedding, you can ask your daughter to visit you on Anima as often and for as long as you see fit."

At these words, Ophelia's mother's complexion returned to normal, her father sat back down in his chair, her uncles and aunts exchanged questioning glances. As for Ophelia, she couldn't believe her ears.

"It seems to me," she said, trying to be patient, "that I could at least . . ."

"I have your word?" her mother cut in. "I will be able to summon my daughter back home as often as I like?"

It was too much for Ophelia. She was starting to find the way they all talked about her as if she weren't there intolerable. She had faced the audience at the Optical Theatre dozens of times, and yet she was incapable of making herself heard by her own family! She breathed in as deeply as her blocked nose allowed, determined to assert herself, but Thorn's irrevocable reply deflated her lungs:

"I promise that you will."

"You will never go against my wishes?" Ophelia's mother had underlined each syllable by hammering the tablecloth with her index finger; the pepper shaker, somewhat panicked, wisely distanced itself in a few jumps.

"No," said Thorn. "I will never go against them." His eyes then sliced through the air like a blade to fix themselves on to Ophelia's glasses. Parents, grandmothers, brother, sisters, uncles, aunts, and cousins all scraped their chairs as they, in turn, swiveled around to look at her.

"If my opinion still interests you," Ophelia said, annoyed, "I think that . . ."

"You're too obliging, Mr. Thorn." This time, it was the Rapporteur who had cut her short. She had spoken with an indulgent smile, cup of tea in hand, her metal stork nodding its beak in agreement on the crown of her hat. "It's most honorable of you to want to reassure us," she continued. "But you shouldn't be making such promises to us. Our little Ophelia's place is right here, by your side. If you allow her too much freedom, she'll never honor her duties to you and will make a mockery of this diplomatic alliance."

Thorn snorted disdainfully. His eyes went slowly from Ophelia to her mother, without stopping at the Rapporteur's weather vane, which was pointing its beak at him.

"To sum up the situation," he said clearly, pressing his long fingers together, "I offer you my most profitable possession, my worldly goods, and I spare you from my least attractive possession, my company. In exchange, I ask for these four days, during which you will not interfere in my affairs."

The Rapporteur was no longer smiling, frightfully offended at having been ignored. As for Ophelia's mother, she contorted every feature on her face. She screwed up her eyes, knitted her brows, tightened her lips in such an effort of concentration, searching over and over for any jiggery-pokery, that the pins in her enormous bun shook to the rhythm of her thoughts.

Her muscles finally relaxed into a triumphant smile. "I would love a little more dessert. Another slice of tart, Mr. Thorn?"

In the cable car, Ophelia silently stared at Thorn over her darkened glasses. Having folded himself up as best he could on the opposite bench, his briefcase on his knees, he said nothing either. Agatha took it upon herself to make conversation on their behalf for the duration of their ascent:

"Nine castles, that's ex-traor-dinary! There's not a single castle on Anima, is there, sis? Just little buildings that are temperamental and, at best, per-fect-ly boring. Whoa, our cabin's creaking a lot, don't you think? I'm looking forward to seeing something grand at last, Mr. Thorn! I've been all over Opal Sands—that grey sea, those sinister rocks, all those factories, it's so lu-gu-brious . . . Swings alive, aren't we swaying rather too much? The fact is, I don't understand why your aunt is forcing us to stay here so long, Mr. Thorn. I'd so love to meet some real society ladies, like the ambassador's sisters. They're so beautiful, so graceful, so de-li-cate! A little strange, admittedly. I passed them this morning on the walkway, and wondered whether they hadn't overdone it with the vapors: they looked to-tally washed out. Ah, phew, we've arrived!"

Agatha's prattling accompanied Thorn and Ophelia right up to the cable car's landing stage, and rang out through all the brick arcades of the Opal Sands railway station. It died on her lips when, instead of going down to the platforms, Thorn plunged into a very drafty tunnel.

"Where are we going?" stammered Agatha, holding on to her feathered hat. "Isn't Mr. Thorn taking the train? He's surely not walking home, is he?"

"He has a private location outside the station, up on the wall," Ophelia replied. "That's how we returned from the circus, earlier."

"A location? On the wall? I . . . I don't understand."

"As Treasurer, Thorn possesses special keys. Well, the keys aren't special in themselves, but they allow access to the Compass Roses, and the Compass Roses, you see, are kinds of shortcuts. Although, shortcuts . . . One obviously mustn't take a wrong turn in the maze of doors."

From the way her sister was staring, wide-eyed, Ophelia knew she'd completely confused her with her explanations. "The location's not far," she summed up, simply.

Agatha let out a small, terrified cry while clutching her hat with both hands. The tunnel had just opened onto a rampart wall, protected by a double row of crenellations and adorned with statues too eroded still to bear any resemblance to human beings. If the width of the path was perfectly comfortable for walking, the view was certainly much less so.

To the right, the wall looked down upon the shore of Opal Sands from so high up that one could admire every trace of foam on the silvery surface of the sea. The thermal resort looked like a small town-planning model, and its hotel, standing in the distance on its rocky headland, had something of the miniature factory about it. This vista alone would have been enough to give one vertigo, but what lay on the other side of the wall was even more spectacular. To the left, nothing existed of the world but vapor. The clouds were forever building up and breaking up, in perpetual motion. Through their fluctuating filigrees, they occasionally allowed one to see slivers of sky, a flash of sun, but never, absolutely never, the ground. This is where the ark ended, this is where the void began. Even the most desperately suicidal wouldn't have thrown themselves from that side of the wall.

Thorn advanced between these two infinities as indifferently as along the pavement of an avenue. He had wasted no time—already all one could see of him was a distant black coat flapping like a flag in the wind. He ended up half-turning, however, when he realized that there was no longer anyone following him.

"I just can't," Agatha declared, flatly. "Impossible. Let's say goodbye to Mr. Thorn from here."

"He's just signed a peace treaty with Mommy," countered Ophelia, "it wouldn't be very diplomatic." She indicated the stone projection of a sentry box, further along the wall, to show her sister where they were aiming for.

"I just can't," repeated Agatha, leaning against the wall of the tunnel, as if the whole world had become unstable. "The cable car, just about. But that, it's beyond me."

"Stay here, I won't be long. I'll accompany Thorn and then be back—you'll be able to see me the whole time."

"I . . . Alright. You won't tell Mommy that I left you alone together, will you? You know what a stickler she is for principles."

"Promise."

Thrown off balance by the wind buffeting her dress, Ophelia had the impression, as she caught up with Thorn, of walking along a stone tidal wave that would split the universe in two. Even for her, who didn't suffer from vertigo, the experience made quite an impression.

Thorn set off again as soon as Ophelia was by his side, but at a less hurried pace this time. "I now understand better why, of all the possible chaperones, you picked that chatterbox." There was an almost admiring note in his voice, but Ophelia, for her part, didn't feel proud of herself. She'd counted on her sister's fear of the void, which was pretty meanly manipulative.

"I had something to ask of you," she said, "and I wanted to do so in private."

"What, then?"

"An apology."

Hindered by gusts of wind, Ophelia stuffed as much hair as possible under her scarf, and did her best to ignore the sidelong look Thorn shot down at her. She had tried to instill

278

hardness into her words, to rekindle the embers of a justified and deserved anger, but she hadn't succeeded. The strange melancholy that had swept over her on the beach at Asgard wouldn't leave her.

"Why would I apologize? You asked me for a home, I offer you a castle. I have kept all my promises to you."

"I'm talking about my parents. You were supposed to reassure them. All you had to do was make a good impression for an hour, Thorn. One small hour. Instead, you clinch a deal with my mother."

"And she is reassured."

"Reassured? She's exultant, yes. You've given her total control over my life."

"I promised her that I wouldn't oppose her will. That promise binds only me."

Ophelia gave herself a moment to think, long enough to do a few steps along the wall's path, and she had to admit that Thorn had indeed chosen his terms carefully during the meal. Curiously, that didn't make her feel any better. So, the choice of staying or leaving was down to her, and her alone? It just couldn't be that simple.

"Say I take you at your word," she muttered. "Say I leave the Pole straight after the Ceremony of the Gift, and I never return. That would make you the most ridiculous of husbands."

"First, I am going to see to it that you survive until our marriage," Thorn grumbled, sullenly. "You will pass your Animism on to me, I will free you from your conjugal obligations, we will be even. What you decide to do next will be your business."

Ophelia sensed that he was going to add something else, but he was interrupted by successive explosions, cutting through the moaning of the wind. In the distance, beyond the seashore and the industrial quarters, where the wall ran along the boreal forest, two plumes of smoke were rising from the crenellations. It was never reassuring to hear the wall's cannons. It usually meant that a Beast was getting too close to the town. A few days earlier, a giant wolverine had charged at the ramparts; it had taken much cannon fire to rout it. Its growling had been so loud, it could be heard as far away as the baths. The staff and bathers might not have been concerned, being used to nature's outbursts, but it had been a pretty shocking experience for Ophelia's family. Life in the Pole was like that: wherever one went, whatever one did, danger was part of daily life.

And yet, Ophelia reflected, she didn't hate it that much, that life.

"What about the diplomatic alliance? You and Berenilde were forever waving that argument in my face to keep me quiet. Do you think Mr. Farouk will accept it, if I spend my time at the other end of the world?"

"He will forget you, as long as he doesn't have you continually in front of him," asserted Thorn. "All that counts is his Book, and the Book, that's . . . "

"Your business, I know." With her cold returning, Ophelia noisily blew her nose, before summoning up a serious tone. "You have only given yourself three months for tackling this reading," she reminded him. "Do you really think you can do it without anyone to teach you how to master your new power? Stop wanting to carry the whole world on your shoulders."

Ophelia suddenly became intensely interested in the immense swirls of clouds, but out of the corner of her eye, she could tell how deeply perplexed Thorn was.

"What happened to the outer wall, over there?" she asked. Leaning on the parapet, Ophelia indicated a distant part of the wall, barely visible to the naked eye in the silvery mist.

The fortifications followed the outline of the edge of the ark, between a sea of water and a sea of clouds, but their course seemed to stop suddenly at the edge of the void, picking up again a bit further along. This gave the impression that there was a large hole full of clouds in the middle of the scenery.

"It collapsed," said Thorn, who was looking much more attentively at her than at the wall in question. "A section of land fell away at that spot, four years ago."

Ophelia immediately pulled away from the parapet, as though it threatened to crumble suddenly under her weight. "A collapse?" she repeated, incredulous. "Of that size?"

"That one wasn't that big," Thorn corrected. "A section several miles long broke away from a minor ark of Heliopolis, two years ago. Don't you ever read the interfamilial newspapers?"

Ophelia shook her head. She'd always thought of the arks as solid and unchanging little planets. It came as a shock to discover that whole pieces could fall away into the void, from one day to the next. "We're living in a *bizarrre* set-up, y'know," her great-uncle had said.

As their conversation suddenly came back to her, Ophelia felt herself being swept up in a whirlwind of questions. Was the Rupture of the world really over? What alone had caused it? One of those wars that the Doyennes just didn't want to hear about anymore? Had the family spirits known something important on the subject before forgetting it? Did their Books contain information about what had happened? And what if it was that very truth that disturbed certain people?

Ophelia was distracted from all her questions by the rain. A drop fell on her forehead, another on her nose, and in a few seconds a cold downpour was pounding the whole wall.

"We're living in a truly enigmatic world," she said, shielding her glasses with her hand. "I've been reading all sorts of objects for years, and yet I feel as if I know nothing. An Earth

shattered to pieces. Deliberately forgetful family spirits. Indecipherable Books. You."

A glimmer crossed Thorn's eyes, a muscle flexed along his
jaw, and in a flash, Ophelia was certain that he was finally
going to confide in her. Just as he was ungritting his teeth,
a new explosion rose in the distance—the gunners must be
tackling a particularly obstinate Beast—and that interruption
seemed to bring Thorn back to reality. He protected his briefcase under his big, black coat.

"Let's get a move on," he said, gruffly. "I can't linger any
longer and you are going to catch cold again." As Thorn headed
for the sentry box, its old stones and bulbous roof outlined
against the cloudy backdrop of the sky, Ophelia was more
disturbed than ever by the lonesome aura that surrounded
him, from head to foot. "Help Thorn," Berenilde had implored
her. How was she supposed to accomplish that feat with such
a stubborn individual?

Ophelia signaled to Agatha to hold on, as she was making
great exasperated gestures at her from the station tunnel; seen
from here, through the rain, her sister was reduced to just
waves of white dress and red hair. Ophelia then ran to join
Thorn under the canopy of the sentry box. It was only a relative shelter: the gaps between the slates let water seep through,
and the proximity to the void created a stronger draft here
than elsewhere.

"When will you return?" she asked.

"I still have many inspections to carry out in the provinces."

With her glasses being splashed from all directions, Ophelia
could now only make Thorn out as a large, blurred shadow.
His voice seemed to her to have a more cavernous ring than
usual, and that wasn't just due to the echoing acoustics of the
sentry box.

"When would you like me to return?"

"Me?" asked Ophelia, astonished; she hadn't expected him to ask her for her opinion. "I suppose it depends mainly on your duties. Just try not to forget the wedding."

It was said in jest, obviously, but Thorn responded with his unfailing seriousness: "I never forget anything."

"You've just reminded me," Ophelia exclaimed, after wiping her glasses, "I forgot to inform you of your aunt's latest whim: Berenilde has asked me to be her child's godmother."

Thorn arched his brows, and his unsightly scar moved with them. "That's far from a whim. You are now part of the family."

Ophelia's stomach lurched. Why on earth make such a declaration with such solemnity?

"That request doesn't surprise me," Thorn continued. "My aunt is going to bring Farouk's direct descendant into the world. Those close to this child will be assured a choice position at court. It's also my position she's reinforcing, at the same time."

Ophelia suddenly realized that, had Archibald not imposed himself as godfather by force, that role would have probably been Thorn's.

"That said, my opinion is that you should decline the offer," he added, after consideration. "Your place isn't, and has never been, at court."

My place is wherever I have chosen to be, Ophelia almost retorted, with some annoyance, but she heard herself reply: "I met your mother yesterday."

Ophelia instantly wondered what had come over her. It was neither the place nor the time to tackle the subject, but she had a feeling that that taboo was the central cog within Thorn's entire mechanism. If Ophelia managed to grasp the depth of the bond that attached him to his mother, she might finally understand him. And perhaps even help him.

"Berenilde told me what happened to her," she continued, less confidently as she saw Thorn totally cloud over. "I was wondering . . . If you really inherited her memory before her Mutilation, might it be possible for you to . . . well . . . to give it back to her? I don't mean to imply that she deserves an affectionate gesture from you," she hastened to clarify, as Thorn's face visibly hardened. "I know that your mother didn't have a single one for you. It was mainly that I felt that her memory was an additional burden."

"You know nothing."

Thorn had said these three words with icy composure. Electricity flickered visibly all around him; his claws were ready, at the end of his nerves, as sharp as his razor-blade eyes. This hostile reaction had the same effect on Ophelia as the rain that continued to stream over her head through the cracks in the canopy.

"Indeed," she admitted between her teeth. "I know nothing."

There was, however, something that she was beginning to understand. Thorn's mother had been close to Farouk and she was in possession of a secret; wasn't it because of this, and this alone, that Thorn wanted to decipher the Book? The link between these two elements seemed obvious.

Thorn took out the Treasury keys, and after inspecting them, inserted one into the sentry-box lock. The interior of the place was identical to all the Compass Roses that Ophelia knew: a circular room consisting almost entirely of doors, each one leading to a faraway destination. The Compass Roses often led to other Compass Roses, which offered a wide range of options for moving around.

"Do not leave the hotel anymore," ordered Thorn. "Be careful about the people you frequent, the food you swallow, and the air you breathe until my return. The Invisible is looking out for your safety, avoid making her task more difficult. If you follow my recommendations to the letter, nothing will happen to you."

Ophelia glanced behind her, wondering whether Vladislava was, at that very moment, on the wall with them, but she saw nothing but the thick curtain of rain. She shivered all over as she felt the wind flattening her soaked clothes. Now that she could no longer make out either her sister or the abyss, she almost had vertigo.

"Wait," muttered Ophelia, as she took the fob watch out of her coat pocket. "Before you go, I would like to return this to you. You need it more than me, and, in any case, I won't read it. I've chosen to trust you—you, not your watch."

These words would certainly have been more effective had Ophelia's voice not left her for the last few. She'd just noticed that the second hand wasn't moving anymore.

"I . . . I don't understand," she stammered, as Thorn closed his fist around the watch with a strained expression. "I wound it again this morning . . . A grain of sand must have got into the works." Ophelia felt a total idiot. Her intention had been to mollify him, not make him really angry. "My great-uncle can heal any object," she said, ineptly. "All things considered, you should leave it with me a little longer."

Thorn leant over, in a sustained vertebral extension, but he didn't return the watch to her. Instead, he placed his mouth on hers.

Ophelia stared wide-eyed, her breath taken away. It was a totally unexpected kiss that left her in a state of stupor. She was incapable of thought, but, conversely, sensed all surrounding stimuli with a new acuity: the lapping of the rain on the stones, the wind caught in her dress, her glasses digging into her skin, Thorn's wet hair against his forehead, the clumsy pressing of his lips. And suddenly, as she finally became aware of what was happening, Ophelia was gripped by ferocious vertigo. A surge of panic rose up inside her and her hand flew out of its own accord.

It was the first time Ophelia had slapped a man, and although her gesture had been more instinctive than aggressive, she was shocked by her own reaction. Thorn, however, appeared to be much less so. He straightened up, stiffly, while pensively rubbing his cheek and looking away, as if he had prepared himself for this eventuality from the start.

"Listen," she stammered, after an embarrassed silence. "I didn't want . . . You shouldn't have . . ."

"I had my doubts," Thorn interrupted her, still looking away. "You have dispelled them."

Ophelia did her best to control the frantic jerking of her scarf. Had she really behaved in a way that could be misleading? Mortified, she saw Thorn's big body bending to pass through the sentry-box door, with not a backward glance.

"I will do everything possible so that you survive until the wedding," he promised her for the second time. "When it is all over, return home with your family. Ridicule has never killed me."

With these words, he closed the door behind him, and the loud clicking indicated that he had double locked it. With ears burning and glasses crimson, Ophelia stared at the faded letters on the old wooden panel—"STAFF ONLY"—as if Thorn might, at any moment, retrace his steps, take back his kiss, and leave his fob watch with her, as she'd suggested in the first place. Agatha's loud, hysterical cries interrupted her thoughts:

"Hey! Hey! Sis! Come back im-me-diate-ly!"

Ophelia thought at first that Agatha had achieved the improbable feat of seeing the whole scene despite the distance and the rain. She finally understood that something else was happening, as she went back along the rampart wall. Her sister was indicating the surroundings with overexcited gestures, which was surprising considering her fear of the void, and the cannons on the wall boomed for the third time. Ophelia leaned over the parapet. The downpour had stopped as suddenly as it had started, and already the sun was tearing through the clouds to spread its light over the salt marshes of Opal Sands. There was unusual activity in the streets, and, for a moment, Ophelia feared a wild animal had got into the town.

She blanched when she looked up at the horizon and saw, above the sea, between two moving clouds, a gigantic and chaotic interlacing of turrets, flying buttresses, and chimney stacks. It wasn't the arrival of a Beast that the gunners were announcing; it was that of the Citaceleste.

"Madam Vladislava, are you here with me?" Ophelia called out.

"Yes, miss," a slightly distant voice, with that characteristic military ring, finally replied.

Right now, Ophelia could almost detect the presence of a red shadow out of the corner of her eye, but she saw no one when she turned her head. Maybe later she would be embarrassed at the thought that this Invisible had witnessed what had happened between Thorn and herself, but right now, there was something more urgent.

"Could you have Thorn alerted that something unexpected has occurred?"

"Yes, miss."

FRAGMENT: THIRD REPRISE

God could be so cruel in his indifference, he horrified me. God knew how to show his gentle side, too, and I loved him as I've loved no one else.

"Why?"

This memory starts with that question. As he concentrates on it, and his memory supplements the "why" with a tone of voice and a silhouette that becomes increasingly defined against the light, he understands that it is being said by Artemis. She has changed a good deal since the last memory; several years must have passed by. She no longer wears glasses, her voice has deepened, and her body, despite the incongruous masculine clothes she wears, is definitely that of an adolescent girl going through puberty. A very tall adolescent: her height and build are way beyond normal. Artemis is sitting on a window ledge that's a bit narrow for her; her Animism is turning a terrestrial globe that's balanced on her knees. The sun lights up her serious profile and her long red plait.

"Why are you asking me why?" His voice has also changed. It is even deeper than that of Artemis, as if his rib cage had reached extraordinary proportions.

"Why are all the caskets you give me empty?" Artemis

clarified. "Every time I do you a favor, you give me one, and it's empty. If you're going to give a present, do it properly."

She explains that to him in a tone devoid of reproach. It sounds more like advice from big sister to little brother. She continues to make the globe turn on its axis without needing to touch it. A round world, still in one piece. The world at that time?

"I think caskets make an ideal present," he hears himself reply, after a moment of silence. "If there was something inside them, how likely is it to be exactly what you were hoping to find there? You would inevitably be disappointed. I give you the container, you put in the contents you want."

As he is saying these words, he knows that that's not the only reason. The truth is that he's totally lacking in imagination. Sometimes he feels as empty as the caskets he gives his sister.

"I wonder where I will go and live when I reach adulthood," Artemis says, scanning her globe without enthusiasm. "If it were possible, I'd choose the stars. Ironic, no? My power only works on artificial matter, and I'm only interested in the celestial world. Who knows, the stars might be as disappointing as your empty caskets. The only way of being certain," she added, pensively, "would be to learn to know them better. When I'm an adult, I'll start by selecting a mountain on which I'll have them build the best observatory in the world. And you?"

Him? He's content just to stare at Artemis's globe without replying. He doesn't know. He doesn't relish at all the prospect of having to leave home one day, like when he was made to do his apprenticeship among the humans.

"You should practice like the others, instead of lazing about," Artemis suddenly declared, ceasing to make her globe turn. "You're still far from mastering your power, Odin."

The others? His angle of vision changes direction, returning to its starting point, before Artemis had asked him, "Why?", and he notices that he's got his face partly buried in his sleeves. He's slumped over a table, arms folded in front of him. Between the parted curtains of his white hair, there's just fog, a haziness due to the failing of his memory. The observer lurking deep inside him, that awareness that, today, is trying to piece together the puzzle of the past, keeps replaying that turning of Artemis's eyes towards "the others," from the window to the rest of the room, in the hope of grasping a detail, of triggering something in his mind that would enable him to recreate the scene.

Lead soldiers.

Yes, he can see them lined up on the neighboring table. The lead soldiers aren't his; they belong to Midas, his brother. Midas is busy attempting transmutation, squinting with all his might at his colonel to turn him into gold. For the moment, he looks more like copper.

Okay: to his left there's Artemis and her globe; to his right, Midas and his lead soldiers. And then?

Pastel crayons. They are flying through the air, but in no disorderly way . . . Like miniature satellites, these colored sticks are orbiting his other brother, Uranus, the artist of the family, sitting a bit further along the table.

Okay: to his left, there's Artemis and her globe; to his right, Midas and his lead soldiers; in front of him, there's Uranus and his pastels. And then?

The breadth of his vision expands the more he recaptures the scene. He can make out the silhouettes of the twins, Helen and Pollux, doing acoustic experiments with a tuning fork, and also that of Venus, trying to charm a beetle that glitters like a jewel in the sunlight. Where are they, all of them? Beyond the tables and the sunlit windows, he can't remember.

All those big, awkward adolescents, busy doing their

practical work like model students, are they aware that one day they will be the kings and queens of the world, a world that will no longer bear any resemblance to the globe resting on Artemis's knees?

He wonders this while his eyes try to reach the shadow looming right at the back of the room, where the fog of his memory still hasn't lifted.

Who is God? What does God want? What does God look like?

All of his memories gravitate around this central character, and yet none of them can put a face to him. But the emotion choking him when, as now, he observes God from his table, from his folded arms, through the parting of his hair, is only too clear.

Fear.

He doesn't understand, he has never understood, what God expects of him. For his brothers and sisters, everything seems so simple! They accept their powers, they follow every instruction, they do what is written in their Books without asking themselves any questions. He, Odin, hasn't got a clue. He is scared of becoming what God expects of him, and he is also scared of never becoming it. These are emotions that are far too complex for him.

The memory is suddenly hit by turbulence. It comes from a shudder coursing through his body. God has just begun to move and is coming towards him. He's more afraid of him than ever, so why does God remain merely a shapeless shadow? He absolutely must remember him, it's essential.

God advances very slowly between the tables—unless this slowness is memory playing tricks. God goes past Helen's and Pollux's acoustic experiments, Venus's beetle, Uranus's pastels, Midas's lead soldiers. God is coming for him, and him alone. God has seen that he doesn't work on his power like the others do. God is disappointed. God is going to take back his Book. God is going to disown him and throw him out of the house.

God raises his hand.

The hand of God: it's the first physical manifestation of him that he manages to remember. This character, for whom he feels such intense emotions, does he really have a hand that's so small and ordinary?

He thinks God's hand is coming down to hit him, but it ruffles his hair, teasingly.

And as God moves off without a word, and still without a distinct form, he, himself, is filled with a searing heat. Fear has been replaced by boundless love. A truth dawns on him, the only one that matters in the whole world: today, again, he can remain at home with God and the others.

The memory ends here.

Nota bene: "Try your dears." Who said these words and what do they mean?

THE ABSENTEES

If the Citaceleste gave the illusion of being immobile, like an architectural beehive suspended in the middle of the clouds, in reality it was continually moving. Partly driven by the wind, partly by thousands of propellers, in the main, it moved around randomly. Right now, the great orbiting city was already plunging the industrial quarters of Opal Sands in darkness. With her nose pressed to the window of the cable car slowly descending towards the hotel, Ophelia didn't take her eyes off it, clinging to the small hope that the capital's presence here was pure chance, and a headwind would soon propel it northwards.

"For pity's sake," groaned Agatha, "don't tell me the court is right up there!"

"You see the highest tower," said Ophelia, "it's there."

"That's not possible! First, that in-ter-min-able journey in the airship, then the train on the high wall, the walks along the cliffs, the ups and downs in cable car, and now that? I'm starting to miss our little valley . . . Gadzooks!" Agatha suddenly cried, slapping her lacy glove on the cable car window. "People are falling from the city!"

She pointed at a large, gleaming sleigh that was sliding through the air, pulled by reindeer.

"They're not falling," Ophelia reassured her. "The Citaceleste is served by highly efficient airstreams."

"Oh, the sleigh has landed right in front of our hotel!" exclaimed Agatha. "Men are getting off. Their uniforms are mag-ni-fi-cent! If only Charles could dress like that, all in white and gold! Are they princes?"

"No," muttered Ophelia, with far less enthusiasm. "They're policemen."

"They haven't come for us, have they?"

They had barely alighted from the cable car when Agatha got her answer. The policemen, who were busy questioning their family, asked Ophelia to get into the big police sleigh, all gilt and fur, that was parked outside the hotel.

"Lord Farouk requests to see you, miss."

"Me? Why?"

"Because he requests to see you," she was told, with impassive courtesy. "Madam Berenilde isn't with you?"

"No, you won't find her here," Ophelia said, staying evasive.

"That's regrettable. Get in, Miss."

Ophelia did her best not to show her anxiety to her family. Had Farouk finally lost his patience? Was he going to ask her to read his Book, for real this time? Thorn was, no doubt, already at the other end of the ark, and Berenilde hadn't yet returned from the sanitarium; just the thought of facing Farouk on her own gave Ophelia a stomach cramp.

She was both surprised and reassured to see that Archibald's sisters were also sitting on the sleigh's fur-draped benches. Neither their hair nor their makeup was done, and their dresses had been laced with unusual carelessness.

"What's going on, Miss Patience?" Ophelia whispered, as she sat opposite the eldest. "What do they want from us?" Patience's only response, totally unexpected from such a refined young girl, was to yawn in her face.

Looking up at the hotel, Ophelia noticed the bulky form of Cunegond, watching them from the window of her room.

She immediately pulled the curtains, as though not wanting to be seen. Nervous illness or not, that Mirage behaved really suspiciously.

"One person only to accompany miss," a policeman announced, in a formal tone, when all the Animists rushed towards the sleigh.

"Me," decided her mother. "Family spirit or not, Mr. Farouk is still a man. If he wants to frequent my daughter, he will first have to ask my permission."

Given the choice, Ophelia would have preferred to be accompanied by Fox. He was leaning on the handrail of the sleigh and bombarding her with documents and recommendations:

"These, here, are your identity papers. You forgot them in the pocket of your other coat, you'll need them. This is the facsimile of sir's, your fiancé's, contract with Lord Farouk, and this your professional license for your reading consultancy, but importantly, only get it out if Lord Farouk raises the subject. I'll take care of alerting Madam Berenilde and your aunt. In the meantime, don't do anything rash, kid."

With one hand holding on to her feathered hat, and all the dignity of a duchess, Ophelia's mother took her place on the bench. A few moments later, as the police sleigh rose in an airstream at the speed of the wind, her hat was swept far away.

After landing on Citaceleste's main square, there followed an interminable ascent in a lift, floor by floor, under police escort. Every time they had to change lifts—a considerable number of times—an officer in a white-and-gold uniform checked their identity papers and then indicated for them to take their places in the next lift. Never had Ophelia seen such security measures, and no one bothered to give them the slightest explanation.

Her mother got a little redder from one floor to next, and kept asking the same outraged question: "What do you want with my daughter?" To which a policeman, unperturbed, offered her the same reply: "Lord Farouk has requested to see her, madam. Her and the young ladies from the embassy. He has also asked for Madam Berenilde, but as she's not here . . ."

"This is no way to behave towards young ladies, all the same!" Ophelia's mother responded, indignantly. "You would have told me, my dear, if you'd done something foolhardy, wouldn't you? Dear, oh dear, if I'd known I'd have gone to the lavatory first. How many more lifts must we take like this?"

Ophelia didn't answer her because she was herself a bit lost. She realized that they were making them take a diverted route, so they went up to Farouk's tower without going through Clairdelune, which she didn't even think possible. The embassy was officially the antechamber of the court, which should have made it unavoidable.

"Cornets alive!" Ophelia's mother suddenly exclaimed, covering her mouth with her varnished fingernails. The lift's golden gate had finally opened onto the fifth floor. Ophelia, who was used to the dazzling light and blazing colors of the court, was herself startled by the change of scene. The sun, which she'd always seen here at its zenith, like a gold needle fixed on midday, was now sinking into the sea, leaving a long fiery trail on the water. The sky was an ever-changing symphony of pinks, blues, purples, and oranges. Even the air felt different, at once gentle, warm and sweet, like the balmiest of summer evenings.

"So is this where you spend your days, my dear?" Ophelia's mother asked, her voice totally transformed, as they followed the policemen along the seafront.

"For the most part, yes."

Ophelia had replied distractedly, totally focused on the floating palace of the Jetty-Promenade, every window of which reflected the sunset at the other end of the seafront.

What on earth was being cooked up here? And why, she wondered, looking at Archibald's sisters, why had they all been summoned together? The seven young girls were moving like sleepwalkers, eyes half-closed, not even looking at this splendid part of the court from which their brother had always kept them away.

"You should have told me!" exclaimed Ophelia's mother. "If I'd known you had access to such a fantabulous place, I wouldn't have given such a hard time to Mr. Thorn! Come on, it looks just like a picture postcard! But what are those people doing up there?"

She had just noticed the men in tailcoats standing on scaffolding along the promenade, facing the sea. They were all making the theatrical gestures of conductors, but they weren't directing any musicians; they were putting the finishing touches to the sunset, extending a streak of cloud here, adding a halo of light there, adjusting the colors again and again. They looked like Impressionist painters using fingers instead of paintbrushes.

"They're Mirage artists, Mom. They're perfecting the scenery." Ophelia could clearly see, in her mother's amazed eyes, that she was considering her marriage under a different light. As for her, she was already missing the authentically grey sky of the real outdoors.

The few amblers that turned round as they went by were courtiers of little influence, which wasn't a good sign: all the powerful ones had gathered in the place where they were heading. *Never set foot in the court ever again*, the writer of the letter had ordered her. If he or she was among the people Ophelia was preparing to face up to, they would know soon enough that she had disobeyed them. She glanced around her, wondering whether Vladislava was still escorting her right now, or whether she had personally undertaken to alert Thorn.

That was the slight inconvenience of an invisible bodyguard: one could never be sure whether they were there or not.

The policemen made them cross the large bridge on piles that led to the Jetty-Promenade. The palace's main rotunda was full of women and of murmuring. Ophelia's mother, who hadn't expected to rub shoulders with the sophisticated outfits of the court ladies, nervously readjusted her enormous bun, as though she felt naked without her hat.

"Good evening, madam, good evening, miss," she greeted every person she passed, concerned to make a good impression. "Is it customary to say good day or good evening?" she whispered, as she got closer to Ophelia. "We're right in the middle of the day, but with that sunset I'm confusing my clock hands, and I get the impression I'm putting all these snoots out of joint."

Ophelia noticed the dangerous glint in the looks being directed at them. "When you go back there, expect to face hell," Cunegond had predicted.

"They never say either good day or good evening," Ophelia explained, passing her arm under her mother's, determined not to lose sight of her. "The servants are the only polite people that you will come across here."

The policemen helped them to make their way through the crinolines, and to cross one of the five main galleries that formed a star around the rotunda. Since Ophelia had first been on the Jetty-Promenade, she'd had many an opportunity to visit its numerous gaming rooms. None of them made her more uneasy than the one they had just been brought into. The Roulette Chamber. It was a room of vast proportions that had the feel of an auction room, with its countless chairs turned towards the rostrum where Farouk sat. Or rather, where Farouk *slouched*. At the sight of this great slumped form, long white hair rippling down to the floor, Ophelia felt her legs shaking; from their last confrontation she'd retained an irrepressible desire to run away.

"So that's him, the famous Mr. Farouk?" asked her mother, somewhat puzzled. "A fine specimen, but he doesn't hold himself very well."

The Roulette Chamber owed its name to a decorative illusion adorning the ceiling with a huge spinning tray divided into numbered sections, around which a white ball was forever rolling. One merely had to look up at this giant roulette wheel to feel as though one were handing one's life over to chance. This wasn't unfounded, since it was here that Farouk arbitrated disputes, gave his verdict, and handed out sentences once a month. His decisions were so contradictory and so random that they were the subject of continuous betting, as though justice were a gamble like any other.

The case being heard concerned the Minister of Centralized Heating, who was in charge of all Citaceleste's stoves. From the witness stand, opposite Farouk's great throne, he was complaining about a document put out by Thorn. "Yes, it so happens that I am the fortunate owner of a coal mine!" he was pleading, in a voice full of injured pride. "Yes, I humbly proposed myself to be the court's official supplier of fuel! So where are these conflicts of interest of which the Treasury accuses me? If my company can serve my ministry, I would be failing in my duty if I refrained from doing so!"

Slumped on his gold and velvet throne, like a child made to sit there against his will, Farouk was reading the problematic paper with a look of profound boredom. His favorites were standing behind his throne, immobile and silent, like diamond statues. The court clerk was typing up all that was being said.

Stuck between her mother and Archibald's sisters, Ophelia twisted around on the bench to take a good look around the room. She knew most of the members of the assembly—they were nearly all magistrates, ministers, and top civil servants. Baron Melchior, today wearing just a plain white suit, was drumming his fat, beringed fingers on the knob of his cane, propped between his legs. No smile lifted his waxed moustache, and his blond hair wasn't slicked back, which was about as unusual as the sobriety of his attire.

Ophelia sighed, disappointed not to see Thorn. She had been surprised, however, to observe that all the rows to the front were occupied by members of the Web. With arms crossed, they were struggling to listen to the plea of the Minister of Centralized Heating. Ophelia frowned on studying them more closely: they were stifling yawns, continually rubbing their eyes, or jumping when they caught themselves sleeping. What, then, was this strange drowsiness that seemed to have taken over the entire family? And why hadn't Archibald been summoned along with his sisters? Did he even know that they were there?

"I can sum up the alternative in a few words, my Lord," the minister said, unctuously, noticing that Farouk was struggling to make a decision. "If you ratify, expect to be very cold next winter."

Farouk nonchalantly tore up the Treasury document. In the Roulette Chamber, blue sandglasses were then exchanged depending on who had won their bet and who had lost it. Ophelia hoped for Thorn's sake that the Family States wouldn't proceed like this.

"Next case!" shouted the court steward with a bang of his gavel.

Ophelia stood up, and then immediately sat down again. It wasn't her turn yet; to her great surprise, it was the Knight that two policemen were leading to the witness stand. Since he was too small for it, he was made to stand on a chair. Once installed, he stared down at his patent shoes while biting his nails. Without his dogs, he looked as vulnerable as any other child.

"What's such a young boy doing here?" asked Ophelia's mother, to disapproving looks from the closest nobles. "He's Hector's age! Poor little boy, it must be terribly daunting!"

Ophelia would have found it tricky to reply to her, but she was spared by Baron Melchior. As soon as he had seen them, in the shadow of their alcove, he had left his chair and tiptoed over to them as discreetly as his portliness permitted.

"How are they?" he inquired, anxiously, looking closely at Archibald's sisters.

"I don't know," whispered Ophelia. "They reply to no one and react to nothing. Baron, what is going on? Why have we been summoned? Where is Archibald?"

"What?" Melchior asked, astonished. "You haven't been told?"

He didn't have time to continue; the steward had launched into reading the statement. "Mr. Stanislav, here present, stands accused of having put his power to inordinate use, with the said use involving the Beasts and compromising the safety of your subjects. A request for Mutilation has been submitted by the Treasury following an incident that caused life-threatening injuries . . ."

Several Mirages turned to glare at Ophelia's alcove: her mother had just produced an incredulous splutter at the mention of Mutilation.

"Please note," the steward continued, with a cautious look at Farouk, "that the events seem to involve the responsibility of Madam Berenilde."

"That's not true!" the Knight protested, speaking for the first time.

"What?" grumbled the steward, "You are denying the events?"

301

"I'm not denying them," the Knight stammered, fiddling clumsily with his large glasses. "I just wanted to say that Madam Berenilde never asked me to do anything. Everything I did, I did it for her, but without her permission."

He turned around, tilting precariously on his chair, and searched the alcoves, stopping at Ophelia once he found her. She couldn't see the Knight's eyes clearly at this distance, behind his thick glasses, but she saw him biting his lips with a distraught look. Squeezing her scarf with her fingers, she realized that he had hoped to see Berenilde with her. He was afraid, and that fear was sincere.

"It so happens that Madam Berenilde was also injured by my behavior," the Knight finally stuttered, in an uncertain voice, but loud enough to be heard by all.

Ophelia felt a jolt of surprise. Had the conversation she'd had with him shaken him more than she'd thought?

"Will it . . . be painful?" the Knight added in a small voice as he got down from his chair.

"Remove your glasses," Farouk said, simply, rising from his throne with predatory slowness.

Barely had the Knight removed them, blinking his myopic little eyes, than he let out a sharp cry. Farouk's huge body had leant forward and he had smothered the child's whole face with the palm of his hand, his fingers buried in the blond curls. The Knight convulsed and clung to the family spirit's sleeve, as though no longer able to breathe. His body, reduced to its tiniest form before Farouk's gigantic proportions, didn't stop writhing. It was impossible to tell whether it was from pain, asphyxia, or panic.

Ophelia was not exactly fond of the Knight, but she really started to fear for him. And there was no one among the Mirages, among the members of his own family, who seemed to care. She got up instinctively, elbowing Baron Melchior's belly as she passed. "Don't get involved," he whispered to her. "All will be fine, I give you my word."

And indeed, a phenomenon then occurred that Ophelia had never previously witnessed: a silvery vapor rose from the Knight's body, as if some substance were escaping from it. His family power had just left him, like a soul departing the body of a dead person. Farouk finally, and casually, released him, and the Knight collapsed, gasping, onto the floor of the stand. A big, black cross spanned his face, as if Farouk's hand had imprinted it on his skin.

"From now on," Farouk said slowly in his thunderous voice, as he returned to his seat, "you will never hurt Berenilde ever again."

In Ophelia's mother's eyes, all trace of amazement had disappeared. Her feelings had even rubbed off on her jewelry: Artemis's profile, outlined against the red background of her favorite cameo, had its mouth wide open in horror.

"Mr. Stanislav," the steward started up again, monotonously, without even allowing the Knight time to get back on his feet, "you have been found guilty of the betrayal of your own family. Your power has been taken back from you. Where is your legal guardian?" he asked, looking gloomily at the assembly.

"He disappeared from his bath." The Knight replied himself in a weak voice, searching on the floor for the glasses he had dropped. What little one could see of his complexion, around the mark of infamy, was so green, he looked as if he were about to vomit. Ophelia was disturbed to see blue sandglasses being exchanged from hand to hand in the room. Now that the Knight had been dispossessed of the power he had put to such bad use, the general relief was palpable.

As for the mysterious disappearance of Count Harold, it seemed more to annoy the steward than concern him. "Indeed,

indeed, I have a file here that mentions that established fact," he grumbled, examining the documents on his lectern. "Well, Mr. Stanislav, since your guardian has elected to disappear unexpectedly, you will be sent to Helheim from today."

"No!" implored the Knight, who had never seemed so pathetic, his hands sweeping the ground of the stand to find his glasses. "I want to stay close to Madam Berenilde, I will be good, I beg you!"

"Helheim?" Ophelia muttered to Baron Melchior, as the assembly was already applauding.

"It's a very specialized establishment," he explained to her. "Helheim is on a minor ark of the Pole. Disruptive children are dispatched there when there is no desire to see them anytime soon."

The policemen led away the Knight, who continued to scream for Berenilde until his voice had faded into the distance. Ophelia should have felt relieved at the thought of never having to deal with him anymore. And yet, her only satisfaction was that Berenilde hadn't witnessed the scene; it would have broken her heart.

"Next case!" announced the steward, scouring the room. "Ah, you're there?" he added more gently when he recognized Ophelia. "Come forward, dear miss, it's your turn. Bring over Mr. Ambassador's sisters, too," he instructed the policemen.

As they all went up the stairs of the rostrum, Ophelia felt more uncomfortable than she had ever felt on the stage of the Optical Theatre. Cunegond hadn't exaggerated: that glint in the Mirages' eyes, it was pure hatred.

As for Farouk, he studied Ophelia intensely from his great seat, with fist under chin. His mental emanations were already setting her nerves on edge. The young Aide-memoire stood on tiptoes to whisper in his ear and make him reread certain passages in his notebook. Ophelia was a little shocked to notice that it wasn't the same adolescent as usual; this one didn't have the Web tattoo between his eyebrows.

"Why have we been summoned?" she asked, feeling increasingly anxious. The steward gave her an apologetic smile. Ophelia was surprised at this bewigged man's courtesy towards her; it did nothing to reassure her.

"A very peculiar business, dear miss! We appreciate your coming so promptly . . ."

"Where is Berenilde?" Farouk had interrupted the steward in an extremely slow, extremely heavy voice, his big hand pushing away the Aide-memoire as it would have got rid of an annoying fly. He didn't seem at all happy, but, luckily for Ophelia, he hadn't left his seat. Even at a distance, his eyes gave her such a bad headache, she felt as if her glasses were about to crack.

"She is taken up with various obligations, sir," she replied, choosing her words carefully.

"And you? What obligations have taken up so much of your time and energy that I have heard nothing more from you?"

Ophelia refrained from pointing out that it was rather she who had remained with no news from him, and that it hadn't done her any harm.

"I have my family visiting. We are taking the waters together."

"I would have placed my baths at your disposal, had you asked me," drawled Farouk. "Instead, you oblige me to move myself to come to you."

Was it, then, to find them, Berenilde and her, that Farouk had made the whole capital migrate southwards? Ophelia was starting to understand why the atmosphere was so toxic.

She wanted to restrain her mother, who was suddenly moving towards Farouk with an imposing swish of her dress, but she dismissed her attempt with a slap on the fingers.

"We have not been introduced, dear sir," she said, solemnly. "I am Ophelia's mother. I confess to appreciating the obvious interest that you show my daughter, but I have a few observations to make to you. To begin with, I am not sure I appreciate how women are considered in your little gathering," she said, indicating the exclusively male assembly, which, in turn, was sizing her up. "Next, I find you too harsh on your youngest descendants. And finally," she concluded, this time addressing the favorites, "you should learn to dress appropriately, ladies. At your age, one doesn't hide one's private parts behind diamonds! What a deplorable example you are giving to my daughter! So much for my observations," she said, in a more measured tone, returning to Farouk. "Now, kindly tell us why your policemen came to snatch these young ladies from their occupations. Oh, and could someone serve me an aspirin?" she asked, rubbing her forehead. "I don't know if anyone has already told you, dear sir, but your eyes give one a bit of a headache."

Along the rows of chairs, monocles had popped off faces, so wide-eyed were the stares of the nobles. The steward dropped his gavel, the favorites pursed their lips, and Dulcie, the youngest of Archibald's sisters, let out a long yawn into the now awkward silence.

Ophelia contemplated the candy-jar silhouette of her mother, and had to admit that that she'd never felt so proud to be her daughter. All that remained now was to hope that they would survive this court sitting.

Drumming his fingers on the armrests of his chair, Farouk honored Ophelia's mother with neither a response nor a glance.

"Little Artemis, I have a new occupation for you. I . . ." He stopped himself, frowned at length, and then reread the last page of his notebook, as if it were the most tedious of novels.

"Ah, yes. I would like you to find my ambassador. He has disappeared," he said, as an afterthought, realizing he had forgotten to mention it.

Ophelia's heart missed a beat. Archibald had disappeared? No, Archibald *couldn't* disappear. He belonged to that category of demanding men one just can't get rid of. It was with growing incredulity that Ophelia listened to the steward, nose buried in papers, outlining the facts:

"It is pointless to make a mystery of it, we all know that unexplained and worrying abductions have occurred in recent weeks. The Provost of the Marshals disappeared on the 20th of April, from a billiard room. The editorial director of the *Nibelungen* disappeared right in the middle of a costume ball, on the 25th of June. Count Harold, of whom we spoke a bit earlier, disappeared from the actual interior of a bathroom on the 29th of July. And now it is Mr. Ambassador who, in turn, has just disappeared from his own bedroom. Four disappearances," the steward summed up, closing a file, "but no ransom demand, no sign of struggle, and no evidence of breaking and entering. The victims all disappeared within the walls of Clairdelune, a place that is, however, known for its high level of security, and, with the exception of Mr. Ambassador, they are all Mirages. A bit of quiet, gentlemen!" the steward sighed, with weary bangs of his gavel.

While he had been speaking, Mirages had got up from their seats to demand justice, but a single look from Farouk restored their silence. Increasingly slumped in his chair, his fingers drumming again and again on the armrests, he was clearly starting to find that time was dragging.

"There," he said, not allowing the slightest emotion to show. "Little Artemis, I ask you to find all these people, as soon as possible."

"Me?" Ophelia asked, choked.

"Her?" her mother added.

Farouk slowly turned the pages of his notebook. "I have written that you wish to run your own reading consultancy."

"That has nothing to do with it," Ophelia said, panicking. "I can evaluate objects, not elucidate criminal activities. And in any case," she added, after a sudden thought, turning to Archibald's sisters, "shouldn't it rather be these young ladies you ask? They are best placed to know where their brother is right now."

Ophelia was starting to suspect that Archibald's disappearance and the drowsiness of his family were linked, but she got the full measure of it when the steward leant his great bewigged head over his lectern to address Archibald's sisters directly.

"Young ladies!" he said, loudly, as though dealing with the hard of hearing. "Did you listen to what has just been said? Does one of you feel able to speak here and now?"

Neither Grace nor Relish, nor Gaiety, nor Melody, nor Clarimond, nor Dulcie reacted. Only Patience blinked a little, as though her instinct as the eldest was telling her to pull herself together, but she immediately sank back into her torpor. With their glazed eyes and their arms, paler than candles, hanging limply, the seven sisters only seemed able to remain upright on the rostrum because their legs agreed to. Right now, more than ever, they resembled a collection of fragile china dolls.

"Don't rush them."

In the front row, a diplomat from the Web clan had risen so unsteadily to intervene, he had knocked his chair over. Ophelia had come across him a couple of times in the Jetty-Promenade gaming rooms. Normally, he was a man of keen intelligence and formal manners, but today he gave the impression of having abused narcotics. For a moment, he appeared not to remember why he had intervened, raising his eyebrows with a dazed expression, but then his eyes regained a little clarity behind his pince-nez.

"Don't rush them," he repeated. "Their empathy with Mr. Ambassador is superior to our own, they are even more affected than we are."

"Affected by what?" Ophelia asked, impatiently. Her mother looked at her with astonishment, but Ophelia was in such a state of turmoil, she no longer cared about good manners. In this jumble of emotions, anger was starting to dominate. Only the previous day, she had advised Archibald to be careful. Why hadn't that idiot listened to her? Into what soup had he gone and put himself?

"All that we *sense* is that Mr. Ambassador is plunged into a sleep verging on unconsciousness," the diplomat replied, as his neighbors weakly nodded assent with their chins. "That is at least proof that he is still alive, and thus maybe the others who are missing are, too. But there we are, the nature of his sleep is abnormal and it provides us with no indication of where he is to be found, how he got there, or even because of whom."

"More than anything, he is contaminating us all!" grumbled the man seated beside him, between two yawns. "His sleeping around, his debauchery, his difficulties—that rogue will have spared us nothing!"

"Our Lord's Aide-memoire is himself out of service," the steward stressed, indicating the adolescent now standing beside Farouk as though he were merely a poor substitute. "Normally, only a member of the Web is authorized to fulfill that function. Are you starting to gauge the seriousness of the situation, miss?"

Yes, Ophelia was gradually grasping the implications of what she was being told. It wasn't only Archibald's life that was in danger, it was the entire equilibrium of his clan, and, consequently, of the whole court.

"I will help you if it's in my power to do so," she promised, wringing her hands, "but I'm not the most skilled person . . ."

"You are."

Farouk had said this in his thunderous voice, spreading a renewed respectful silence across the Roulette Chamber.

"I appoint you Great Family Reader," he declared, scratching his quill on a page of his notebook. "Your sole priority will be to find my missing people. I give you until . . ." Farouk then paused at length, enough to reread his last notes " . . . until midnight tomorrow," he said, with more laborious quill scratching. "After midnight, it will be the Family States, and I can't look after everything at once."

There was stiff applause across the room and an extra level of hatred in the eyes of all present. The Mirages, in particular, didn't greatly appreciate seeing the fate of their family placed in the hands of a foreigner.

Ophelia felt her knees knocking. This court session was like a nightmare. She couldn't believe that, only this morning, she was taking her little brother to the circus.

"Come now, you can't ask such a thing of my daughter!" protested Ophelia's mother. "She's still just a girl, and clumsy with it! She can't even find a pair of stockings in a drawer, so your poor gentlemen . . ."

"My mother is right in one respect," Ophelia interrupted her. "It's too weighty a responsibility for me."

"You are the Great Family Reader," said Farouk, returning his quill to the hat of the Aide-memoire. "No responsibility is too weighty for you. If it is all that is required to reassure you, I will officially appoint an assistant for you."

His half-closed eyes scanned the rows of nobles, who each, in turn, suddenly took great interest in their shoes, their watches, their wigs, or their snuffboxes. Being Ophelia's assistant seemed as degrading to them as a public Mutilation.

Farouk's eyes stopped at Baron Melchior, probably because he was the most visible, with his bright-white outfit and hot-air-balloon figure.

"You are?"

"Your Minister of Elegance, my Lord." Baron Melchior had bowed low with infinite grace, despite his corpulence.

"I charge you with assisting Little Artemis in her task."

"I will do so to the best of my ability, my lord."

The baron was probably not thrilled at this prospect, but, being an exemplary minster, had the courtesy not to show it. Ophelia herself had nothing against him, but couldn't really see how he could be of use to her.

"And if I fail anyhow?" she asked. "If, at midnight tomorrow, I haven't found any of the missing?"

"Then we will stop looking for them." Farouk had wielded neither threats, nor blackmail, and yet Ophelia found his reply worse than all those he might have given.

"I request more time."

"We cannot, alas, afford it, miss." It was the diplomat in the front row again. Holding his pince-nez in one hand, with the other he was vigorously rubbing his eyes to wake himself up. "We won't last long in this state. What is happening to Archibald affects the integrity of the entire Web, and we must be in full possession of our faculties to take part in the Family States. If, between now and then, you haven't found him, we will break the empathetic bond that links us to him. An irreversible procedure that will probably prove fatal to him."

Ophelia felt her heart quickening even more. With a slowness in inverse proportion, Farouk got to his feet, and then lifted his pale eyes up to the huge roulette wheel spinning on the ceiling. "If I were you, Miss Great Family Reader, I would not waste a minute."

THE SEAL

The parquet floor shone like the wood of a violin. It reso-
nated musically with Ophelia's and the Keeper of the Seals's
every step as, together, they went through the antechamber.
The crystal chandeliers made all the gilding on the bookcases,
paintings, clocks, chairs, and windows glimmer; it was like
entering a world of solid gold. And yet no surface shone as
brightly as that of the door to which the Keeper of the Seals
was leading Ophelia.

"We are here, Miss Great Family Reader," he declared in a
voice both sad and solemn, as though it were a coffin they were
standing beside. "The bedroom of our unfortunate ambassador."

Ophelia nodded, unable to utter a word. She had gone past
this door hundreds of times, when Berenilde had been living
here, on Clairdelune's second floor, but never had she crossed
its threshold.

"You will have to wait just a trifle longer, Miss Great Family
Reader," cooed the Keeper of the Seals. "I have to obtain the
family's permission in order to remove the seal."

He had indicated the red wax seal, as big as a plate, that
had been affixed right in the middle of the panel of the door.
It was supposed to deter anyone from entering the bedroom,
but there was no ribbon, no string linking it to the door-handle
mechanism.

"Do not touch this door as long as I have not deactivated the seal," the Keeper of the Seals nevertheless insisted. "The illusion that would be triggered, in that case, would be most unpleasant. May I invite you to familiarize yourself with the particulars of the inquiry?" he said, handing a thick dossier to Ophelia. "That should keep you occupied, Miss Great Family Reader, while I see to the final formalities."

Coming from his mouth, Ophelia's title sounded like a tasteless joke. This Mirage compensated for his short stature with an imposing beribboned wig and a bombastic tone. He left the antechamber hammering the parquet floor with his high, silver heels.

Ophelia sat at a small table that was as gilded as the rest of the furniture, and opened the dossier. She soon gave up on the interminable report—the text was so larded with legal jargon, she couldn't even understand the first line. She did, however, pay very close attention to the letters slipped into protective sleeves. They were typed messages, some addressed to the director of the *Nibelungen*, others to Count Harold, and Ophelia even found one addressed to the Provost of the Marshals, which had probably come to light after a thorough search of his belongings. The messages always ended with an injunction: *GOD DEMANDS YOUR SILENCE; GOD CONDEMNS YOUR ATTITUDE; GOD SEEKS YOUR PENITENCE.*

No room now for any doubt. It really was the same person who'd been blackmailing Ophelia. She was even more disturbed when she noticed, on each letter, the same pincer marks. The blackmailer had left absolutely nothing to chance, not even the possibility of Ophelia being called on to evaluate these letters.

"Here is the register, Miss Great Family Reader."

Seeing Philibert right in front of her, Ophelia wondered

how long he'd been standing like that, leather-bound register in hand. This dull and unassuming steward always succeeded in taking her by surprise.

"Thank you," Ophelia said, leafing through the register.

"As Miss Great Family Reader can see," commented Philibert, "Clairdelune hasn't welcomed any regular guests for some time, apart from the unfortunate Count Harold. Those ladies and gentlemen of the court now only pass through briefly, between two connecting lifts."

"I daresay they're afraid of disappearing themselves," Ophelia said, giving Philibert back his register. "So Archibald . . . I mean Mr. Ambassador, entered through this door and never came back out?"

"Yes, Miss Great Family Reader. Sir declared that he wished to rest, and requested to be woken for supper. When the servants entered, his bed was empty."

"And . . . um . . . he was resting on his own?"

"Yes, Miss Great Family Reader."

"And . . . um . . . he couldn't have come out without being seen?"

Ophelia considered herself rather unfortunate, being so at ease when it came to reading objects, and so ill at ease when it came to questioning people.

"No, Miss Great Family Reader. The Clairdelune sentinel is permanently on guard in the corridors."

Ophelia jumped. At these words, the policemen present in the antechamber had clicked their heels in unison.

"And . . . um . . . he couldn't have left through another door?"

"No, Miss Great Family Reader. There are no doors other than this one to access sir's bedroom."

For a moment, Ophelia wondered whether Philibert, too, wasn't rather making fun of her, but he seemed far more distressed at Archibald's disappearance than she would have thought him capable of being.

"Do you know whether Mr. Ambassador received letters similar to these?" she asked, indicating the papers spread out on the table.

"Not to my knowledge, Miss Great Family Reader."

The slight quaver in Philibert's voice made Ophelia wonder whether he was telling her the whole truth.

"Let's forget these formalities," she suggested. "Do you have your own idea as to what may have happened?"

Philibert stared at her, looking shocked. "Is miss insinuating that I abducted my own master?"

"No, of course not," stammered Ophelia, somewhat flustered.

"Just as well," said Philibert, bowing. "With Miss Great Family Reader's permission, I am going to see whether my services aren't required elsewhere."

With exaggeratedly hurried steps, he left the antechamber and knocked on the door opposite it, in the corridor. He couldn't have closed it properly behind him, as Ophelia suddenly heard what was being said on the other side of it:

"For pity's sake, Philibert, don't impose that funereal face on us! As far as I know, my brother isn't dead yet."

Ophelia's eyebrows rose as she recognized Patience's stern voice. Of Archibald's seven sisters, she was the first to have resurfaced thanks to the "miracle coffee," a novelty perfected by the Minister of Gastronomy. It was only ever hot water, but it was instilled with a stimulating taste illusion that was more effective than regular coffee.

"How is miss feeling?" enquired Philibert's voice, barely audible from where Ophelia was sitting.

"More serious than my sisters. Everyone lets themselves go in this place, so someone has to show a good example."

"Does miss have any news of sir?"

"Philibert, you're not going to keep asking me. I tell you, and repeat to you, Archie is out of my reach at the moment. I'm already finding it hard enough to keep myself awake—focusing on him makes me unbearably sleepy."

"But maybe a memory . . . some detail, could have come back to miss?"

"It all occurred so quickly, I didn't have time to understand what was happening to us. Come on, make yourself useful and pour me a little more of that miracle coffee."

The clatter of china echoed in the silence. The acoustics of the place, all polished wood and gold plating, amplified every sound. Even if Ophelia hadn't wanted to listen to them, she couldn't have stopped herself from doing so.

"What is our Great Family Reader doing?"

"She is waiting, Miss Patience."

"She'll be waiting some more. I won't make a hasty decision, especially since it's the first time I'm having to do this. Usually, it's Archie who deals with all these things . . . So you recommend, Mr. Keeper of the Seals, that I not agree to this reading?"

The dossier Ophelia was carefully going through almost fell from her hands. Wasn't that man, on the contrary, supposed to be obtaining permission for her?

"Be sure not to, dear miss," said the syrupy voice of the Mirage. "We are dealing, quite obviously, with a total amateur. Wait, instead, for the return of Mr. Treasurer. He's also an incompetent, but to a lesser extent."

"I won't allow anyone, not even you, dear cousin, to call Mr. Thorn incompetent. He's lacking in good manners, I grant you, but he's the most capable man I know."

This time it was Baron Melchior's voice, recognizable by its precious tone, that had intervened. Ophelia felt so oppressed by the weight of her new responsibilities, she would have liked to hear her assistant take her defense with the same fervor.

"I would, personally, feel easier if Mr. Treasurer were here with us," the baron added, anxiously, "but for the moment, no one knows either where he is, or when he'll return. Furthermore, our Lord Farouk would be angered to know that we, the Mirages, are obstructing the smooth running of this inquiry. Don't forget that I am personally involved, now. As are you, dear cousin."

"An inquiry? What inquiry, Mr. Minister of Elegance? That little foreigner hasn't the slightest idea of what she's supposed to be doing."

"Maybe, Mr. Keeper of the Seals," admitted Baron Melchior, "but it was to find that little foreigner that our Lord Farouk had the whole of Citaceleste moved. Speaking of foreigners, do we know where Madam Architect is? She's always been quite close to Mr. Ambassador, and she knows Clairdelune better than anyone; her assistance could be valuable to us."

"Mother Hildegarde is a very independent lady, sir. For weeks now, she has neglected all her building projects in Citaceleste . . . not to mention the improvements she's been due to make at Clairdelune for months! Barely do we cross her, at the turning of a corridor, before she disappears into the nearest Compass Rose."

Ophelia raised her eyebrows. Even at a distance, she could detect a certain hostility in Philibert's voice.

"That's strange behavior," commented Baron Melchior. "Is she even aware of our ambassador's plight?"

"I don't know, sir, just as I don't know where she's to be found right now. My master was lamenting not being able to have a simple meeting with his own architect anymore."

"There's nothing more elusive than an Arkadian who

doesn't want to be found," the Keeper of the Seals said, sarcastically. "Between you and me, I find it all pretty suspicious."

"And then there's another thing, sirs. On the subject of the interfamilial Compass Rose linking the Pole to the LandmArk. I am personally in charge of the key that opens that passage—a passage to which access is strictly controlled at Clairdelune."

"Well, Philibert?"

"For one reason or another, sirs, the passage has been blocked up. I only noticed it earlier. The door now leads to a simple storage room.

"Well that's most unfortunate," Baron Melchior said, after a moment's silence. "Let's hope Madam Hildegarde hasn't returned to her native ark. Without that route, we won't be seeing her anytime soon."

"I have never understood why my brother became so besotted with that old woman," Patience's composed voice suddenly declared. "She's pushy and scheming. And I think our Great Family Reader is equally so," she added, to Ophelia's surprise. "Behind her innocent airs, that foreigner is infiltrating our lives the same way that Madam Hildegarde infiltrated our homes. She . . ." A yawn stopped Patience mid-sentence. "A little more miracle coffee, please. She now occupies a choice position at court, just as she carved herself one in my brother's confidence. Is it desirable to allow those hands to poke around our embassy?"

Ophelia was dismayed. Pushy? She'd never asked for four men's fate to depend on her! The entire court hated her for having been chosen to find them; it would hate her even more if she didn't find them, and Farouk would only give his protection, to her and her family, if she fulfilled her part of the contract. And it didn't help that she'd received the same threats as those she was supposed to rescue. In truth, her main ambition was to remain alive as long as possible.

"Even you, Mr. Minister," Patience continued, sounding somewhat baffled, "I suspect you of having allowed yourself to be 'infiltrated' by that reader. And I'm not referring to your position of assistant."

"Me?" protested Baron Melchior. "Come now . . ."

"Miss Patience is not wrong, dear cousin. You have been caught several times colluding with that bastard Treasurer and his little foreigner. You should watch the company you keep. You are neglecting the interests of your own clan."

Ophelia jumped when she heard Baron Melchior's voice, normally so refined, exploding like a thunderbolt: "The clan, the clan, the clan! I am the minister of a government, not of a clan! I dedicate my life to just one cause, Mr. Keeper of the Seals: turning us all into a civilized society, and you don't make my task any easier! Close that door, Philibert," he added, in a more moderate tone. "All we need now is for Miss Great Family Reader to hear us."

The voices stopped and Ophelia was suddenly returned to the silence of the antechamber. For want of anything better, she nibbled the seams of her glove, furiously thinking. While those people tried to decide whether she was incompetent or pushy, Archibald was dying somewhere.

"Stay well away from illusions." Those were his last words to her, but what had he meant to say to her, exactly? Why hadn't Archibald told her what he'd learned, instead of playing games?

Ophelia nibbled even harder at the thumb of her glove. She had twenty-four hours. Twenty-four hours before the opening of the Family States. Twenty-four hours before the link with Archibald would be severed. Twenty-four hours before the enforcement of her own ultimatum. She contemplated the pages of the dossier spread on the table. Would her own name soon feature within them?

Ophelia straightened her glasses on her nose. In wanting to run her own reading consultancy, hadn't she wanted to put her hands in the service of the truth? Well, it was now or never. If she had the slightest chance of discovering the identity of this blackmailer, who used God's name to terrorize people, she had to seize it.

"Three times!"

Ophelia turned around. Her mother had just charged into the antechamber, hammering the floor loudly with her heels.

"Three times I was almost arrested by the policemen between the lavatory and here! And of course you, you weren't worried at all! It's getting really late," she added, consulting a pendulum clock. "Read quickly whatever you have to read, my dear, and let's get back to the hotel."

"Mommy, you should go back first," Ophelia advised her. "I'm likely to be some time."

Her mother approached her in a great swirl of dress, not stopping until they were nose to nose. "We both know perfectly well that you're not cut out to do what this strange Mr. Farouk expects of you. Don't take this farce too much to heart. Play the game until your wedding, one reading or two, just for show, and then I'll take you back home."

Play the game? That was certainly the last advice Ophelia wanted to receive, particularly from a woman who had always taught her the importance of a job well done.

"Mommy, please, this is the first time I'm asking you: show a little confidence in me. I really need it this evening."

"What on earth is all this clutter?"

Ophelia quickly tidied away the dossier her mother was already peering at. She didn't want her happening upon the threatening letters. "It's confidential, Mom."

Incapable of staying still, Ophelia's mother darted over to Archibald's door. "Is this where you have to do your reading?"

"No, Mom, don't touch that . . . " Ophelia didn't hear the end of her own sentence. Barely had her mother put her fingers on the handle than a chorus of bells resounded throughout the antechamber and the seal started to glow like molten metal. It was the most earsplitting sound illusion Ophelia had ever experienced. She saw her mother putting her hands over her ears and mouthing wildly at her, but not a word reached her. Her skull had turned into a bell tower.

Immediately, Baron Melchior, the steward Philibert, and the Keeper of the Seals rushed in from the room next door. The last crossed the antechamber with mincing little steps, silenced the seal with a mere flick, and then checked that his huge wig hadn't gone skew-whiff.

"You must not open this door, Miss Great Family Reader," he cooed, unctuously. "We haven't yet finished deliberating. Why don't you read the dossier, as I suggested, hmm?"

"Maybe Miss Great Family Reader would like me to get on and make a decision?" With china saucer in one hand, pretty cup in the other, Patience now entered the antechamber. With her long, fine neck, white dress, and silvery-blond hair, silky as plumage, the young woman resembled a large swan. Patience was, as her name indicated, the most moderate and thoughtful of all her siblings. The black teardrop between her eyebrows helped to make her face look more serious than it already did naturally. Even though she was trying not to show it, she seemed exhausted.

"Or then," she continued, after a gulp of miracle coffee, "maybe Miss Ex-Vice-Storyteller would like to make that decision in my place?"

Ophelia tensed at these words. Miss Ex-Vice-Storyteller? Of course, it could be a coincidence, but that was exactly the formula the anonymous writer had used in the last letter.

"It's me who is deciding for her," Ophelia's mother intervened, puffing out her enormous chest. "I understand that you are shaken by the misfortune befalling you, but leaving us hanging around like this, it's not polite. Come on now, my dear, let's leave these people to do as they like."

"No." Ophelia pulled her spotty handkerchief out of her dress pocket, blew in it several times, determined not to let her cold get between her and her interlocutors, and then raised her chin with determination. If just once in her life her experience at the Optical Theatre were to help her to make herself heard, it was now.

"I heard what you were saying about me earlier on."

There was an exchange of embarrassed looks between the Keeper of the Seals and Baron Melchior, but Patience, she just calmly drank another gulp of miracle coffee. Ophelia focused all her attention on her, pointing at the sealed door.

"You think I'm incompetent? If there's a single object in that room that witnessed what happened to your brother, I will make it talk. You think I'm pushy? I am a professional reader, and as such, I have an ethical code. The embassy's private affairs will remain private. I will not leave before I've done what I've come here to do, but I won't do it, either, without your agreement. Ask for the seal to be removed, Miss Patience, and ask now. I only have twenty-four hours left to find your brother. Don't do it for me, do it for him."

Ophelia's mother, with a hand on her heart, stared at her daughter in shock, as if she didn't recognize her. But no one had a chance to react: a creaking of floorboards made everyone's eyes turn to the entrance of the antechamber. A huge shadow was leaning against the gilded frame of the door.

As his coat dripped rainwater, Thorn caught his breath.

THE PIN

Ophelia felt her blood throbbing against her eardrums, but couldn't have said whether it was due to sudden relief or, on the contrary, heightened tension. Despite the circumstances, she couldn't set aside what had occurred on the path of the wall. She had to breathe in several times to speak to Thorn in a voice she wasn't too ashamed of:

"You have turned up at just the right time. We were all waiting for you."

Ophelia's smile soon faded from her lips. As Thorn advanced through the antechamber, scattering puddles that were discreetly mopped up behind him by a Clairdelune valet, his eyes flashed like two thundery skies.

"Do not authorize this reading," he ordered Patience. "I will take over the inquiry myself. As for you," he said, turning to Ophelia, "I am relieving you of your duties. Return to the hotel immediately."

Ophelia's glasses paled on her nose. It wasn't exactly the support she'd hoped for. "You can't ask such a thing of me."

Thorn straightened to his full height before Ophelia, and that was saying something: she was literally engulfed by his shadow. She instinctively stood on tiptoe to continue holding the incandescent look he was bearing down on her.

"I am the Treasurer and your future husband. Of course I can."

"I must do this reading, whether it pleases you or not."

Under the coat drenched in rain, Thorn's chest was rising at an irregular rhythm, but it was hard to know whether he was breathless due to his frantic dash across Citaceleste or to the fury electrifying his entire body. What had got into him? Ophelia could imagine that he was annoyed, but why did he appear to be this angry with her?

"I forbid you to read anything whatsoever to do with the disappearances," Thorn said between his teeth. "None of these issues concern you in any way, do you hear? And you, be quiet," he said, irascibly, cutting Ophelia's mother short with a wave, as she was already opening her mouth to give her opinion. "Remember our agreement: you meddle in nothing at all until the wedding. *Nothing.*"

Ophelia had once seen her mother catch her fingers in the door of a carriage; the look on her face then had been exactly as it was now.

Baron Melchior interrupted with a little embarrassed cough. "Well . . . technically, Mr. Treasurer, you can't forbid your fiancée from fulfilling the mission that's been entrusted to her. It is Lord Farouk in person who appointed her Great Family Reader, and I was selected to be her assistant. As this responsibility has never been borne by anyone prior to her, no one yet knows the prerogatives. Our Minister of Protocol is looking into the matter as we speak."

Thorn looked daggers at Baron Melchior, who just responded with a moustache-raising smile, before spinning around to Patience as smoothly as a hot-air balloon. "The decision rests with you. Does Miss Great Family Reader have your authorization, or not?"

Now, everyone was hanging on Patience's lips. The young woman contemplated the bottom of her empty cup for a long time, and then looked up at Thorn.

"You have been incapable of finding anyone at all up to now, and it's my brother we're talking about today. It hurts me to admit it, but if he had been here, he would have entrusted this reading to you," she said, addressing Ophelia this time. "I thus give you my permission. Let the seal be removed."

Thorn stared at Patience as if fighting the desire to shove her china cup down her gullet.

The Keeper of the Seals briefly swept the air with his hand; the seal, despite having all the appearance of a thick piece of wax, was erased from the door like chalk from a blackboard.

"Thank you for giving me your trust," muttered Ophelia.

Patience herself opened the door and the light from the antechamber cut through the darkness like a gold blade.

"I'm not giving it to you. Fail to find my brother, and I will make your life hell."

With these words, said astonishingly calmly, Patience switched on the electric light. Ophelia was speechless when she saw Archibald's bedroom for the first time. If she'd been asked to imagine the private quarters of a man such as him, she would readily have pictured a jungle of cushions, instruments of pleasure, libertine tomes—in short, a shameful mess over which the perfume of all that is taboo would permanently waft. She certainly hadn't expected to go into an empty room.

There was nothing in there but an old wrought-iron bed, standing proud in the middle of the floor. Cracks crept across the walls and ceiling—Archibald's room's neglected appearance was in keeping with the way he dressed. Even the ambient temperature was chilly, compared with the antechamber, as if the thermal illusion didn't work here.

"I don't understand," Ophelia said, looking around. "Where are Archibald's personal belongings stored?"

"Nowhere, Miss Great Family Reader," Philibert declared from the doorway. "Sir has always kept this place in this state."

"All the same," Baron Melchior sighed, casting the critical eye of a great couturier over the place. "It's a little too conceptual for my taste. Couldn't Mr. Ambassador have ordered an illusion or two? A mere touch of rococo, and your interior is transformed."

Everyone was now gathered at the threshold of the room, so as not to interfere with the searching of the premises. Ophelia felt as though she had to prove herself before a jury. The great confidence she had displayed earlier slipped between her fingers. A room without objects? They couldn't have given her a thornier challenge! She took off one of her gloves, determined not to lose heart before she'd even started.

"Are you obliged to read the bed?" asked Patience. "It would be indecent for a girl of your age."

Her stern expression didn't come close to the one on Thorn's face; he didn't take his eyes off Ophelia, as if at any moment she could do something irredeemably stupid. As for her mother, she squinted back and forth between the two of them, as if she still couldn't decide which of them had insulted her the most. Curiously, the person who seemed to have the highest hopes of this reading was Philibert.

"I don't really have a choice," Ophelia finally replied.

"What about the floor?" asked Patience. "And the walls? It can't be that different from your *usual* readings, can it?"

"It is. Those surfaces are far too vast and far too vague. We leave our trace on objects when we have direct contact with them. One rarely touches the walls of a room, and when one walks on the floor, one wears shoes. Soles make remarkable insulators."

Ophelia went up to the wrought-iron bed, unsure exactly how to tackle it. It didn't appear to have been slept in. Only the moth-eaten bedcover was lightly dented in the middle, suggesting that a body had lain on it long enough to leave its imprint. One didn't have to be a detective to work out that Archibald had just stretched out on it, without even sliding between the sheets.

What interested Ophelia were Archibald's last moments before his abduction, not the thousands of nights he'd spent under the covers, alone or with company. This, of course, narrowed the scope of the investigation even more.

Ophelia laid her hand flat on the bedcover and felt the tiniest tingle at the tips of her fingers. The feeling was still too distant to be definable. She slid her palm slowly over the fabric, like a divining rod, seeking the areas most marked by Archibald's emotional imprint. Suddenly, Ophelia felt overwhelmed with ennui, an ennui so profound she felt as if she were sinking into the very essence of melancholy. And the more Ophelia drowned her sorrows at parties, the more intoxicated she became with pleasure, the more she defied convention, the greater the ennui.

The thoughts weren't her own, they were Archibald's. She would have found witnessing his lovemaking less indecent. Discovering what was hiding behind his carefree smiles made her feel she'd been around him without ever making the effort really to know him. And yet Ophelia persisted, on and on, covering every inch of the bedcover with her fingers in the hope of finding an anomaly, a shock, a surprise, anything that might indicate a disturbance in the bottomless depths of ennui permeating every thread of the fabric.

When a shudder of panic coursed up her spine and turned her glasses yellow, Ophelia knew that, this time, the emotion was definitely coming from her. This bed was teaching her nothing, absolutely nothing, about Archibald's disappearance!

"I know you can no longer enter into communication with your brother," Ophelia said, half-turning to Patience. "But might it be possible for you to 'possess' him? I once witnessed

Archibald . . . um . . . *borrowing* the body of a Valkyrie. Maybe you could . . ."

"No," Patience interrupted her, her tone categorical. "A member of the Web can only possess another with that person's informed consent. Don't see it as a question of principle—if my brother doesn't give me access, it's physically impossible for me to take his place."

"Should we conclude from this that your reading has failed?"

Ophelia gave Thorn a hard look. With his raptor's eyes, his black coat dripping rainwater, and his large nose, the triangular shadow of which swallowed up half his face, he was like a bird of ill omen. She didn't expect encouragement from him, but he could have at least spared her this sort of comment.

"No. I haven't finished."

Ophelia was just wondering whether, in the end, she shouldn't extend her reading to the sheets, pillows, and mattress, when Baron Melchior approached her.

"Ah, it's not a figment of my imagination! There really is something here that's catching the light."

With the golden tip of his cane, he pointed to a metal ring on the bedcover, which Ophelia was mortified not have noticed before. She carefully picked it up with the fingertips of her still-gloved hand, to examine it closely. What was it? A ring? A key ring? An earring?

Ophelia breathed deeply to calm the turmoil of her emotions. This reading was probably her last chance to understand what had happened to Archibald, she mustn't let it slip away. When she felt sufficiently focused, she touched the ring lightly with her finger.

An image burst into her head like a soap bubble. In the space of a single heartbeat, Ophelia was Archibald. She saw, felt, and thought what he had seen, felt, and thought.

Sandglass. Jubilation. Danger.

"It's not a ring," she muttered, to herself more than to the others. It was the pin from a sandglass. Ophelia "saw" very clearly the light from the ceiling lamp duplicated in the glass of the phial, as though it were she who were there, lying on the bed. The blue sandglass bore the usual stamp: "Family Manufacturer Hildegarde & Co." Ophelia stroked its pin pensively with her thumb. At last she'd found one. This sandglass looked ostensibly like any other one, but for one detail, a tiny difference that was terrifyingly insidious: a complex and minuscule mechanism, at tipping level, barely visible to the naked eye. Ophelia herself could see it because she'd been searching for it on every sandglass for weeks on end. And now that she'd found the trap, what was she supposed to do with it?

When she looked up, Ophelia realized that everyone had gathered around her, in a shared state of tension.

"So?" asked Patience, who, for the first time, was starting to lose her cool. "What is it? What did you see?"

Keep well away from illusions.

"The blue sandglasses," Ophelia whispered. "They're the things that took away the missing people. And Archibald knew it."

THE WORKSHOP

Ophelia sneezed into her scarf. Stinking puddles oozed over the cobblestones, and the more she tried to avoid them, the more she put her shoes in them. Her stockings were starting to feel damp—she wasn't even sure if it was water—but she kept walking as fast as her little legs allowed. That was the least she had to do to keep pace with the squad of policemen, whose hobnailed boots rang out in unison across the street.

"Is the sandglass workshop still far away?" asked Ophelia.

"Another two lifts, miss," one of the policemen replied, without looking at her or slowing down.

She searched, right to the end of the street, for the gate of their next connecting lift. Never had Ophelia ventured this deep into the basements of Citaceleste. The more floors they descended, the more she felt as if she were plunging into the city's sewers. The air here was so thick, saturated with cooled vapors and foul smells, that it absorbed any light from the rare street lamps. Occasionally, Ophelia glimpsed faces pressed to the misted-up windows of the engine rooms and industrial workshops. In the capital's basements, hundreds of workmen, mechanics, and artisans maintained radiators, repaired piping, evacuated wastewater, in addition to producing the silverware, porcelain, and soft furnishings required for daily life in the higher quarters.

Ophelia raised her glasses at Thorn, who was walking on her right, saying not a word.

"The more I think about it, the less I understand," she whispered to him. "Why would Mother Hildegarde want to use her own sandglasses to abduct courtiers? Not everyone likes her," she conceded—she'd just remembered that the Provost of the Marshals, the editorial director of the *Nibelungen*, and Count Harold heartily detested foreigners like her—"but I can't imagine her going to such extremes. There must be something else."

Thorn's eyes remained out of bounds. Was he even listening to her?

"On the other hand," Ophelia continued, raising her voice, "Archibald had detected a trap. That I clearly sensed. But if he was right, why did he allow himself to be taken all the same?"

"How should I know?" grumbled Thorn.

Ophelia didn't persist. She had an atrocious headache and didn't know whether it was due to her cold, her lack of sleep, or Thorn's claws. Maybe he wasn't aware of it, but his anger radiated out of him and then rose up her spinal cord, in the form of a painful throbbing.

Since they'd left Clairdelune, she could no longer change direction, enter a lift, or tie her shoelaces without knocking into Thorn at some angle. He was following her everywhere, like a second shadow, as if the squad of policemen weren't sufficient. His proximity—all grinding of teeth and frowning—was uncomfortable. He seemed truly furious with her, and perhaps even more so since she'd read the sandglass pin.

What did Thorn really imagine? That she'd waited for his back to be turned to rush before Farouk, beg him to make her his official reader, and boast that she could save the missing, all on her own? She was petrified at the thought of finding only corpses, or, even worse, finding nothing at all. And to top it all off, instead of being annoyed with Thorn for his lack of understanding, she actually felt at fault, as if, in some way, she deserved his fury.

Ophelia knew that it was because of what had occurred on the wall, but she couldn't even think back on it without her ears burning.

"Would you . . . give me . . . a moment . . . please?"

Ophelia, Thorn, and the police squad all turned around as one, all banging into each other. Behind them, under the flickering light of a street lamp, Baron Melchior was dabbing his triple chin with a lace handkerchief. He was perspiring so much, his cheeks were glistening. He had stopped right outside the entrance to an Imaginoir. What must have once been an Imaginoir, at any rate. The strings of red lanterns framing the sign, *Erotic Delights*, had long been switched off. As for the windows, they were covered in dust and outdated advertisements.

"You wouldn't be . . . trying to shake off . . . your moral guardian . . . by any chance?" Baron Melchior gasped while fanning himself with his top hat, not without a touch of mischief.

That had been Ophelia's mother's latest brainwave. She had agreed to return to the hotel on the sole condition that the Minister of Elegance would personally serve as chaperone to her daughter. Ophelia already found it embarrassing enough that he was her assistant.

"We have to get to the workshop as quickly as possible," grumbled Thorn. "If they hear that we're on our way, this surprise inspection will no longer be one."

"I don't make a habit of walking this much," apologized the baron. "I'm going to end up dirtying my new shoes."

All this wasted time was torture for Ophelia. On every floor, every connecting lift, every sidewalk, new policemen asked for their papers, as well as official justification for their presence beyond the zones of authorized movement—a pass that only their personal police escort was able to supply. The security measures were such that it would have been impossible for an Arctic lemming to cross the road without being arrested.

"This is all rather tricky," declared Baron Melchior. "You're aware of that, Mr. Treasurer?" He glanced several times around him, through the street vapors, as Ophelia had often seen him doing before. Behind his seeming placidity, and despite the heavy protection they had been given, he seemed permanently afraid of being stabbed in the back.

"Of course, as a Mirage, I feel concerned by the disappearance of my cousins, and I want justice to be done," he continued in a hushed voice. "But as a minister, I should remind you that it is thanks to Madam Hildegarde that we have an interfamilial Compass Rose, and that that route is currently blocked. If we mistreat one of their own, the Arkadians will never reopen that route, and we'll have to wave goodbye to their spices and delicious citrus fruits. The blue-sandglass lead is now taking us to Madam Hildegarde, but as long as her guilt isn't established, we must ensure that she is treated *elegantly*," trilled Baron Melchior, tunefully stressing the last word for the policemen's benefit. "If we're lucky enough to find her at her workshop, I suggest we put her under arrest, in a cell that even her power can't get her out of, but only long enough to sort this business out, and with absolutely no brutality. Do we fully understand each other, gentlemen?"

The policemen remained standing to attention, chins up, exchanging neither a word nor a look; it was probably their way of saying "yes."

"If Madam Hildegarde is implicated, one way or another, in the disappearance of Archibald," said Thorn, "I will get flowers personally delivered to her in prison."

"I didn't hear that," Baron Melchior said, diplomatically. "We can go now, I've caught my breath. Are you coming, Miss Great Family Reader?"

Before diving back into the street vapors, Ophelia had a last look at the Imaginoir, with its grimy windows and unlit red lanterns. She had just suddenly remembered an important detail. She waited until they were all in the lift, after an umpteenth identity check, to ask Baron Melchior the question she was itching to ask: "Did that Imaginoir belong to your sister?"

Baron Melchior, who was combing his hair while gazing at himself in the lift's mirror, made an embarrassed face. "To my great shame, yes. Thankfully, it has been closed. Cunegond is a remarkable artist, but she should devote her art to the service of estheticism, not vulgarity."

Ophelia shook her head. That wasn't what she was getting at. "Your sister claims that her Imaginoirs are failing due to competition. The competition from Mother Hildegarde's sandglasses," she specified.

Baron Melchior took a pretty little metal pot out of a pocket, scooped a knob of perfumed wax from it, and stiffened his lengthy moustache with a deft slide of the fingers.

"That's tough market forces," he sighed. "Dare I confess that I myself invested in a few shares in Madame Hildegarde's workshop? Indeed, I'm starting to wonder whether I got such a good deal," he added, after a moment's thought. "If we have proof, later, that the blue sandglasses are dangerous, you can just imagine the scand . . ."

"The last time I came across her, Madam Cunegond was in possession of blue sandglasses," Ophelia interrupted him. "Far too many for personal use. She asked me not to mention it, but, given what's going on, I can no longer keep it to myself."

Baron Melchior's moustache collapsed with astonishment. If the situation hadn't been so serious, it would almost have been comic. "Are you sure about that? Well, that's most embarrassing! I admit that my sister isn't beyond reproach, but I swear on my new shoes, she is neither a trafficker nor a criminal."

Ophelia looked searchingly at Thorn to get his opinion, but he turned his face away and cranked up his frown, as if she just wouldn't stop riling him. Had she made a new blunder?

A final lift and three identity checks later, they were going through a porch on which it was written, in large, faded letters:

FAMILY MANUFACTURER HILDEGARDE & CO

The factory was such a huge building, it took up a whole basement to itself. Its size was the only noteworthy thing about it; its facades were just gloomy, grey, and windowless walls, and there were old mattresses dumped on the damp flagstones of the courtyard.

Thorn had to bang the knocker on the main entrance several times before a woman porter came to open it for them. "Yes? What is it?"

"I'm the Treasurer," declared Thorn. "I must see Madam Hildegarde most urgently."

"The Mother's not in her workshop," said the porter.

"How long has she been gone? When will she return?"

The porter just shrugged her shoulders, half-heartedly.

"Who is responsible for the workshop in Madam Hildegarde's absence?" insisted Thorn.

The porter left without a word. A few moments later, an elderly gentleman turned up instead and whistled with admiration as he peered up at Thorn. He straightened his work cap with his thumb. "Mr. Treasurer himself!" he exclaimed, with a half-smile. "I'm the foreman. What can I do to help you?"

"Allow me to inspect the building," Thorn said, handing him his search warrant.

If he was surprised or concerned at the request, the foreman didn't show it. Ophelia felt he didn't seem particularly nervous, for someone finding a whole police squad at his door. She noticed a badge in the form of an orange on his cap. The orange was Mother Hildegarde's favorite fruit, and it served as a rallying symbol for all those who were in alliance with her. Ophelia was unlikely to forget it—it was after delivering a basket of the fruit that she herself had ended up under the policemen's truncheons.

Once he had checked the search warrant, the foreman considered Thorn, Baron Melchior, and Ophelia in turn, with amused curiosity. "Well, well, but I recognize the little young lady. I've never gone up to the high floors, but I do read the papers. You're that little storyteller, the one from Anima. And you," the foreman continued, turning to the baron, "you're a minister. The Minister of Haute Couture, or something of the sort. Well I never, all very grand! Come in, come in! When my workmates get to see what I'm bringing them . . ."

Thorn indicated to Ophelia to go first. "You stay where I can see you," he hissed between his teeth. "No escaping, no big ideas, no disaster. Is that clear?"

"I will do whatever I deem necessary for the inquiry," Ophelia said, annoyed. She was really starting to see red. Literally: her glasses had turned crimson on her nose.

As for Baron Melchior, he was wiping his feet meticulously on the doormat, muttering: "Minister of Haute Couture . . . no, but really . . . we'll have heard it all."

"May I at least ask the reason for this search?" the foreman enquired, amiably.

"The ambassador has disappeared after pulling the pin on one of your sandglasses."

"That's the whole point of the sandglasses, Mr. Treasurer."

"The ambassador never reappeared," grumbled Thorn.

"Well that's unfortunate," the foreman commented, without dropping his half-smile. "It's probably a terrible misunderstanding. I suppose you'd like to inspect the sandbeds? We generally don't allow anyone access there, but since you have a warrant . . ."

Ophelia got the disturbing impression that this man was reciting—very badly, in fact—lines learnt in advance. She wondered, in passing, what on earth a sandbed might be.

"I want to inspect everything," Thorn corrected him.

The workshop's interior bore no relation to the lugubrious façade of its exterior. The hall led to a corridor of impeccable cleanliness. Its walls comprised countless wooden compartments. Each one carried a pretty label: "luck of the draw," "breath of fresh air," "ladies at home," "the red boudoir," "place your bets," "an exotic evening," and so on. They were all sandglass destinations.

"This is where our sandglasses are made," the foreman announced, entering a room illuminated by fine lamps hanging from the ceiling. "At this stage of production, they're just ordinary sandglasses that will be of no interest to you. It's only at the next stage that Mother Hildegarde gives them locomotion properties."

The first thing that struck Ophelia was the shelves behind glass. Tens, hundreds, thousands of little sandglasses lined up as far as the eye could see, and each one a true work of craftsmanship.

The second thing that struck Ophelia was the workers sitting at their workbenches, despite the lateness of the hour. Not one of them looked up from their articulated magnifier, screwdriver, or glass-grinder as the policemen circulated among them. It was just old men and old women here, and their aprons all bore the symbol of an orange. That the ambassador had disappeared, that their sandglasses were involved, and that an army of policemen had besieged the premises, none of it seemed to make any difference to them.

The third thing that struck Ophelia, right in the heart this time, was an eye twinkling from a dark corner at the back of the workshop, through a mess of black curls. Gail was perched on a stool. With a cigarette wedged between her teeth, and overall straps hanging over her tool belt, she seemed to be repairing what looked like a transmitter-receiver radio set. Her monocle reflected the light from the lamps like a lighthouse, and that brightness didn't compare with the blazing of her electric-blue eye.

Ophelia had to summon all her presence of mind not to rush over to Gail and shake her by the shoulders. What exactly was she doing here now? Where was Mother Hildegarde, in the end? And why the heck did no one in this workshop seem surprised by anything? Ophelia stifled, with difficulty, all the questions she was dying to ask; she would have got Gail into trouble by drawing the policemen's attention to her. A false identity, these days, could cost her very dearly.

"The sandbeds are over here," the foreman said, opening a door right at the back of the room. "If you would care to follow me."

Gail had a quick look over her radio set, and, for a brief moment, seemed surprised. Her astonishment wasn't prompted by either Ophelia or Thorn, or Baron Melchior, or the policemen, however; its sole focus was a point suspended in midair, somewhere behind them.

Ophelia tensed under her scarf. She'd completely forgotten about Vladislava! Had the Invisible finally managed to follow them all the way here? Gail was a Nihilist, which meant that the family powers of other descendants of Farouk had no effect on her. Had she just caught out the bodyguard, well and truly, behind her veil of transparency? Did she realize that she wasn't supposed to see her? Could she even tell the difference between reality and illusion? It would have taken just one word for her to give herself away, so Ophelia breathed a sigh of relief when Gail buried her nose back in her radio set, and the policemen left the workshop without having noticed anything.

The workshop led to an administrative office, where Thorn cast around his prying eyes. Ophelia herself looked for anything resembling "sandbeds"—sand reserves? sandglasses without sand?—but there was nothing here but accounting documents.

"I am confiscating these," Thorn declared, seizing a set of ledgers.

"I doubt you'll find anything interesting in them, but do as you please," the foreman said, with his unshakeable smile. "The sandbeds are through here," he added, opening another door of frosted glass.

Ophelia shivered as soon as she left the office. Her sneeze resounded like a thunderbolt in the silence, reverberating in endless echoes. They had just come to a metal gangway that overlooked, and from quite high up, a huge hangar, in which the temperature had suddenly plunged. The place was lit by lamps with blue glass shades, barely allowing one to distinguish, in the aquatic light, an impressive quantity of very large boxes. They were really strange, these boxes, with their elegant carved-wood roofs and curtains of white muslin. It took Ophelia a few seconds to realize that these boxes were in fact canopied four-poster beds, and a few more to realize that, behind the muslin curtains, there were recumbent figures. It couldn't be possible— people were *sleeping* here?

"The sandbeds," declared the foreman, rather amused at Ophelia's flabbergasted face.

THE SANDBEDS

"Trompe-l'oeils alive!" exclaimed Baron Melchior. "So this is where they lead to, your famous blue sandglasses? The hygienic conditions are appalling!" he said, shocked.

Thorn, on the other hand, didn't even bat an eyelid; he had already buried his big nose in the workshop's ledgers.

"Oh, that's because you're seeing the sandbeds from the outside," the foreman said, calmly. "I can assure you that each one conforms entirely to public-health standards. And we give the place a sweep every day," he stressed, with a hint of mischief in his voice. He moved over to the metal staircase adjoining the gangway. "It's this way to access the hangar, lady and gents. We do have a goods lift, but it's in need of a little mechanical servicing."

"Watch where you put your feet," Thorn warned, for Ophelia's benefit.

She didn't suffer from vertigo, but she took the warning seriously. There were many steps and they were narrow and badly lit, and there were many flights to tackle before reaching the ground. At each landing, she leaned over to take a better look at the hangar's beds, from which some figures emerged, and into which others disappeared, through the muslin curtains, after one turn of a sandglass. Ophelia was still too high up and too far away to make them out clearly in the bluish

340

light of the lamps, but she wondered how these people managed not to be conscious of their surroundings. Had none of them ever had the curiosity to open the curtains of their four-poster bed?

As she was continuing her descent, Ophelia felt a hot breath against her ear. She turned around and saw Thorn crossing the landing above. It wasn't his breath Ophelia had sensed; he was too far away. Was it Vladislava following her that closely? She'd just had this thought when she was winded by a violent blow to the chest. She was so surprised that she didn't immediately understand why the banister was slipping from under her fingers, why her feet were leaving the ground, and why her hair was splayed across her glasses.

She was falling. She was going to break her bones on an endless flight of steps.

With a feeling of complete unreality, Ophelia toppled backwards, unable to cling to anything but the sight of Thorn turning another page of the ledger. As she landed with all her weight, her lungs emptied of their air and a pain shot through her elbow like an electric current. She stared blankly, through her almost knocked-off glasses, at the mustachioed face looking down at her.

A policeman had rushed to catch her in his arms. "Okay, lung yady . . . young lady? Nothing broken?"

The policeman's speech was a little garbled, under his handlebar moustache, and he was slightly cross-eyed, making him squint. Ophelia wasn't about to forget that face; she probably owed her life to it.

"Y-yes," she stammered in a tiny voice, still winded from the impact. "Thank you. Really."

Finally looking up, Thorn frowned on seeing the policeman helping Ophelia to her feet. "I told you to watch out."

"I did watch out," Ophelia said, defensively. "It wasn't

my . . . " She went quiet before finishing her sentence, and looked at the stairs she'd almost come flying down on her back. She was certain she'd been shoved by an invisible presence, but she refused to believe it was a deliberate act on the part of Vladislava. The disgraced Invisible had protected them from the Chroniclers, and Thorn was about to defend the cause of her clan. Laying into Ophelia now made no sense at all. *Never set foot in the court ever again.* And what if it wasn't Vladislava who was in their midst right now?

Ophelia took the precaution of staying close to the policemen, particularly the one who had caught her in midair, while the foreman showed them around the place.

"It's the principle of 'pull pin—enjoy!'" he explained in a cheery voice that echoed across the hangar. "For a long time, we only produced the regular sandglasses, of the green or red collection. Round trips to standard destinations, you know. One day, Mother Hildegarde said to us, just like that: 'Hey, *viejecitos*, what if we invented a sandglass that transported people straight into a dream?' That's what she's like, the Mother. She always has completely crazy ideas, and she always finds a way of making them a reality."

Chilled thanks to the hangar's ice-cold temperature, they all moved together between the rows of beds. Ophelia found them impressive, close up: they looked like real boats, with their frames carved like prows and their vast white curtains like sails. The only way not to get lost in the middle of this stationary naval fleet was to follow the direction panels: "STANDARD ILLUSIONS FOR LADIES," "STANDARD ILLUSIONS FOR MEN," "ILLUSIONS OF YOUTH," "SPECIAL CHILDREN'S ILLUSIONS," "ILLUSIONS JUST FOR SERVANTS," "LOYALTY BONUS ILLUSIONS," etc.

"To create a sandglass," continued the foreman, "Mother Hildegarde just has to take a sample of space on a mattress and slip it into a sandglass phial."

"A sample of space?" Ophelia interrupted him.

"Yes, miss. I'd find it very tricky to explain to you what that looks like, but Mother Hildegarde has never got it wrong. The workshop makes the sandglasses so that all she has to do is seal the cover and prime the pin, once her work is done. We then place the mattress in here, in its pretty wooden frame, with suitably nice, clean sheets," the foreman stressed, turning his smile towards Baron Melchior. "And when that's done, a professional illusionist goes over there, to the depot," he added, indicating a large industrial double door, at the back of the hangar. "He transforms these ordinary beds into wonderlands. I'll let you be the judge of the result."

Ophelia looked carefully at the sandbeds surrounding her. It was the most grotesque phantasmagoria she'd ever witnessed. Shadows kept on appearing and disappearing behind the muslin curtains: a crinoline dress tipped back from which there emerged two legs shaking with laughter, an old fogey bouncing on his mattress like a schoolboy, a bewigged silhouette sobbing with joy into his pillow. Some of them, in more than compromising positions, let out lascivious moans. Ophelia felt embarrassed for all these people as the policemen pulled aside the bed canopies, just for a brief inspection, but nothing, seemingly, could rouse them from their bewitchment.

"When I think that only yesterday I was here, among them!" Baron Melchior sighed, with dismay.

"But you're a Mirage yourself," Ophelia said, startled. "Isn't it possible for you to break this kind of spell?"

"A Mirage is immune only to his or her own illusions, Miss Great Family Reader. They're also the only ones with the power to cancel them. Hence, all of a Mirage's creations disappear when they die. Ours is an ephemeral art," he said with a melancholy smile, under his moustache. "It upsets me every time to think that neither my musical ties nor my perfumed jewelry nor my kaleidoscopic dresses will survive me!"

"Illusions all need a helping hand to work, you see?" the foreman continued. "A signal, if you like. It enters first through the eyes before reaching the brain. As long as you're not looking at our 'helping hand,' you don't see the illusion and don't feel its effects."

"You're oversimplifying," the baron protested, in a professorial tone. "Our illusions work *preferentially* by sight, but there are also auditory, tactile, or olfactory stimuli. We can create highly complex works of art, even if we don't all specialize in the same areas. Depending on whether one is a landscape gardener, an interior designer, or a couturier, one will favor certain sensations over others. I grant you, however, that the eyes remain our preferred amplifier."

Ophelia thought of Gail's black monocle, which had the ability to filter all illusions.

"May I know the name of the professional illusionist who works for you?" asked Baron Melchior, indicating the nearest bed with his cane. "Having sampled these illusions from the inside, I can confirm that they are devilishly effective. I've always emerged deeply moved, and I've never been able to recall exactly why. It's like waking from a marvelous dream that just leaves you with a very powerful impression."

"I haven't the slightest idea. We've never come across him in the workshop; he only goes to the depot. Only Mother Hildegarde could tell you his name."

Ophelia jumped. A policeman was suddenly shaking with an uncontrollable fit of the giggles while inspecting a sandbed. He threw his cocked hat into the air, did a little jig, and blew kisses to an imaginary audience, proclaiming at the top of his voice: "Life is beautiful, ladies and gentlemen!"

"Ah, that one has found our 'helping hand,'" commented the foreman. "He must have looked up into the bed's canopy."

Thorn was so engrossed in his ledgers that he paid no attention to the policeman, who was now trying to entice one of his colleagues into a passionate waltz.

"With all this, we still haven't found anyone," Ophelia muttered to him. "What exactly are you looking for in those accounts?"

Thorn let out an exasperated groan, and Ophelia thought how she herself would have liked to have an object to read, anything to help her to accelerate the inquiry and feel less powerless.

"And the yellow sandglasses?" she asked, turning to the foreman. "Foster . . . A friend told me about them once. He said they were exactly like the blue sandglasses, but only one way, with no time limit. Do you produce them here?"

"Certainly not," the foreman said, categorically. "It would be far too dangerous. The yellow sandglasses are a myth contrived to make servants dream, nothing more. Just imagine if you remained stuck within one of those illusions," he said, indicating the policeman, who was still smiling beatifically. "You would die of pleasure, before even dying of dehydration! That said, someone with even the slightest skill could modify any sandglass," he admitted, with a mischievous glint in his eye. "Installing an automatic turning mechanism isn't simple, but it's not impossible, either."

Ophelia nodded, pensively. An automatic turning mechanism? That was probably it, the trap Archibald had detected on the sandglass, of which she'd read the pin.

"We have inspected all the sandbeds, sir," announced a policeman, clicking his heels in front of Thorn. "Those reported missing are not to be found here."

"Nothing in the depot to report, either," said a second policeman, returning from the other side of the building.

Ophelia felt her throat tighten. Of course, she'd expected that, but she'd really hoped to see Archibald emerging from the canopy of a bed, yawning.

As for the foreman, he didn't seem at all disappointed. He broke into a smile, revealing teeth in pitiful condition. "Jolly good! As you can see, our factory isn't implicated in your case."

"That is not true."

Thorn had declared this as a simple statement of fact.

THE DEAD END

Thorn strode over to the foreman, forcing him to look up at him, and held out three of the ledgers he had just been going through.

"This ledger," he growled, shaking the first one, "records the number of sandglasses made in your workshop every day of this year."

"Indeed," said the foreman. "But I don't see . . ."

"This ledger," Thorn interrupted him, this time shaking the second one, "records the number of sandglass-bed links carried out by Madam Hildegarde, also this year."

"That's correct, but I . . . "

"And this ledger," continued Thorn, shaking the third, "records the number of beds furnished with illusions, once linked to their sandglasses."

"So?"

"So these figures don't tally. Four blue sandglasses and four beds have got lost in transit, somewhere between leaving the workshop and being put into service."

"Oh, that can be explained very easily," the foreman said, still not dropping his half-smile. "That stock must still be lying around at the depot. Our illusionist casts his spell on the beds when he has the time, and we don't sell sandglasses whose beds haven't yet been treated by him."

"You keep a register of the beds waiting to be treated by him," Thorn said, rigidly. "I have, of course, taken them into account in my calculations, and the total still doesn't tally. Four sandglasses and four beds have disappeared from your stock."

For the first time, the foreman appeared to take Thorn seriously. From a pocket on his apron, he pulled out some spectacles that were as old as he was, and scanned the columns of figures. "Are you quite sure you're right?" he asked, turning the pages. "Maybe some sandglasses got broken and were considered unusable. We keep a register of damaged stock."

"I am absolutely sure. I searched to establish exactly when the discrepancy in your accounting occurred, and pinned it down to the date of May 23rd. See for yourself," insisted Thorn, returning one of the ledgers to the foreman. "Under the number of sandglass-bed links carried out by Madam Hildegarde on that date, the number '9' has been changed to '5'. The ink is different, so this correction was made after the event."

"Would someone have falsified our accounts?" the foreman muttered, seeming not to consider it possible. "But, come on now, who would do such a thing?"

"A colleague, an intruder, you yourself, or Madam Hildegarde in person," Thorn reeled off, without a second thought. "This factory is an open house, anyone can just come and go here without anyone else knowing."

"But still . . . pilfering beds right under our noses."

Thorn snorted in annoyance. "If you kept your books properly, with unique serial numbers for each sandglass and each bed, this error wouldn't have been missed by you."

Ophelia stared at Thorn in disbelief. How had he managed to pick up such a small anomaly in such a short space of time?

"The fact is, those sandglasses and those beds have left your factory after having been linked and before being treated by the illusionist," Thorn recapped. "Our abductor planned to use them only for sending specific people to a destination of his or her choice. They would have modified the sandglass mechanism themselves to make any return impossible."

"Four sandglasses, four beds, four people missing," Baron Melchior summed up. "It doesn't tell us where they are, but we shouldn't have any other abductions to lament." He smoothed his moustache, looking relieved, as if Thorn had just told him he no longer had to fear for his own life.

"But how could the abductor be sure his sandglasses would actually have their pins pulled?" asked Ophelia. "Giving one as a present is one thing. Being certain it will be used is quite another."

"That wasn't a hard bet to win," countered Baron Melchior, tapping his frock-coat pocket, bulging with his own sandglass. "When an item becomes fashionable, up on high, you can count on the courtiers going to town on it. Starting with me."

The foreman couldn't stop rechecking the falsified ledger and comparing it with the others. He wasn't smiling so much.

Frozen to the bone, Ophelia lifted her scarf over her nose and did her own tally of what they'd discovered so far. If she disregarded the particular case of Archibald, those who had disappeared were in the grip of extreme anxiety, so were susceptible to taking tranquilizers. After all, hadn't each of them sought sanctuary at Clairdelune, precisely because they feared for their lives? They'd all received threatening letters. The writer had used them very effectively to put pressure on his victims: the more anxious they were, the stronger their desire to pull the pin on the blue sandglasses. It was a truly malicious manipulation.

"And yet," Ophelia thought, out loud, "I can't really imagine the director of the *Nibelungen* using sandglasses. He gave them very negative publicity, and exhorted his readers not to use them."

"Contradictory old Cousin Chekhov!" Baron Melchior sighed, with a bittersweet smile. "If you knew him privately, you'd know he's an avid puller of the pin. Those most fiercely opposed to a temptation are sometimes its greatest adepts."

"But Archibald wasn't supposed to be the fourth target," Ophelia reminded him. "When I read the pin, I saw that he'd appropriated someone else's sandglass."

'Was it destined for me?' she suddenly wondered, struck by the very thought.

Baron Melchior maintained a wary silence, and then let out a sigh so prolonged, it was as if his body was deflating like a balloon. "It was mine."

"Yours?" Ophelia asked, amazed.

At that, Thorn did allow himself a raising of the eyebrows, which, briefly, relaxed his features.

"Mine," confirmed the baron. "I had inexplicably mislaid a blue sandglass following my last visit to Clairdelune. Mr. Ambassador must have taken advantage of a moment of distraction to pick my pockets."

"He may have saved your life," said Ophelia. "But why would someone want to abduct you, in particular? The Provost of the Marshals, the director of the *Nibelungen*, and Count Harold all took political stances that were . . . well . . . somewhat extreme."

Baron Melchior's smile was joyless and couldn't even raise his moustache. "You're flattering me, but I'm not the saint you think I am, Miss Great Family Reader."

Ophelia recalled how many times she'd seen him glancing anxiously behind him, as if he feared being attacked by his own shadow. Even now, he didn't seem entirely at ease.

"Did you receive threatening letters?"

Baron Melchior suddenly looked away, and Ophelia was struck by the loneliness she caught in his eyes at that moment. It was the very same loneliness she detected in Thorn.

"Forgive me, Miss Great Family Reader. With all due respect to you, I can't reply to that question."

To Ophelia, it was as if he'd replied, "Yes." She wanted to dig deeper, but Thorn stopped her with a look, clearly telling her to mind her own business. Ophelia's scarf lashed the air like the tail of an annoyed cat. Why did everyone double-lock themselves into their own secrets? Wouldn't it be so much easier for them, in the end, to trust one another?

"Take great care of yourself, please," she whispered, ignoring Thorn's grimace of irritation. "I think you're in danger."

Baron Melchior looked back at Ophelia, his moustache taut with perplexity. With the great distinction typical of him, he leant with both beringed hands on the knob of his cane and tilted a body as round as the full moon towards Ophelia.

"Danger is part of our life," he told her, solemnly. "I'm fighting for a different future, and I believe you are, too, at your own level and in your own way. I will not abandon my post, just as you didn't abandon yours. It's up to us to see our choices out to the end, am I not right?"

Ophelia silently considered him, in that aquatic light, and couldn't help but find him magnificent, in his own way. "Forgive me for persisting," she said to him, gently, "but if you are a victim of blackmail, you really should talk about it to us. I myself also recei . . . "

"That is enough," Thorn cut in, fiercely. "If the minister has a statement to make, it's to the Treasury that he will address it."

Ophelia went quiet, rather shocked, and Baron Melchior also seemed ill at ease.

"Can we consider my sister to be in the clear?" he inquired, gently. "Really, the quantity of blue sandglasses you caught her with is her own business, isn't it? Cunegond probably put in an order, in the usual way, like any of Madam Hildegarde's clients. Of course," he hastened to add, swiveling his spinning-top body round to Thorn, "Mr. Treasurer could check them, one by one, should he deem it necessary."

Thorn pulled a legal notebook from an inside pocket of his coat. "We'll see about that. The running of this workshop is under official scrutiny. It matters little whether Madam Hildegarde was or wasn't the instigator of the abductions, she will have to face justice forthwith. From now until light has been shed on this affair, I order work to cease at this workshop. Sandglasses, of whatever color, are prohibited from sale and use until further notice."

"Such a measure won't make you popular, Mr. Treasurer," sighed Baron Melchior. "You're going to deprive a lot of people of their little treat."

Thorn signed the writ, tore it from his notebook, and handed it to the foreman. "As for you, you are remanded in custody."

"Me?"

"Madam Hildegarde is away and you are her deputy," Thorn said, as if that explained everything.

The old man seemed increasingly confused, and Ophelia felt a surge of compassion for him. Indifferent, Thorn took the ledgers from his hands without further ado, entrusting them to the cross-eyed policeman, who squinted at them, clearly wondering what he was supposed to do with them.

"From now on, these are case exhibits. If Madam Hildegarde wants these documents back, she will have to submit an official request to the Treasury."

"Thorn. Please." Unable to bear it any longer, Ophelia had tugged on his coat sleeve to make him look at the foreman, who was swaying to and fro, eyes glued to his writ, as if the ground were giving way beneath him.

"Oh, you, no point fainting over it!" Thorn said, annoyed. "It's an order of provisional detention, not a conviction. You will be released as soon as Madam Hildegarde has been heard, and the inquiry has established that you are not compromising public safety. If Madam Hildegarde is the model employer you claim she is, she will volunteer to face justice, in your place."

"Well I never," the foreman exclaimed, scratching the gray hair under his cap. "It's my wife who's going to give me a right telling-off, you know. And my artisans, what are they going to do while I'm away?"

Thorn's eyes flashed like lightning. "They can employ an accountant worthy of the name and sort this place out. For your information, you have fourteen spent bulbs, twenty-three beds that aren't perfectly aligned with the rest of their row, and I find it absurd that there is a different number of steps between each landing of your stairway."

Ophelia raised her eyebrows. She had no idea what was going on behind Thorn's massive forehead, but he was definitely not his normal self. As for herself, she wasn't remotely inclined to count the steps, as they all trooped back up to the workshop. With her hurt arm folded on her stomach, she just wanted to be sure not to tumble down them a second time. As long as she didn't know who had pushed her earlier on, she wouldn't feel at ease. If all of Thorn's days resembled the one she'd just lived through, she understood why he had such shadows under his eyes.

Ophelia still felt too anxious to think about resting, and was exasperated when, once they'd reached Mother Hildegarde's administrative office, Thorn pointed, in an authoritarian way, at a chair for her to sit on, as if dealing with an unruly child.

"I must get on with an in-depth inspection of the accounts. You don't move from here, you touch nothing until I have finished. As for you," he said, addressing the policemen, "confiscate all the sandglasses in the workshop, including those in the process of being made."

The policemen clicked their hobnailed heels in time as they marched through the workshop, like soldiers off to battle. Baron Melchior followed them, begging them, on behalf of the Ministry of Elegance, above all, not to ill treat anyone.

Thorn's mood was so terrible, Ophelia didn't want to worsen it. She sat down, frustrated and with nothing to do. A glance at the clock revealed that only eighteen hours remained before the Web severed its link with Archibald. Ophelia still didn't know where he was, and she no longer had a single lead, a single clue.

It was a dead end, once again.

While Thorn combed through the books, she examined the room. It would have looked like any old accounts office, with its metal filing cabinets, cash register, and three telephones, if it hadn't belonged to Mother Hildegarde. Every storage space proved much bigger than it logically should have been. Thus, on several occasions, Ophelia saw Thorn's long arm buried up to the elbow inside the tiny drawers of the desk. There were also still lifes on every wall surface, and they always featured, without exception, baskets of oranges. Ophelia had never known anyone else so obsessed with one fruit.

"And me, Mr. Suretreat . . . Treaterer . . . Treasurer?" stammered the cross-eyed policeman, after a while.

Loaded down with the ledgers Thorn had entrusted to him, he had remained in the office and was twitching his handlebar moustache as if fighting the need to scratch his nose.

"You, don't distract me," grumbled Thorn, depositing a load of extra notebooks on top of his pile.

If Ophelia had, initially, felt gratitude towards this policeman, who had, after all, saved her life, now he made her feel ill at ease. It wasn't his crossed eyes that bothered her, but the way he stared so intently at her, without kindness, as though looking at some strange creature on the shelf of a cabinet of curiosities.

Ophelia got up from her chair and pressed her nose to the glass panel that allowed one to see the workshop from the office. Following Thorn's orders, the policemen were throwing all the sandglasses into large canvas sacks. The old artisans watched them doing so without protest, but with perhaps just a dazed look in their eyes. As for the foreman, his wrists were already in handcuffs.

Only Gail was moving amid this inactivity, banging her palm on a table. She was shouting at Baron Melchior, and Ophelia could clearly read the word "innocence" on her lips. Would they remain friends after all this? Ophelia had the unpleasant feeling of finding herself on the wrong side of the fence, as though justice was the real guilty party. In the end, weren't Mother Hildegarde's employees the victims, more than the accomplices, in this affair?

Ophelia turned resolutely towards Thorn, banging her knee on the chair as she did so. "The Treasury is currently the owner of the ledgers, isn't it?"

"I refuse."

"Excuse me?"

Thorn's lightning response had thrown Ophelia. He was flicking rapidly through the pages of an address book, instantly memorizing Mother Hildegarde's list of contacts.

"You were going to ask me permission to carry out a reading," he said, without looking at her. "I don't give you that permission. End of story."

Ophelia couldn't believe her ears. "Not even if that reading could establish the identity of the abductor? Not even if it could save lives and jobs?"

Thorn closed a drawer with an exasperated shove. "If you read the falsified ledger, would you be able formally to identify the author of the aforementioned falsification, dated the twenty-third of May?"

"No," Ophelia had to admit. "When I penetrate a person's state of mind, it's rarely kind enough to reveal their name, face, and the date they came into contact with the object. But I can try to piece together an identity from a range of clues."

Thorn opened another drawer and had to extend the desk's piston lamp to see the back of it. Warily, he armed himself with a handkerchief to pluck several moldy oranges out of the drawer, and they instantly gave off a ghastly smell.

"Do you have the remotest idea of the number of people who might have circulated in this office and handled that ledger since May? Am I supposed to consider as guilty all those of whom Miss Great Family Reader thinks she has 'pieced together the identity'? You are proposing evidence to me that is inadmissible by law," he replied, instead of Ophelia, with no patience whatsoever. "It is objectivity and facts we need right now, not suppositions that will make us waste precious time."

Ophelia wasn't particularly proud, but she had rarely felt so humiliated. She felt it even more because she knew, deep down, that Thorn was right. The more layers of "experience" an object had been through, the less precise the evaluation of it. The pin of a sandglass and an accounting ledger, those were two totally different readings. And right now, human lives were at stake.

"I just wanted to make myself useful," she said.

"You already have been, more than enough if you ask me. I am just looking forward to the wedding being over and you leaving the Pole with your whole family."

In the workshop, someone must have switched on the radio, as a crackly voice started to sing: "Why sleep when I can dance at the ball? Why go to bed when I can play cards? It's my, my, my splendid miracle coffee!"

Ophelia felt a powerful rumbling, the nature of which she didn't understand, rising up the length of her body. Her stomach began to vibrate, her lungs to fill, her temples to throb, her eyes to mist up. Despite her blocked nose, she forced herself to breathe deeply to stem this rising tide, but the dikes finally gave way and her voice burst forth from her body in an uncontrollable flood:

"A lot has happened to me since you made me your fiancée. I've received an unbelievable number of death threats, and almost as many indecent proposals. I've been imprisoned, disguised, tricked, insulted, enslaved, infantilized, booed, subjected to hypnotic manipulation, and I've seen my aunt losing her mind, before my very eyes. And yet, I've never been as afraid as I am right now. I'm afraid for my family, I'm afraid for myself, I'm afraid for Berenilde, I'm afraid for Archibald, too. And for all of that, Thorn, it's you I have to thank. So could you, please, stop speaking to me as if I were the cause of all your problems?"

Surprise had extended Thorn's brows in one go, and his facial scar, pulled by this sudden movement, seemed ready to burst.

Ophelia was as stupefied as he was. Her voice, lips, hands, legs continued to shake, and she even felt a tear might escape her. She hadn't the faintest idea what was actually happening to her, but knew she'd best get a grip immediately. This was no time to make a scene.

Thorn was looking at her so fixedly, one might have believed that his great body had been jammed. Only his jaws were half-opening and closing without a sound, as if he wanted to say something without knowing what that something was.

The cross-eyed policeman was so fascinated by the spectacle

that he didn't notice that the pile of ledgers in his arms was teetering more and more, about to collapse at any moment.

It was in the middle of this uncomfortable silence that the voice of the radio presenter rang out from the workshop wireless: " . . . tonight, in a sanitarium close to the seaside resort of Opal Sands, which Citaceleste is now hovering over. The nurses are deaf to our questions, but we detected anxious murmurings among them. The outcome of this delivery is looking more than doubtful. Let's be clear, dear listeners, the number-one favorite in the Pole isn't as young as she tried to make out, and the way she fled the court fooled no one. But no problem—if you don't come to the court, the court will come to you! Because this event is important, ladies and gentlemen. This baby, presuming it makes it into the world safe and sound, is the first direct descendant of our Lord Farouk for three centuries. But does that guarantee it a bright future? Nothing is less sure when one knows our Lord's aversion to children. Stay tuned, dear listeners! *Tittle-Tattle*, your favorite program, will keep you informed as soon as we know more."

Ophelia had shot up like a spring. Berenilde was giving birth! She was giving birth and already, journalists were lying in wait behind the door of her room.

Thorn instantly regained control of his movements and speech. He opened the glass door separating workshop and office, and addressed all the policemen: "Requisition all that is transportable and have an airship on standby. Six volunteers will stay here to go through the factory with a fine-tooth comb. If you find anything at all of interest—a cuff link, a footprint, a feather from a pillow, whatever—you cable the Opal Sands sanitarium. I will be away only as long as is strictly necessary."

Thorn had spoken in a detached, almost mechanical way, but Ophelia wasn't fooled. He had compulsively pulled his fob watch out of his coat, and only then remembered that it had stopped. For someone who never forgot anything, this absent-mindedness alone betrayed great inner turmoil. *Tittle-Tattle*, with its macabre dramatizing, had had its effect.

"Your master key?" she asked, trying to calm the twitching of her scarf.

"No Compass Rose serves the sanitarium, and going via the station access will waste time," Thorn stated, categorically. "The airship is our quickest option. I'll get us a safe passage."

Thorn picked up the telephone, and spoke to the operator as though to a policeman under his command.

"I'm going ahead," Ophelia decided. "Security checks or not, there's no law in the Pole that forbids people from passing through mirrors."

She went over to the office's wall mirror and leant with both hands against her reflection. Not entirely convinced, she concentrated on a mirror in the sanitarium waiting room, in which she'd already reflected herself. The mirror wouldn't let her pass though it; the destination was too far away. Ophelia was more disconcerted, however, when she encountered the same resistance on trying to access her hotel room. Citaceleste was hovering above Opal Sands; the distance wasn't that great, surely? Her anxiety increased as she tried ever closer destinations: the room at the airship landing stage, the hall of mirrors near the main square, the last lift they'd taken. She didn't even manage to access the mirror in the hall of the factory, just a few yards away, although she was sure that, on entering, she'd reflected herself in it.

"Well?" Thorn grumbled, putting the receiver down. "You're still here?"

"I don't understand," stammered Ophelia, staring at the shocked face of her own reflection. "I can't pass through mirrors anymore."

FRAGMENT: FOURTH REPRISE

I think we could have all lived happily, in a way, God, me and the others, if it weren't for that accursed book. It disgusted me. I knew what bound me to it in the most sickening of ways, but the horror of that particular knowledge came later, much later. I didn't understand straight away, I was too ignorant. I loved God, yes, but I despised that book, which he'd open at the drop of a hat. As for God, he relished it. When God was happy, he wrote. When God was furious, he wrote.

The memory has launched into a new image. A children's book.

Although the memory gives him no indication of where he is, it is abundantly detailed on this book. So it must be important.

The large, colored illustrations depict, in turn, an overdecorated oriental palace, an oasis lost in the sand, naked women under turquoise veils, and, in each scene the same character: a horseman with skin illuminated in gold.

At first sight, of no interest.

Through the density of the memory, he manages to fathom the emotions these images trigger in him. Fascination and jealousy. The Odin of the past would have liked to resemble the character in the children's book. He doesn't like himself as he is.

And is that it?

The images tell him nothing, so he decides to focus his effort on remembering the text. It's an old language, one of those spoken before the Rupture. It's not the language Odin speaks, the one God taught them at home, the one that, one day, with few exceptions, all their descendants would speak. And yet, one way or another, he must have tried to assimilate the language of this children's book, since he can see himself deciphering the letters in the title, with no comprehension problems:

THE EXTRAORDINARY ADVENTURES OF PRINCE FAROUK

So that's it. He understands now the underlying point to this memory. An identity crisis. He would have liked this children's book to be his own Book.

For the first time since he's been delving deep into his memory, he finally sees it. His Book. Not Artemis's, not anyone else's—his. Very carefully, he takes it out, and turns its thick pages made of skin. Revulsion. The Book is written using an alphabet that God never taught him. That language, only God understands it; it's not spoken, but written. God uses it every time he is seized by a new creative impulse.

He places Prince Farouk's beautiful book and his own hideous Book side by side. A work on paper and a work on skin. The first speaks to him of hot lands, the second destines him to a world of ice.

He feels it suddenly, right through his body, this call pushing him northwards, to a world as white as he is, with no oasis and no oriental palace. When the time comes, he, like a migratory bird, will have to go there. Because it's written. Why? Why should he follow orders in a language he doesn't even understand? He wants nothing of this destiny dictated by God, of this story that doesn't belong to him, of this power that he can't master. He doesn't want to leave home, leave God and the others; he doesn't want to become what he is supposed to become; he doesn't want to be what he's supposed to be. He doesn't even want his name. Odin.

The memory is now taking an interesting turn. Something happened on that night, something essential. What was it again?

Ah, yes. The knife. It's coming back to him now. He's brandishing a knife. He looks, in turn, at *The Extraordinary Adventures of Prince Farouk* and his hideous Book of flesh.

"I will call myself Farouk," he hears himself whisper.

He stabs his Book and the pain completely overwhelms him.

The memory ends here.

Nota bene: "Try your dears." Who said these words and what do they mean?

THE CRY

Outside, the sun was changing by the minute. It had spent the night suspended just above the landscape without ever tipping below the horizon, shrunk to the size of a candle flame, casting a twilight hue on the rocks and water of the fjords. Now, it was slowly rising above the boreal forest, brighter than an Olympic torch.

Ophelia didn't look at it once. Hunched up on a folding seat, nose pressed to the cockpit window, she was desperately searching for the sanitarium, as if that could help the airship to reach it quicker. It was still too soon to see it. They had only just taken off, and right then, the pilot was slowly maneuvering above Opal Sands in order to fly around the Citaceleste, and then head north.

Stuck between Thorn and Baron Melchior, Ophelia had cramps all over from being so tense. Berenilde's delivery was likely to be difficult; Archibald's life now just hung by a thread; and mirrors had suddenly closed, like doors. She felt as if everything solid in her world threatened to shatter, from one moment to the next.

When the airship was rocked by a strong west wind, Ophelia was thrown first against Baron Melchior and then against Thorn. The pain in her elbow was making her see stars. The small airship wasn't designed to carry so many passengers.

Totally professional, the policemen were as busy in the cockpit as they would have been at the police station. Half of them were going through the items requisitioned at the factory, the other half putting each artisan through a detailed interrogation. For some obscure reason, Thorn had opted to take all of Mother Hildegarde's personnel with him, rather than entrusting them to the policemen who had remained at Citaceleste. Uprooted from the familiar world of their workshop, the elderly craftsmen were disorientated, but showed remarkable consistency in their answers: none of them had ever noticed anything suspicious either about Mother Hildegarde or their colleagues.

Brought on board with the rest of the employees, Gail was squatting in a corner of the cabin, arms wrapped around legs, electric-blue eye looking daggers from under the peak of her cap.

With his lace handkerchief covering his nose, Baron Melchior kept looking, in turn, at his pocket watch, at Ophelia, and then at Thorn. "Far be it my intention to question your methods, but are you quite sure that this diversion won't prejudice the inquiry? We only have until midnight. Our sole serious lead is Madam Hildegarde, and I doubt very much we will find her in a delivery room."

Ophelia didn't really know how to respond. She felt she wouldn't be able to think straight until she'd seen Berenilde and her baby doing well. Turning to Thorn, she immediately knew that he wouldn't respond, either. Twisted like barbed wire on the next folding seat, with his coat collar turned up against his cheeks, he was looking deep inside himself. Stubble was starting to encroach on his face. He hadn't uttered a word since takeoff, and his thumb kept opening and closing the cover of his watch, with an obsessive click-click. His anger, it seemed, had completely dissipated. And with it, all his vital energy.

"You still can't manage it?" Baron Melchior asked, politely. He had just noticed how Ophelia kept tapping the little double-sided mirror an artisan had lent her.

"No. Still can't."

"But, with all due respect, Miss Great Family Reader, he continued, gently, "are you at least still able to . . . well . . . to read objects?"

"I checked," muttered Ophelia. "I can still read objects, I can still animate objects, but for some inexplicable reason, I can no longer pass through mirrors. Each branch of power demands a specific frame of mind. I've lost that one."

And that was precisely what was tormenting her. "Traveling through mirrors," her great-uncle had once told her, "that requires facing up to oneself. Those who close their eyes, those who lie to themselves, those who see themselves as better than they are, they could never do it."

Since when had Ophelia stopped being honest?

At last, the airship began its descent, and all the passengers toppled over like dominoes. It took a good many crushed toes and elbowed ribs before everyone could leave the airship by the rear gangway.

The fresh air outside, permeated with salt and resin, hit Ophelia like a salutary slap. However, as she stepped onto the lawn, her dress billowing in the draft from the propellers, she thought for a moment that the airship pilot had gone to the wrong place. Instead of the clients stretched out on loungers she'd encountered on her last walk in the sanitarium garden, today she saw only Mirages swirling joyfully between the caviar and vodka buffets, buoyed by the lively music of a ball orchestra. Cascades of flowers, firework ballets, perfumed fountains: a multitude of illusions had been conjured up across the whole garden, as if a veritable nuptial celebration were in full swing.

On a stage worthy of a theatre, a commentator was describing all that was going on behind the round windows of the sanitarium:

"I can see another nurse," his smooth voice boomed from the carbon microphone. "She's coming up to a window on the second floor. Is she going to give us an official announcement? False hope, dear listeners, she's closed the curtains. Is that the room Madam Berenilde is in? Would so many precautions be taken if the birth were progressing normally? What unbearable suspense, but what suspense! Stay close to your wirelesses, dear listeners, *Tittle-Tattle* will, as ever, be your eyes and ears!"

"What are all these courtiers doing here?" asked Ophelia, amazed. "Isn't coming and going beyond the Citaceleste strictly controlled? It took us an hour to obtain a safe passage."

Baron Melchior pointed out to her, up in the sky, an airship with a gilded fuselage moored to the roof of the clock tower. Blinded at first by the reflection of the sun on this flying bullion, Ophelia finally recognized the family coat of arms. Farouk was here in person!

"And there I was, thinking he didn't care about this child . . . "

"A father remains a father," the baron said, philosophically. "Particularly when he's a family spirit."

Gloomily, Thorn surveyed the celebrations. "Proceed with the immediate confiscation of all sandglasses in circulation here," he ordered the policemen. "Give no explanation. Two of you, stay with me to escort Madam Hildegarde's employees. Whatever happens, you are all sworn to silence; the ongoing inquiry must remain confidential. The first person to contravene my orders will share the foreman's cell at the police station."

Gail dug her hands into the pockets of her overalls. "In short, we open and close our valve at your whim."

Thorn didn't react. He cleaved his way through the whirling dancers and party illusions like a shadow cutting through a world of light. His procession of old men didn't go unnoticed: with their dazed expressions and work aprons, the artisans soon prompted a wave of hilarity across the garden. The laughter turned into protestation, however, when the policemen circulated among the Mirages to seize their sandglasses.

"Merely a control measure, ladies and gentlemen," they repeated, with totally professional courtesy.

Thorn honored no one with a look; neither the ministers who came up to him with furious little steps nor the servants who offered him culinary illusions nor the photographers who rushed at him in a flash of magnesium.

Trying to make herself as small as possible, under her thrice-wound scarf, Ophelia followed hot on Thorn's heels. She noticed, not without some concern, that he had become visibly stooped. She might find him insufferable sometimes, but she did rather regret what she'd told him to his face in anger. It had happened at the wrong time.

Ophelia noticed a few Web diplomats and their wives among those waltzing. They were stumbling more than dancing, but their drowsiness was a sign that Archibald was still clinging on to life, somewhere, in a mysterious twilight world.

Taking advantage of the general confusion on the sanitarium lawns, Ophelia moved closer to Gail. "You have no idea where we might find Madam Hildegarde? I accuse her of nothing, but what she knows could really help us."

The Nihilist blew her nose on her sleeve. With her workman's garb and her scowl, it was hard to believe that she was noble herself. "I've already told you once before," she whispered. "Why is Hildegarde called 'Mother'? Because she never abandons her children."

Ophelia couldn't make head or tail of this reply. She

wanted to go further, but her voice was drowned out by that of *Tittle-Tattle*:

"It's anyone's guess, dear listeners! What faculties will the child to be born have? Will it inherit just the maternal claws? Will it develop a new type of family power? With direct descendants, everything is en-tire-ly possible! Oh, but hold on!" the commentator suddenly exclaimed, making his microphone crackle. "Whom do I see, hiding in our Treasurer's shadow? Is it not the Great Family Reader who honors us with her presence?"

In an instant, the journalists harassing Thorn rushed over to Ophelia and encircled her, bombarding her with questions on the case of the missing. She would never have managed to extricate herself had Baron Melchior not diverted the general attention on to himself.

"As assistant to the Great Family Reader, I would be delighted to answer your questions!" he intercepted, in a bombastic voice, while his cane discreetly pushed Ophelia in the direction of the sanitarium. "Those, at any rate, that won't compromise the ongoing inquiry. I'm all ears, gentlemen!"

Ophelia slipped among Mother Hildegarde's employees and quickly went through the entrance with them. As soon as Thorn had closed the heavy double doors, the dancing music and *Tittle-Tattle*'s speculating became as distant as the wind whistling through the conifers. The sanitarium may have been a world of tiles, windows, and colonnades, but its thick walls protected its clients from all outside disturbances.

The person on reception, who was busy sending a telegram, took off her earphones, put on her white headdress, and emerged from behind her counter with a stern clicking of her clogs.

"I repeat that you cannot come in," she whispered. "Our

patients need quiet. Only close relations are allowed to visi . . . Oh, it's you!" she said, calming down as she recognized Thorn. "We're not accustomed to Mr. Treasurer coming with so much company."

"Where is my aunt?"

"Madam Berenilde is in full labor. But really," she added, with a disconcerted look at the old artisans who had invaded her hall, "that's a lot of visitors for one health establishment. Might you not be able . . ."

"These people are witnesses in an important case," Thorn interrupted her. "I don't want to just let them loose."

Placed under the watch of two policemen, the artisans were passively contemplating the sanitarium's luxurious white expanses. Since their foreman had been placed under arrest, they seemed incapable of taking the smallest initiative.

Only Gail could contain her outrage no longer, and spat on the white tiles.

"Let's call a screw a screw. We're your hostages, not your witnesses!"

"I forbid you from shouting here," the employee scolded, in a low voice. "And if you spit again, I'll wash your mouth out with soap."

"Where is my aunt?" Thorn asked again, unperturbed.

"You can't see her for the moment, Mr. Treasurer. I suggest you wait in the waiting room . . . Oh, no," the employee corrected herself with a sigh, "it's just been completely rearranged to accommodate Lord Farouk. You see, we weren't expecting him to visit Madam Berenilde in person."

"How is she?" Ophelia interrupted her.

"I couldn't tell you, miss. I'm not in her room, as you can see."

"But me, can I see her? I'm the godmother of the baby." It was as she said these words that Ophelia realized that she'd decided to accept that responsibility. If there was a future to which she was ready to commit herself, that was certainly it.

"Are you married?"

"Excuse me?" asked Ophelia, nonplussed. "Well . . . not yet."

"In that case, no, you can't see her. Our internal rules are clear: men and young girls are not allowed to attend births. Lord Farouk, here, can you believe it?" the employee continued, as if she had never been interrupted. "Our nurses are bubbling over with excitement. Our clients have all been confined to their rooms until further notice. On the subject," whispered the employee, bringing a hand to her mouth, "allow me to present all my condolences to you, Mr. Treasurer. Your grandmother passed away during the night. Her lungs, you understand? I know it's not the ideal time, but could you help us with the necessary procedures? The death certificate, organization of the funeral, notification of your lawyer, all those kinds of things. I can't really see us asking Madam Berenilde to do them in her current state, and since you are the grandson . . . "

"Where is my aunt?"

Something in Thorn's voice prompted the nurse to reply: "Upstairs, east wing, room 12."

Ophelia's legs started moving of their own accord. She went up the staircase on the right, and heard, above the ringing of her steps, Thorn's voice resounding behind her:

"Keep the artisans in the hall," he ordered the policemen. "No one must enter the building, or leave it, without my being informed."

The spiral staircase led, inevitably, to the rotunda, so Ophelia and Thorn put the peristyle's colonnade to good use, to go around the rotunda without being seen. The big picture windows had all been covered, plunging the whole floor into a soft half-light, and a gigantic velvet sofa had been installed, on which the favorites, reclining in languorous positions, sucked on the tips of hookahs.

The sanitarium's waiting room had taken on the appearance of a brothel.

Ophelia had no difficulty finding Farouk in this profusion of bodies and cushions. Without really seeming to see it, he was staring at a show of animated images that an illusions projector was endlessly rolling out on a screen. Lost, his brow furrowed, he seemed to have neither the remotest idea of where he was nor why he was there.

And yet, thought Ophelia, he was there. Despite all his negligence and his appalling memory, his instinct had told him to come here.

She followed Thorn along the corridor of the sanitarium's east wing. They had go past a whole succession of numbered doors and round windows before finding Berenilde's particular room. A sign saying "MIDWIVES, MARRIED WOMEN, AND WIDOWS ONLY" had been hung on her door. Thorn grabbed a chair from the corridor and posted himself close to the entrance with, evidently, the firm intention of remaining there.

Incapable of sitting down, Ophelia felt so febrile that her Animism would have made any seat leave on the double. She pressed her ear to the door and heard, through the thick wood, vigorous cries.

Aunt Rosaline's voice dominated all the others: "Breathe like bellows . . . Like that, that's good, carry on . . ."

Her heart pounding, Ophelia held her own breath, the better to listen. Why couldn't she hear Berenilde? She resisted the temptation to break the rules. The thought of attending a birth terrified her, but she found staying in the corridor even worse. When the door started vibrating on its hinges, Ophelia had to resign herself to stepping back. As long as her Animism hadn't calmed down, she'd have to avoid all close contact with objects; and the last thing Berenilde needed right now was a panicked girl at her bedside.

Ophelia paced up and down the corridor, wiped her glasses several times, nibbled the seams of her gloves, half-opened the balcony curtains to look outside, and closed them as soon as the *Tittle-Tattle* commentator pointed at her from the stage while screeching into his microphone, prompting a fusillade of camera flashes.

The sanitarium clock chimed ten times, then once, then eleven times. Ophelia wondered how Thorn managed to stay calm. "Your aunt is awfully quiet," she said to him.

The Treasurer emerged from the well of his thoughts and agreed, almost imperceptibly. "She wouldn't cry under torture."

He was hunched over on his chair, elbows pinned to knees, coat flaps hanging like crow's wings. It was a rare spectacle indeed to see him like this, features relaxed, without a frown, or a twisted mouth, or a taut jaw. Only the steel of his eyes glinted intensely under the dark eyelids of an insomniac.

Ophelia suddenly recalled the familiarity with which the employee had spoken to him. Thorn had already come to the sanitarium in the past, and he'd come often. Somewhere in this establishment, on one of the floors, in a closed room, behind a tattoo in the form of a cross, was his mother. A woman who had rejected him like a bad experience, and to whom he remained attached all the same.

Ophelia hesitated. Was there some link between Thorn's mother's memory, Farouk's Book, and the criminal activities that were plaguing Citaceleste? She was tempted to take advantage of Thorn being more relaxed to ask him the question, but she finally decided that it wasn't the best way to reconcile with him.

"You're on guard," she said, instead. "Do you think Bere-nilde is in danger?"

"In a vulnerable position. If I managed to get here, anyone else could do the same. The Web is currently no longer in a position to guarantee her any protection."

Ophelia didn't find that hard to believe. If the Valkyrie was in the same state as the diplomats staggering around out-side, she'd be no great help with any attempted murder. And also, Ophelia didn't forget that the friendship of the Web was dependent upon that of Archibald.

"We have only thirteen hours left to find the ambassa-dor," she said, nervously massaging her arm. "I feel as if each second that I don't dedicate to looking for him is a form of abandonment."

Ophelia contemplated the long corridor. Doors painted white, walls paneled in white, floors tiled in white, windows draped in white: she found this silent whiteness totally chill-ing. On Anima, when a woman was giving birth, the atmo-sphere was different. The rooms were crawling with people. Neighbors were endlessly coming for news. The furniture never stayed in one place. The whole neighborhood was in a frenzy.

"And yet," Ophelia muttered, after a while, "I can't help but think that our place is here."

Thorn looked away. It was a simple movement of the eyes, without the use of a single bodily muscle, but it was as if he were suddenly sitting at the other end of the corridor.

"I had no idea you were that attached to my aunt."

Ophelia almost told him that she'd thought the same about him. Thorn had got her used to treating Berenilde like an adult capable of protecting herself on her own. And yet he'd just sus-pended an investigation and jumped into an airship for her.

"You would, however, be wrong to think that we are com-promising the inquiry," Thorn continued. "We had no chance of finding Hildegarde within the Citaceleste's walls. Here, anything is still possible."

"The Mother never abandons her children," repeated Ophelia, finally understanding what Gail wanted to say to her. "The artisans . . . are they really your hostages?"

"Hildegarde would never have left the Pole without them. I'm convinced that she hasn't entered the interfamilial Compass Rose, and that she's somewhere around here. She will soon come out of her hole. All I can do is wait."

Ophelia twisted her mouth; Thorn and his compulsive use of the singular!

"She has total control over space," she reminded him. "Couldn't she herself snatch her employees away from your policemen, and then disappear with them with a click of the fingers?"

"Hildegarde isn't half as powerful as you think she is. Apprehending her is difficult, but it's certainly not impossible."

Thorn had spoken with detached composure. Far from feeling that calm, Ophelia returned to pacing up and down. Despite her sleepless night, or perhaps because of it, she couldn't stop her thoughts from furiously ricocheting, one against the other. Even if Thorn did find Mother Hildegarde, even if she were implicated in the business of the abductions, what guarantee did they have that she would help them? And what would they do if she *couldn't* help them, and if people continued to disappear? If the writer of the letters employed methods other than the blue sandglasses? After all, Baron Melchior would have been next on the list, had Archibald not been trapped in his place. Without even mentioning herself, Ophelia.

Because she'd been gnawing away at it, she split a seam of her glove. And why, darn it, could she no longer pass through mirrors?

"Unbutton your dress."

Ophelia stopped still and stared at Thorn. With fingers linked before him, he was observing her, impassively, from his chair. She wondered whether she'd heard correctly.

"The sleeve will be enough," Thorn specified, in a steady voice. "You seem to be bothered by your arm. Let me have a quick look at it."

Ophelia undid the buttons of her sleeve, and rolled it up as far as she could. Her elbow joint had almost doubled in size and the skin had gone a very ugly color. Ophelia was used to bad knocks, but she hadn't expected it to be that impressive.

"I must have banged the banister as I fell down the stairs. If the policeman hadn't been there, I would have broken my neck."

Thorn felt her swollen arm. "No dislocation, even partial," he muttered between his teeth. "Are you able to stretch out your arm?"

"With difficulty." Ophelia closed her eyes so she wouldn't have to watch Thorn's fingering anymore. Maybe it was due to pain or hunger, but her stomach started to clench. "Is Madam Vladislava still escorting us?"

"No," Thorn replied, without hesitation. "She alerted me when you were summoned by Farouk, but she wasn't able to join us in Citaceleste. I don't know where she is right now. When I press, do you get a shooting pain? Tingling?"

"Both." Ophelia kept her eyes firmly closed. She hoped Thorn would soon be done; burning sensations were now spreading right across her stomach. "I didn't lose my balance on that stairway. I was shoved."

Thorn's fingers and voice tensed at the same time: "By an Invisible?"

"By someone I didn't see, at any rate. And neither did you, apparently. I'm not saying it was intentional, but if it wasn't clumsiness on Madam Vladislava's part, I have some questions. The writer of the letter strictly forbade me to return to the court," she reminded him in a hushed voice. "I disobeyed him."

Ophelia thought fleetingly of the Knight. That child had got her so used to nasty tricks that she would have considered him entirely capable of threatening people's lives, even when he'd been mutilated and banished. But they were undoubtedly dealing with someone whose intentions were far more complex.

"The Family States take place this evening, after midnight," declared Thorn. "It wouldn't be in the Invisibles' interest to provoke me when I'm defending their case."

"I know. Don't change anything that's been planned."

Ophelia reopened her eyes when she felt Thorn letting go of her arm. One of the favorites had just slipped away from Farouk to rush furtively down the corridor. She stopped dead the precise moment she saw Thorn and Ophelia. Especially Thorn, in fact. Without even attempting to hide her annoyance, she immediately turned tail in a clatter of diamonds.

"There's one whose conscience isn't clear," muttered Ophelia. "You were right, some people really are ready to take advantage of Berenilde's vulnerability."

Thorn positioned Ophelia's forearm at a right angle, as if nothing notable had just happened. "I don't think it's fractured, but, while in doubt, keep the joint bent like this and avoid making it carry the weight of the arm."

Ophelia buttoned her sleeve with difficulty. She thought it best not to ask Thorn where he got his medical expertise from. In any case, he was, once again, hunched on his chair. Even though he was saying nothing about it, she could clearly see that she'd shaken him by revealing what had really happened on the stairs at the factory.

She gave a flick to her scarf, which lazily uncoiled itself, slid off her shoulder, and positioned itself like a sling to support her arm. Ophelia had to admit that it was much less painful like this. And yet, somewhere deep inside, her stomach was still dying.

"Thorn, about what I said to you earlier . . . " She stopped of her own accord. Thorn had moved neither an eyebrow nor a feature nor a scar, but his eyes alone had been enough to halt her in full flow.

"I am responsible for you, and I'm far from proving myself up to it. You were right from start to finish, so let's say no more about it."

"You had pushed me to the limit. I would mainly like to understand what riled you to that extent."

"You would like to understand what riled me."

Thorn had repeated these words slowly, his accent making both "r"s grate like the cogs of a clock. He gave himself a moment to think, seeming to search for the best way to put his response. To Ophelia's surprise, he ended up taking out some dice from an inside pocket of his coat. They were finely crafted dice, very different to those Thorn's half-brother had carved when they were children, but Ophelia couldn't help but make the comparison.

"I believe neither in luck nor in destiny," he declared. "I trust only the science of probabilities. I have studied mathematical statistics, combinatorial analysis, mass function, and random variables, and they have never held any surprises for me. You don't seem fully to grasp the destabilizing effect that someone like you can have on someone like me."

"I'm not following you at all," Ophelia stammered, with total sincerity.

Thorn rolled the dice around in the palm of his hand, and then put them back in his pocket.

"I can't turn my back for an instant without you ending up where you should never have been. I think you have . . . how can I put it . . . a preternatural predisposition to disasters."

"And that's it?" she insisted. "There's nothing else? That's why you want me to leave the Pole? That's why you got yourself into such a state?"

Thorn shrugged his shoulders and said nothing, his eyes turned to his deepest thoughts. The silence between them was such that they no longer heard the muffled cries of the nurses in Berenilde's room and the distant waltz music through the windows.

Ophelia couldn't hold back any longer: "Are you angry with me because I rejected you?"

"No," Thorn replied, without looking at her. "I'm angry with myself because I had the conceit to think for one moment that you wouldn't do so. You were very clear, message received. Pointless to go back to that episode, too."

And with those words, he plunged back into his thoughts as though into deep water.

Ophelia no longer knew what to say. She was suddenly certain, without understanding on what grounds, that it was Thorn, more even than her, who was heading for a disaster. Was it linked to the abductions? To his mother's memory? To Farouk's Book? To all that at once? The fact is, Ophelia had a sudden premonition that Thorn was going to end up crushed by a mechanism that was much too powerful for him. And that it was from that very mechanism, of which only he seemed to know the true nature, that he had been trying, at all costs, to keep her away since the start.

"Thorn . . . against whom are you fighting, exactly?"

"I made you a promise," he muttered, as though speaking to himself. "I will conceal nothing more from you that directly concerns you. As long as I'm not absolutely sure that a link exists between what is threatening you and what I myself know, that promise will be respected."

If Ophelia had suspected for one moment that Thorn would apply their agreement to the letter, she would have used a different formula.

"Are you Miss Ophelia?" A nurse had just burst into the corridor with a tray. She was bringing a telephone, the long line of which was unwinding behind her.

"Er . . . yes?"

"A call for you, miss."

Ophelia exchanged a brief look with Thorn, and then grabbed the brass receiver, which was already off the hook.

"Hello?"

"I'm delighted to see that, for once, *Tittle-Tattle* isn't talking nonsense. So you really are at the sanitarium, my dove."

"Madam Cunegond?" Ophelia asked, amazed.

Thorn picked up the second earpiece to follow the call, and signaled her to continue.

"Can I do something for you?" asked Ophelia.

"No, no, my dove. On the other hand, me, I can do something for you. Meet me in an hour in front of the Opal Sands lighthouse. That dear Mr. Thorn is obviously invited, but let's avoid the policemen and the journalists, do you mind?"

"I . . . Excuse me?" stammered Ophelia, increasingly stunned. "It's just that, for the moment, we can't really go anywhere."

"In an hour, my dove. I'm sure that nothing in the world would make you miss an appointment with Madam Hildegarde."

Cunegond hung up. At the same moment, a resounding cry filled the whole sanitarium. The cry of a baby. The cry of life.

THE NON-PLACE

Farouk had a daughter! In a matter of seconds, the news had travelled to every floor, spread across the gardens, and taken over the airwaves. It took even less time for all the assembled nobles to besiege the sanitarium, despite the desperate protesting of the nurses. Each wanted to be the first to present their congratulations to the father and send their compliments to the mother—the most eager were those who, an hour earlier, were already burying Berenilde.

Berenilde? Buried? Sitting beside the cradle, her hair neat, her face radiant, and with a smile on her lips, she was already prepared to receive her visitors. That, at any rate, was the brief vision Ophelia got when the midwives opened the door to her room. The courtiers then arrived so quickly, and in such great numbers, that she was pushed to the other end of the corridor before even managing to glimpse the baby. Squashed between crinoline dresses and fur coats, and coughing from the camera smoke, Ophelia would have ended up asphyxiated had Thorn not come to extricate her.

"Let's go," he growled. "My aunt is now capable of defending herself on her own, and we're expected elsewhere."

Walking against the current of a crowd, and in a narrow corridor at that, demanded great perseverance. But Ophelia and Thorn did finally reach the waiting room, which was swarming with people, and where nobles were queuing right up to the family spirit's sofa—his daughter had only just been born and engagement proposals were already flooding in, with one man highlighting his personal wealth, another praising his sons' valor. Staring blankly around him, Farouk clearly didn't understand what all these fathers wanted from him.

Ophelia followed Thorn down the stairs. There they came across policemen from the squad and the old artisans from the factory, swept along against their will by the momentum of the crowd. Gail had hoisted herself up onto the guardrail, like a sailor on the bowsprit of a ship; above human concerns, she was puffing away on a cigarette right beside the sign that said: "SMOKING STRICTLY FORBIDDEN."

It took Thorn and Ophelia several more scrambles to get out of the establishment. Baron Melchior, whose portliness had prevented him from entering it, immediately came over to them, tapping the face of his pretty watch. "Not wishing to panic you, but it's midday. We only have twelve . . ."

"Your sister telephoned," Thorn cut in. "She has arranged a meeting with Madam Hildegarde. Don't ask me how," he added, as Baron Melchior dropped his watch in surprise. "Where is our pilot?"

Apart from a few servants tidying the buffet tables, there was no one left in the garden. The festive illusions were starting to fade as rain started to fall.

"I will be your chauffeur!" It was Gail who had made them this offer—more of an order—raising the peak of her cap with a finger. She had followed them and listened to them unnoticed. Without waiting for assent, she stubbed out her cigarette, climbed the airship's gangway, and gestured at them to join her on board. "The boss has given you an appointment, don't make her wait."

A few minutes later, the airship was leaving the sanitarium, propellers humming. Ophelia had a last look at its grand facade, and at the twelfth window of the first floor of the east wing, where a new life had begun, for which she already felt responsible. "I still haven't even chosen a name for her," she muttered.

The rain drumming on the fuselage stopped as soon as the airship flew over Opal Sands. Above it, hovering much higher in the sky, the Citaceleste served as a giant umbrella for the entire resort. The shadow cast over roofs, salt marshes, and rocks was so heavy, it felt like winter, right in the middle of summer. Gail maneuvered the tiller to avoid the steam from the thermal baths and the cable-car system, and then began the descent towards the lighthouse. Glued to the window, Ophelia wondered where she would land the airship, given that there was neither plain nor park at Opal Sands. Gail chose the largest rocky beach, about a hundred yards from the Great Jetty, and let down the gangway. Instantly, the wind, full of salt and sea spray, surged into the cockpit.

"Off you go, I'll moor the machine."

"Let's hope it's not a trap," Baron Melchior said, anxiously, clutching his hat as he made his way down. "Are you absolutely sure that it really was my sister's voice on the telephone?"

Ophelia pushed away the hair catching on her glasses, and looked out beyond the shore, to the very end of the jetty, at the foot of the white tower of the lighthouse, where the sea swirled its foam. An outlandish figure was watching them.

"It's definitely her," said Thorn, striding off.

All around them, the sea rumbled like a liquid thunderstorm. The further they went along the jetty, the rounder and more eccentric the figure waiting for them at the foot of the lighthouse became. Cunegond was wearing what Ophelia supposed was a holiday outfit. With her feathered turban, cascade of necklaces, black veil, and gold-brocade dress, she would have looked more at home in a tropical setting.

"I knew I could count on your unerring punctuality, Mr. Treasurer!" Cunegond cooed as soon as they were within earshot. "Time, you see, is not something that dear Hildegarde has an endless supply of." As she said this, the Mirage pulled out, from under her veil, an impressive bunch of black sandglasses.

"But really, Cunegond, would you mind explaining to me what all this is about?" Baron Melchior demanded, his splendid moustache demolished by the wind. "Since when have you been consorting with Madam Hilde . . . So it was you!" he suddenly exclaimed, eyes popping out. "The anonymous illusionist of the sandbeds, that was you!"

Cunegond's smile extended her large red lips. "My Imaginoirs are failing, little brother; I offered my services to someone who really appreciates them. Hildegarde is not only my competitor, she's also an excellent businesswoman. Of course, I knew this collaboration would be disapproved of, and that's why I remained discreet, but anyway," she sighed, "I daresay that, now, it no longer really matters. Sandglasses are already a thing of the past."

"I savored your delights so many times without realizing it!" Baron Melchior said, revolted, as though speaking of some incestuous act.

"So I'm evidently not the failed artist you thought I was."

"Where is Hildegarde?" Thorn cut in, sharply. Cunegond unhooked three black sandglasses from her bunch and gave one to each of them. Hindered by her arm in the scarf, Ophelia grabbed hers awkwardly.

"Is this a joke?" Baron Melchior asked, indignantly, holding up his black sandglass with the tips of his fingers. "Do you seriously think we're going to pull the pin on such dubious objects in the current climate?"

"We will not touch these sandglasses until we have an explanation," said Thorn. "You can start now by telling us about your personal involvement in the case of the abductions."

With feathers frolicking atop her turban and countless necklaces clattering, Cunegond draped herself in a parody of dignity as she solemnly laid her hand on her ample bosom. "I am not involved in any respe . . . "

Ophelia never heard the end of the sentence. Cunegond, Thorn, Baron Melchior, the lighthouse, the wind, the sky had all disappeared and the entire sea had fallen silent.

Ophelia found herself plunged into a shadowy room. Her dazed eyes made out the cracks in the floorboards at her feet, looked up at the beams of the ceiling, and squinted at the black sandglass she was still clutching. Despite the weak lighting, she saw that the grains of sand had started to run. When Ophelia found the pin hooked on a stitch of her scarf, she understood that she had triggered the mechanism without even meaning to. And of course, that had happened when no one was paying attention to her . . . How long would it take for Thorn to notice that she'd disappeared?

It took Ophelia a few blinks to get used to the half-light and work out the contours of the room. It was built entirely with beams and smelt strongly of damp pine, like some old, abandoned chalet. A chalet without a door or windows, as far as Ophelia could tell. Right at the back of the room, hunched behind a desk, weakly backlit by a lamp, was a motionless shadow.

The floorboard creaked hideously as soon as she ventured a step. The shadow moved behind the desk, as if roused from its slumbers.

"You can come closer, *niña*," muttered the guttural voice of Mother Hildegarde. "You can come closer, but don't cross the line."

Ophelia put the sandglass in a pocket. She made the floorboards creak until she reached a security cordon, which kept
her at a respectable distance from the desk. Mother Hildegarde
ceased to be a shadow. She now possessed two little black eyes,
sunk into an old, blemished skin, that were looking at her
with sustained attention. Elbows on desk and fingers linked,
she was wearing a ghastly dress with wide pockets and chunky
buttons. There was a sealed envelope lying in front of her, and
an ashtray overflowing with cigarette butts.

"Welcome to my non-place. You're alone, *niña*?"

"Not for very long," Ophelia replied, hoping to goodness
she was right.

"You're nervous," Mother Hildegarde observed, with satisfaction. "Don't think about breaking your sandglass to shorten
this meeting. It's unbreakable glass from Leadgold, you'll
remain here until all the sand has run through."

Ophelia decided not to beat around the bush. "Do you
know where those who disappeared are?"

"No, but I know why they disappeared."

Mother Hildegarde's reply, spoken with her very particular
accent, profoundly disappointed Ophelia.

"Well, that doesn't get us much further. We also know . . . "

"No," Mother Hildegarde interrupted her. "You, you know
how. Me, I know why."

All the wood in the room creaked furiously, and a panel
on the wall split just behind the architect. Ophelia was too
absorbed in their conversation to worry about the caprices of
the non-place.

"Why, then, according to you?"

Mother Hildegarde unlinked her fingers to shake them
around like puppets. "With the right hand, one rids the court
of its greatest agitators. With the left, one makes Mommy Hildegarde carry the can—or, I should say, the sandglass."

"So it's a frame job?" Ophelia asked, cautiously.

"Yup. One might even say a coup d'état."

There was a great crashing noise in the room. For a moment, Ophelia thought Thorn was at last joining her, but it was nothing more than a shelf that had just fallen off the wall.

"You know space like the back of your hand," she remarked, returning to Mother Hildegarde. "Couldn't you at least help us to find Archibald and the Mirages? It would be the best way to exonerate yourself."

"What do you think I've been doing with my time, *niña*? I've looked everywhere for him, your Augustine. Alas, I did my job as architect a bit too well, Citaceleste is a real warren. Might as well hunt for a needle in a haystack."

"I've heard that the route to LandmArk has been blocked."

"Yup. I heard that, too."

"So it wasn't your doing?" Ophelia asked, amazed. "Your own family has abandoned you here?"

Barely moved, Mother Hildegarde shrugged her shoulders. "That's the rule. At the slightest danger, the border controls close the Compass Rose. I promised them that Clairdelune was the safest place in the Pole. I was betrayed by my own sandglasses. That, I must say, I didn't see coming."

"But the missing," insisted Ophelia. "What if someone moved them to LandmArk before the route was closed? If they are all over there, at the end of the world, while we're looking for them here?"

"That would be hard luck."

Ophelia almost went over the security cordon. The floorboards had started to buckle under her feet and all the panels in the room roared in unison. The jolting stopped as quickly as it had started. The non-place seemed subject to an exterior pressure that was trying to crush it like a nut.

"You were saying that it was a put-up job against you," she

muttered, massaging her arm in her scarf. "I can't see which clan would benefit from such a twisted plot. And who would hate you to that extent?"

"Don't go seeing it as an affair of feelings, *niña*. Love and hatred have no place in this story." Mother Hildegarde cut off the end of a cigar, then lit it with a match that highlighted every wrinkle on her face. "It's more a game of hide-and-seek. A game I'm going to lose, as I haven't seen the mug of the other player. I'm getting on. You just have to look at this place," she said, blowing a cloud of smoke around herself. "It's my very latest creation, and it's visibly shrinking. I've broken too many laws of nature. I won't be able to hide here much longer. With all these policemen and all these security checks, I'll get myself arrested the very moment I set foot outside. I'm trapped, kid. It's now only a matter of hours. The other player will end up finding me, and will want to deliver me to the only master he serves."

"Which master are you talking about?" Ophelia whispered, gripped.

With her cigar, Mother Hildegarde indicated the security cordon between them. "The one who's dying to cross this line."

"The God of the letters?"

"That fellow, my dear, best to avoid crossing his path," Mother Hildegarde sniggered, by way of a reply. "And yet, that's what ends up happening to those whose interest in the Books gets a little too keen."

"The Books?" repeated Ophelia. "Because you, too . . . "

Mother Hildegarde's little black eyes lit up like coals and her smile spread waves of wrinkles right across her face. "No, me, I have nothing to do with all that Book malarkey. I'm wanted for a totally different reason, but I can't tell you about it. Let's say it's an affair of the *familia*. If you want to live a quiet little life, let me give you some good advice: don't ask questions and nose around as little as possible. Look what happened to Augustine. Look at what will soon happen to Mr. Thorn."

An icy shiver ran through Ophelia. She looked at Mother Hildegarde, and then at the envelope on the desk, increasingly disturbed. "Why did you make this appointment with us?"

"I told you, *niña*. I'm old and tired."

There was an extraordinary creaking of floorboards. This time it really was Thorn who had just appeared in the middle of the room, sandglass in hand. His towering figure knocked into a ceiling beam, and his eyes, squinting due to the change in lighting, searched in all directions before finding Ophelia.

"How long have you been here? Couldn't you have waited for me?" Baron Melchior, in turn, burst out of nowhere and twirled around like a disorientated spinning top. His whole body jumped when the floor split under his lovely white shoes. "Where are we? Ah, Madam Hildegarde!" he sighed, noticing her behind her desk. "Here you are at last!"

Without moving from her chair, Mother Hildegarde stubbed her cigar out in the ashtray and immediately lit a new one. "Do not go over the line, gentlemen, *por favor*."

"Madame Hildegarde has told me some very troubling things," Ophelia said to them. "You should let her speak."

"The *niña* is right, let's not waste any more time. This," Mother Hildegarde declared, tapping the sealed envelope on the desk, "is my written confession. I admit absolutely all of my crimes. I used my factory to abduct Mirages, and I ran away as soon as it went wrong."

"What?" stammered Ophelia. "But . . . "

"I acted alone from start to finish," she specified, throwing the envelope to Thorn as if it were a discus. "It's all written down in there. So I thank you in advance for freeing my foreman, leaving my artisans in peace, and not making trouble for Cunegond."

Ophelia felt as if she had missed a step. She knew that Mother Hildegarde was capable of playacting to protect her own, but she hadn't seen that coup de théâtre coming.

"Well, that sorts that out," Baron Melchior said, drumming his fingers on his belly and looking pleasantly surprised. "Perhaps, madam, you would further oblige us by telling us where the prisoners are?"

Mother Hildegarde took a long drag on her cigar. "They're fine where they are. Let them stay there."

"Don't listen to her," Ophelia said, gripping Thorn's arm. It's not at all what we spoke about."

Thorn didn't reply to her. Under the black sleeve of the coat, Ophelia could feel that all his muscles had become tense as springs. He was staring intently at the security cordon separating him from Mother Hildegarde's desk. In fact, from the moment he had set eyes on it, he had not looked away, as if this cordon were the most fascinating thing in the world. He didn't even seem to notice that the non-place was shrinking around them, minute by minute, inch by inch, with an appalling rumble of breaking wood.

Thorn finally put the sealed envelope into an inside pocket of his coat. "Madam, you are under arrest. Given the gravity of the deeds and your propensity to run away, you will be placed in a maximum-security prison cell. I will personally see to it that you receive no visitors for as long as the investigation requires."

Ophelia was dismayed at Thorn's decision. Mother Hildegarde, on the contrary, seemed highly amused.

"Oh, no, I don't think so, sonny. And don't you dare cross that line," she warned, as Thorn grabbed the security cordon. "You will just hasten the inevitable." She savored a last drag of cigar before stubbing it out in the ashtray. This time, she didn't light another one. "I'd like to say a word about all the space I've distorted here, these past hundred-and-fifty years. The duplications, the shortenings, the enlargements, and the secure locations will all remain operational. I did some good work, it's solid stuff. On the other hand, you can kiss goodbye to the interfamilial Compass Rose. The route to LandmArk will never be reopened."

Baron Melchior's moustache collapsed. "What? Farewell spices, citrus fruit, coffee, and cocoa?"

Ophelia didn't like the way this conversation was going, but Madam Hildegarde continued, unperturbed: "The Cita-celeste shouldn't fall from the sky for centuries. Back in the day, I signed a contract with some chaps from Cyclops. They can supply you with one or two bursts of weightlessness, if necessary. As for this non-place," she said, looking around it with her little black eyes, "it will disappear of its own accord, in a few hours from now. Your sandglasses will make you leave the place much before that." Mother Hildegarde sniggered, briefly. "I've never made anything so shoddy, it was about time I retired."

All the tendons in Thorn's hand tightened around the security cordon, as if he were struggling not to go through it. It was with an electrically charged voice that he insisted: "Madam, I ask you to be reasonable and to follow me."

Mother Hildegarde got up from her chair with difficulty, her joints protesting as loudly as the non-place's floorboards. "I'm starting to see through your game, sonny. You're tall, but, believe me, you don't have the caliber. As for you, *niña*," she added, turning her smile on Ophelia, "tell my Gailita that she's going to have to learn to peel her own oranges."

With these words, Mother Hildegarde plunged a hand into one of her pockets. This action would have remained banal had her whole arm not followed, as though sucked into a vacuum. Mother Hildegarde's wrist, elbow, shoulder, entire torso twisted under her dress with a horrifying cracking of bones. The spine snapped in two the moment the head finally entered the pocket, and then the rest of the body contorted, shriveled, dislocated until it was entirely swallowed into the vacuum with a grotesque sucking noise.

All that was left of Mother Hildegarde was a chunky button from her dress, bouncing on the floorboards.

The scene had unfolded with such speed, Ophelia hadn't even had the reflex to scream. When she realized what she had just witnessed, the room started spinning around her, and this time it wasn't due to a shrinking of space. Ophelia held on to a chair. A spasm shook her stomach. Never, in all her life, had she been gripped by such a feeling of horror.

Baron Melchior pushed the security cordon with his cane, picked up the dress button, and then looked at Thorn with eyes full of reproach.

"You hounded that lady with your ways, Mr. Treasurer."

Thorn didn't respond. With his hand still clutching the security cordon, frozen to the spot, he was staring at where Mother Hildegarde had been standing, a moment earlier.

Ophelia was incapable of saying a word to him, for the simple and good reason that her sandglass had just run out. The half-light of the non-place shattered and a squall of salty wind engulfed her mouth, her hair, and her dress. She found herself back where she'd started. Alone. Cunegond had left and neither Thorn nor Baron Melchior would be able to break their sandglasses before they had run their course.

It was all over. Mother Hildegarde alone possessed the power to locate the missing before midnight, and she'd just turned it against herself. So who on earth was this God, for her to choose this hideous death over him?

Ophelia turned to the airship, floating above some rocks on the beach. Curiosity had drawn a few people around the gangway. Among them, despite the distance, she recognized the fiery head of Fox, who was leaning over Gail. Gail . . . would Ophelia have the heart to pass Mother Hildegarde's last words on to her?

She didn't get the chance to consider the matter for long. An invisible force threw her against the wall of the lighthouse, and then dropped her flat on her face. Her elbow sent a shock wave right through her body, but that pain was nothing compared with the panic that gripped her when she stopped breathing.

"This time, your number's up," panted a familiar voice against the nape of her neck.

THE DARK

Sparks in her eyes. Thunder in her ears. Deprived of air, Ophelia could see and hear almost nothing. Sitting on her back, the Invisible was crushing her with his, or her, weight while gripping her throat in an armlock.

"Please forgive me . . . had no choice . . . for Mr. Archibald . . . "

These mutterings reached Ophelia through miles of fog. She knew that voice. But her field of vision was shrinking at the speed of a camera shutter.

Ophelia would have ended up losing her hold on the world if air hadn't suddenly rushed into her lungs. She inhaled, coughed, hiccupped. For some reason, the Invisible had loosened his grip, but his body continued to weigh down on hers. With the help of her undamaged arm, Ophelia tried to tip on to her side to throw the Invisible off balance, but she only succeeded in turning her head. What she glimpsed over her shoulder at least enabled her to understand what had saved her.

The scarf was squeezing the void in the manner of a boa constrictor.

"Let go of me, and it will let go of you," Ophelia promised, in a hoarse voice.

This deal was a waste of time. Judging by the writhing of

the scarf, the Invisible was fighting back and would soon have the upper hand. Ophelia searched around her for a solution. She was too far from the beach to call for help, and there was no lighthouse keeper in the summer. How could she attract Fox's and Gail's attention, at the other end of the jetty? She noticed a white canister beside her, linked to a wide red trumpet. A foghorn.

The scarf was starting to stretch, its stitches losing their shape, as if fingers were pulling furiously at the knitted fabric.

Ophelia stretched her arm as far and as high as she could in order to lower the hatch of the foghorn. The compressed air in the canister escaped, making the trumpet's aperture vibrate, but the siren only sounded for a fraction of a second. A transparent hand had just slammed down on to Ophelia's.

"Why are you forcing me to do this to you?" whispered the familiar voice, winding the scarf around Ophelia's neck. "That fall on the stairs wasn't enough for you, then? I'm not a criminal, all you had to do was leave the Pole. I would have fulfilled my mission and Mr. Archibald would have been freed, as agreed. You condemned yourself to death on your own."

The scarf was endeavoring, with every one of its stitches, not to strangle its mistress. Ophelia wanted to hit the Invisible, but she could only hit out randomly in the air. She was running out of oxygen again. Just when she thought she was done for, she felt a weight throwing itself on the Invisible and forcing him to let go.

For the second time, Ophelia felt as if she were coughing up her lungs. She tugged on the scarf in order to release her throat. In the midst of the luminous dots dancing in front of her eyes, she finally made out Fox. He must have run back along the jetty at full speed when he'd heard the foghorn, because he was out of breath. Crouching on the ground, he was hitting the void with rage. His fist hit the paving three times out of four, but when he hit the Invisible, the latter let out a groan of pain.

Ophelia wanted to help Fox, but her numb legs didn't respond. All she managed was to direct a strangled groan at him.

"He's going to escape from you!" cried Gail, who was next to arrive, clutching at a stitch in her side. "Knock him out!"

"And how do I do that?" roared Fox, sweeping the air with his enormous hands. "I don't even know where his noggin is! Ow . . ."

Fox was bent double, as if he'd just received a violent punch right in the stomach; Twit, the kitten, who until then had been clinging by his claws to his hair, rolled on to the ground, spitting. The next moment, a figure suddenly appeared from nowhere. A small man in a grey frock coat, breathless and bruised, was flattening himself against the wall of the light-house. Ophelia struggled to recognize Philibert, the very respectable steward of Clairdelune. When the latter realized that all eyes were on him, he seemed the first to be astonished at having lost his cover of invisibility.

Once he had got over his surprise, Fox promptly grabbed him by the lapels of his frock coat and lifted him off the ground. "It wasn't enough to let me rot in the dungeon, Papier-Mâché? You also had to lay into my little lady? And first of all, you, since when are you an Invisible? Looks like your little power is on the blink, hey!"

Philibert was struggling to escape Fox's grip, but in losing his camouflage, he had also lost the advantage. Ophelia better understood now why this man had always given her the impression of melting into the background. Right now, he was barely recognizable. His wig was completely disheveled, and his eyes, so inexpressive normally, were glinting with rage.

"You betrayed me!" he hissed between his teeth. "For a foreigner and a person with no powers!"

Ophelia only understood the meaning of these words as she saw Gail approaching. The wind had swiped away her mechanic's cap and was making her black curls swirl, as if trying to uncover the face that she continually tried to hide.

Right now, however, Gail wasn't hiding anymore. She had removed her monocle, revealing the true nature of her eye: the eye of a Nihilist, as dark, as unfathomable as the other eye was bright. Gail stared at Philibert without blinking. As long as she kept him in the sights of her eye, her power would nullify his.

"It's you who betrayed us," she declared, solemnly. "Since when are foreigners and people without powers enemies? If I'd known what you were planning when I saw you shadowing the girl, I would have denounced you sooner."

"Hold on, hold on," stammered Fox. "Have I missed something?"

He couldn't stop staring at Gail, going from her differently colored eyes to the monocle she held between two fingers. Fox then started to shake Philibert, while still eyeing her, as if he wanted to force him to return to being invisible, and then he let out an exasperated sigh: "I thought the Nihilists had all snuffed it. Well, that's just my luck. Years I've been lusting after her, that woman, and she had to go and be an aristocrat!"

Gail's cheeks blazed, from both embarrassment and anger.

"Don't insult me, Foster! And don't get involved; this is between this traitor, the little reader, and me. The Mother didn't give us her protection for us to shame her," Gail said, returning to Philibert. "You chose to renounce your clan years ago, and it was your right to do so. You wanted a new life—the Mother gave you one. The past shelved, remember? So pulling out your family's power now, to settle your scores, well, that's unacceptable."

Philibert had stopped struggling. He hung now like a dead weight between Fox's strong hands, and kept his eyes resolutely lowered, so as not to meet anyone else's. His face was torn by such contradictory emotions—rage, distress, guilt, bitterness—that it really did seem to be made of paper.

"The Mother's protection is worthless," he said in a lugubrious voice. "She wasn't capable of saving my young master, and he's my new life. This meeting with the black sandglasses, you know as well as I do what that means."

A shadow crossed Gail's face, and her blue eye became almost as dark as the other one.

"It was her choice," she grumbled. "The Mother died as she lived: right up to the last moment, she protected us."

"She abandoned us," Philibert somberly contradicted her. "I was forced to manage on my own. I received a letter, yesterday. Mr. Archibald will be freed if I get rid of this reader."

"A letter?" screamed Gail, seeing red. "You were prepared to kill over a letter?"

Ophelia's head was spinning so much, she was really struggling to follow this conversation, but she felt she had to intervene. Her elbow gave her an electric shock when she tried to get up. She managed only to slump, wheezing, on the parapet.

"That blackmailer . . . dealing with him . . . me, too."

Ophelia breathed in several times to regain some kind of voice. Her nose started to run, but this time it wasn't from her cold; it was bleeding profusely. Even her poor scarf was cowering at her feet like a wounded animal. Philibert certainly hadn't pulled his punches.

"The writer of thith letter," she continued, pressing her sleeve to her nose. "If you know anything about him, tell uth."

"What's going on here?" Thorn had just appeared at the foot of the lighthouse in a flapping of black coat. It took him one second to capture the scene, and another to draw his pistol. He aimed it first at Gail, then at Fox, then at Philibert. "Which of them put you in that state?" he asked Ophelia.

There was something dangerously methodical in his voice that prompted Ophelia not to reply too quickly. "Firtht, put away your pithtol," she suggested, nose in sleeve. "We'll exthplain everything to you calmly."

That was the moment the third sandglass chose to return Baron Melchior to where he had started. The minister materialized right in the middle of the scene, which immediately resulted in the severing of the eye-to-eye link between Gail and Philibert. The latter took advantage of everyone's surprise to become invisible again in Fox's hands.

"What a way to behave, young lady!" complained Baron Melchior.

Gail had just pushed him roughly aside, but it was too late. Fox was now holding just a grey frock coat; shed by its owner, it had instantly regained its opaqueness. Much as the Nihilist turned her black eye in all directions, letting out a volley of expletives, Philibert reappeared nowhere.

"It's all over," Fox said to her, furiously throwing the frock coat down. "Either he's hidden, or he's far away."

"Who are you talking about?" asked Baron Melchior, increasingly perplexed. "In the name of my moustache!" He had just noticed Ophelia, slumped on her corner of parapet, hair a mess, glasses bent, and chin smeared in blood.

"It was Mr. Philibert," she answered in a croaky voice. "Archibald's steward."

"It's barbaric!" exclaimed Baron Melchior, grimacing. He would have used the same tone faced with an illusion in poor taste. Ophelia would have liked to get up to put on a better show, but she felt as if the entire jetty were rocking around her. She wound her scarf, which was visibly unraveling, and reflected that they must both be an equally sorry sight.

"He's the Invisible that pushed me on the stairs," she said to Thorn. "Except that he didn't do it on behalf of his clan. He's also a victim of blackmail." On the verge of losing her voice, she coughed several times into her sleeve. "That doesn't excuse his actions, but that also means he's not the only guilty one."

Ophelia had hoped that these explanations would prompt Thorn to put away his pistol. Although he had deigned to lower the barrel towards the ground, he continued to hold the weapon with both hands, ready to use it at the first sign of trouble. His sparrowhawk eyes kept darting from one side of his field of vision to the other, as if the enemy was everywhere at once. His coat and hair flapping in the wind made him look even wilder. Ophelia reflected that Thorn hadn't got out of the non-place unscathed.

"Gail and Foster saved my life," she told him. "You can trust them."

This statement would have had more effect had Gail not instantly looked away to avoid any questions, and Fox not looked down and fallen into a sulky silence. Even Twit showed no goodwill: he was furiously sharpening his claws on Baron Melchior's fine white trousers.

The latter paid no attention. He tugged on the chain of his watch and then looked over to the airship, at the other end of the jetty, around which an increasing number of onlookers were flocking. With forehead creased and moustache drooping, Baron Melchior seemed deeply despondent. Ophelia noticed his ringed fingers shake as they closed the cover of his watch. He, too, seemed to have been shaken by the unexpected suicide of Mother Hildegarde.

"I think all we can do is give up," he sighed, putting his watch away with a fatalistic flourish. "We have a written confession, and for everything else, nothing more can be done. Unless you have a suggestion, Mr. Treasurer?"

Thorn didn't reply. He was totally frozen around the grip of the pistol, eyes wide and focused on some powerful inner thought. Ophelia frowned. The Thorn she knew would have already taken control of things, set in motion a new plan of action, given out orders, made phone calls.

"Miss Great Family Reader?" Baron Melchior said next. "A suggestion?"

Ophelia felt as if she was in possession of nearly all the pieces of the jigsaw puzzle. If only her head could have stopped spinning for one moment, she might have been able to fit them together . . .

"I know," Thorn suddenly declared. The shadow of a smile, a smile that was neither grimace nor snarl, floated on his lips, while he examined his pistol closely. "It may have taken me some time," he continued, calmly, "but I finally know what must be done."

Not only had Thorn recovered his sangfroid, but his entire body seemed galvanized by a renewed determination. Ophelia could even have sworn that he had just gained a few extra inches, before realizing that he had simply stopped stooping.

"You really know what must be done?" she repeated, full of hope.

When Thorn turned towards her, brows arched with satisfaction, Ophelia knew that it wasn't a figment of her imagination: he was smiling. An almost imperceptible smile, certainly, but a smile all the same.

"I just need to eliminate you from the equation," he said to her.

Ophelia got up, fired with emotion. The next moment, the ground started to shake and all went dark.

THE ANNOUNCEMENT

Ophelia held out her cup to Archibald, for him to pour tea into it, and then watched him take a seat on the other side of the table. He was smiling with a cheery nonchalance that she found, without knowing quite why, rather out of place.

"How's your line?" she asked, while sugaring her tea.

Archibald plunged his hand into the gaping mouth of his top hat and pulled out a telephone receiver. The cord was cut.

"Looks like scissors have passed that way!" he guffawed.

Ophelia didn't share his amusement. A broken line was always a nuisance. Insoluble sugar was, too. She stirred away with her teaspoon, but hers refused to dissolve. Maybe it was due to the fact that her cup was full of sand.

"I hope you've remembered a monocle," said Archibald, casually resting his elbows on the table. "It's starting to rain."

Ophelia looked where he was looking, and saw that, indeed, mattresses were falling around them like meteorites. She sipped at her cup of sand. She knew that something was odd, but couldn't quite put her finger on it.

"Have you changed your décor?" Ophelia had indeed just noticed that there were neither floor nor walls in the room. Their table was floating in the middle of the sky, flying very high above a town of the old world. She hoped the downpour of mattresses wouldn't injure anyone down there.

"It's good old Hildegarde who had the idea," explained Archibald, pouring her another cup of sand. She redid it all entirely in memory."

"You mean *from* memory?"

"No, *in* memory. Memory is a much more solid material than it seems to be."

"That depends which memory," Ophelia commented, sounding professional. "Thorn's or Farouk's?"

Archibald leaned across the table and, playfully, whacked Ophelia's head with his hat. "Yours, little scatterbrain."

Knocked off balance, she tipped backwards. There was no more Archibald, or table, or sand, or mattresses, or old world. She was in her dressing gown, in front of the mirror of her childhood bedroom, on Anima. Her reflection was moving its lips. *Release me.*

Ophelia opened her eyes, heart pounding.

She had once fallen off a moving streetcar, and had come to in the hospital with an indescribable blend of pain and confusion. That was nothing compared with how she felt at this precise moment. Her head hurt, throat hurt, back hurt, stomach hurt, arms hurt, knees hurt, and she had no recollection of what had got her into this state.

From her pillow, Ophelia gazed myopically around her. The room was bathed in an orangey light, filtering in through all the slits in the shutters. The sea was rumbling like a volcano and a smell of sulfurous water permeated the atmosphere. Ophelia realized that she was in her room at the thermal hotel.

Without moving her head, she looked over to the door. Despite her poor sight, she made out that it was half-open, and Thorn's voice, distant and cavernous as the rumbling of the sea, seemed to be reaching her from a lower floor.

"Awake?"

Ophelia turned her eyes in the opposite direction and made out a slim, hazy figure, perched on the edge of a chair, right beside the big bed. She smiled on recognizing her father. This small man wasn't what one could call an intrusive parent; he never asked personal questions and nothing embarrassed him more than having to meddle in the private lives of his daughters. And yet, at the slightest fever, the first bump, he was clamped to his child's bedside.

She had to make several attempts before managing to breathe out an audible sentence: "You were also a Mirror Visitor, Dad."

Disconcerted, Ophelia's father rubbed his bald head. "Er . . . I passed through a few mirrored wardrobes in my youth, yes, but I wasn't as talented as you."

"Why did you stop? You've never told me."

"Oh, it wasn't really a choice," he whispered, with a kind of modesty. "Rather . . . how can I explain it to you . . . a change of outlook. One grows up, and then one grows old, and that's it, from one day to the next, one's forever angry with one's mirror."

Ophelia turned her eyes to the ceiling and stroked the scarf, which was slowly waking up beneath her fingers. During a long silence, she listened to Thorn's distant voice, with its solemn and monotonous tone, unable to recognize a single word of what he was saying. She was curious to know to whom he could be speaking like that.

"A while ago, I got stuck in several mirrors," she said, picking up where she'd left off. "It's going to seem strange to you, but it reminded me of my very first passage. Or rather, something that would have occurred at that time. As if . . . as if, on entering the mirror, I'd allowed someone else to get out of it. And yet it can't be possible, can it? A mirror visitor can't allow any other living being to accompany them. Even if they wanted to, they wouldn't be able to."

Ophelia saw her father's blurred silhouette shaking its head. "We found only you that night. To be precise, two parts of you, each stuck in a different mirror, and that was already quite enough for our liking." He rubbed his bald spot once more, hesitated timidly, and then leaned over the bed. "My dear girl, does Mr. Thorn make life hard for you?"

"Thorn?" Ophelia asked, surprised.

"One couldn't say you were in great shape when he brought you back to the hotel. He gave us no explanation. You know . . . this marriage . . . If you ask us to, we'll do the impossible, me and your mother, to cancel the whole thing. We'll displease the Doyennes, that's for certain," her father admitted in a fearful voice, "but we . . . well . . . we'll displease them together."

Ophelia raised herself, painfully, on her pillow. She suddenly noticed that Hector, Domitilla, Beatrice, and Leonora were all sound asleep around her, in an unlikely tangle of arms, legs, and nightshirts. Ophelia felt as if she had a windmill between her ears, but she was starting to think more clearly. For all her siblings to feel they must invade her bed, she really must have caused them concern. Her old mirror story suddenly seemed very much of secondary importance.

"What am I doing here, Dad? Who is Thorn talking to right now?"

"You don't remember anything?" Her father handed her glasses to her, as if they could bring back her memory. It worked. From the moment she could see her scarf in the smallest detail—its pulled stitches, its unraveled wool, its dirty fringes—it all came back to her.

Ignoring the protests of her entire body, Ophelia got herself out of bed, avoiding waking her brother and sisters, and buttoned up a dress directly over her nightgown.

"You should rest a bit more," her father suggested, cautiously. "It's late, we'll talk about all that tomorrow morning."

Now that Ophelia could see him more clearly, in the twilight glow from the window, she realized just how anxious he seemed to be. She would have hastened to reassure him had she not herself been devastated. She'd just consulted the mantel clock: it *couldn't* be three o'clock in the morning. Farouk had given her until midnight to find the missing . . . to find Archibald. What right had Thorn to let her sleep like that?

She slipped on her scarf and grabbed her shoes. "I've rested too much."

Ophelia rushed out, head down, and passed Fox, who was standing right outside her door, vigilant as a sentinel, a black monocle stuck in his eye socket. Was he standing guard?

She had plenty to say to him, but Fox placed a finger on his lips. Thorn's voice boomed through the hotel stairwell like roaring thunder:

" . . . representation within the Ministerial Council needing to be proportional to the demographic weight of each family branch. The Council currently includes five representatives of the Mirage clan, three representatives of the Web clan, and one representative of those without power. The Dragon clan lost its only delegate with the death of Mr. Vladimir, last March. These figures in no way reflect the social realities of the ark, and favor a monopoly scenario . . ."

Perplexed, Ophelia tracked down Thorn's voice, stair by stair, corridor by corridor. Her father kept offering her his arm, terrified at the thought of her losing consciousness again.

"Don't stray too far from yours truly," Fox muttered behind them. "Papier-Mâché could come to finish his nasty job. I've only one monocle for watching your backs, me."

"Did Gail give it to you?" asked Ophelia. "Where is she?"

"Went off again in her airship. Better things to do elsewhere."

Ophelia observed Fox over the banister, at the turning of a landing. He was in such a bad mood, he didn't notice Twit, the kitten, descending the stairs at his rhythm, and nearly flattened by his every step.

"Do you hold it against her that much, her being what she is?"

"No," muttered Fox. "I hold it against her that she never told me. An upper-crust lady, not really in my league, you see."

Ophelia's father couldn't stop rubbing his head now; all this talk of monocles, papier-mâché, and crusts was beyond him.

They reached the ground floor and went through the hotel's large foyer, where all the brass gleamed in the light of the setting sun. Despite the lateness of the hour, the place was full of people. All the adult members of Ophelia's family and some of the hotel staff were huddled around a large radio set, whispering in muffled tones. The Animists' nervousness was even more noticeable because it contaminated all the objects in the foyer: carpets quivered, chairs stamped their feet, lamps flickered, and display cases spilt their pamphlets over the floor.

Ophelia was barely surprised to find Berenilde there. She was sitting in a velvet armchair, fresh as a rose, as if she hadn't actually given birth that very morning. It was incredible to think that the tiny, pale baby she held in her arms was the daughter of the giant Farouk.

Ophelia looked around for Thorn, before realizing that his voice was emerging from the enormous loudspeakers of the radio set:

" . . . which brings us to the current state of the larders. The facts are as follows: the interfamilial Compass Rose won't be reopening its doors, and importing food by air would come at exorbitant cost. Please hand these round, one copy per person." There was a rustling of paper and murmurs of impatience rose, both from the radio and in the hotel foyer, but Thorn proceeded, unperturbed, with his meeting: "As you can see on the document I have just distributed, the rate of exchange of our family currency is not moving in our favor. We must rely on our own resources. The intensive fishing in recent years has emptied our lakes. Hunting season starts soon, and the post of master-of-the-hounds remains unfilled to this day. Given that the disgraced are, for the most part, highly qualified hunters . . ."

"Is he going to spit it out, his blasted announcement!" Ophelia's great-uncle said, exasperated, while slapping the radio with the flat of his hand.

"What announcement?" asked Ophelia.

Everyone turned to her at once. A few seconds of uncomfortable silence hung in the air, and Ophelia wondered whether her bruises, tousled hair, holey scarf, shoes in hand, and nightdress sticking out under her dress mightn't have something to do with it. Aunt Rosaline was the first to react. She made Ophelia sit on a chair and, without asking, stuffed a flatbread into her mouth. "You skip meals, you stay out all night, you get attacked, and then you're surprised when you pass out? It's a whole army of godmothers you need, my girl."

In no time, all the family surrounding the radio gathered around Ophelia's chair. Her grandmothers each brought her a coat, her brother-in-law served her maple-syrup liqueur, and her uncles, aunts, and cousins asked her so many questions at once that Ophelia didn't understand a single one of them.

With the tips of her fingers, as if it were seaweed, Agatha lifted her thick, tangled hair. "Oh, sis!" she groaned. "You're looking la-men-ta-ble."

Her mother jostled everyone with her big red dress to secure prime position. "Chew well, and tell us everything," she ordered. "Did Mr. Thorn say something in particular to you?"

Ophelia swallowed her flatbread with difficulty, and directed a reproachful look at the radio, now churning out an interminable legal text, as if it were Thorn himself. *I just need to eliminate you from the equation.* The only declaration this man had deigned to make to her, he'd already put into practice.

"No," Ophelia replied, to general disappointment. "What's going on?"

"We're listening to the public broadcast of the Family States, live from Citaceleste," Berenilde calmly explained to her, from her armchair. "A plenary session is taking place now at the court, and they are dealing at the moment with the question of the disgraced. Thorn informed them at the start of the session that, after his appeal in favor of their rehabilitation, he would make an announcement. A *personal* announcement," she specified, stroking her sleeping baby's cheek with her finger. "Are you sure he didn't confide in you, my dear child?"

Ophelia's heart skipped a beat. "Perhaps it's about the disgraced?"

"Really, I couldn't give a flying petticoat about that lot," snapped her mother, raising her eyes to the ceiling. "Have you not seen the state you've returned to us in? Covered in bruises from head to toe! Foster told us how you were attacked because of Mr. Thorn."

Fox tapped his monocle with embarrassment. "All due respect, I don't think I said 'because of.'"

"Thorn has nothing to do with it," Ophelia stated categorically.

Her great-uncle huffed and puffed under his moustache. He grabbed Ophelia's chair by its back and, with remarkable strength for his age, swung it right round to face the Rapporteur. "Just look at her little face! You're here to observe, right? Then report that to the Doyennes!"

Seated beside the radio set, the Rapporteur refrained from

making any comment. She was keeping unusually quiet, under her weather vane hat, and her stork was spinning above her without settling anywhere, a sign of some confusion.

"My daughter was in good health when I entrusted her to Mr. Thorn!" her mother piped up again, pointing at the radio with an accusing finger. "That sinister individual has returned her to me completely damaged, and then just returned to his little concerns as if nothing had happened!"

"The Family States are not 'little concerns,' Madam Sophie," Berenilde corrected her. "They take place once every fifteen years, and each matter dealt with during them is of capital importance. This is the first time my nephew is attending them as Treasurer. It's a weighty responsibility, and I would appreciate it if you bore that in mind."

Thorn's voice continued, tirelessly: " . . . Invisibles, Narcotics, and Persuasives, to name just a few, have been recognized as being of public service. If one refers to the actual rehabilitation law, article 16, paragraph 4 . . . "

Ophelia pulled her chair over to the radio and listened to it with her closest attention. So what was this personal announcement he was due to make?

"He must have discovered something," she muttered to herself. "Has the Web given news of Archibald?"

Berenilde exchanged a fleeting look with Aunt Rosaline, who gritted her horsey teeth, before returning to Ophelia in a graceful swirl of blond curls.

"The Valkyrie responsible for protecting me was recalled by the Web earlier this evening. I only learnt the reason for this two hours ago, listening to that radio. Archibald's sisters have made a statement on the subject of their brother. A very sad statement," she warned, looking deep into Ophelia's glasses. "I don't know all the details of the affair, but Archibald couldn't be located. His state of consciousness was, it would seem, disturbing his entire family. The Web proceeded with the severing of his link at a private ceremony. Yes, my dear child," Berenilde whispered, seeing her turn pale, "I fear we will never see our eccentric ambassador again."

Ophelia wrapped her arms around her self; her bodily temperature had suddenly plummeted. She saw Archibald again in her dream, shaking the cut cord of his telephone receiver.

"An irreversible procedure that will probably prove fatal to him," the diplomat had warned, in the Roulette Chamber.

First Mother Hildegarde. Now Archibald. Ophelia felt cold, truly cold.

"Why did you let me sleep?"

Aunt Rosaline poured her a little more liqueur.

"You can't blame yourself, child. Your mother told us everything. Mr. Farouk should never have put that burden on you."

"In the meantime, I'm going to need another godfather for my daughter," sighed Berenilde, kissing the baby's forehead. "As well as a name, my dear Ophelia, as soon as you have recovered. Come, come, get ahold of yourself," she said, with a bittersweet smile. "I, too, had developed a certain affection for that rascal, but we have to remain focused on our future."

Frozen to the core, Ophelia went right up to the radio's loudspeaker. She couldn't stop herself from still expecting a miracle from Thorn. He had seemed so determined, so confident, earlier, on that jetty; he must have had a plan at the back of his mind. Ophelia clung to his deep voice, now just concluding his address by reciting the interfamilial Constitution, recalling the paternal duties of a family spirit towards each member of his lineage.

"That's it!" exclaimed the hotel's telegraphist. "The Treasurer's finished his speech!"

Everyone around the radio held their breath. Thorn's presentation had been replaced by the sound of scraping chairs and a vague hubbub. Silence fell as soon as Farouk's voice rose, half-heartedly, from the back of the room: "We thank you for that long speech. Your request of . . . er . . ."

"Of rehabilitation, my Lord."

Ophelia recognized the characteristic whispering of the young aide-memoire. Now that the link with Archibald had been cut, the Web hadn't taken long to get back to business.

"That's right," said the family spirit. "Your request of rehabilitation has been taken thoroughly into consideration and written into the register of . . . er . . . "

"Of grievances, my Lord."

"That's right. It will be the subject of deliberation, then of a vote of . . . er . . . "

"Of members of parliament, my Lord."

"That's right. You may go now."

"I had an announcement to make," Thorn's voice reminded him.

A lengthy rustling of paper. Ophelia could almost see Farouk searching through his notebook. "Is that on the schedule?"

"No, replied the Treasurer. "I would ask you to grant me three extra minutes of speaking time. I will not require more for what I have to announce."

"Be brief."

From the radio one could hear a clinking of glass and a flowing of liquid. Thorn was drinking a glass of water. He cleared his throat, and continued in a clearer voice:

"What I have here, in my hand, is the contract I signed with you last year. I agreed to marry a reader from Anima, to combine her family power with my own, and to supply you with a complete analysis of your Book, in exchange for a title of nobility."

"What's all this tosh?" Ophelia's mother exclaimed. "What this stuff about a contract?"

Ophelia indicated to her to be quiet and pressed her ear closer to the radio. Berenilde herself had frozen in her chair, like a porcelain figure.

"Yes," said Farouk's voice, after a moment's hesitation. "I remember that. Incidentally, I'm finding the wait interminable."

There was a tearing sound and shocked cries rose from the entire assembly.

"There," Thorn declared, calmly. "I have just destroyed my contract. I cancel the marriage, I will not read your Book, and I offer you my resignation. I would like to stress that this is a decision I made alone. So it is alone that I will accept all the consequences. I thank you for your attention."

Through the loudspeakers, the cries turned into a general outcry, but no sound was as fearsome as Farouk's silence. The banging of a gavel rang out, while someone called for calm, and then the broadcast was finally replaced with a musical interlude.

Around the radio set, there was total astonishment.

"Why?"

Everyone turned towards Berenilde's chair. With her bulging eyes, quivering chin, lined forehead, knitted brows, and convulsive lips, she was barely recognizable. Her perfect society-lady mask had just smashed to smithereens.

"Why?" she repeated in a flat voice. "Why has he done that? He's lost his mind!"

She had begun to shake so hard that Agatha rushed to take the baby from her arms. Bent double in her chair, as though punched in the stomach, Berenilde looked imploringly at Ophelia. "I beg you. Don't abandon my boy."

On the surface, Ophelia was completely still: she didn't move, didn't blink, didn't say a thing. And yet every molecule in her body had already started moving. Thorn's announcement had just released an internal breaking mechanism, and the dark material blocking her head for hours, for days, suddenly disappeared in a cloud of vapor. Ophelia breathed in deeply.

All at once, everything seemed wonderfully clear to her. She rose from her chair and went over to Berenilde, who was staring at her, looking distraught.

"I promise you two things, madam. I won't abandon Thorn, and I will find a name worthy of your daughter."

"Might I know what you are intending to do, exactly?" her mother asked, astonished, fists on hips. "You heard Mr. Thorn. This bad joke is over, we're going home."

"I'm not going home, Mom. I'm going back up there." Ophelia's announcement prompted general incredulity: there was blinking, snorting, outrage, even nervous laughter, but no one seemed to realize that she really was serious.

No one apart from Fox. "Up there?" he repeated, somewhat panicked. "You mean to Citaceleste? With the Family States and that whole caboodle, there's not a single airship, not a single sleigh available. Even the folk from the Carnival Caravan, over there at Asgard," Fox said, thumbing towards a window, "they're not authorized to set off for now. In any case, your fiancé . . . your ex-fiancé ordered me not to allow you to go through the hotel door anymore," he concluded, crossing his muscular arms. "It's become far too dangerous out there."

"You won't have to disobey him," Ophelia reassured him. "I won't go through that door. I'll go through there." And she indicated a foyer mirror. She could sense, with her entire body, that she would manage to pass through it. She had lied to herself, she understood the reason why, but it was over now.

"Oh, but no, no, no!" Fox protested, gripping her shoulders. "I wouldn't be able to go in there with you, kid!"

Ophelia requested a pocket mirror and a small writing set from the receptionist. She gave the first to Fox, and kept the second for herself.

"Check this mirror regularly. I'll send you messages, you'll be able to follow me wherever I go."

Fox frowned, his brows like two burning bushes, and then finally removed his monocle. "Take this in exchange. And take great care not to let yourself be strangled again, hey?" he grumbled. "You're my boss, I'd like to keep my job for a long time yet."

"Thank you," Ophelia said to him, with an irrepressible smile. "For the monocle, and for what you did back there, on the jetty."

Ophelia's mother opened her mouth as wide as a hearth, but Aunt Rosaline interrupted her before she exploded. "I think I express the general consensus when I say that your plan is most unreasonable. You think you're going where, exactly, like this? To the Family States assembly? I doubt you'd be allowed entry. All the policemen have been summoned to the court to maintain security."

"So much the better," said Ophelia. "I'm not going to the court, so I'll avoid being checked."

Aunt Rosaline was taken aback. "Well now, I don't follow you at all anymore. Where are you going?"

"The mattresses," she explained. "Do you remember that article in the *Nibelungen*? The one that told of a logjam of mattresses in the lift? I found it ridiculous at the time, but I've just finally understood it. Four beds linked to sandglasses were stolen from Madam Hildegarde's factory. We know they were used for the abductions. They're what caused the logjam, do you see? If I find the mattresses, I find the missing. If I find the missing, I can still save Thorn. I've made my decision," Ophelia stated firmly, to halt the protests of the entire family. "I'm going, whether you agree to it or not."

"My daughter has fallen on her *noggin*!" Ophelia's mother finally burst out. "So you didn't understand that he publicly repudiated you, your dear Mr. Thorn? I forbid you to go and once more put yourself in danger for him!"

Ophelia tied her scarf securely around her neck, so her hair wouldn't bother her anymore, and looked her mother straight in the eye.

"You're the one who hasn't understood, Mom. Thorn isn't the egotistical monster you think he is . . . that I once thought he was, too," she had to admit. "I convinced myself that he wanted to read Mr. Farouk's Book out of personal ambition, but it's something else, there always was something else. Thorn has just given it up to protect us, we can't let him down now."

"But what are you talking about?" Berenilde asked anxiously, shaking in her chair. "What is this 'something else?'"

"I don't know," Ophelia admitted, "but I will find out."

She had already sensed that there was a link between what Mother Hildegarde had revealed to her in the non-place and the God of the letters: "That fellow, my dear, best to avoid crossing his path. And yet, that's what ends up happening to those whose interest in the Books gets a little too keen." The more Ophelia considered the matter, the more obvious it seemed to her that Thorn had been investigating it from the very start. When he'd wanted to place Mother Hildegarde under arrest, it was protection he was offering her.

As Ophelia walked purposefully towards the foyer mirror, her mother made an imperious flourish with her arm to stop her. Her father talked her out of it. "I think, my dear, we should let our daughter make her own decisions for once. We've already imposed our own on her too much."

The Rapporteur, who, until then, had maintained the

utmost discretion, couldn't hold back any longer. She reared up across Ophelia's path, in a swirl of black dress. The weather vane on her hat was aimed at Ophelia, while her protruding eyes looked coldly at her over her gold spectacles.

"Since your parents evidently have no authority over you, I find myself obliged to intervene. You will get mixed up no further in the affairs of this individual. If I had known sooner that he was involved in dubious activities, I would have sent an unfavorable report to our dear mothers. He has deceived the Doyennes and insulted our entire family. You will not pass through this mirror for him, do you hear me clearly, my dear?"

Ophelia held the Rapporteur's glare unwaveringly, ready to defy her even more than any of the others, but her great-uncle stepped in. "If you want to stop her, it will be over my dead body. Off you go, m'dear," he muttered into his moustache. "Your queer fish strikes me as also being a serious *sympathizer*, in his own way, no? Just for that, I will help you to help him."

"Thank you, dear uncle."

Ignoring the outraged expression of the Rapporteur and the flabbergasted faces of the rest of her family, Ophelia neared the foyer mirror until she was reflected in it. She looked straight at her determined face, beyond its scratches and bruises, finally ready to face that truth that she hadn't wanted to see.

It wasn't Thorn who needed her. It was she who needed Thorn.

Ophelia plunged, body and soul, into the mirror.

THE MATTRESSES

Ophelia re-emerged in the administrative office of Family Manufacturer—Hildegarde & Co. The lights were off, the premises silent.

She made her way, in the half-light, to the piston lamp, and then searched in Mother Hildegarde's absurdly deep drawers. After a few minutes of looking, she found what she'd come for: the public transport leaflets that Thorn had handled that very morning.

Seated in the light of the lamp, Ophelia set aside the network of metropolitan Compass Roses—these shortcuts had only been installed on Citaceleste's highest floors, and she knew they were too narrow for mattresses.

She unfolded the leaflet of Citaceleste lift lines.

The factory was situated in the town's underbelly, between the sewers and the countless engine rooms. For maintenance reasons, several lifts serviced these basements and Ophelia didn't have time to inspect them all. She had to restrict her field of inquiry to a minimum. The factory only had access to one lift stop, the other two lines descended and ascended without stopping at that floor. The factory's lift itself allowed access only to the floors above it.

The bed thieves had thus, inevitably, ascended.

Ophelia had the start of her lead, but was still without any particulars, some trail she could follow.

She opened the door to the hangar and went onto the gangway of the stairs on which Philibert had pushed her the preceding night. Looking down from on high at the sand-beds lined up between the rows of lamps, Ophelia saw there wasn't a single shadow behind the beds' curtains—the blue sandglasses had all been removed from circulation. She leaned over the railing and looked for the goods lift the foreman had spoken to them about. It was much further along, to her right, out of bounds, blocked halfway between the hangar floor and a large portcullis. Currently being serviced, the foreman had said. But that wouldn't have been the case back in May, and Ophelia was convinced the four stolen beds had been trans-ported in it to get them out of the factory. All she needed to know now was where exactly that goods lift ended up.

Having crossed the office, the workshop, and the hall, Oph-elia landed at the large courtyard outside. Luckily, the door was neither locked nor sealed by the Keeper of the Seals. Piles of old mattresses had been soaking up the damp here for years; clearly, they were not the ones she was looking for. She walked along the factory's grey facades. The administrative depart-ment and the workshop adjoined a huge industrial building; its high doors were fastened with a chain, but Ophelia could peer through the gap between them. She made out, at the back of the room, the large portcullis that she'd seen from the hangar stairway. So here was the precise destination of the goods lift; the stolen beds had come this way.

It was mattresses that had caused a lift logjam, not whole beds. The thieves had probably got rid of the frames, bases, and canopies right here, rather than under the windows of the workshop. She poked around the junk rotting away on the flagstones, and ended up finding a length of muslin. A bed curtain. It didn't take her long to unearth some blocks of fine wood, just like that framing the sandbeds in the hangar.

Ophelia unbuttoned her gloves. She didn't make a habit of reading objects without their owner's permission, but this was dumped junk, and her position as Great Family Reader authorized her to work on public property.

One by one, she probed the bits of bed. As she'd expected, the last people to handle them were the thieves themselves. Images flashed in her mind, as she delved into their perceptions. Leather gloves. Faces half-hidden by beards. Rapid breathing. Repeated glances towards the workshop, at the other end of the courtyard. There were three of them, maybe four. She couldn't penetrate their thoughts, but a very particular state of mind emanated from these objects: extreme vigilance, a certain efficiency, and a lot of nervous tension. She had her particulars.

A noise made her jump. A stoat was nosing around in the debris, doubtless in search of food. To be on the safe side, Ophelia took Gail's monocle out of her pocket, and, closing her right eye, stuck it against the left lens of her glasses. She turned around several times to be sure no hidden Invisible was around, no illusion that was a trap, and then made for the only lift on that floor.

Consulting the lift lines leaflet, Ophelia realized that this lift only served two floors. According to the map and its key, one of them was a dead end, used just for storing coal. The thieves had probably gone up to the next floor and, from there, taken a connecting lift.

She moved the lever, went up two landings and came out onto a foul-smelling road where a tangle of machines and pipes sent out jets of boiling-hot steam. Things were now getting serious: she was at a junction of connecting lifts. Here there were five lift stops, in addition to the one from which she'd just emerged. The mattress thieves could have chosen any one of them. Ophelia had no option but to read each lift to find their trail.

She searched in her dress pockets, scribbled a message in her notebook, and slipped it into the little double-sided mirror lent to her by one of the sandglass makers. If Fox had kept his own mirror in sight, he should already be reading this message: *All well, making progress in my research.* It wasn't lofty prose, but it would at least reassure the whole family.

Ophelia went to the nearest lift and pulled the request cord. On the lower floors of Citaceleste, there were no liftboys circulating on fixed schedules. At least Ophelia would be at leisure to do what she had to do.

Once inside the lift, she took a deep breath and grabbed hold of the floors lever with her bare hand. She felt instantly overwhelmed, as if a procession of ghosts were taking possession of her being, one after the other. She went from being irritated to exhausted, excited, worried, tired, annoyed, moved, disillusioned, impatient, distracted, tormented, concerned, offended, demoralized, and weary, with not a single one of these feelings being her own. Ophelia had already read objects in the public domain, but nothing that came close to this lift lever, raised and lowered several dozen times every day of every week of every month of every year. All she could do was go back in time in reverse, in the hope of happening, sooner or later, on the particulars of her thieves.

When she finally released the lever, none the wiser, it took her a few seconds to remember who she was and why she was there. She left the lift, cut through the road's hot vapors, and pulled the request cord of the next lift. Another fruitless reading.

At the third lift, Ophelia had to allow herself a rest. Her hand was shaking and her glasses had become blurred. All those extraneous emotions went through her like galvanic currents, putting her nerves under great strain. She was starting to question the validity of her method when, at last, in the

420

fourth lift, she recognized the particulars. Vigilance, efficiency, nervousness.

Ophelia had her thieves.

Now she had to refine her reading and determine to which landing, precisely, they had traveled. She probed the lever for a second time, going back in time, day before day, week before week, month before month. As soon as she found the particulars, she would immerse herself as deeply as possible in the minds of the thieves.

Finally, the last one . . . Too bulky, these mattresses . . . Think of the bounty. . . Just three more . . . The workmen again . . . They're moaning, we're making them late . . . Think of the bounty . . . Just two more . . . Damn, some workmen . . . No room to bring them all up . . . Think of the bounty . . . Right, the first one . . . Now's our chance, the coast's clear . . . Think of the bounty.

Ophelia released the lever and all her muscles at the same time. The effort of concentration had given her a migraine, but she had enough material to piece together the scene. She examined the half-moon dial that indicated floors, which she'd seen through the thieves' eyes; they had done four return journeys, one for each mattress, between the twenty-fifth and thirteenth underground floors. She closed the lift gate and engaged the lever to make the same journey.

The thirteenth basement floor gave Ophelia a sense of déjà vu. It had the same dark alleys, the same stinking pipe systems, the same damp vapors that were the norm throughout the underbelly, and yet she had the familiar feeling of having already been here.

According to the leaflet, there was only one connecting lift for this floor. And yet, when Ophelia embarked on a detailed reading of the following lift carriage, she no longer found the particulars. The characteristic combination of vigilance, efficiency, and nervousness had disappeared. This phenomenon could only be explained by a radical change in mindset.

The thieves had off-loaded their cargo right here, between two lift stops.

Ophelia felt her heart ticking like a metronome: one beat for joy, one beat for fear. Carefully, she went back down the road, checking each smoky window. Despite it being so late at night, she could make out figures hard at work, amid the showers of sparks and clouds of smoke. Where had the mattresses been deposited? In this lead foundry? In this porcelain workshop? In this gasworks?

Ophelia stopped in front of a facade with switched-off red lanterns and windows plastered in old advertisements. So it wasn't just a feeling, she had already been here. *Erotic Delights*, the Imaginoir that Cunegond had closed down due to bankruptcy.

The ideal hiding place.

There was no one about, on either side of the steamy road. The thought of going in there alone left her mouth dry, but time was limited. Her writing was shaky as she scribbled a new note for Fox, and slipped it into her pocket mirror.

Imaginoir red lanterns, 13th-floor basement: I'm having a quick look, then coming back.

Ophelia had expected to have to break in, so she was taken aback when the door opened with a mere push. It was the first time she was seeing what an Imaginoir looked like on the inside. The only lighting came from the strings of lanterns on the ceiling, probably illusions of emergency lighting in case the gas was cut off. Red carpets, red drapes, red velvet, red upholstery, red stairs: the hall gave the impression of entering some organic universe.

For the moment, Ophelia could see no mattresses, or the missing, anywhere.

She moved quietly to the front desk and picked up the telephone receiver. No dial tone. Ophelia calmed down her scarf, which was flapping nervously. They really would just have to manage on their own.

Signs in the form of long red gloves all pointed up to the Imaginoir's only floor. They bore suggestive titles, probably the names of rooms:

THE GENTLEMAN WITH A FAN
THE QUADRILLE OF HANDS
THE BLACK VELVET STOCKINGS
THREE LADIES SEEN FROM THE BACK

Ophelia took the stairs on the left—those on the right, having collapsed from the damp, had been closed off. Although the first floor was bathed in the same soft half-light, its atmosphere was very different. Large statues of white marble, with bodies bared and faces masked, flanked four black doors. The lanterns projected their doubled and distended shadows across a labyrinth of screens.

Ophelia slipped between the screens of the central aisle. Each one was a work of art in which suggestive illusions winked at visitors, bared a shoulder, or blew kisses from fingertips. She went up to the door marked THE GENTLEMAN WITH A FAN. An uneasy shiver ran through her when, behind the masks, she noticed the eyes of the sculptures following her every move. She got out Gail's monocle and stuck it against her glasses. Reality instantly reasserted itself, reducing the illusions to just pale filigrees of images.

Having put her monocle away, she opened the door and went in without making a sound.

Barely had Ophelia laid eyes on the dark room than her migraine intensified. Her thoughts became muddled, like tangled wires, to the extent that she caught her foot on the cushions heaped on the floor and only just grabbed hold of a pedestal table, knocking over the vase of artificial flowers on it. She cast a dazed look around her. The room was just an ever-changing collection of cushions, pedestal tables, carpets, drapes, shadows, and lights.

Ophelia no longer recalled why she'd come in here, but had the vague intuition that it would be best to get out. Clinging to her pedestal table, the consistency of which was turning increasingly gelatinous, she searched for the door, in vain. The room had suddenly become hermetically sealed.

She looked around for a mirror, with the unpleasant feeling of going through endless quicksand. Tripping on a bolster, she fell flat on her face, and was so totally stunned, she paid no attention to the explosion of pain in her arm.

After several blinks and a few contortions, Ophelia had to revise her opinion. It wasn't on a bolster that she'd tripped, it was on a man, wearing a long beard and a satin dressing gown. What on earth was Count Harold doing, sleeping in such an uncomfortable place?

In fact, he had the right idea. That sea of cushions was far too choppy; better just to keep lying on the floor. Ophelia would have stayed like that, stretched out on the carpet, eyes to the ceiling, for a long time had her scarf not tried to slap her, even knocking her glasses off.

The monocle, she thought, weakly. I must put on the monocle. She fumbled in her pocket, closed her right eye, and stuck the black lens into her other socket. While the world around her darkened, her thoughts, on the contrary, became clearer, and the ground became firm again. Illusions capable of producing the same effect as inebriation: Cunegond had already spoken to her about them. This place was a Confusion Bubble.

Ophelia kneeled beside Count Harold, stretched out

between the cushions, and examined him as best she could through the combined opacity of room and monocle. The tattooed eyelids of the Mirage were closed.

"Count?" whispered Ophelia.

He didn't respond, plunged in deep lethargy. A few glances through the monocle showed Ophelia that he enjoyed every creature comfort here: the pedestal tables were loaded with books, snuffboxes, sweet jars, carafes of water, and bottles of perfume. There was something excessively thoughtful and ironically refined about this scenario that chilled her blood.

She noticed bedding on the floor, probably one of the four stolen mattresses. She got confirmation of that when she made out, hanging over the bed, like a mobile over a cradle, the blue sandglass linked to it. Without a minimum of lucidity, it was impossible to reach it and break it.

As for the door, Ophelia now understood why she'd stopped seeing it once inside the room. The monocle enabled her to see, in light outline, the illusion of the wall camouflaging it. The height of perversity.

"Count?" she repeated. "Can you hear me?"

Not a hair stirred in the Mirage's long, blond beard. This man might be hard of hearing, but his failure to respond was worrying. Ensuring that she kept her monocle in place under her glasses, Ophelia moved her ear close to his mouth. He was no longer breathing.

Ophelia felt her own breathing become panicky. Had she arrived too late? Count Harold showed no sign of injury or expiring. Had he succumbed to the shock of the illusion? Frantically, she removed her glove and took his pulse at the wrist, then at the neck, but she had to accept it. The Knight's former guardian was dead . . . and he'd died recently, his bodily warmth testified to that.

Ophelia got up. She could do nothing more for him, but she

might still be able to save the others. She went to the second dark room, THE QUADRILLE OF HANDS. Holding the monocle between thumb and index finger, this time Ophelia took the time to survey the scene from the doorway. Nothing remained of the old projection room as it must have been. Every corner had been stripped of the merest sign, real or illusory, of debauchery. There was the same seeming respectability as Count Harold's room: a profusion of flowers, snuffboxes, confectionery, cushions, books, flasks, and, tauntingly suspended above a mattress, out of reach, a self-turning blue sandglass. Despite the monocle filtering the illusion, Ophelia could feel a heaviness in the atmosphere that made her head hum. Another Confusion Bubble was in action here. Being trapped in this perpetual delirium tremens, surrounded by a thousand and one refinements, was a torture worse than any corporal punishment.

Ophelia rushed over when she noticed a man collapsed on a pedestal table. She didn't recognize his face, but he bore the Mirage tattoo on his closed eyelids. Probably the Provost of the Marshals, the first of the abduction victims.

He wasn't breathing, either. This man was dead without any trace of blood, without any sign of a struggle, like a puppet whose strings had just been cut. And yet, his skin was still warm.

Ophelia moved away very slowly, palm pressed to mouth to quell a surge of panic. It wasn't due to negligence that the front door downstairs had been left open. There was someone else inside the Imaginoir right now. Someone who had come specifically to finish off the prisoners.

She hastily left THE QUADRILLE OF HANDS, slipped between the screens and took to the stairs, keen to put as much distance as possible between herself and this place. She stopped still in the middle of the stairs. Her whole body was urging her to run away, but she couldn't reconcile herself to doing so. Not this close to the objective. Giving up now, that would be abandoning both Thorn and Archibald. Archibald . . . He was bound to be here, in one of the two remaining rooms.

With infinite care, ready to scarper at the first suspect noise, Ophelia went back up the stairs and pushed open the door to THE BLACK VELVET STOCKINGS. She checked out the place through the prism of her monocle. This room was, in every respect, the same as the other two. Her heart skipped a beat when she spotted, between pedestal tables and cushions, a body slumped deep in an armchair, head lolling to one side.

Archibald!

In her haste, Ophelia almost knocked over a record player. She had to crouch in front of the chair to see the ambassador's face, collapsed against his shoulder, behind a tangle of fair hair. He was looking frightful. Ophelia shook him so hard, she nearly lost her monocle.

"Please," she whispered. "Be alive, I beg you."

An arm fell from the armrest and just dangled, limply. Archibald did not wake up. Feverishly, Ophelia searched for his pulse. If she'd arrived too late for him as well, she'd never forgive herself.

She stifled a gulp of relief. His heart was still beating— weakly, but it was still beating. Archibald had survived both the Imaginoir killer and the severing of the link with the Web.

"I'm getting you out of here," Ophelia promised him.

Beneath the jumble of cushions, she looked for the mattress by which Archibald must have arrived here. Keeping her monocle in place while keeping the other eye closed was getting increasingly tricky. Ophelia found the mattress, but it took her a little more searching to find the unpinned sandglass. It had rolled onto the carpet. Apparently, there hadn't been time to hang it above the bed, as had been done for the others.

Ophelia broke the sandglass; Archibald's body disappeared from the armchair.

All she could hope now was that he would be found in his room at Clairdelune without delay, and be given first aid. With a bit of luck, his witness account would be decisive in enabling the blackmailer to be identified. Ophelia slipped the pieces of sandglass into her dress pocket for a future reading. Maybe they, too, would enable her to go back to the source.

Only Mr. Chekhov remained, in the final room. Would Ophelia have the courage to try to save him, too? Wasn't it best to leave as quickly as possible, while she still could?

Ophelia crossed the dark room on tiptoe, slipped through the half-opened door, and, with the help of the screens, concealed herself by making herself smaller than ever.

All these precautions proved pointless: a figure the shape of a hot-air balloon was blocking her path.

"Miss Great Family Reader," sighed Baron Melchior. "I would have dearly liked to spare us this situation."

THE GENTEEL DEATH

Baron Melchior came forward, making his gold-knobbed cane tap against the floorboards. He wore a voluminous frock coat of peacock feathers, which gave Ophelia the feeling of being watched by dozens of staring eyes. Those of the baron expressed deep regret.

"Keep your hands clearly in sight," he said, very gently.

Ophelia was obliged to let go of the notebook she'd been trying to reach in her pocket. She should have sent a warning to Fox when she still could. It was too late now.

"Did you come alone?"

"No," she whispered.

Baron Melchior's pointed moustache stood up, under the impetus of a smile. And yet it was a smile devoid of irony, almost pained. "You came alone. No disrespect to you, but you're a bad liar."

Ophelia felt anger knotting her innards. She'd seen this man as being preyed upon when he'd never ceased to be the predator.

"That's not the case for you. You're a remarkable actor."

"Don't judge me too harshly. My intentions have always been excellent."

"Does your sister know what her Imaginoir is being used for?"

"Her former Imaginoir," stressed Baron Melchior. "No, Cunegond knows nothing of what's going on here. This place was a disgrace, with all those decadent illusions." He grimaced, indicating a screen on which a nymph was emerging from the water lilies to beckon them to join her. "I refurbished it as best I could to make it almost respectable."

Ophelia moved backwards as he moved towards her, until she found her back against the labyrinth of screens. The baron stood between her and the stairs. Jumping over the landing guardrail would mean breaking one's bones down below. The other staircase had been blocked with an impassable barrage of planks. And as far as Ophelia had been able to see, there was no mirror downstairs. Things were looking pretty bad.

With his black-gloved and gold-ringed hand, Baron Melchior indicated the pediment, supported by statues, saying THREE LADIES SEEN FROM THE BACK. "I was just finishing with that dear Chekhov when I heard a noise from the room next door. I certainly wasn't expecting to fall on you. What led you all the way here? And how did you manage to get through my Confusion Bubbles? Truly, Miss Great Family Reader, you catch me off my guard."

An icy chill swept through Ophelia. Baron Melchior wouldn't let her leave this Imaginoir alive.

"And there I was, thinking you detested violence."

"I do hate it. Indeed, had I known that Philibert would mistreat you that way, I would never have requested his services."

Ophelia stared at the baron in the red light of the lanterns. He seemed sincere. She might have been swayed by that had she not noticed the way he was moving, slowly but surely, so as to cut off any possible escape route, and distance her as much as possible from the stairs.

"I attach great importance to the genteel life, miss, but I attach just as much to the genteel death. We can kill each

430

other decently, between civilized people, and that's what I expected of Philibert. I would have readily taken it on myself," he said, with a resigned shrug of the shoulders, "but Mr. Thorn always had his eye on you. Until now, at any rate."

"All that to keep him from reading Mr. Farouk's Book?" whispered Ophelia.

"I find it infinitely regrettable that a man of his abilities should wish to poke his nose where it doesn't belong. This marriage to you was a mistake—a mistake that I've endeavored to correct. Of course, I could have chosen to kill Mr. Thorn instead of you," Baron Melchior readily admitted. "Don't take it too much to heart, but I find you less indispensible than him."

"That doesn't tell me why you yourself are afraid of the Book."

The baron gently nodded his head, looking melancholic. "Afraid? Come, come, don't speak about what you don't understand."

"You are afraid," she insisted. "You're afraid of what another person thinks of you. Afraid of your God. Afraid of not living up to his expectations. You speak endlessly of human dignity, but you remind me of a slave who thinks only of satisfying his master."

There was a moment of silence, during which Ophelia heard her heart beating like a drum.

"If I had to judge by your expression," Baron Melchior finally muttered, "I would say that you're much more afraid than I am."

He moved around with deliberate patience, like an enormous peacock, as though he expected Ophelia to give herself up. Was he going to throw a surprise illusion in her face? Keeping her back to the screens, Ophelia tightened her grip on the monocle, which she'd kept in her hand, ready to use it at any moment. She needed to play for time, to find a way out.

"Who is God?"

"That, dear miss, is not for me to answer."

"You have killed your own cousins to please him."

Baron Melchior looked offended. "I did it *decently*," he insisted. "Not a single drop of blood was spilled, not a single injury inflicted upon them. I promise you that, if you don't cause difficulties for me, you will experience an equally appealing end. Tut-tut, watch out for your scarf," he warned her. "It's got energy to spare, for a rag of badly knitted wool."

The scarf was, indeed, becoming so agitated, Ophelia was struggling to control it. "You're making it nervous."

"That's mutual. Tie it up, please." Baron Melchior indicated with his cane the leg of a screen. Ophelia had to grapple with her own scarf, while trying not to drop the monocle. For a moment, she'd hoped to knock over one of the screens, onto the Baron, but they all turned out to be screwed to the ground.

"I don't understand," she muttered. "How could you have lowered yourself to do that?"

Baron Melchior emptied of air like a balloon. "It saddens me to hear you put it that way. I've already told you: I'm fighting for a different future. A murderer who spilled innocent blood, and a slanderer who manipulates public opinion," he specified, indicating, in turn, the doors of the Provost of the Marshals and of the director of the *Nibelungen*. "As for that unreasonable Count Harold, not satisfied with perverting the child in his care, as well as an entire kennel, he made scandalous remarks in public. All three of them had tarnished the Mirage coat of arms for too long. The Family States take place only once every fifteen years, do you realize that? That was the occasion finally to see the court opening itself up to new horizons! My cousins would have imposed their force of inertia; I had the moral duty to remove them."

"And Archibald? Was it also a moral duty to keep him here, while his family severed his link? You very nearly killed him."

Looking aggrieved, Baron Melchior drew in his head, making his triple chin stick out, as if he were himself the victim of some wrongdoing. "Mr. Ambassador put us both into a difficult situation. That sandglass he stole from me was the only way I had to come and go here as I wished. I'm rather good with my fingers, you see. I inserted a mechanism of my own invention to be able to reuse my sandglass whenever I liked, without having to pull its pin. That boy used it any which way! Of course, I had foreseen the possibility of some pest unpinning my sandglass, intentionally or accidentally, and that's why I'd installed a Confusion Bubble, right there. What I hadn't foreseen was that the pest would be the ambassador himself. His disappearance triggered maximum-security measures, with policemen around every corridor corner. I was obliged to wait for the Family States, finally to be able to visit my guests, without the fear of identity checks and awkward questions! I think your scarf is adequately secured," Baron Melchior suddenly said, in a friendly tone. "Stand up, please, hands still in view. Dear, oh dear, believe me, this situation doesn't please me any more than it does you!"

Tied up, the scarf was squirming like an eel, worsening the hole in the knitting. Ophelia moved away from it, as though avoiding its flailing. This step to the side allowed her to reposition herself; she was no longer backed up against the screens, giving her an opening to the left of Baron Melchior. He was heavy, he was slow—if Ophelia managed to get around him, she could reach the stairs before him.

"On the contrary, I think this situation does please you."

433

The baron's moustache collapsed. "How can you claim that?"

"The staging of the rooms. The tone of your letters. The way you embraced your role as the perfect assistant. You pushed your malice as far as to speak to us, Thorn and me, right in front of this Imaginoir, mere steps away from your victims." Word by word, inch by inch, Ophelia was moving so as to widen the space between them. "You say that you disapprove of our marriage? I heard you once, putting yourself forward to make my wedding dress. The truth is that you're playing with us like a child plays with dolls. Does that make you feel less like a doll yourself?"

Baron Melchior didn't lose his cool, but Ophelia could have sworn that the feathers on his frock coat had begun to quiver. He gripped his cane with both hands, enough to make the bamboo creak.

"You weren't so disapproving when I did what was necessary to neutralize our impetuous Knight. Since you want to know everything, miss, I hadn't planned to kill anyone at all. My initial intention was to keep my cousins quietly out of the way, here, until the end of the Family States. The same went for you, my dear; I hoped you would be reasonable enough to leave the Pole on your own initiative. I sent letters to each of you, friendly letters, to avoid a painful confrontation between all of us. You have no idea of all the precautions I took, for months, to avoid the shrewdness of your little hands. I admit that I took a risk in allowing you to read the pin of my sandglass, but I knew it was minimal."

"If murder was just one option among others," countered Ophelia, "why choose it?"

The glimmer of sadness that shone in Baron Melchior's eyes went out like the flame of a candle. "Do you recall what I said to you yesterday? 'It's up to us to see our choices out to the end.' By ignoring my letters, you all accepted the idea of being killed. So me, I accepted that of being your killer."

The scarf lashed out, violently, which, for a brief moment, distracted Baron Melchior's attention. Ophelia might not have another opportunity. She charged towards the stairs as fast as her legs allowed.

She had counted on Baron Melchior's heaviness. And yet it was with a lithe, almost nonchalant movement that he held her by the wrist and then tipped her onto the floor. Ophelia cried out when he methodically twisted her elbow behind her back; the bone, already damaged by the fall in the stairs, emitted a horrible cracking sound.

"I've broken your arm," he noted, wearily. "You could have avoided that by just complying nicely."

Through the tears of pain clouding her eyes, Ophelia saw the black monocle rolling across the floor and spinning like a coin. Without even relaxing his grip, Baron Melchior smashed it with his cane. "A Nihilist monocle," he commented, appreciatively. "I didn't know any still existed. Those things are infallible against illusions that are optically triggered. So that's how you managed to come and go in my Confusion Bubbles! Right, Miss Great Family Reader," he muttered, applying all his weight on Ophelia, "do you still think I'm afraid? I grant that you may have been right on one point." He leaned closer, his moustache stroking her ear. "In fact, this situation doesn't displease me as much as all that."

"Permit me, however, to interrupt you."

Squashed against the floor, arm bent backwards, Ophelia looked up at the shadow climbing the stairs.

THE HEART

Ophelia could only make out the reflection of the red lanterns on the buttons of a uniform. Was it really Thorn standing there on the stairs, or was she the victim of an illusion?

Baron Melchior must have asked himself the same question, as it took him several seconds to recover his facility for repartee: "For such a mismatched couple, you certainly are inseparable. I thought you were dozens of floors above here, Mr. Thorn. How did you find us?"

Thorn walked calmly, unhurriedly, up the last stairs between him and the landing. From the floor, Ophelia couldn't raise her eyes as high as his face; she did, however, have a great view of his shoes.

"Thanks to that woman you are pinning to the floor," Thorn's deep voice replied, above her. "She communicated her position to her assistant, who communicated it to me by priority telegram. I had to slip away from a cohort of civil servants and policemen to join you. Don't worry, I came alone. I wish to negotiate with you, without bothersome witnesses."

Ophelia couldn't believe her ears. With all the policemen present at the Family States, Thorn had decided not to bring a single one? She bit her tongue when Baron Melchior pulled on her arm to make her get up, unconcerned about the unbearable pain he was causing her. He clasped Ophelia to the plumage on his paunch, in a parody of a waltz.

"This way it will be more comfortable for *negotiating*. I'm listening to you, Mr. Thorn."

Ophelia's hair had spilled over her face, but she could see enough to notice that Thorn was studiously avoiding looking at her.

"Why?"

"Why do you ask me why?" Baron Melchior replied, on his guard.

"I have benefited from your support since the start of my career. I would probably never have become Treasurer had you not slipped the right word into the right ear at the right time. You have often helped me, for proceedings and matters in which you had no personal interest at stake. And never, at any moment, did you come to ask me for anything in return. Why?"

Baron Melchior softened, his expression suddenly tinged with a paternal kindliness, which didn't stop him from crushing Ophelia's arm. "Because I always sensed the great things you were capable of achieving. I believe in you, my boy, more than in any Mirage."

"You believe in me," Thorn repeated. He was maintaining a respectable distance between them. Without moving an inch, he looked around him, at the screens whose illusions winked enticingly at him, then at the four doors, framed by their masked statues. Ophelia realized that he was trying to determine whether there were any accomplices hidden in the place.

"That sandglass pin that you miraculously found on Archibald's bed," Thorn continued, after a silence. "You found it because you knew it would be there. You seized that opportunity to push me to carry out a search of the factory, and if it hadn't been the pin, you would have thought up some other ploy. You were clearly counting on me to bring to light the falsification of the ledgers, and, consequently, the implication of the factory in the abductions. Every aspect of your behavior dictated my conduct, up to the indictment of Madam Hildegarde. You didn't support me in my career because you believed in me," he concluded, in a steady voice. "You did it the better to manipulate me when the time came."

"Come now," sighed Baron Melchior. "Are you now telling me that I have disappointed you, too, Mr. Treasurer?"

"I am no longer Treasurer. And that woman," Thorn added, without even looking at Ophelia, "is no longer my fiancée. Her parents are waiting for her, to take her back to Anima. Our little family affairs in no way concern her, from now on. Let's discuss between ourselves, just you and me, would you mind?"

The baron gave himself some time to think, which gave Ophelia time to hear the bones in her arm cracking even more.

"Have you given up the idea of marrying for good?"

"And of reading the Book, yes. That's what you sought to obtain from me, isn't it? You have nothing more to fear from that Animist."

"Excellent!" Baron Melchior exclaimed, gleefully. But he didn't release Ophelia for all that, tightening his grip to the point of smothering her in his lace jabot. "You possess three essential qualities, Mr. Thorn. You are efficient, honest, and peaceable. The way you got involved in the business of the disgraced was ex-em-plary! These clan wars, these endless acts of revenge, all that blood spilled over trifles," he intoned, his voice quivering with indignation, "we must bring an end to it. We need men such as you, capable of solving the thorniest problems within the framework of a civilized administration."

"I am no longer Treasurer," Thorn reminded him. "And I will remain forever a bastard."

Baron Melchior swung his cane around so vigorously, Ophelia heard the air whistle right beside her. "A mere detail! I, myself, am offering you a new life! Or rather, should I say, a new responsibility, which will place you above Lord Farouk, and shield you from his pathological obsession with his Book. You will benefit from total protection, and you will never have to worry, either for yourself or for your aunt, ever again. Do you understand me clearly, Mr. Thorn? I'm not proposing that you become my pawn. I'm proposing that you become my partner."

Thorn slowly raised his eyebrows, his scar seeming to get even bigger. "My mother also benefited from that responsibility and that protection. Look where she is today. I would like to know," he continued, with utmost seriousness, "is it you making me this offer, or is it the God you serve?"

Baron Melchior burst out laughing, all his peacock feathers jiggling with him. Ophelia bit her lip so as not to cry out— each shake made her feel her arm would explode into a thousand pieces.

"Ah, Mr. Thorn, if your mother had half your clear-sightedness, she wouldn't have ended up disgraced and mutilated," he said, fervently. "So the rumor is true, you have inherited her memories? That makes you the perfect initiate. We will succeed, *you will succeed*, where she failed. You and me, we will save the Pole from all this corruption blighting it. Just as we will save Lord Farouk from the bad influences on him." As he said this, he kept hammering Ophelia's shoulder with the knob of his cane. "Right now, Mr. Thorn, I'm going to ask you a question that few of the elect have the privilege to hear: would you like to meet God?"

"It is my dearest wish."

Ophelia stared at Thorn in the hope of finally capturing his attention. He had replied with such spontaneity, his eyes were shining with such keen interest, that it was clear to her that he was very serious.

"I will arrange a meeting," promised Baron Melchior. "It will permit me at least to compensate for the one I was unable to arrange with Madam Hildegarde. Right now, we must deal with this young lady," he sighed, lifting Ophelia's chin with his cane. "Murder is as repugnant to me as it is to you, but I fear she's seen too much and heard too much."

Thorn stroked his bottom lip with his index finger. Unlike Ophelia, whose glasses were turning bluer by the minute, he didn't panic in the slightest. "I share your opinion, but I would propose falsifying her memory instead. I am partly Chronicler, I can cause her to forget all that took place here."

Ophelia knew that wasn't true. By his own admission, Thorn had never indulged in those kinds of practices, but she had to admit that, right now, he was very convincing. Baron Melchior appeared to consider the matter carefully, while twirling his cane around his index finger. Finally, he returned Ophelia's arm to its natural position, bringing an end to the torture, and even extended his gallantry to kissing her hand. "I have been honored, miss, to make your acquaintance."

With these words and a theatrical flourish, he let her go, like a bird taken from its cage and returned to the sky.

Far from being relieved, Ophelia was a nervous wreck. Hesitantly, she walked towards Thorn, who waited for her, impassively, in front of the stairs. The more distance Ophelia put between herself and Baron Melchior, the more she dreaded him changing his mind and smashing her, like Gail's monocle, with one strike of his cane.

He did nothing of the sort.

She sensed that something wasn't right. Her arm felt terrible, and it wasn't just due to the fracture. An intense heat was rising up to her shoulder and chest. The baron's kiss on her hand had seemingly lit a fire under her skin. Ophelia's heart was beating so hard and so fast, it was becoming uncomfortable.

The moment Thorn noticed how she was seizing up, he grabbed her by the shoulders. "What have you done to her?"

"You may have the power to alter her memories, but you don't have one to alter her fundamental nature," Baron Melchior replied, casually. "This child has been endowed with a curiosity and an obstinacy that will lead her, sooner or later, to cause us fresh difficulties. Take no offense, dear partner, but I prefer my methods."

Ophelia barely heard him. Little by little, the heat was turning into pain, as if the blade of a knife were slowly plunging between her ribs. She slid out of Thorn's hands and fell to her knees.

"It's an illusion of my making," Baron Melchior explained, approaching as calmly as he was speaking. "I inject it directly into the organism. It speeds up the heart to the point of cardiac arrest. A clean death, without violence, without a flaw, in due form. Of course, we'll disguise it afterwards as an accident, to avoid any problems. The interfamilial High Court doesn't joke with such matters."

Prostrate on the floor, in the grip of a cold sweat, Ophelia hugged her chest with both arms to control the pounding. 'It's an illusion, an *illusion*,' she repeated to herself. 'It's not real. My heart's perfectly fine. It's an illusion, an illusion, an illusion.'

The pain felt unbearably real to her.

"So, about my offer?" the baron said, holding his hand out to Thorn. "Is it a deal, dear partner?"

A spurt of blood spattered Ophelia's glasses. She saw five gloved fingers fall to the floor, right beside her, in a cascade of rings. Baron Melchior looked, incredulously, at his mutilated hand. "I . . . What?"

"Cancel your illusion." Thorn's voice came from deep within, like an animal's growl. He hadn't moved a finger, but, despite her inner turmoil, Ophelia could see the static electricity with which he had suddenly charged himself.

Baron Melchior stared wide-eyed, increasingly dumbfounded. The sight of his own blood, pouring over his frock coat, his trousers, and his shoes, made him turn pale. Only then did he emit a horrified cry, as if finally becoming conscious of the pain. "You have used your claws against me? Have you lost your mind? I was going to fulfill your dearest wi . . ."

Thorn grabbed him by his lace jabot with such violence that he winded him. "I gave up that wish the very moment I resigned," he hissed between his teeth. "Cancel your illusion!"

Baron Melchior went from deathly pale to crimson. He whipped Thorn's cheek with a enraged lash of his cane.

"You never intended to ally yourself to me, never! You deceived me to get your little hussy back. A hussy when, me, I was offering you God! I'm spilling blood everywhere, just look at that," he said, indignantly, shaking his mutilated hand. "It's the peak of poor taste, Mr. Thorn, you profoundly disappoint me."

Baron Melchior was about to bring his cane down on Thorn a second time, but it fell to the floor with the rest of his fingers. Thorn's claws had struck again. Thrown off balance by the surprise and the pain, the baron staggered backwards to the landing's railing, which, held up by just a few screws, leaned precariously under his weight.

Kneeling on the ground, Ophelia observed the scene through her tangled hair and the spattered blood on her glasses. Her sight was becoming increasingly blurred. Her heart, beating insanely fast, wouldn't hold out much longer.

"Cancel your illusion!" ordered Thorn.

Baron Melchior, both hands dripping blood, shook with

skeptical laughter, as though all this was a tasteless joke. "Come, come, you're not planning on killing the Minister of Elegance and God's delegate. That would be quite the opposite of a genteel death."

With a kick right in the belly, Thorn projected him against the railing, which, this time, gave way under his weight. Ophelia closed her eyes on hearing the sound of the fall, a medley of metallic clattering and broken bones.

In the darkness behind her eyelids, she felt a great silence wash over her. Her blood rushed back like a flooding river. The fire beneath her skin died out. The pain diminished until it had totally gone. Her heart rate slowed down, beat by beat. *An illusion disappears with its creator.* Ophelia's heart would live because Baron Melchior's had stopped.

When she reopened her eyes, Thorn was kneeling in front of her. He pushed back her hair, took off her glasses, and closely examined her pupils, without uttering a single word. In the rather brusque manner of a medic, he swiveled her chin first one way, then the other, to check that her eyes stayed well focused on his own.

Ophelia hoped that Thorn wouldn't notice that she was on the verge of tears. Even without her glasses, she could see that he himself had a nasty gash across his cheek, intersecting the line of his old scar, where the baron's cane had struck him. He was frowning so much, and his jaw was so tense, Ophelia would have preferred that he explode once and for all, instead of containing his anger.

His question was terse: "Your heart?"

"It's fine," she stammered. "The illusion has passed. I feel be . . . "

Ophelia didn't finish her sentence. Thorn had wrapped his arms around her with a vehemence that took her breath away. She opened her eyes wide on this darkness, which was making her blink rapidly. She didn't understand. Thorn should have hurled reproaches at her, shaken her furiously. Why was he hugging her?

"When I told you that you had a preternatural predisposition to disasters, it wasn't an invitation to prove me right."

Ophelia couldn't hold back her sobs any longer. Thorn's arms stiffened with surprise when she clung to him. She pressed her face against his chest and howled as she'd never howled before, in all her life. It was a cry that came from the depths of her being and surged up her body like a tornado. Thorn let her sob, hiccup, sniff against his uniform until she'd used up all her breath. They remained for a long, silent moment on the floor of the Imaginoir, bathed in the red light of the lanterns.

"I wanted to help you," Ophelia finally said, her voice hoarse. "I've ruined everything."

"You have regrets? I don't."

Stripped of its wintry coldness, the sound of his accent was very different.

"You turned both our families against you, and you've just killed a man," she whispered to him. "All that because of me."

She felt Thorn's fingers lightly touching her hair, her nape, her shoulder blades, tentatively, as if he didn't know where and how to place them. It hadn't happened to him often, having to console someone.

"I should never have involved you in my affairs. I knew it would be dangerous. I convinced myself that I had the situation under control, and that mistake almost cost you your life." Thorn maintained a long silence, which Ophelia presumed was hesitation, from the way he was holding his breath. "There is one thing that I have tried to tell you several times. I'm no good at these formalities, so let's get on with it and speak no more of it." He cleared his throat, as if the words were stuck there, and finally muttered: "Please forgive me."

Ophelia contemplated the hot darkness she was nestled in. At that second, she finally knew with absolute certainty where her place was. It wasn't in the Pole, it wasn't on Anima. It was precisely where she was now. At Thorn's side.

She found her own voice changed when she asked: "Who is God?"

Thorn remained silent, but Ophelia felt the muscles in his arms tense up.

"Your mother's memory," she replied for him. "By passing on her memories to you, she made you a witness, didn't she? It's this past that you're privately investigating? You uncovered the existence of a person even more powerful than the family spirits? Mr. Farouk's Book might contain some information on the subject?"

"What you have heard tonight," Thorn interrupted her, "tell no one about it and endeavor to forget it. Melchior was but a link in a very, very long chain. I'm convinced there are other links on each ark, in each family."

With a jolt, Ophelia suddenly remembered the "strange stranger" that the Rapporteur had once spoken to her about, a man capable of influencing the Doyennes' decisions. So, her intuition had been right: a common denominator did exist between the events taking place in the Pole, and those taking place on Anima.

"You promised me," she said. "You promised me not to conceal anything anymore that directly concerns me. I'm more than concerned now. You owe me the truth."

"I'm breaking that promise," Thorn declared, without the slightest hesitation. "It's much more than a court intrigue," he insisted, his voice heavy. "It's a spiral and the moment you get involved you will never know peace again, and I speak from experience. There's still time for you to back out."

Ophelia had no desire to. She came back, however, to immediate reality when she heard the scarf, still tied to its screen, slapping the floor with impatience. Causing a searing pain in her arm, Ophelia pulled away from Thorn and put her glasses back on. Her sight was blurred from having cried too much, but as for her thoughts, they were perfectly clear. "We can't stay here. There are three corpses in this Imaginoir, four counting the baron. I managed to free Archibald in time, but he suffered the effects of a Confusion Bubble; he can't be counted on to testify. We must flee."

"No," replied Thorn.

"No? You have another idea?" Through the bloodstains on her glasses, Ophelia's eyes met Thorn's unyielding ones.

"There is no more 'we.' The marriage is canceled. You will return home with your parents and lead the life that I should never have interrupted. As for me, I am going to hand myself in to the Pole's legal system, and face the consequences of my actions. That is, in any case, what I was preparing to do when I received the telegram from your assistant. Where that individual is concerned," Thorn added, looking at where the railing had given way, "I did what I had to do. It's not the first time I've killed someone in legitimate defense, and that's never stopped me from facing up to my responsibilities."

"That's different, and you know it," Ophelia protested. "This is about a Mirage, and for all those people, you are just . . . just a . . . "

Thorn's lips twisted in the way that was so hard to interpret. "A bastard, yes. I'm under no illusions—I won't have the right to an impartial trial. I fought to stop the nobles from putting themselves above the law," he said, firmly stopping Ophelia as she was just opening her mouth. "I won't flee from justice today." He seized her by the shoulders to look deep into her eyes. "Will you respect my decision?"

After a long, obstinate silence, she gave in. "I will respect it."

THE DEAL

At court, the turmoil was at boiling point. Whether the nobles were under the hanging gardens, in the steam of the thermal baths, on the balconies of the Family Opera House, or in the gaming rooms of the Jetty-Promenade, they just couldn't keep still. They kept gathering around the newspaper kiosks to follow each revelation about the sensational "Imaginoir Affair," in which Thorn played the part, in turn, of traitor, murderer, and liar. The Mirages, who were particularly shocked, were desperate for details, but they didn't have time to mourn. Their world was changing, and changing fast.

From one day to the next, a new community had appeared on the scene. The Invisibles, the Narcotics, and the Persuasives, formerly disgraced, were parading around everywhere with heads held high. Three new clans, three new rivals in the race for Farouk's favors. It was a nobility of a very different kind, having suffered the trials of both the cold and hunger over several generations. These people possessed neither the refinement of the Mirages nor the diplomacy of the Web, preferring the sword to lace, action to conversation, hunting to salons. They were so practical that barely had they returned to the court before they were already reclaiming their former family possessions, long redistributed among other branches of the aristocracy.

And as if the atmosphere weren't feverish enough, the Carnival Caravan troupe had turned up in Citaceleste, with no one knowing who, exactly, had actually invited them. One could no longer walk a step in the higher quarters without crossing a furious noble, a hysterical lawyer, or a tamer of chimeras.

Only Farouk was conspicuous in his absence. At the conclusion of the Family States, he had locked himself away in his private apartments, with the order that no one be allowed in.

And yet it was he whom Ophelia, with resolute step, had come to find today. She was making her way along the Jetty-Promenade, where the fake sunset was forever setting over the fake sea. Every jostle was an ordeal due to her arm in its scarf sling, but Ophelia continued to walk at a brisk pace and, as soon as a courtier bombarded her with questions, she dived back into the crowd. She had already repeated her version of events to her family, to the sergeants, to the law, and to the press; right now she no longer had a second to lose.

Aunt Rosaline turned up just as the liftboy was about to close the gate of Farouk's private lift. Ophelia had thought she was at the hotel with the other Animists.

"You may have managed, once again, to give the slip to your whole family, but you won't pull that mirror trick twice on me. You need a chaperone now more than ever, dear girl."

"Mr. Farouk wishes to meet me alone," Ophelia told her.

"That won't stop me from accompanying you until the very last moment."

The lift, decorated like a reception room, slowly ascended, making its crystal chandeliers tinkle.

"The Rapporteur is keeping her weather vane pointed at you," Aunt Rosaline warned her. "She has sent her report to the Doyennes and is expecting their response at any moment.

Anima's Familistery won't approve of what you're planning on doing. I'm not even sure that I approve of it myself."

"As long as their telegram hasn't reached us, I've not yet disobeyed anyone," Ophelia retorted, firmly. "It's for that reason that I urgently requested a meeting."

"Mr. Farouk agreed far too quickly, which doesn't bode well to me. Berenilde has asked to see him a hundred times without him even doing her the courtesy of replying. The actual mother of his child! She is reduced to running from salon to salon, baby in arms, in search of support. Berenilde beseeching, can you imagine? I've never seen her so desperate." Aunt Rosaline noticed that Ophelia was remaining stubbornly silent, her hand clutching her arm in its sling, her eyes staring straight ahead. "I don't have much sympathy for Mr. Thorn," she added more gently, "but what's happening to him is revolting. No visiting rights, not allowed to appear in court, and a trial so cursory that the jury probably hadn't had time to sit down. Even the disgraced . . . sorry, the former disgraced, are dissociating themselves from him. I understand your being distressed."

Ophelia didn't respond, leaving it to the music from the gramophone to fill the silence for her. Distressed? It was beyond that. She'd not often hated anyone, but what she felt at the thought of Baron Melchior, even postmortem, was getting closer to that by the hour. No one at court had wanted to believe that such a quiet man could have organized the abduction of his own cousins and the murder of a young girl; conversely, everyone was in agreement that Thorn himself was perfectly capable of doing so. The bad impression he had made by handing his resignation to Farouk and breaking off the diplomatic alliance with Anima hadn't worked in his favor. Thorn had become the culprit par excellence, accused not only of the murder of the Minister of Elegance, but also of those of

Count Harold, the director of the *Nibelungen*, the Provost of the Marshals, and even Mother Hildegarde, who had disappeared in very murky circumstances. Her written confession had also mysteriously disappeared.

Ophelia had obviously asked to testify, but had not been allowed to do so inside the courtroom. A court clerk had merely taken down her statement, and she was convinced the document had never left the drawer it had been slipped into.

The verdict had come early that morning, swift as a cleaver. Declared a traitor to his family, Thorn had been sentenced to the Mutilation of his two family powers, following which he would be thrown out, beyond the city walls. Delivered to the Beasts without his claws and without his memory. And as if this judicial procedure weren't summary enough, the enforcement of the sentence had been set for the following week.

Ophelia swallowed the wave of panic and anger that had surged up inside her. She would not allow it. When Thorn had elected to face justice, she'd told him that she would respect his decision; at no time had she promised not to get involved.

"The Gynaeceum!" announced the liftboy. Ophelia was about to ask him to carry on up, but someone pulled the bell at the gate to get on board. It was Archibald.

"My humble respects," he said in greeting, raising his old top hat. Badly coiffed, badly shaved, badly dressed—he looked like a tramp. The liftboy himself couldn't suppress a frown as he took his place in the lift.

"You look wretched," Aunt Rosaline told him. "How are you feeling?"

"The same as I look, dear madam." Archibald's phony smile gave way to his deadened eyes. He didn't look like a tramp; he looked like the ghost of a tramp. Not only had the Web severed his link, but it had also continued to mourn him, as though his bodily presence were no longer enough to make him a living person. His own sisters treated him like a stranger, his steward had disappeared into thin air, and Mother Hildegarde, an integral part of his world since his birth, was dead. His own world had also changed from one day to the next. Ophelia would have wanted to feel sorry for him, but she didn't have the time.

"Do you have any news?" she asked.

Archibald served himself a glass of champagne at the lift's buffet. "I have just been *conversing*, to put it politely, with Madam Nadia. At first she seemed rather reticent, once she knew what had brought me. Thorn has never been so unpopular. Mercifully, that's not the case for me: no one resists Archibald for long!"

Ophelia could well believe it. No other man could have entered Farouk's Gynaeceum, and then got out unscathed, as he had just done.

"Madam Nadia is a very interesting favorite," Archibald continued, after a gulp of champagne. "Not only does she have the loveliest legs at court, but also a fabulously long arm: with a few telephone calls, she managed to get me a five-minute meeting in the visiting room. For a state prison, I couldn't have hoped for more."

"We'll be able to speak to Thorn?" Ophelia cried, her stomach lurching.

Aunt Rosaline observed her with a slight shudder, somewhat disturbed, but said nothing.

The ambassador shook his head, with a half-smile. "Not you, no. Madam Nadia agreed to do this favor just for me. I will use those five minutes as best I can," he promised, making an effort to appear serious. "If Thorn has a message for you, I promise I will pass it on to you."

"Tell him that we're not abandoning him," Ophelia muttered,

gripping Archibald's sleeve. "It's really decent of you, what you're doing. Thorn will appreciate it."

Archibald fluttered his eyelashes. His eyes began to sparkle like the champagne in his glass, only to die once more—a brief resurgence of his former self.

"Thorn will appreciate it?" he repeated. "Until a second ago, I wouldn't even have thought it possible to put those two words together. Let there be no misunderstanding, Ophelia, I'm not doing this for him. I am indebted to you, and I loathe that idea. It's much more fun when the roles are reversed."

It was his way of thanking her.

Since Archibald had resurfaced, they hadn't spoken much, and Ophelia suspected him of feeling a little ashamed. He had only a delirious recollection of his time at the Imaginoir. The last time he'd had anything to do with Baron Melchior had been at Clairdelune, when he had stolen the baron's sandglass. Archibald had seen him as the next victim of Mother Hildegarde, who he was convinced—mistakenly, of course—was responsible for the abductions. He had decided to unpin the sandglass in secret, without telling anyone, thinking that it would lead him to the architect. He had thought that, once there, it would be possible for him to make her see reason, and sort this situation out without a scandal. Today, he was still paying for that error of judgment.

"Last floor!" announced the liftboy, jamming on the brake and opening the golden gate. "Farouk's private apartments. Only miss is authorized to enter."

Aunt Rosaline gripped Ophelia's shoulder to keep her back a moment. "I was wrong, you're no longer a girl . . . Go on," she said, gruffly, letting her go. "Show Mr. Farouk what an Animist is capable of."

Ophelia really wasn't in the mood for smiling, but she couldn't suppress the smile that came to her lips. "Count on me."

She stepped out onto the tiled floor of an antechamber. The liftboy closed the gate and Ophelia saw the lift going back down, taking Archibald, raising his glass to her, and Aunt Rosaline, making encouraging signs to her, with it.

It was the first time she'd set foot on the seventh floor of the tower. On entering the family spirit's lair, she'd expected to find the ultimate in comfort and extravagance. The antechamber was merely an unfurnished room, higher than it was wide, very cool, and serving the sole purpose of leading to an immense gold door. Since there was no servant around and Ophelia didn't feel like waiting, she opened the door without having been announced.

Farouk's apartments proved even more surprising than his antechamber. Giant shelves of books crisscrossed the room, forming corridors as wide as roads. Ophelia's steps rang out on the checkered tiles as she walked between the rows of tomes, which were three times her height. This private collection was almost worthy of Anima's big Family Library, where her parents worked. Some books were in such poor condition, despite their obvious patching up, that they seemed on the verge of falling to pieces.

Ophelia felt disorientated in this world comprising only vertical and horizontal lines. "Hello?" she called out. Her voice echoed between the checkered tiles and the high ceiling without getting a response.

She did, however, finally find Farouk, in one of the last corridors of books. He was standing, completely absorbed in the volume he was reading, so silent, so still, and so white that Ophelia at first took him for a marble statue. "Sir?"

With infinite slowness, Farouk dragged his pale eyes away from his book to lower them on Ophelia. The power of his psyche instantly swept over her like freezing rain.

"Thank you for having accepted to receive me, sir."

As he didn't reply, Ophelia felt her scarf tightening nervously around her broken arm.

"Is your Aide-memoire not here?" she asked, looking around for the young man.

"I've dismissed him. I wanted to be alone with you."

Farouk's flaccid voice sent shivers right across Ophelia's skin, but she didn't let fear get the better of her. Not this time. "Sir, I have come to see you because . . ."

"Look." Farouk had cut her short to show her the book he was holding. Ophelia noticed that it was his notebook. On the very last page, the family spirit had stuck, rather clumsily, in fact, a photograph cut from a newspaper. A baby with pale skin and closed eyes. Between two ink blots, Farouk's handwriting captioned it, succinctly: "Berenilde's little girl."

Ophelia had to admit that she hadn't expected that. "Sir, I came . . ."

"I would like to forget this kid," Farouk said, cutting her short again, and returning to his pensive contemplation of the photograph. "Children are so noisy, so tiresome, so easy to make cry," he listed, languidly. "I can't stand their company in general, but I'd like to forget this kid even more than all the others. She's taken my place in Berenilde's life, and I sense she's going to cause me a whole lot of trouble. I really would like to forget her, so why can't I manage to get her out of my head?"

He closed his notebook and put it on the shelf in front of him. Ophelia then realized that the library was comprised solely of notebooks—hundreds, thousands of notebooks. This place was Farouk's written memory.

"Sir," she insisted, "I've come to suggest to you . . ." The end of her sentence died on her lips. Farouk had leaned over her in an endless flow of skin, fur, and white hair; Ophelia felt as if she were watching an avalanche of snow heading for her. He lifted her glasses with a finger to stare at her with a curiosity that bordered on fascination. The proximity of his psyche was now so oppressive that Ophelia felt her ears blocking up, as if she'd just sped through a railway tunnel.

"And the same goes for you, Artemis's girl," Farouk murmured, slowly, very slowly, articulating each syllable. "I can no longer manage to get you out of my head. You look angry," he suddenly observed.

Ophelia released the breath she'd been holding too long. "The man that I should have married will be mutilated and thrown to the Beasts in a week's time. Thorn always served you with the utmost honesty, and you, you didn't so much as bother to assure him a fair trial."

Farouk let go of the glasses, which fell back suddenly onto Ophelia's nose. His seraphic face, without a wrinkle, without a line, without a blemish, had hardened like ice.

"I'm not bitter, for the simple and good reason that I have a very bad memory. But the way that ungrateful man broke his promise to me," he muttered, with thunder at the back of his throat, "I am not, however, prepared to forgive him for that. I hope, in your interest, Artemis's girl, that you haven't come to ask me to grant him a pardon. I don't like you to the extent of humiliating myself for you."

The threat, barely whispered, was accompanied by a psychic wave that triggered neuralgia throughout Ophelia's body. She knew it was utterly pointless to explain to Farouk that Thorn had torn up his contract to protect her, not to defy him.

"No," she replied, calmly. "I asked to see you to propose a deal." With increased clumsiness due to her broken arm, Ophelia unfolded a sheet of paper that she'd guarded preciously on her person. "It's the facsimile of Thorn's contract," she explained, "the one in which he committed to marrying me, appropriating my family power, and deciphering your Book. I've come to honor this contract in his place."

Farouk frowned, wearily, as if suddenly making a supreme effort of concentration. He took an inordinate amount of time to peruse the facsimile, looking for a technicality or a hidden clause. When he raised his eyes back at Ophelia, a dangerous glint had been sparked in them. "You want to read my Book?"

"I want what was agreed upon in this contract to be respected," Ophelia corrected him. "In exchange for my services as a reader, you uphold the marriage for today."

"You have no other demands?"

"No, sir."

A smile spread slowly, very slowly, across Farouk's face. Far from softening its features, it made them even harder and even icier.

"It's a deal."

THE READING

With elephantine slowness, Farouk invited Ophelia to follow him through an immense door leading to another wing of his apartments.

The ordered, rectilinear world of the library gave way to complete chaos. Carpets of every color were buried under a bric-a-brac of miscellaneous objects: furniture of gigantic proportions, human-sized automatons, pyramids of caskets, hookah pipes as big as trees, and a bed the size of a house. The walls had completely disappeared under layers of pages badly cut out from picture books.

Ophelia tripped several times on enormous jigsaw-puzzle pieces, and her sole got stuck on what must have once been caramels; she was starting to understand why Farouk saw the birth of his daughter as that of a rival.

"Take a seat here," he said. "You will be more comfortable."

He righted an overturned chair and, with a mighty sweep of his hand, cleared a table of all that was cluttering it: teapot, sugar bowl, milk jug, saucers, and dirty cups scattered across the carpet in a clatter of china.

With difficulty, Ophelia hoisted herself onto the chair, which was far too big for her, as Farouk laid the Book on the table. He passed his hand over it as though dusting it off; the binding inlaid with precious stones, all just an illusion, disappeared in a puff of smoke, leaving the Book's skin totally bare.

Focusing, Ophelia pushed her glasses up her nose, and flexed her fingers to soften her reader's glove—she'd put on a new pair for the occasion. Impatience was gripping her stomach, but she would put that feeling aside until she had fulfilled her part of the contract. Thorn's fate depended on her performance.

In a professional manner, she lifted the first page. Disturbingly, Farouk's Book resembled the one Artemis had stowed in Anima's family archives. It appeared to be made entirely out of skin, a supple and smooth texture without a trace of mildew, not even a whiff, and yet this object was several centuries old. By the light of the table lamp, Farouk's Book looked paler than Artemis's, but this was just the subtlest of differences

Ophelia leaned forward to examine the text. Was it merely a text? That particular alphabet, all intricate arabesques and diacritical marks, had no known equivalent. It had been printed indelibly onto the skin of the Book, using a technique similar to that of tattooing. Certain symbols occasionally reappeared at the start of a line, but that was the only sign of any logic in the midst of this textual chaos.

Upon turning a page, Ophelia frowned.

"Well?" asked Farouk.

He had settled himself at the end of the table, brand-new notebook open before him, fountain pen in hand, ready to record all that his own memory didn't enable him to recall. It was an extraordinary spectacle, seeing this giant emperor in schoolboy mode. His long, white hair, rippling around him like a river of milk, allowed barely a glimpse of the fixed beam of his eyes.

"Has this Book deteriorated since it has been in your possession?" she asked.

Farouk didn't reply. Ophelia slid her gloved finger over a long, barely visible tear along the binding, between two pages. What little skin remained resembled a badly healed wound.

"A page is missing. I've already had the opportunity to handle Artemis's Book several times, and it features the same anomaly at the same place. A strange coincidence, you must admit."

Farouk remained impassive for a long time, and then his fountain pen slowly scratched the paper of his notebook. "Is that all you have to tell me?" he said, in a voice as labored as his handwriting. "That would be very, very disappointing."

"It was a mere observation. I haven't started yet." Ophelia unbuttoned her glove and pressed her palm to the Book, skin against skin.

Nothing.

Farouk's Book was as unreadable as a living organism would have been. This wasn't entirely unexpected, since Artemis's Book had that same idiosyncrasy, but how was Ophelia supposed to do her evaluation? She made sure not to show her disappointment in front of Farouk, whose undivided attention she sensed from the other side of the table. Ophelia turned the pages one by one, touching every inch of skin, but without managing to feel anything other than her own anxiety. Thorn would never have proposed a reading if that weren't possible. There must be some flaw that could be exploited.

She ended up finding it after turning the final page, embedded in the actual spine of the book: a small, pointed, metal tip, so old that it was completely rusty.

"Has this always been embedded here?" Ophelia asked, with surprise.

Farouk looked at her through the gap in his hair, fountain pen suspended over notebook.

"It seems to me that it's more for you to tell me that."

"Right. I can't guarantee to provide you with a translation of the textual content of this work, but I'll go back in time as far as this sliver of metal takes me."

He said nothing for so long, and his aura was charged with such tension, that Ophelia feared a refusal. So she was taken aback when she heard his response:

"There is, with regards to this Book, a certain something that I've forgotten and that I shouldn't have forgotten. I sense that it's of primordial importance. If you help me to discover what it is, Artemis's girl, I will consider your contract honored."

Ophelia untied her scarf, because it risked distracting her. She positioned her broken arm as best she could; she'd have to put aside the pain until the end of her reading.

"Could you turn your eyes away, sir?"

Farouk arched his eyebrows in one endless movement. "Why?"

"Your family power is too strong. Every time you look at me, it's . . . unsettling," she explained, choosing her words very carefully. "If you want a high-quality evaluation, relax your attention a little."

After an uncomfortable silence, Farouk turned his head until it was at an angle that would have snapped the vertebrae of any normally built human.

Barely had Ophelia placed her finger on the little rusty tip than she knew this reading would be among the longest and most testing of her career. Most objects went through periods of inactivity—they were forgotten on a shelf, in a drawer, at the bottom of a trunk—and these long stretches of silence allowed readers to make a few stops on their journey through time. That was not the case with this Book. From clutching it to his heart, day after day, month after month, year after year, decade after decade, century after century, Farouk had charged the embedded metal with an accumulation of lived experience as deep and dense as a succession of geological strata.

Who am I? What am I?

The further Ophelia went back in time, the more she felt herself sinking into an abyss, whose murky waters contained nothing but dissatisfaction. That sense of the unfinished gave her a feeling of dissolving into eternal nonfulfillment, as if condemned never to be either nothing or something. Yes, Ophelia felt it fully now, in her flesh, in her stomach, in her veins: there was a central piece of the Farouk jigsaw puzzle missing, a void yearning desperately to be filled.

Sometimes, briefly, her viewpoint shifted. Scientific curiosity, hope of a reward, profound puzzlement: these were the occasional traces of all the experts that had preceded Ophelia.

Who am I? Why am I?

Ophelia was going back down the river of time for what seemed an eternity when, with no warning sign, intolerable suffering took her breath away. It was a horrendous feeling, as if an invisible hand had plunged into her stomach to tear out her entrails. 'My page!' thought Ophelia, overcome by a terror that wasn't her own. *The* page, she immediately corrected herself. The page missing from the Book: Farouk had experienced its being torn out like an amputation of himself. Much as Ophelia tried to step back, remain a spectator, repeat to herself that this suffering and this terror were Farouk's in the past, extremely long ago, she almost let go. She thought of Thorn. She saw Farouk's enormous hand on his head, drawing away his family powers, emptying him of his memory, stealing even his recollection of himself, and throwing him, vulnerable as a child, into the clutches of a giant polar bear.

She gritted her teeth and continued with her reading.

The suffering stopped as suddenly as it had started, and Ophelia had the overwhelming feeling that her internal vision had become considerably clearer. The fog that had shrouded Farouk's existence for centuries had lifted: there had been a before and an after the tearing of the page. Ophelia visualized the family spirit's beautiful white hand dreamily stroking the metal tip, no longer rusty, within the skin of the Book. She felt filled with more powerful emotions, more lucid thoughts. She couldn't see Farouk's face, since she was reliving the past through the filter of his perception, but she sensed his youth, his hopes, his doubts, his questioning deep within her, as he gazed intently at his Book.

Who am I? What am I?

Ophelia encountered fleeting images of great intensity. A headless soldier standing in the sun. Shouts in the corridors of an old school. And a scent, a scent that Ophelia had never smelled in her life, but could still identify with certainty: that of golden mimosa.

Suddenly, after a leap in time, Ophelia saw Farouk. Or rather, an adolescent version of Farouk, halfway between childhood and adulthood. He was crouching on the ground and raising up to her a face on which conflicting emotions clashed: defiance and fear, revulsion and adoration, pride and helplessness. She saw him because she had ceased to be him. The Book had changed hands and this new protagonist was studying sometimes the tip of metal embedded in the skin, sometimes Farouk at her feet, who was looking avidly at her. Ophelia had become someone else without even noticing it, as if she'd simply slipped into an older skin of her own, as if it were her, her in person in this bygone time, who was leaning over the young Farouk. She'd never experienced anything like it, and the shock she felt briefly clouded the scene with her personal emotion.

"Why?" Farouk asked her, with a defiant look. "Why do I have to do what is written? What am I to you, God?"

'God?' asked Ophelia's internal voice, with surprise, over Farouk's voice. She would have liked to rewind the scene, keep showing it again and again, like old Eric's projector of illusions. Instead, she was dragged deeper into the past, back to that night when Farouk had stabbed his own Book with a kitchen knife, lodging the metal tip in it. On that night, as the pain pierced his body, he became fully aware of who he was, what he was. And he also knew that he would never, ever accept it.

Ophelia finally released the pressure of her finger on the little metal tip, and slowly, and rather shakily, pulled on her reader's glove. Her reading was over. And her life would never be quite the same again.

She cleared her throat. Farouk returned his head to a humanly acceptable angle, his fountain pen still suspended above the notebook.

"I'm listening."

Ophelia endured the psychic pressure of his gaze without blinking. She didn't return his Book to him, as was usual after an evaluation, preferring to leave it on the table. Now that she knew what she was dealing with, she would no longer be able to touch it without a feeling of defiling something supremely personal.

"That 'certain something' that you had forgotten with regards to this Book, I've discovered what it was."

"I'm listening," repeated Farouk. The words were the same, but his voice had completely changed: deeper by a few octaves, almost inaudible.

No doubt Ophelia should have taken precautions, prepared him gently for what she had to tell him, but she had neither the time nor the aptitude. She heard herself reciting what her reading had revealed to her, as though listening to a perfect stranger:

"This Book is an extension of your body. Its skin is your skin, its story is your story. It describes, down to the smallest details, what you are, and what you will be led to become."

Farouk moved not a line of his face, wrote not a word in his notebook.

"In other words," she continued, still with that curious feeling of hearing herself speak from afar, "you were not conceived in the natural way. This is probably the case for all the family spirits."

Stubborn silence at the other end of the table. Ophelia herself found it hard to believe she was actually saying what she was saying.

"Then there's the question of the missing page. At one time in your past, you were amputated of part of yourself. I have every reason to suppose that that page contained some . . . er . . . some *instructions* relating to the functioning of your memory. It didn't affect your family power, since you were able to pass on great capacities of recall to several of your descendants."

Farouk seemed to have turned into a statue for good. As for Ophelia, she had turned into a gramophone and her record was continuing to turn on its own:

"What I'm trying to tell you, sir, is that your problems with amnesia were caused deliberately. Those of Artemis likewise, since the same page is missing from her Book, and I don't think it would be going too far to say that all the family spirits were victims of the same amputation. Someone, in the past, wanted to condemn you all to perpetual forgetfulness."

Farouk remained impassive.

"I don't know who that someone is," continued Ophelia. "Perhaps it is the same someone who engendered the Books . . . who engendered you, the family spirits." She swallowed, before concluding: "The someone you call 'God.'"

Ophelia got a shock: Farouk had just stuck his face right up to hers. He had grabbed the back of her chair to make it tip backwards, and all of Ophelia with it. How could such a slow giant move with such prodigious speed? The wood of the seat creaked under the pressure of his fingers, but that was nothing compared with the pressure his mind was exerting on Ophelia's. She felt as if her skull were going to shatter like a nutshell.

"Give me a reason not to kill you, here and now." Farouk's voice was no more than a murmur, his eyes no more than two predatory slits. He was so close to Ophelia that his breath misted up her glasses as he spoke to her. "You stole my memory," he whispered. "You dispossessed me of myself. What am I to you?"

"You're confusing me with someone else," Ophelia said, in a tiny voice.

The terrifying glint in Farouk's eyes flickered, and then flared up even more. "What you have told me, Artemis's girl, is not what I wanted to hear. There must be something else."

"You wanted to know the secret contained within your Book. I have revealed it to you."

The wooden back of Ophelia's chair creaked even more under the pressure of Farouk's fingers. Their proximity was too oppressive—Ophelia wouldn't be able to endure it for long. Her ears were ringing, her eyes seeing double, and she felt as if an invisible blade were trying to pierce her skull. She had just survived a fall down the stairs, an attempted strangulation, and cardiac arrest, but her body did have its limits, all the same.

"You're hurting me," she said, firmly.

Farouk released the chair, which fell abruptly back on its four legs, and Ophelia thought he was about to finish her off. Instead, he turned away. With slow, almost methodical movements, he knocked over, one by one, all the objets d'art in his room: vases, lamps, cabinets, clocks, daybeds, hookah pipes, dragée dishes, automatons, and caskets all smashed into a thousand pieces on the floor. When Farouk had finished, only Ophelia's chair and the table were still standing.

"A problem, my Lord?" asked a polite little voice. It was the Aide-memoire. His youthful, dainty figure was outlined in the doorway. He looked at the surrounding chaos with total neutrality. Never had Ophelia been so pleased to see a member of the Web.

"Escort Artemis's girl back," muttered Farouk. He was standing to one side, fists clenched, resolutely facing a wall plastered in pictures, his long white hair concealing any facial expression. Ophelia felt sure that, right then, anyone who met his gaze would have found themselves struck down on the spot.

She wound her traumatized scarf around her arm as best she could, and slid off the chair. Her legs could barely carry her, but she couldn't leave without being sure she'd won her case. "Will you keep your promise?" she asked.

There was a slight stir in Farouk's hair, but he remained facing the wall. "What promise?"

"The contract, sir," Ophelia reminded him, with all the patience she could still muster. "You committed to upholding my marriage to Thorn today, in exchange for the reading."

Rustling of paper. Farouk had just pulled the facsimile out from his fur coat to reread it once more. It took him a considerable time.

"Marry Mr. Thorn," he finally declared.

Ophelia took in a big gulp of air. She'd waited for the verdict with such apprehension, she'd forgotten to breathe. "Thank you."

"Marry Mr. Thorn," Farouk repeated, without turning either

from his facsimile or from his wall. "Transfer your power to him. I give him until tomorrow morning to learn to use it."

"Learn to use it?" Ophelia repeated, flabbergasted.

"What you told me," he murmured, stressing each syllable, "is not what I wanted to hear. There is something else. So you haven't entirely honored your contract. I entrust your husband with the task of completing it in your stead tomorrow morning. If he succeeds, I pardon him. If he fails, I mutilate him. Aide-memoire?"

"Yes, my Lord?"

"Ensure that my decision is applied to the letter. Go, now."

Ophelia was appalled. "You're asking the impossible! My evaluation was already very thorough. Thorn will never be able to become a professional reader in just one night. You cannot . . ."

"I can everything," Farouk cut in. The tone of his voice, as he returned the facsimile of the contract to his coat, brooked absolutely no reply. Ophelia replied all the same:

"You know better than anyone in the world what it is to be deprived of one's memory. How could you condemn Thorn to the same fate?"

"One word more, Artemis's girl, and I'll give him no time at all. Until tomorrow."

Ophelia contemplated Farouk's back for a long time, and then the Book on the table. She had to resign herself to following the Aide-memoire, who escorted her back to the lift. He reported to the liftboy what had happened, charging him to convey the news at every floor, and then pivoted round to Ophelia with a graceful sliding of his heels.

"Appointment at the police station, miss. I will take care of the formalities."

Ophelia was in such a state of shock, she didn't notice either the golden gate closing on her or the crystalline tinkling of the lift. She paid as little attention to the sudden jolts of the lift, caused by the unusual clumsiness of the liftboy, who seemed to be using his lever like a novice. Throughout the interminable descent to the lower floors, Ophelia stared wide-eyed, unable to see anything other than the unspeakable feeling of horror that had seized her.

When the liftboy opened the gate for her to leave the lift, she did so like an automaton.

"Try your dears."

After a moment's hesitation, Ophelia turned back to the liftboy. It was the same man who had brought them up to the seventh floor, Aunt Rosaline and her, and yet he was barely recognizable. He was holding his lever in an unlikely position that bent his arm backwards, and his lips were twisted into a strange smile, as if he'd lost all his professionalism.

"Excuse me?"

"Try your dears," the liftboy repeated. "I mean, dry your tears. What's done is done and what must be done will be done."

The liftboy closed the gate and took the lift back up. Ophelia had understood absolutely nothing.

Fragment: Fifth Reprise

And one day, when God was in a really bad mood, he did something enormously stupid.

A door that slams. It's with that image that the memory begins. He replays the scene several times, revisits that slamming of the door, again and again, in the hope of bringing to light the detail that will trigger a new memory process. Who slams that door? Is it him? No. He witnesses the slamming of the door. So it's someone else.

Right.

The door slams violently. Anger? Yes, the memory is becoming clearer. God is angry. It is he who slams the door. What made God angry? He can't remember.

Right.

Proceed methodically, one question after the other. Does God slam the door when he arrives or when he leaves? This time, the answer is self-evident: when he leaves. Yes, it's coming back to him now. The day of the slammed door was a day of separation. Life was never, ever the same after that.

Right.

Where did God go? Did he go outside, or did he enter some other place? Impossible for him to recall that. And yet

470

he senses that it's essential. He absolutely must know what is to be found on the other side of the door.

Right.

Approach the memory from a different angle. Him, Odin, where is he to be found at that precise moment? There again, the answer that springs up is self-evident: in the house. This thought has barely formed in his mind when he manages to associate images with it. Shards of glass on the floor. Broken mirrors. Windows blown out. The spoons were all thrown around. Even the water was cut off. Why? What had happened?

He must open the door.

He will open the door.

He opens the door.

The void.

On the other side of the door, where God went, there's nothing but sky, as far as the eye can see. A sky with no earth. A world torn apart.

The memory ends here.

Nota bene: "Try your dears." Who said these words and what do they mean?

THE MEMORY

The police station was a large establishment, adorned with a facade worthy of an ancient temple. It was situated at the heart of Citaceleste and served by eight lifts that were spacious enough to transport several squads. It was under the escort of one of those that Ophelia climbed the big main staircase and crossed the waiting hall. The Aide-memoire had been remarkably efficient: she found that all doors opened for her, without her having to say a word.

After leaving Farouk, she had immediately been taken into the charge of the police. They hadn't allowed her either to make a telephone call or send a telegram or speak in public. Ophelia had desperately searched for Aunt Rosaline among the gaggle of onlookers that had formed around her, but she'd found only courtiers peering at her through their gold lorgnettes.

They were going to marry her in prison, behind her own family's back.

Ophelia was led to the basement, where State prisoners were held. After being searched by an old lady, she was asked to stay in a waiting room under the watch of four policemen. She sat on the marble bench, which was ice-cold, and gazed at the large pendulum clock, the sum total of the furnishings. Three hundred and seventeen minutes later, the squad superintendent returned, accompanied by a young magistrate in black gown and white wig.

"Ah, here's the lucky girl!" he exclaimed on seeing Ophelia, frozen stiff on her bench. "Please follow me, dear miss, I will be your celebrant. Oh, I see that you're wounded. It's not your writing hand, I hope? I have a whole pile of papers for you to sign." He tapped the red leather briefcase under his arm. "Please forgive us that little wait, we had to get the prisoner ready, summon the master of ceremonies and the witnesses, all those kinds of things. A marriage remains a marriage, and the law's the law!" he sang out, cheerily.

Ophelia walked down several high-security corridors, protected by a succession of reinforced doors, before arriving at Thorn's cell. The last door was the most impressive she'd ever seen. It was round, some three yards in diameter, and appeared to be entirely molded out of a gold so pure, one could see one's own reflection in it. The door was bolted with a complex mechanism of bars and cogs, as if it were securing public enemy number one.

Ophelia was surprised to see Archibald among the security guards, his hands deep in his pockets, relaxed as a tourist. He must have been brought in along a different route to the one she'd taken. The magistrate bowed down to him with deference.

"Thank you for volunteering to come, Mr. Ambassador! You met with the prisoner just a few hours ago. It does you great credit to have returned here a second time to celebrate this impromptu marriage. That's the way of the court! Dramatic events are our daily bread. Colonel," he continued solemnly, this time addressing the squad superintendent, "you can give the order to open up."

Unbolting the strong room door required three men, each turning a key and a wheel. The loud metallic clicking reverberated across the marble of the hall.

"What are you doing here, Mr. Ambassador?" murmured Ophelia, during the unlocking process.

Archibald pressed his old top hat to his chest. "I am your master of ceremonies and your witnesses."

"All on your own?"

"All on my own. If you were dreaming of a grand wedding, you're likely to be disappointed."

"I'm pleased you're here," Ophelia declared, with such spontaneity that Archibald raised his eyebrows. "But . . . the ceremony of the Gift? Will you be able to do it?"

Archibald's smile broadened and, conversely, his eyes seemed even blanker. He replied to himself: 'My link with the Web is severed, but that doesn't mean I've lost my family power; you and Thorn will soon be united by more interesting bonds than those of marriage.'

The door of the strong room, more than a foot thick, was finally open. It led, in turn, to a golden gate that the squad superintendent unlocked with his key.

The interior of the cell was fitted with the same marble and gold cladding as the rest of the basement. Ophelia felt all her innards lurch when she saw Thorn in the middle of the room. He had been seated at a table that was too low for him, and the leather straps restraining his wrists forced him to stoop. On his face were traces of blows, which they had tried to hide under several layers of powder. Even the fine white shirt he had been made to put on wasn't his size, and his unbuttoned sleeves came halfway up his forearms, revealing his old scars. Was that what "getting the prisoner ready" meant?

"Please be seated, miss," the magistrate said, indicating a chair to Ophelia. "We may begin."

He kept at a good distance from Thorn, as if he feared being decapitated with a single clawing. The policemen and security guards had surrounded the place, truncheons in hand, ready to intervene at the first sign of trouble. As for Archibald, he was squinting at the toe poking through a hole in his shoe; for someone supposed to be a witness, he wasn't very attentive.

Ophelia took her place on the other side of the table. When her eyes met those of Thorn, sitting opposite her, she found them as inscrutable as a raptor's. The only light in the room came from an incandescent lamp, placed on the table, which created disturbing shadows around the angles of his face.

The magistrate sang out his address: "We are gathered here today to celebrate the marriage of Mr. Thorn, descendant of our Lord Farouk—although by way of an unconventional lineage—and Miss Ophelia, descendant of Madam Artemis. Marriage is more than the celebration of family, it is at once its foundation and its crown, it is the family itself, in essence and in perpetuity!"

The magistrate threw himself into an endless diatribe on the duties of marriage, and then proceeded to recite a very lengthy legal text. He was certainly sparing no effort to waste as much time as possible.

Frozen in Thorn's stare, Ophelia had never felt so uncomfortable. Not only had she disobeyed him, but also, she hadn't helped the situation at all. When the time came to sign the legal documents, she was so nervous that she snapped the nib of a pen, tore a sheet of paper, and knocked over the ink pot twice. As for Thorn, he signed each page mechanically, hardly bothered by his restraints, without uttering a word or ceasing to stare at Ophelia.

"I declare you husband and wife!" exclaimed the magistrate. "I will let Mr. Ambassador take over for the ceremony of the Gift."

Archibald sauntered up to the table. "Move your chair closer to your husband, miss . . . oops . . . Madam Thorn. That will be perfect. Now, I am going to serve as a bridge between you both in order to allow your family powers to combine. You may experience slight discomfort, but it will soon pass."

Ophelia squirmed on her chair. She'd spent the last few months dreading this moment and, now, she was hoping for a miracle. If Farouk was right, if there was "something else" in the Book that she hadn't been capable of finding, then Thorn had to become a better reader than her. And he had to do it fast—by dragging everything out, the magistrate had already robbed them of part of the night.

Archibald placed one hand on Ophelia's head, and the other on Thorn's thoroughly morose one. Ophelia shuddered when Archibald's thumb pressed her forehead, between the eyebrows, where he himself bore a tattoo. She felt nothing in particular at first, and then, little by little, a hot flash crept over her body, which itself seemed to be traversed by an electric current whose intensity increased, second by second. Ophelia looked up at Thorn. Could he feel it, too? Stooped before her, strapped to his table, he let no emotion show. Ophelia tensed as a tingling spread along her every vein, as if the very substance of her blood were changing. The tingling was finally confined to just below her forehead, at the precise spot Archibald's thumb was pressing. Images, of which she knew neither the nature nor the source, flooded her mind at such dizzying speed, she couldn't grasp a single one.

When, at last, Archibald withdrew his hand, Ophelia felt a terrible migraine hammering on her temples.

"Good, good, good," sang out the magistrate, putting the papers into his briefcase. "I think everything is in order. We're going to withdraw, to leave you to . . . well . . . to do what you have to do. The squad superintendent will come to release you tomorrow morning, at six o'clock, dear madam," he concluded, turning to Ophelia.

"Six o'clock?" she said, indignantly. "We need more time."

"The rules are the rules, dear madam," the magistrate replied, departing in a swirl of gown.

Archibald raised his top hat to take his leave, in turn.

"I'll take care of informing your parents and Berenilde. All my compliments, Mr. Ex-Treasurer!" he congratulated Thorn as he shook his strapped hand. "Make the most of your short honeymoon!"

"Move away from the prisoner, Mr. Ambassador," advised the squad superintendent. "He's dangerous." He waited until Archibald, the magistrate, and the policemen had left the cell to release Thorn's hands and then lock the gate. He cast a concerned look at Ophelia, as though abandoning her to the claws of a criminal of the worst kind. He indicated a telephone fixed to the wall of the cell. "If you have the slightest problem, madam, call security."

The heavy, reinforced door closed on the strong room and, after countless mechanical clicks, a deafening silence descended.

Ophelia found herself alone in front of Thorn and his leaden stare. Although his straps had been removed, he still had his fists on the table, with back stooped, as the light from the lamp accentuated the gashes and bumps under the powder on his face.

"This isn't at all what I wanted," she finally burst out. "Well, yes, I wanted to maintain the marriage, but I didn't want to precipitate your sentence. I was counting entirely on that delay of a week to appeal, do you see? Baron Melchior spoke of the interfamilial High Court, and . . . and that gave me an idea. It's not only to me that you're now linked, but to all the Animists. I swear to you that if Mr. Farouk had allowed me the time, I would have made sure that you were put under a different jurisdiction. You would have had the right to a real trial, no one would have mistreated you, I would have testified, and . . . and . . . Thorn," she whispered, drawing her chair closer, "what I read in that Book, I don't even know where to start."

Ophelia gave a garbled account of all that had taken place on the seventh floor of the tower. The deal she'd made with Farouk. The delving into the past. The true nature of the family spirits and their Books. The missing page responsible for their memory lapses. She also told him of the headless soldier, the old school, and the scent of the golden mimosa, convinced that even these preposterous details had their importance.

Thorn listened to her without unclenching his teeth. He didn't even bat an eyelid when Ophelia told him of her vision of "God."

"I've been left with a feeling of uncertainty about that memory," she admitted. "I feel as if I missed something, and it's that something that you're going to have to find in my place. Do you think it may have something to do with what you spoke of with Melchior?"

Ophelia got a start when Thorn finally sat up straight, straining the seams of his ill-fitting shirt. "Could I have a glass of water?"

"Er . . . yes, of course," stammered Ophelia.

She caught her foot in the wire of the lamp, banged her knee against the iron bed frame, and then knocked herself on the porcelain washbasin. Her migraine was making her clumsier than ever. Did it stem from the injection of the new family power within her? She stared at her wild reflection on the wall, made of the same reflective gold as the door's armor-plating. Her glasses were looking off-color, but otherwise, she felt no different.

Turning towards Thorn, Ophelia almost spilled the tumbler over the floor. She hadn't noticed it until that moment, but the bony outline of his left leg was horribly distorted.

"What . . . what have they done to you?"

Thorn shifted awkwardly on his chair, and his leg took on an even more horrifying angle.

"Baron Melchior had many friends," he said, sounding little concerned. "If you hadn't 'precipitated my sentence,' to use your words, my whole skeleton would have suffered the same treatment. Don't look at me like that," he grumbled. "My resistance to pain is excellent."

Ophelia was shaking like a leaf; she didn't dare imagine what the leg looked like under the trousers.

"I don't want to hurry you, but we must begin your lesson," she said anxiously, glancing at the cell's clock.

Thorn took all his time to drink his water, one gulp after another. Ophelia couldn't fathom how he managed to stay so calm at such a time; as for her, she was making a considerable effort not to succumb to panic. When he had finished drinking, Thorn stared at the bottom of his empty tumbler, his other hand still clenched in a fist on the table. He seemed lost in deep thought.

"In the beginning, we were as one," he suddenly declared. "But God felt we couldn't satisfy him like that, so God set about dividing us."

"Sorry?" Ophelia stuttered, totally disconcerted.

"My mother was mutilated fifteen years ago," Thorn continued, in a faraway voice. "It took place shortly after the previous Family States. The last time I saw her was right here, in this prison. I still don't know why she chose me, considering that I never meant anything to her. I presume she had no other choice. The fact is, she made the most of the three minutes of visiting time she'd been allowed, to communicate a fraction of her memory. A very small fraction," Thorn stressed, contemplating the void within his tumbler, "but it was sufficient to change my life forever." He looked up at Ophelia with a

479

metallic glint. "Farouk's personal memories. A few fragments, at least, which I've spent years dissecting, to extract all their substance. What your reading taught you, I already knew it, but for a few details. A bit more than that, even."

Enthralled, Ophelia inhaled deeply, having held her breath for too long.

"A bit more than that?"

"God broke the world." Thorn had announced this as others would comment on the weather.

Feeling dizzy, Ophelia had to lean on the table. "The Rupture . . . it would be the work of a single person?"

"I don't know how, but God broke the world," Thorn repeated, with supreme composure. "Since then he's had an absolute stranglehold on the fragments that remain of it. Melchior sold his soul to him, and he's not an isolated case. Men and women are watching, from the shadows, to ensure that the family spirits, along with all their descendants, behave according to the plan laid out by God. My mother was one of them, and it corrupted her to the core, to the extent that God himself finally disowned her. I wouldn't be surprised if your Doyennes weren't among them, perhaps even some members of your own family, and that's why I ask you to take utmost care."

Ophelia closed her eyes. Her migraine was building into a storm in her head, as though something within her were resurfacing. "Who is God, in the end?"

"*What is he* would be the appropriate question," Thorn corrected her, leaving his tumbler on the table. "I've been asking myself that question since the day I inherited my mother's memory, and, to date, I have no satisfactory answer. I only know that he possesses a knowledge that brooks no possible comparison with our own. He created the family spirits, broke the world to pieces, and placed humanity under supervision.

He is endowed with exceptional longevity, and, for one reason or another, he doesn't want us to know his true face. Unfortunately, the few memories I have in common with Farouk become confused as soon as God is involved."

"So, is that why you're so keen to read his Book?" murmured Ophelia.

Thorn frowned. Maybe it was an effect of the table lamp, but a menacing flash of lightning crossed the leaden sky of his eyes.

"Every man should have the right to play his life with a throw of the dice. They produce random results that transcend all predermination. That ceases to makes any sense if the dice are loaded. The entire court cheats. It's inevitable since our family spirit, the mold itself of our society, is a cheat. Farouk hands out favor and disgrace according to his moods, not to ensure that the rules are respected. What this world-breaker is up to is even worse," Thorn hissed between his teeth. "He stole humanity's dice without ever—absolutely never—emerging from the shadows."

Ophelia felt intimidated. It was the first time he was confiding in her in this way. He was at last speaking to her for real, eye to eye, equal to equal.

"So you were investigating God from the start," she said. "And then? What were you planning to do?"

Thorn shrugged his shoulders as if it were obvious. "Give the world back its dice. What the world would have then done with them, that wasn't my problem."

Ophelia was increasingly flabbergasted. "You mean . . . confront God?"

"I stopped at nothing to draw his attention to me. Melchior was prepared to go to any lengths to prevent me from reading Farouk's Book. And for a very good reason: Farouk and God have a past in common. I hoped secretly to provoke an encounter by encroaching on that territory. God must have a weak point, everyone has one. I just had to discover which one, and the matter would have been sorted."

"But why you?" insisted Ophelia. "Why should it be up to you, and you alone, to sort that matter out?"

Thorn grimaced as he tried to change position. Beads of sweat stood out on his hairline. Whatever he said, his leg must be putting him through real torture.

"I'm conditioned by my job," he finally grunted. "See it as a ridiculous sense of duty, or incurable intellectual rigor."

Fascinated, Ophelia considered Thorn for a long time in the twilight glow of the lamp. Never had she felt so small, and never had he seemed so big; it made no difference that she was standing and he was folded in three on his chair. This man was a total misanthrope, but he viewed everything in broader terms, deeper terms, than others, way beyond his personal interest.

"You've kept all that to yourself for fifteen years?"

Thorn nodded, eyes narrowed to two silver slivers.

"I totally refuse to mix my aunt up in this. Ignorance is less dangerous than knowledge. In your case, that has ceased to be true since you read the Book. Bear in mind, however, that the truth has a price, and it's high. Never forget what happened to Hildegarde. She probably knew more than me, and preferred to commit suicide rather than accept my protection. I can't help wondering why Melchior was so keen for God to meet her," he added, pensively. "He took that secret to his grave, too."

A flash suddenly burst through Ophelia's migraine. Due to a delaying mechanism, Thorn's family power poured into her now, fanning the embers of her own memory. She saw once more the young Farouk kneeling at her feet, looking avidly up at her, as if expecting to get from her, from her and her alone, a meaning to his life. *Why do I have to do what is written?*

What am I to you, God? Countless little details came back to her, details she was certain she hadn't seen during her reading: windows without their glass, mirrors draped in sheets, and her, God, addressing Farouk, explaining something essential to him.

The striking of the clock brought Ophelia abruptly back to the here and now.

"We mustn't waste any more time."

"I never waste my time," Thorn asserted, arching his eyebrows. "Everything I've said to you, I had to say it to you now. It will be up to you to make better use of it than I did."

With these words, he unfurled the fingers he'd kept clenched in a fist: they held a small pocket pistol. Ophelia's heart lurched when she saw it. She was sure Thorn had been empty-handed at the time of signing the magistrate's papers.

"Archibald," she said, finally working it out. "When he congratulated you . . . "

"He may not be funny, but he is efficient. I asked him to do me this favor during his time in the visiting room."

Ophelia felt herself going from ice cold to burning hot. "Why ask him for a gun?"

"I have no intention of ending up like my mother," Thorn declared, categorically. "I want to decide myself when and how I die."

"You won't end up like your mother, I promise you, so throw that idea away immediately." She had spoken so angrily that Thorn's stern features relaxed in surprise.

"You need not promise me anything. There's a detail about this object that will surely interest you." Thorn looked intently at the pocket pistol, gleaming in the light of the lamp. "Since I've been holding it in my hand, I've not yet read it."

"What?"

"I'm not reading it," repeated Thorn. "I'm touching it, but

I'm feeling nothing special. I'm obviously not an expert, but I would tend to think that that's not a good sign."

Ophelia noticed the tinplate tumbler on the table and pushed it in front of him.

Thorn took it, turned it in his fingers, and put it back down. "Nothing."

"Concentrate hard," she advised him, trying not to show her panic. "Reading an object is like picking up the telephone. You must be ready to listen to what it has to tell you."

Thorn replicated the fingering, this time on the lamp switch, turning it one way, then the other, increasing and decreasing the light emitted by the bulb. "Nothing."

"No image?" stammered Ophelia. "No particular sensation? Not even a vague impression?"

"No."

She took off her glasses. "Here. It's easier to read an object that isn't already steeped in one's own state of mind."

Thorn returned her glasses to her after fingering them a little.

"Still nothing. It's pretty ironic, but it would seem that I'm definitely not gifted at reading. Right now, give me all your attention. I have a favor to ask of you."

"No." The reply had escaped from Ophelia almost despite herself, but it didn't stop Thorn from continuing, unperturbed: "Take my aunt with you to Anima. Neither of you should have to suffer Farouk's outbursts in my place. Speak of what you know to no one, and live your life as before. The truth is a weighty burden; it shouldn't be placed on all shoulders."

"No," repeated Ophelia. She looked around for any objects that could still be used for reading, but the prison cell didn't offer much choice.

Thorn slipped his little pistol into a pocket of his shirt. "I won't use this gun in front of you. Call security and be off with you."

Ophelia shook her head so vehemently that her bun gave way and her hair streamed down her back. Terror was starting to get the better of her.

"No, no, no," she stammered, with increasing incredulity. "You must still try . . . We must still try. I'm going to convince Mr. Farouk to let me read his Book a second time. There's bound to be a solution, there's always a solution."

"Ophelia." Thorn's hands framed her face to force her to look straight at him. Seated awkwardly on his chair, he was looking at her with extreme seriousness. The scars that criss-crossed his arms shone out like crescent moons in the subdued lighting of the place. "Don't make the task harder for me. Neither of us is capable of satisfying Farouk, and you know it. He's going to take my memory from me, and, with it, all that I am. I don't want to end up like my mother, you understand?" His fingers pressed harder on Ophelia's cheeks. "I won't suffer," he promised her.

"Please . . ." Ophelia's voice was no more than a beseeching whisper. Thorn stared at her with obvious puzzlement, and then his lips twitched, half-smile, half-grimace. With a hesitant, somewhat timid movement, he invited Ophelia to come closer to his chair, to find the best compromise between her broken arm and his smashed leg. When she was close enough, he rested his forehead on her shoulder.

"The first time I saw you, I formed a very poor opinion of you. I thought you had no common sense and no character, and wouldn't make it to the marriage. That will forever remain the biggest mistake of my life."

Ophelia felt torn between distress and fury. He didn't have the right! He didn't have the right to come into her life like this, turn everything upside down, and then leave as if nothing had happened. She felt as if she were breaking inside when Thorn tightened his embrace around her.

"Don't go falling down any more stairs, avoid sharp objects, and above all, above all, keep away from disreputable people, alright?"

A tear rolled down Ophelia's cheek. Thorn's words were carving out an abysmal void inside her. She knew with absolute certainty that from the moment they separated, she would never know warmth again.

Thorn swallowed against her shoulder. "Oh, and by the way, I love you."

Ophelia's sob caught in her throat. She could no longer speak. Breathing hurt her.

Thorn's hands disappeared into her thick mass of curls. She became even shorter of breath. He clasped her body against his own, as close as was physically possible, and then pulled away from her with almost brutal briskness. He cleared his throat, suddenly hoarse. "It's . . . it's a little harder than I thought it would be."

He pushed his pale hair back, his eyes studiously avoiding Ophelia's. The rims of his eyes had reddened; this sight, more than all the rest, moved her as she'd never yet been moved.

"Leave, now," muttered Thorn. "I loathe tearful farewells."

He unclasped Ophelia's hand, which had clung to his shirt. She wished she had both her arms, the better to hold on to him.

"Away with you," Thorn insisted, his voice muted, when he saw that she wasn't moving. "The more you linger here, the harder it will be for me to . . . "

The end of his sentence died on his lips. Slowly, his eyes widened, and his facial scar kept lengthening. With a start, Ophelia turned around and saw it, too.

A foot had sprung out through the golden reinforcement of the door.

THE PARENT

Ophelia wasn't dreaming. A body really was emerging through the sixteen-inch thickness of the door. The gold was glowing like molten lava, and yet the man extricating himself from it bore no sign of burns. Once in the cell, he dusted off the golden specks that had ended up on his clothes. His skin was black and he wore a tartan typical of the alchemist clan of Leadgold. The metal of the door had already returned to being solid, but an unsightly crust had formed where, a minute before, the gold had been flawlessly smooth.

The man calmly contemplated Ophelia and Thorn, through the bars of the security gate, as if there was nothing unusual about passing through a prison door as though it were made of butter. He then began to turn pale, his eyes narrowed, and his clothes became more exotic in style. In but a moment, he became a totally different person. He slipped between the bars with supernatural suppleness, as if his whole body were made of rubber.

"We meet again, little Animist," he sang out, tunefully.

Ophelia half-opened her mouth, but her lips formed the word without a sound escaping: Milliface! A performer from the Carnival Caravan coming and getting lost in such an unlikely place, it was beyond her comprehension. But her surprise was nothing compared with Thorn's. He had leaned on the table to try to stand on his good leg, and this endeavor alone was soaking his shirt in sweat. With jaws clenched like pliers, he was looking at Milliface with a gleam in his eyes.

With supreme indifference, Milliface grabbed a chair. Between the moment of moving to sit and being seated, his body had stretched like an elastic band. A large handlebar moustache sprouted on his face like a mushroom, his clothes changed into a frogged uniform, and one of his eyes veered to the side of its socket. Increasingly flabbergasted, Ophelia recognized the cross-eyed policeman who had caught her on the stairs of the sandglass factory.

He crossed his legs and linked his fingers around his knee in a stance that was no longer remotely military.

"I've followed vecent erents . . . recent events with a certain curiosity," he said in a completely different voice, this time inflected with the Northern accent. "You two, in particular. I've been intrigued by you for some time."

Ophelia's heart skipped a beat. In an almost inaudible whisper, Thorn articulated for her the incredible thought that had just formed in her mind:

"You are God."

Milliface's handlebar moustache rose with the push of a smile. It was the least human smile Ophelia had ever witnessed, and a shiver coursed across her skin when she noticed that it was directed at her.

"So, you have read my son's Book. Or at least, you tried to. My works are not accessible to the first reader to turn up."

Milliface squinted around the cell, and then focused all his attention on Thorn, who was making a considerable effort to remain standing. He had gripped the edge of the table so hard, his finger bones seemed on the point of snapping.

"You, on the other hand, are not the first reader to turn up. Using your memory as an amplifier, that was a daring idea."

As he said this, Milliface hiccupped loudly and put his hand to his mouth. Out of it, naturally as anything, he pulled a small piece of rusty metal.

Ophelia was overtaken by a whirlwind of alarm, terror, and rage. The last time she'd seen that object was in the skin of Farouk's Book. If it had come into this individual's possession, no matter whether he was called "God" or "Milliface," he was an enemy: he had just made any reading totally impossible.

"I hold more knowledge than all the libraries put together," declared Milliface. "But this small detail," he said, calmly contemplating the rusty tip of the knife in his fingers, "I must admit that it escaped my attention." He gulped it back down with a moist swallowing sound.

"The liftboy," murmured Ophelia. "That was you, wasn't it? You went to see Mr. Farouk after me."

Milliface half-lowered his eyelids in the shadow of his cocked hat. "Ordinarily, I avoid getting involved in my children's affairs, but Odin has been causing me problems since his punctuation . . . his conception. He never shared his brothers' and sisters' obedience. I think today's lesson won't have been wasted: from now on, he will do all that I will write to him to do."

Milliface's squinting eyes looked up at Thorn, who was clinging to his table, his smashed leg, a ghastly mess of broken angles, dragging behind like a dead weight, as though standing up, here and now, had become more important than everything else.

"As we speak, Odin is making his way here. He's coming to carry out your sentence, my boy. You milled a can . . . killed a man. And not any old man." As he said this, Milliface's body was inflating on his chair, the ends of his moustache tapering like exclamation marks, his cocked hat turning into a top hat, and his police uniform being replaced by the most elegant of frock coats. Ophelia felt her stomach lurch. Seeing Baron Melchior sitting there, right in front of them, was spectacularly macabre.

"This poses two interesting questions," Milliface continued, in the baron's cooing voice. "The first: did this man deserve to live? The second: you, do you deserve to die? In fact, I think you would make a much better Guardian than him."

Ophelia held her breath and looked up at Thorn. Precariously balanced on his leg, he was remaining obstinately silent. His jaw was so clenched, its bone structure showing beneath the skin, that he seemed incapable of unclenching it.

Milliface twisted his triple-chinned head into a hazardous position, to study his interlocutor from a different angle. Ophelia was struck by the similarity between his grotesque positions and those of Farouk, as if they both had bodies that didn't obey the same natural laws as ordinary vertebrates.

"You're hesitating? You don't seem to appreciate quite what an honor I'm doing you. The Guardians are the elect among the elect, the only ones to whom I give my template crust . . . complete trust. It's only on this ark that I have yet to find children worthy of representing me. They've all been such a disappointment. Melchior went beyond his duty and threw my name around. As for your mother . . ." At the very moment he uttered those three syllables, Milliface began to shed weight. His body slimmed down until it took on the appearance of a woman of angular beauty. On her forehead she bore the spiral tattoo of the Chroniclers. "Your mother," he continued, in a feminine voice, "had neglected her duty."

Ophelia thought for a moment that Thorn was going to lose his balance altogether. He had totally blanched as he contemplated this younger version of his mother, without her mark of disgrace, or her memory problems.

"Be the Guardian of my son," said Milliface. "Be my eyes

490

and ears on this ark. Help me to put my family back on the narrate and sparrow . . . straight and narrow. Become my most cherished child."

Ophelia felt her blood boil. Using the mouth of a mother to utter such words, it was unbelievably cruel. Milliface forced a smile that altered his beautiful woman's lips without suggesting the least sensuality.

"What do you think of that, my boy? Should I suggest to Odin that he pardon you? Are you ready to give me your life, or must I give you death?"

"What I think of that," Thorn repeated. Ophelia stared wide-eyed as she watched him taking the pistol out of his shirt pocket and aiming it at Milliface. With his other hand he clung to the table, which shook due to the extreme tension in his fingers. "I think that it is high time that humanity got its dice back."

Milliface stared at the barrel of the pistol without blinking. "So you haven't understood, my boy? I am humanity."

"Bullshit!" Thorn spat out, between gritted teeth. "You reproduce the appearance and the power of others the better to hide your own face and your own weakness. I have just finally understood why Hildegarde had put up that security cordon," he added, in a whisper full of antipathy. "You coveted her mastery of space, didn't you? You coveted it because you don't possess it. You are not omnipotent."

Ophelia jumped at the bang: Thorn had shot straight into his mother's face. Her shock turned to horror when Milliface rolled his eyes, squinting up at the entry point of the bullet, lodged in the middle of his forehead, exactly where the clan tattoo was. Not a drop of blood ran from the hole, and the skin closed up until no trace of a wound remained.

"You're as disappointing as your mother. You're as disappointing as Odin."

Thorn snapped. He shot a second bullet, then a third, until he'd emptied his cylinder, aiming at Milliface's every vital organ, but his body absorbed the shots as if it were made of cream.

When Thorn had no more cartridges, Milliface rose from his chair in a graceless swirl of dress. "War," he sighed. "Always war. What must I do to rid my progeny of this nasty habit?"

Thorn threw down his gun, grabbed Ophelia by her scarf, and pushed her with all his might. "Get away!"

Without allowing Milliface time to react, Thorn leant with both hands on the table and released every claw his nervous system was primed with. In but a few seconds, his mother's face, chest, and arms were riddled with gaping wounds, as though dozens of invisible scissors had hurled themselves at every inch of uncovered skin. Barely would one gash close than another would open up elsewhere, leaving the flesh continually lacerated. Some of the cuts inflicted by Thorn's claws were so deep that whole ribbons of muscle fell away, but Milliface's regenerative powers allowed him to reconstruct his body again and again.

With her back to the wall, Ophelia dared only to move step by step. It was the first time she was seeing the power of a Dragon at its full potential, and she couldn't have said who, Thorn or Milliface, shocked her the most. She felt like an insignificant little person cornered between the forces of creation and destruction.

When she finally managed to reach the telephone, Ophelia picked up the receiver to call for help and beg the policemen to unlock the door, but in reply she heard only the sound of her own voice. The line was cut. Her heart stopped when her eyes met their own reflection in the golden surface before her. She could see herself, she could see Thorn, but she could see no one else in the cell. Did Milliface not have a reflection?

Ophelia didn't get time to dwell on the question. A prodigious force, like a ferocious gust of wind, smashed her against the wall. The gold cladding froze her cheek. Her glasses bent. Her arm, in its scarf sling, dug into her stomach. She felt as if, suddenly, she were a pin drawn to a magnet. The phone receiver she was still clutching was also stuck to the wall, crushing her fingers.

All the furniture had scattered to the four corners of the room. The bed had tipped over, with a grating of steel, the chairs were pinned to the ceiling, and the table's legs were caught between the bars of the security gate. Only the desk lamp was bobbing in the air, held by its electric cord like a funfair balloon, its shade spinning around and around. It cast a flickering light on Milliface, who this time had taken on the appearance of a child with a shaved head, typical of the inhabitants of Cyclope. The masters of magnetism and gravity.

Where was Thorn? By wriggling a little, Ophelia managed to spot his big body huddled under the washbasin. Its porcelain had been smashed by his head, and its pipes were drowning him in a seething mix of water and blood. Immobilized by Milliface's repulsive force, he was pinned half to the wall, half to the floor.

"Destroyer of the world."

Ophelia quaked as she saw Milliface approaching Thorn and crouching in front of him. The lamp followed him obediently, floating weightlessly, like a jellyfish.

"I did not deploy the worst . . . destroy the world," said Milliface, his voice small and reedy. "I saved it. I am the father and mother of the family spirits, I am the parent of you all. I have only ever wanted the best for you. You have picked the wrong adversary, my boy."

Thorn pressed on his elbows to push away from the wall,

but Milliface mimed a flick and the strength of the gravitational force threw him violently backwards.

"Do you still think I'm weak?" Right then, Milliface really did look like a child—a child who had caught a grasshopper and was about to pull its legs off.

Ophelia pushed against the wall to free herself; her broken arm, folded against her stomach, was digging into her ribs. Gravity had become so distorted, she could no longer tell the vertical from the horizontal. She looked at her reflection in the gold armor cladding. A mirror. The walls of this strong room were just mirrors like any others.

Letting herself be entirely engulfed by the cladding, Ophelia rebounded through the opposite wall, just beside Thorn. The repulsive field coming from Milliface immediately compressed her lungs.

"That's enough," she panted. "You've made your offer, Thorn has declined, leave it at that." Ophelia could feel Thorn's startled eyes on her, but she focused all her attention on the child crouching in front of them. Milliface turned towards her with a look more of boredom than curiosity, as though contemplating a monotonous landscape through a train window. And yet, little by little, his expression changed. In a single expansive movement, his eyelids, forehead, and entire shaved head lifted. For the first time, a true emotion appeared on the surface of his face.

"You are a villa minister . . . mirror visitor. I knew it. I sensed there was something familiar about you. You bear its mark."

"Mark?" If Ophelia weren't being crushed by the gravitational anomalies, she would have asked a proper question. She sensed her breath escaping, as Milliface again changed shape. Through staring at Ophelia, he had ended up adopting her appearance. A mane of dark curls sprang from his shaved head and glasses emerged on his childish face. Behind him, all the furniture that had stuck to the walls and ceiling fell onto the marble like a hail of meteorites. The lamp went out when it fell, plunging the cell into total darkness for several seconds, and then the bulb came back on, flickering hesitantly.

"You're the one who allowed him to escape," said the second Ophelia in an unfathomable voice. "You freed the Other. Because of you, the balance of this world was disturbed."

As soon as he was freed from the magnetic force, Thorn had gripped onto the washbasin to pull himself up, but Milliface's words had frozen him midway, and the water from the pipes continued to run on his shocked face.

It took Ophelia a few chaotic heartbeats before she understood what Milliface was talking to her about.

Release me.

"My first passage through a mirror," she whispered. "So, it wasn't a figment of my imagination. That night, there really was someone on the other side." Ophelia wanted to get up to look her double in the eye, but she skidded on the wet marble and succeeded only in hurting her arm even more. "Supposing you're right," she said, wincing with pain, "who is this Other, and what was he doing in my bedroom mirror?"

Milliface appeared to be thinking hard. Being sized up so sternly by her own face made Ophelia feel most uncomfortable.

"The Other will cause the collapse king of the arts . . . collapsing of the arks. It's already started, and it's only going to get worse. The longer the Other remains free, the more the world will keep falling apart."

Ophelia thought at first that he was making fun of her, and then a horrified shudder coursed through her and into her scarf. She had just remembered the piece of land that had broken away from the edge of the Pole four years earlier. "That one wasn't that big," Thorn had said to her. "A section several miles long broke away from a minor ark of Heliopolis, two years ago."

No. It couldn't be because she had passed through a mirror. It couldn't be because of her.

Milliface turned slowly to the cell's clock, which had miraculously survived the surrounding mayhem. For someone who had just predicted an apocalypse, he didn't seem particularly nervous. He changed into an old man with bronzed skin, and looked down, indifferently, at Thorn.

"Odin is coming. I'm going to let him decide your fate, as he did that of your mother fifteen years ago. As for you," Milliface added, this time addressing Ophelia, "you should repair what you impaired. From now on, you are linked, you and the Other. Sooner or later, whether you want to or not, you will mead me to limb . . . you will lead me to him. I'll keep my eye on you until then."

At these prophetic words, Milliface's old body turned from solid to gaseous. He rose into the air like a red ectoplasm, and then disappeared through the ventilation grille.

THE SENTENCE

In the strong room, all Ophelia could hear was her own heart beating, the flowing of water on the floor, the flickering of the overturned lamp, and here and there, the rumbling of the upturned furniture. She was so shocked by what had just happened that she would need months, years, a lifetime to recover. Right now, just one thing was clear to her:

"I must speak to Mr. Farouk."

Ophelia turned to Thorn, who remained surprisingly silent. His eyes were hidden behind his hand, which was clamped over his face like a great spider.

"Thorn?" she said, anxiously.

He clenched his long, bony fingers even more, obscuring his face in their shadow. His chest started to heave, as though he were battling a coughing fit, his Adam's apple bobbed, and suddenly, he burst out laughing. It was a harsh, totally incongruous sound, seeming to emerge from the very depths of his body.

Alarmed, Ophelia wondered whether he'd lost his mind. However, when his big hand finally fell away, it revealed eyes sharp as an arrow. An arrow that had finally found its target.

"That divine sham has provided me with a most instructive lesson." Through the strands of hair that water and blood had plastered to his forehead, Thorn's eyes were shining with an intense brightness. "And you, too," he declared. "You have taught me a lot."

His grin faltered the moment he tried to change position. His injuries had just made their presence felt.

"Don't move," Ophelia told him. "I'm going to get help. I'm going to speak to Mr. Farouk."

Her boots skated in vain on the puddle of water—Thorn had gripped her dress to hold her back.

"No. Let him come here. It doesn't matter anymore." He closed his eyes, breathed in deeply, then his eyelids opened enough to let just a glimmer through. "Listen to me carefully. God won't be the only one keeping an eye on you."

Ophelia hadn't the slightest idea what he was trying to say to her, and she didn't want to know. Maybe it was febrility due to what had just occurred, but a burst of determination rose from deep inside her, like boiling hot steam. She gave her dress a hard tug, to make Thorn's hand let go of it.

"We'll discuss it again when you're sorted out, not before. I will stop Mr. Farouk from taking it out on you. I promise you that, so you must promise me to do nothing rash between now and my return."

Thorn leaned his head against the wall as though giving up, and his eyes seemed lost to some distant, internal horizon. The water from the broken pipe continued to swill his blood over the marble floor. He reminded Ophelia of a collapsed puppet, and she suddenly feared leaving him alone. "Promise me," she insisted.

Thorn's large nose let out a sigh. "I never do anything rash."

Without losing another moment, Ophelia plunged into the gold of the wall, and emerged through the external cladding of the door. She saw the crust of molten metal where Milliface had entered, and wondered how the security personnel could have missed it. She knew the answer as she tripped on a uniformed body: the policeman on guard was flat on the ground. Ophelia noticed that he was breathing deeply, but she was unable to rouse him. Milliface must have resorted to narcolepsy to put him into an artificial sleep.

To avoid having to open all the reinforced doors she'd had to go through on arrival, Ophelia used their golden panels like mirrors and passed directly from the first to the last. If Milliface had told the truth, Farouk was already on his way to the police station; where exactly he was right now remained to be seen.

The answer came to her in the form of a great hubbub, as she was climbing the marble staircase that led out of the basement. At the top of the stairs, a procession of courtiers was arriving in the opposite direction, a veritable avalanche of wigs, frock coats, and dresses. They all came in the wake of Farouk, who was descending the stairs with infinite slowness. Try as they might to control this tide of visitors, the policemen were overwhelmed by their number.

"I beseech you, my Lord!" It was Berenilde's lovely voice, rising above all the others. With the long train of her dress sliding from step to step, she was looking up imploringly at Farouk. "Grant my nephew a reprieve. Consider all that he's already achieved for you within the scope of his responsibilities."

She was furrowing her brow in distress, shaking her earrings feverishly, and staring with wide, glazed eyes. Never had Ophelia seen her show such vulnerability in the presence of the court.

If Berenilde was emotion personified, Farouk was the very embodiment of indifference. Without even deigning to look at her, he was impassively descending the stairs, as though made of the same marble as them.

When Berenilde caught sight of Ophelia at the bottom of the stairs, she stopped still, and the whole procession followed suit with a shuffling of shoes. A few voices at the back muttered, "What's going on? Why aren't we moving anymore?" but this impatient hum finally ceased and the silence that fell on the stairs was soon absolute.

Only Farouk listlessly continued his descent, eyes half-closed, long, white hair rippling like a cape of silk.

Ophelia went up the stairs to meet him. She must have been a pitiful sight, with her dripping dress, wild curls, and broken arm, but it mattered little to her. She raised her eyes as high as she could, searching for Farouk's, beneath his lampshade eyelids.

"I, too, have met him," she declared, her voice amplified by the acoustics of the marble. "I know what he expects of you, but you don't have to obey him."

The courtiers exchanged stupefied glances, and Berenilde herself was openmouthed with bafflement. Ophelia was aware that not many people here would understand to whom and to what she was alluding. Farouk continued to descend towards her, one step after another, in slow motion, like a giant sleep-walker. He was so close now that she was surprised that she wasn't yet feeling the first waves of his power. It wasn't a good sign: she didn't have all his attention.

"Assert your freedom," she insisted. "Assert it by sparing Thorn."

The closer Farouk got to her, the more Ophelia had the paradoxical feeling that he was staying far away. He kept his eyes out of her reach and when he finally responded to her, his voice reverberated as though in the crevasse of a glacier:

"I must do what is written."

From that, Ophelia understood that not only would the family spirit not halt his descent, but also that he would make no attempt to go around her. She would have ended up under his feet had Berenilde not moved her from his path just in time.

The procession of courtiers started up again in Farouk's wake. The favorites were shivering under their clusters of diamonds, unsuited to the chilly world of the police station. Even the Aide-memoire, hugging the notebook in his arms, was casting wary glances all around him. When Farouk had reached the bottom of the stairs, the policemen opened the reinforced doors without further ado.

Berenilde led Ophelia to a recess in the stairs where they wouldn't be jostled too much. She took her hands into her own, as a shipwrecked person would cling to a raft.

"I no longer recognize our Lord! He's not in his normal state. 'I must do what is written'—those are the only words coming out of his mouth. It would seem . . . it would seem he's thinking only of punishing my poor boy. Why did you say those words to him? Do you understand what's happening to him? What is going to become of Thorn?"

"I can see them!" exclaimed an exceedingly loud voice. "Let me through! That's my daughter!"

To Ophelia's great surprise, her mother burst out of the crowd of nobles in an explosion of red dress. Her father, great-uncle, Aunt Rosaline, and sister Agatha were hurrying after her.

"So it's not just poppycock?"

"They really married you to Mr. Thorn?"

"In prison?"

"Without all of us?"

"Without a ceremony?"

"Without a lace dress?"

Archibald, in turn, emerged from the procession, his top hat about to topple backwards. He was carrying Berenilde's baby at arm's length, as if he'd been entrusted with a firework that was about to go off.

"We mustn't remain here. Thorn asked me to make you leave this place should things go wrong." Archibald cast a judicious eye over the flood of nobles surging into the basement. "In my opinion, they're not going at all right."

"Let's go home, sis!" implored Agatha, tugging her sister's scarf. "The court, this just isn't how I imagined it would be!"

Dazed, Ophelia turned her back on all of them, closed her eyes, blanked out the noise, and blocked off her mind. Had Farouk really become inaccessible? She swiveled round to her great-uncle, who was swearing in dialect every time a noble elbowed him.

"The tales about objects that you sent me . . . None disturbed Mr. Farouk as much as the one about the doll."

"The doll?" her great-uncle mumbled into his moustache. "The doll who dreamt of becoming an actress?"

Ophelia nodded, more to herself than to him. At the end of the tale, the doll discovers that the dream she hoped to fulfill was in fact that of her owner.

"Mr. Farouk confuses that tale with his own story. I should have made up a different ending for him."

At the very moment Ophelia said these words, a flash of pain darted right across her forehead. The memory from her reading returned to her under the impetus of Thorn's family power. The headless soldier. The old school. The scent of mimosa. The smashed windows. The draped mirrors. Ophelia was swept up in the whirlwind of time, and saw again the young Farouk kneeling at her feet, looking avidly up at her. *"Why do I have to do what is written? What am I to you, God?"*

"I know," muttered Ophelia, turning to Berenilde. "I finally know what I must say to him. Take your baby far away from this place. I will join you later."

As she was already hurrying back down the stairs, her mother grabbed her by the sleeve. "Not so fast!

With a determined look, Ophelia defied her to prevent her from continuing, but her mother came closer and, resignedly, tightened the knot of the scarf around her arm and pushed back her tousled hair, to see her face clearly.

"He's a right one, your Mr. Thorn. I can't help but think that you're clinging to him just because I can't stand him. But anyway, he's your husband now and your place is by his side. My place is to wait for you here. Take care, above all."

Ophelia squeezed her mother's hand before letting it go. "Thanks, Mom."

As she was making her way through the crowd, Ophelia reflected that the message she was now bringing contradicted everything she had seen of God that night. And yet she knew with absolute certainty that there was no possible mistake. It was that, that and nothing else, that she had to say to Farouk.

She finally caught sight of him at the other end of the corridor, towering over the sea of wigs like a snowy peak. Farouk was standing at the door of Thorn's strong room, waiting for it to be opened. A state of general confusion prevailed: the policemen had just discovered their colleague asleep on the floor, and the crust of molten gold on the door. The word "escape" was already flying around, but the squad superintendent was adamant: "The cell remained hermetically sealed, my Lord. There was an attempt at escape, but the door is always locked from the outside. Opening it requires three special keys, and I am personally in possession of one of them."

Now nearing the front of the crowd, Ophelia saw the squad superintendent proudly brandishing the bunch of keys that gleamed at his neck. She could have explained to him that there were all manner of ways to enter and depart from this cell without possessing keys, but it probably wouldn't have been in her interest to do so.

"Open up," Farouk ordered, his voice lifeless.

"Wait!" Ophelia had managed to elbow her way out of the procession, and put herself between Farouk and the reinforced door, ignoring the disapproving murmurs that were spreading around her. She craned her neck and stood on tiptoe in the hope of finally catching Farouk's eye, way up there, at the summit of his lofty stature. She didn't succeed. He was looking straight ahead, through doleful, half-closed eyelids. Ophelia might as well have been a rug.

"Kindly move out of the way, madam," the squad super-intendent intervened. He had given this order in a tone that was polite but authoritarian. For a second, his eyebrows had gone up as he wondered how on earth Ophelia had got out of the cell; he must have decided that the police force had made itself ridiculous enough for today, since he refrained from commenting on the matter.

"Yesterday, I wasn't able to honor the contract," she said, focusing solely on Farouk. "There was something you wanted to remember on the subject of your Book, and I didn't find it. I now know what it was."

Farouk didn't deign to look down at her. He continued to contemplate the vast circular door, all reinforced steel, cogs, and bolts.

"I must do what is written," he said slowly, without the slightest intonation.

Ophelia's glasses darkened. She could imagine only too well how Milliface had gone about putting Farouk back under his control. He had touched his Book. What Ophelia didn't under-stand was why he had done so. It went completely against the truth that he had formerly sought to convey to him.

"You are not a doll," Ophelia asserted, with all the breath she had. "You don't have to fulfill another's dream."

"I must do what is written," Farouk repeated, unperturbed. "Open the door."

The three policemen responsible for the unlocking mech-anism moved towards Ophelia, but she stood firm and God's words emerged from her body, as if they had, inexplicably, always been there, lurking in a corner of her being, waiting for their time to come: "Your Book is but the start of your story, Odin. It's up to you alone to write the ending."

Cries of surprise sprang from every throat. The effect produced by Ophelia's words was as sudden as it was spectacular. Farouk swayed backwards and brought a hand to his chest, at the precise spot he kept his Book under his imperial coat; one might have thought it was his heart that had just broken to pieces. He fell to his knees in a slump of hair and fur. His impassivity was shattered, and his eyes, staring wildly from too strong an emotion, opened wide at Ophelia, as if he were finally seeing her.

She should have felt afraid—afraid of what she had done to him, afraid of what he himself could have done to her. But not at all. The memory in her reading had made Ophelia penetrate Farouk's personal story so intimately that she no longer differentiated between his past and her own past.

She went up to him and, with a gesture that scandalized the whole court, pushed back his long, white hair, just as her mother had done to her in the stairs. Kneeling on the marble, his hand clasped against his Book, Farouk's face expressed indescribable confusion. His psyche was radiating once more around him, like a powerful invisible aura. Ophelia felt pains shooting through her, as her nervous system absorbed the shock wave, but she held steady. Farouk had ceased to be an immortal emperor; he was now nothing but a lost child, and to turn her back on him now could prove fatal to him.

"Artemis's girl," he murmured in a disorientated voice, "what . . . what must I do?"

"It's for you to tell us." Ophelia indicated to the Aide-memoire to come over; after briefly hesitating, the young man brought the notebook with his usual professionalism. All around, policemen and courtiers exchanged concerned glances, divided between the desire to intervene and to run away.

Slumped on the marble, Farouk opened his notebook and slowly turned its pages. There was the court record of Thorn's trial, the facsimile of his reading contract, and a medley of barely decipherable scrawls. Farouk reread his notes with a frantic expression; he seemed to be grappling with internal torment, torn between contradictory instructions. Apart from the rustling of pages under his fingers, and a few nervous coughs from the crowd, a tomb-like silence had descended on the place.

Suddenly, Farouk froze as he was reading. His eyes had fallen on a clipping that he had taken from a newspaper. Although she could only see it upside down, Ophelia recognized the outline of Berenilde sitting beside a cradle.

The crowd all jumped when, finally, Farouk closed his notebook and stood up. "Open the door," he ordered.

For a moment, Ophelia stopped breathing. She felt Farouk's gigantic hand resting, with all its weight, on her head, but it was a gesture of reassurance, not of domination. The roles had just reversed: he was the parent and she was the child.

"You honored the contract, Artemis's girl. I grant Mr. Thorn a noble title and I release him from his bastard status. Consequently, he will undergo a new trial, this time with due process. Open the door," Farouk repeated, directed at the policemen.

The mutterings of protest that rose among the Mirages were extinguished like candles under Farouk's icy stare. With her heart beating like a drum, Ophelia considered him, for the first time, to be a true family spirit. Her relief was so sudden that her legs turned to butter, and it took all her remaining willpower to remain standing. Soon, she would see Thorn again. He could receive treatment, he could be fairly judged, and together, she and he could start afresh.

While the heavy gold door, operated by its three policemen, was emitting endless metallic clicking sounds, Ophelia clung to just that thought. She didn't want to think of Milliface, or the Guardians, or that Other, whom she'd supposedly freed, and who would cause the collapse of the arks. No, she didn't want to think of any of that yet. She just wanted to savor this moment of pure joy with Thorn, even if it were ephemeral.

When the door finally opened on the strong room, Ophelia felt her blood freeze in her veins.

She saw the furniture upturned in the four corners of the room.

She saw the lamp flickering pathetically on the ground.

She saw the water endlessly flowing from the washbasin.

As for Thorn, he was nowhere to be seen.

THE MIRROR VISITOR

The wind was making Ophelia's scarf flutter like a flag. Clutching her little suitcase, she walked along the platform, unable to tear her eyes from the landscape. The airship landing stage was perched on the edge of Citaceleste, offering a towering view of the ark below. Ophelia didn't know when she would see these fir tree forests and white mountains again, so she made sure she filled her lungs one last time with this unique air, in which resin, snow, salt, and coal were combined.

And what about Thorn? Where was he to be found?

"You, too," he had told her. "You have taught me a lot." It had taken Ophelia some time, but she had finally understood the meaning of those words. She had failed to make a reader out of Thorn, but she had made him a Mirror Visitor. He had got out of the prison cell the same way she had, using the reflective surface of the walls. Which mirror had he then emerged through, and how had he managed to disappear from view with a shattered leg? That, on the other hand, remained a mystery.

The platform guard's first whistle brought Ophelia back to reality. She handed her suitcase to her little brother, who insisted on carrying it, and made for the airship's gangway, which all the members of her family were walking up, one by one. She felt a lump in her throat when she saw the little group that had gathered at the end of the platform to bid her farewell.

Archibald came forward first and greeted her with a little tip of his hat, its crown opening and closing like a valve.

"I'll consider requesting your services next time I get myself abducted. For pity's sake, Madam Thorn, don't look like that," he said, leaning towards her with a wink. "If you don't come back soon to the Pole, the Pole will come to you, ambassador's honor!"

Ophelia smiled at him without much conviction, and then held out her hand to Fox, who was resolutely giving her the cold shoulder.

"Please, Foster, let's not part on bad terms." The wind was ruffling his every red feature—eyebrows, side-whiskers, hair, even the fur of Twit, perched on his head—making him look even grumpier than he already was.

"Well, hmm, shouldn't ask too much of me, all the same," he grumbled. "You're my boss, may I remind you. How's it going to be, my life, if I'm not accompanying you wherever you go?"

"It's temporary," Ophelia promised him. As she said the words, she felt an even bigger lump in her throat. The truth was, it was impossible for her to quantify that "temporary."

Ophelia glanced nervously at the Rapporteur, waiting for her a few steps away, and standing there in her black dress like justice personified, the weather vane on her hat pointing sternly at her. As soon as they had been informed of the latest events, the Doyennes had ordered her immediate return to Anima, and Ophelia had no choice but to obey them. Thorn had given no sign of life, not even by telegram, since disappearing from his cell. He had officially become an outlaw, and Anima's Familistery had seized on this pretext to get Ophelia back. She couldn't disobey without worsening diplomatic tensions between Anima and the Pole. She suspected, however, a totally different motive behind this hardened stance. By falling back into the Doyennes' clutches, she would be the object of keen surveillance.

"God won't be the only one keeping an eye on you." Had Thorn been thinking of the Doyennes when he'd come out with that warning to Ophelia?

"Your place is here," she added, insistently holding her hand out to Fox. "Tell Gail, when you see her, that I owe her a monocle."

Fox's enormous hand engulfed hers. "No. You will have to return to tell her yourself."

The platform guard gave a second whistle. Ophelia turned to Berenilde and her pretty white pram. She instantly forgot the words she had carefully prepared for the occasion. "Madam, you . . . I'm going to . . ."

Berenilde hugged her, so hard that her perfume enveloped her like a second dress. "I know," she whispered in her ear. "I know you haven't told me everything, and I know you can't yet tell me. I don't understand everything, Ophelia, but I give you my complete trust, as Thorn gave you his."

The Rapporteur gave a dry little cough, and Ophelia felt her resolve cracking.

"You really don't want to come with me to Anima?" she asked Berenilde, buried in her arms.

"My duty demands my presence here. You had a pretty remarkable influence on our dear Lord, but he's so forgetful! We have to stay beside him, my daughter and I, to remind him what you taught him. Also," Berenilde added, in an even quieter voice, "I must also stay for Thorn. I don't know where he is, as we speak, but don't worry—that boy is pathologically punctual. When the time comes, he will return to us. In the meantime, please, don't forget him."

Ophelia wiped her eyes under her glasses, letting out a small laugh.

"Thorn would have said: 'I never forget anything.' And on the subject, I haven't forgotten the promise I made you. I owe a name to my goddaughter."

The platform guard gave a third and final whistle. Ophelia was going to have to board the airship. Ignoring the Rapporteur's increasingly impatient coughs, and her mother's calls from the gangway, she leant over the baby's pram. Her skin was as white as Farouk's.

Ophelia made a silent promise to her goddaughter. She would find Thorn. And if, to do so, she had to defy the Doyennes, the God of humanity, or a world-breaker, that's what she would do.

"She will be called Victoria."

FRAGMENT: POSTSCRIPTUM

It's coming back to me—God was punished. On that day, I understood that God wasn't all-powerful. Since then, I've never seen him again.

"Try your dears." Thorn understands, now. Those were God's last words before he disappeared from his life. Try your dears. Dry your tears. God rules the world and he muddles his words.

There is now a final piece of Thorn's jigsaw puzzle missing; the one that, in its absence, stops him from finally seeing the truth in its entirety. Why had Farouk convinced himself that God had been punished? Because, should he turn out to be right, that question would raise another, infinitely more disturbing one.

By whom?

Author's Postscript

I wrote this story by animating it with all my personal emotions: excitement, doubt, feverishness, helplessness, euphoria, to name but a few. For your own comfort, I suggest you handle this book with reader's gloves. If, despite your precautions, you notice some malfunction (book pinching fingers, pages turning too fast, etc.), I suggest you consult the website www.passe-miroir.com.

ACKNOWLEDGMENTS

To my dearest Thibaut, who supported me through every word of every sentence of every page of this book. To our respective families, veritable battalions of guardian angels. To my excellent advisers, Stéphanie Barbaras, Svetlana Kirilina, and Célia Rodmacq, and to all my friends at Plume d'Argent, in France and Belgium. To the entire team at Gallimard Jeunesse, who enabled The Mirror Visitor to take flight. To Laurent Gapaillard, who creates the most beautiful covers in the world. And finally, to all the readers, who motivate me every day with their enthusiasm, their comments, and their questions. Without all of you, this book would not have been the same.

THE CLANS OF THE POLE

ARTEMIS
Family spirit
of Anima

Archibald and his sisters
The Aide-memoire
The Valkyries

Gail

The Knight
Lady Cunegond
Baron Melchior
Eric the Storyteller
The Provost of the Marshals
The Director
of the *Nibelungen*
Count Harold

The Doyennes

Berenilde

Ophelia

Thorn